like a
FLOWER
in
BLOOM

May your beauty
always be
your own.

◆ BETHANYHOUSE

Books by Siri Mitchell

A Constant Heart
Love's Pursuit
She Walks in Beauty
A Heart Most Worthy
The Messenger
Unrivaled
Love Comes Calling
Like a Flower in Bloom

like a
FLOWER
in
BLOOM

SIRI MITCHELL

BETHANYHOUSE
a division of Baker Publishing Group
Minneapolis, Minnesota

© 2015 by Siri Mitchell

Published by Bethany House Publishers
11400 Hampshire Avenue South
Bloomington, Minnesota 55438
www.bethanyhouse.com

Bethany House Publishers is a division of
Baker Publishing Group, Grand Rapids, Michigan

Printed in the United States of America

Library of Congress Cataloging-in-Publication Data
Mitchell, Siri L
    Like a flower in bloom / Siri Mitchell.
       pages ; cm
    Summary: "In Victorian-era northern England, Charlotte Withersby, daughter of a prominent botanist, attempts to regain her role as his assistant, despite society's expectations and the presence of Edward Trimble, her father's new assistant"—Provided by publisher.
    ISBN 978-0-7642-1037-2 (softcover)
    1. Young women—England—Fiction. 2. Man-woman relationships—Fiction. 3. England—Social life and customs—19th century—Fiction. I. Title.
PS3613.I866L55 2015
813'.6—dc23   2014031984

Scripture quotations are from The Holy Bible, English Standard Version® (ESV®), copyright © 2001 by Crossway, a publishing ministry of Good News Publishers. Used by permission. All rights reserved. ESV Text Edition: 2007

Cover design by Jennifer Parker

Cover photography by Mike Habermann Photography, LLC

Author represented by Natasha Kern Literary Agency

15 16 17 18 19 20 21   7 6 5 4 3 2 1

For Tony,
who always makes sure I take time
to stop and smell the flowers.

September 1852
Cheshire, England

I shifted, glancing up from the illustration I was coloring to look out the many-mullioned window beside me. Outside, the sea tree mallow tossed its pink scalloped blooms as the goldenrod beside it nodded. Someone who had lived in this house during its hundred-year past had taken a fanciful approach to gardening. At least the sea tree mallow, planted far from its beloved salt spray, thrived upon benign neglect. I was quite happy not to have to coddle or otherwise attend to it. The goldenrod, thick with bees, was a foreign invader, having traveled far from its home in what had once been our American colonies.

The yard beyond, stretching down the lane toward the road, was rife with all manner of plants that had no business taking root in Cheshire. Even I, however, could forgive their impudence when they rewarded our forbearance with such brightly colored flowers. It was enough to make me forget that just the other side of our hill lay the town of Overwich with all its brine pits and the saltworks and its forest of chimneys, which constantly belched clouds of coal smoke and steam.

The wind, having the habit of blowing from the west, kept the noise, the stench, and the peculiarly sticky grime away. Heaven could be thanked for such small mercies. And since nearly every vantage point in the house looked out upon the fields, which tilted toward the horizon, I could easily ignore all the salt-laden carts that trafficked the roads and pretend that I didn't live near a town at all.

Sighing, I pushed my hair from my face with my wrist. Then I picked up my brush again and— Oh dear! In between the waving mallow and goldenrod, the Admiral's ancient carriage came up the lane, proceeding from one mullion to the next in a jerky, shifting progression. I rushed to the old oak door and struggled to pry it open. It always got stuck on the threshold. As the Admiral came through, he bent briskly to kiss my cheek. "My dear Charlotte." Then he moved on past me into the front hall, as if something of urgent import awaited him there.

When we had moved to the county of Cheshire four years after the death of my mother, it was at my uncle, the Admiral's, urging. He called upon us, advertising the town of Overwich as an ideal situation—much less expensive than the city, bounded by farmland and vast fields. Located in the Cheshire Gap, the area's weather was both clement and temperate. The land was composed of barely rolling hills. As my only surviving maternal relative, and having settled upon a permanent state of bachelorhood, my uncle begged the opportunity to spend the remaining years of his life in the embrace of family.

It was not difficult to decide in his favor. London had nearly crept up to our doorstep, and my father had tired of the city. As his work could be done anywhere, we decided to grant my uncle's wish. I had become almost fond of the Admiral since our move, or at least less afraid of his imposing mien. If truth be told, however, he was rather a blight upon the family's good name.

My mother's father had been the author of *The Botanical History of England*, and his father, my great-grandfather, had been the author of *A Natural History of Essex*, with his father before him having published the first *Catalogus* of the plants in the royal gardens. But the Admiral had put aside all of the honor and respect the family had earned over the generations and took himself to the high seas. The possibility of his being a foundling had been brought up a time or two, but my mother always said the Admiral clearly had the nose of my grandfather, so the family had simply done their best to distance themselves from him.

My father, for his part, had tried to keep the Admiral's exploits in the Opium War from reaching the ears of *his* family, but with my uncle's name mentioned in the broadsheets almost daily during the war, and with his being knighted by the Queen herself, it was an impossibility.

Now having established ourselves in Overwich, Father and the Admiral seemed to have arrived at a sort of uneasy agreement to be friends, and for better or for worse, my uncle made it his business to call upon us weekly.

I left him waiting in the central white-plastered front hall, hands clasped behind his back, feet firmly planted on the floor, as I went to fetch my father.

Once in the hall, my father spied the mail and took it up. Opening the letter I'd earlier received from the British Association for the Advancement of Science, he began to read it.

I plucked it from his hands in order to save him the trouble. "I submitted a paper on the flora of the subantarctic islands."

"And what did they think?"

"They refused it when I submitted it under my own name

last year, but they did tell me that, if you cared to address the subject, they might reconsider."

He blinked behind his round, wire spectacles. "But I would never address that subject."

Which had made the rejection all the worse.

"Why would I write about the distribution of plants when my interests lie in the classification of them?"

"My point exactly. But I took the liberty of resubmitting it under your name this year, and they could not praise it enough. They've decided to publish it."

As I spoke, I approached the Admiral for the purpose of taking his coat. He turned around and lifted his arms so I could pull it from his shoulders. I gave it a good shake and hung it from a hook on the hallstand. "I don't know why I expected the decision to be made on the merit of the work alone." Why it was that I kept hoping one day I might be published under my own name.

The Admiral removed his grey top hat and tucked it into the crook of his arm as he stood watching me.

"What point is there in any of this if my sex makes my work unacceptable? Why do I even try?"

Father and the Admiral exchanged a look as I turned and walked from the hall into the parlor, intending to return to my illustration.

The Admiral entered behind me, every wave of his side-parted, steel-colored hair gleaming. Every item of his clothing crisply pressed and his boots shining . . . in great contrast to my father, who was quite the opposite. If anything gleamed on him, it was his spectacles. His hair was an indiscriminate greying brown, his jacket wrinkled, his trousers bagging at the knees. And his boots were off his feet entirely. He was standing before us in stockinged feet.

The Admiral was surveying the green velvet sofa and the table, which were piled, as always, with books and specimens and papers. I'm certain he had not failed to note the dust that covered everything with a grey sort of down, though he seemed to pass no judgment upon us. He merely crossed the thread-worn carpet to the fireplace, grabbed hold of his hat, and waved it in our direction. "It's interesting you should comment on the limitations of your sex, Charlotte. I have been trying to convince your father that it's not right for him to keep you shut up here, nor that you should be so devoted to your collections."

"I wouldn't say that he's shut me—"

"Botany is a pastime that many girls of your generation share." He began to pace in front of the soot-stained hearth from which I really ought to have cleaned the ashes last winter. Seeing, however, that autumn was upon us once more, I reasoned that they might as well stay where they were. "We've been told that it's a virtue to investigate God's creation—though we might be better off, of course, if we begged heaven to save us from the virtues of the virtuous—but even you must have observed that even those who are impassioned of plants and flowers do not fail to find a husband or to partake in God's blessings of children and family. If you want to give yourself to a work better suited to your sex, if you wish to partake in all that life has to offer you, perhaps it is that upon which you should focus."

The Admiral still seemed to suffer from the idea that he could do for me those things that he had failed to do for my mother. He had made the same entreaty every year since we had moved to Overwich, and I found the idea no more attractive now than I had in the past.

I sat down in front of my easel, and he continued, "May I dare to think that you are ready to set aside all of this and take up that role for which you have been created? Marriage. Motherhood."

I looked at my father, who refused to meet my eyes. Why should my answer this year be any different than last year's? Marriage and all it involved had nothing to do with subantarctic islands or the distribution of plants. But if the BAAS was right, *I* had nothing to do with the islands or distribution either. "If I did marry, as you suggest, then who would undertake father's correspondence and keep up with the bills? Who would illustrate his books? And who would classify his specimens?" In short, who would do everything that I had done for years?

"You cannot keep hiding away here, thinking yourself immune to God's great plan."

"My father's work is very important. So why should I not devote myself to its success? Or to the success of my own?"

Father coughed. "What your uncle is trying to say—what he's finally made me come to see—is that I've neglected you for far too long. We have only your happiness as our goal."

"My . . . *happiness*?" He had never been interested in happiness before. His interests lay in lilies and orchids, petals and leaves.

The Admiral smiled at me as he thumped the top of his hat. "You see? We have only your best interests in mind."

We? So they had become united in this effort? I shook my head, intending to resume my work, but discovered that I needed a pen. Going to my desk in the middle of the room, I opened a drawer in hopes of finding it but discovered a pile of specimens and a pocket glass instead. I took them all out and laid them atop the desk. "What is it that you would have me do?" *Where* had I put my pen?

The Admiral picked up the brush I had abandoned. "What any girl in society does. What *every* girl in society does! Do you not think it is time, my dear, to put away your childish things?"

"*Child*ish . . . ?" If he called my pursuits childish, then he was saying the same of my father's pursuits, for they were one and the same.

"Not childish." My father took the brush from my uncle and returned it to my easel. "Charlotte is doing some very interesting work just now. I can't think why the BAAS won't publish it."

"Because they seem to share the Admiral's point of view." I opened another drawer. There it was! I pulled the pen out.

"I did not mean to offend you, my dear girl. What I meant to say is that you must leave off these pursuits that are not worthy of your . . . well . . . your . . ." He grimaced. "What I meant to say was that the blind pursuit of . . . What is it you're working on, again?"

"*Ranunculus.*"

"This blind pursuit of *Ranunculus* is not altogether proper, is it?"

"Proper?" *He* was speaking to *me* of what was proper?

"Not for a girl in your position."

"My position? What position is that?"

"Your age. It's not proper for a girl of your age. I hope you'll think on it, my dear. I can tell you from experience that, if you put off things for too long, sometimes you never actually get around to the doing of them."

Pity that he'd never had a wife or children. If he had, then maybe he would be spending his concern on their behalf instead of mine.

"You're a handsome girl, Charlotte. Sturdy. Sound. Snugly put together. It shouldn't be too difficult to put you to the launch."

Put me to the *launch*?

"And don't worry. I know what it's like to feel a fish out of water. It might take some work to introduce you around and push you out over the surf. But at least all those old lessons I learned in the past will have been good for something. I don't wish to see you expend your life on . . . this." He turned a jaundiced eye on the detritus of scientific pursuit that surrounded us. "Think on it. Promise me that."

My uncle left soon after, and I found myself relaxing. He was a restless sort of man, constantly in motion, and something about him always made me stand up straight and throw my shoulders back.

My father let out a long sigh and then settled himself into a chair. "Your mother would have known what to do about all of this."

Yes, because "all of this" is exactly what she'd done. She'd assisted my father in his work until the day she died. Quite literally. She'd been transcribing his notes right up until the point that she'd fallen over dead.

He shook his head as if I were some recalcitrant child, looking at me through those sad nut-colored eyes that seemed so often to be swimming in tears. The thought that I needed to prevent those tears from spilling over is what had gotten me through those first few years after Mother had died. Through the seemingly endless book contracts. Through the many consultations with him as he lay in the bed they had once shared, claiming that he simply couldn't bear the thought of getting up. Through the sorting of Mother's papers and the editing of Father's discourses.

My desire to protect my father had, in fact, gotten us both here, to Overwich. And if I couldn't say that I looked forward to the Admiral's visits, I was grateful his presence had rallied my father's spirits. Since our move, my father had put off his nightshirt and decided to dress once more. And two years ago, he had taken up his rambles again, coaxing some of the former color back into his cheeks.

"The Admiral says that you really should be out more." He blinked once. Twice. "That you should *come out*—I believe that's how he phrased it. And that you should marry."

"Whom?"

"*Who* whom?"

"Whom am I to marry?" Had he decided that too?

"I don't know." My father's brow furrowed as if in surprise that I would even ask. "There must be someone suitable. Somewhere. Overwich is not some rustic village."

"And I'm to leave off my work, and yours, in order to find this person?"

"It's what nature intended, is it not?" He settled into the chair, as if his words marked the end of our discussion.

Nature intended that flora flourish where the conditions were sufficient to sustain them, but I wasn't so certain that it intended I should marry at the Admiral's command. "Why should his opinions be so important? You've always told me he threw over a promising start in botany in order to join the navy."

"He's been out in society much more than you or I. Courtship and marriage are matters that fall more naturally under his purview. If he says it's time, then I trust his opinion on the matter."

"But he himself never married!"

"He's been around many people who have. And there's a method to the undertaking that I can't pretend to understand."

"But what about you and Mother?"

He opened his mouth, closed it, and then with a squint said, "Actually, I can't quite say for certain how that all came about. . . ." He cleared his throat and shifted in his chair. "It's true, Charlotte. As the Admiral said, you don't have many opportunities here, closeted away, working all day."

"I'm not closeted away. You and I go out for a ramble together every morning. And we go to church on Sunday as well." I trusted our cook, Mrs. Harvey, and Her Majesty's Royal Mail for everything else.

"Be that as it may, your uncle is quite persuasive. And I must admit that I've lost track of time since your mother died. You were fifteen, weren't you?"

"Fourteen."

"And now you're nearly twenty-one."

"I am twenty-two."

"Are you? How astonishing." His brows had arched in surprise. "It's been eight years . . . ? But I always expected you'd marry someday. Surely you must have as well."

I hadn't ever really thought on it. After Mother had died, I seemed barely to manage keeping up with our deadlines. I'd never had the time to imagine a future apart from them. Most of my attentions had been fixed of late on the problem of getting my own work published and paying our bills.

"If you're going to marry, you need to get a start on it, as it were."

"I believe the term he used was launch. I must *launch* myself."

"Yes. Well . . . he is in a position to help you."

"The *Admiral* is?"

"He's quite respected in these parts."

"He is?"

Father's shrug indicated that he was just as puzzled at that news as I was. "He wants to help you. Says he'll manage all the fuss . . ."

There was fuss involved?

"And all the dinners and . . . and . . . other . . . things that it would require. I think that you should do it."

He sounded quite uncharacteristically firm in his opinion, which made me think it was best to nip the idea in the bud. "I haven't the time."

He sat forward, squaring his shoulders as he did so. "You would if you didn't insist upon helping me."

Insist upon it? "But if I don't help you, who will?"

"I'll manage."

Manage? He'd manage to let the bills sit until a collector came, and he'd confuse his letters to Mr. Pierce with the letters to Mr. Peece and jumble up his notes, and he wouldn't get anything done at all. "Are you saying you don't want my help?"

"I'm simply saying that I don't need it."

2

Didn't need it! Didn't need it?

I wanted to know just how much he thought he would have accomplished these past eight years if I hadn't been here. I transcribed his notes and wrote his papers and undertook his correspondence. I paid the tradesmen and the Royal Mail clerk. I kept us in food and boots and sandwiches, which were apparently entirely beneath our cook's dignity to make. And from time to time, on an annual sort of basis, I also dusted.

Marry.

I nearly snorted at the thought. When my father realized how much work I did, he would tremble at the thought. The suggestion was ludicrous, and he would soon come to know it. There was simply too much work to be done for me to marry, so I put the idea aside.

Sometime later, the bell sounded at the door. Sighing, I rose. When I opened the door, a wooden chest greeted me. "For Mr. Withersby."

I had the man place it on the floor in the parlor, then worked a knife under the straps and sawed them off.

"A chest of specimens arrived." I threw the words over my shoulder toward my father's study.

I heard him pad across the floor, and he soon appeared in his doorway. "What's that?"

"Specimens. We've been sent a box of them."

Comprehension rippled across his features. "Splendid. Let's have a look at them, shall we?"

I lifted the lid with no little trepidation. Once I had opened such a chest only to have a lizard dart up and hiss at me before it dropped to the floor and slithered away.

"Where is it from? Does it say?"

"It must be from one of your fine young fellows."

"Yes, yes." He had eased himself to the floor and was already sifting through the contents. "But which one?"

That was the question. My father had a veritable army of fine young fellows who scoured the world, looking for botanic specimens worthy of his work. He went down to Liverpool once a month and canvassed ships bound for foreign parts, soliciting help. It should be noted that his fine young fellows were not all fine. Once or twice he had picked out men who had turned out to be former criminals. And of late, we'd endured the distress of having several of our best correspondents beg payment for their specimens, as if their contribution to science was not recompense enough. It must be said that not all my father's correspondents were young either.

I suspected I knew who had sent this one. "I rather think this chest is from our Mr. E. Trimble." It had that look about it. As many times as I had implored him, in my father's name, to take more care with the conveyance of his specimens, he had disregarded those instructions. These plants of his, as those previous, were not affixed to any kind of sheet, they were not labeled, neither had they ever, apparently, been pressed.

"Useless, the lot of them." He was frowning. "I really should write to that young man about the proper way to preserve specimens."

"I already have." I'd done it many times. Mr. E. Trimble was a sheep farmer from New Zealand who was enamored of numbers and systems and procedures, and I imagined him to be one of those wiry, vigorous men of middle-age. We had enjoyed a regular, if rather spirited, correspondence.

He meant well, but he had sent us a useless chest, filled with worthless specimens for which we must now pay transport. "Next time you go to Liverpool, I really must go with you." Maybe then I could ensure that my father's next recruit would in fact be both fine and young.

"You wouldn't like it. I don't like it . . . all the people, all the boats, all the noise. I don't really know why I bother to go at all."

I had begun to wonder the same thing.

"Here now." He had fished something out from the bottom of the chest and was clutching it like a prize. An envelope. He handed it to me.

I broke the seal and opened it.

To wit: one white flower, called wood rose; one white flower, am told is Mount Cook lily—doesn't look like one; one red flower, species unknown; two suspicious yellow flowers masquerading as ranunculus . . .

Suspicious? Masquerading? Flowers didn't masquerade as anything but themselves. I wished he wouldn't feel the need to be so fanciful in his writing. I finished reading the list aloud and then turned the missive over to see whether he had provided more details on any of them. He had not.

"There's a lily? In there?" Father was peering into the depths of the chest, as if the very thought was inconceivable. I hardly blamed him. He sighed. "I should have liked to have seen a flower from one of those rata trees."

"This might have been one." I held up a bald-headed stem. "It looks as if it might once have had petals."

He took it from me. "He ought to be told that a jumble of specimens isn't particularly useful. It will require too much time to sort them, let alone classify them. And it doesn't look as if he's included any labels."

"I'll send him another letter tomorrow."

"Let's hope he hasn't done too much more collecting in the meantime."

That afternoon, my father went out for a ramble, and I determined to finish my illustration. But just as I was putting my brush to the paper, someone pulled the bell at the door. Really, I'd had quite enough of people for the day.

I wrested the door open. "Yes? What is it?" The words had hardly left my mouth before my eyes registered the glass-sided Wardian case being offered to me. A paradise of plants grew inside of it. I was used to my father's fine young fellows shipping us glass cases, but normally they arrived as a cemetery of dried, dead things, the barest memory of plants that once had been.

And then the case descended enough for me to see that it wasn't the Royal Mail man. Though this man had a thatch of unruly dark hair, he gave the impression of having been carefully cultivated, and his angular face was one upon which all the elements were pleasingly proportioned. A furrow between his eyes was echoed by a cleft in his chin, and beneath dark brows, blue eyes were regarding me.

I blinked. "Why . . . I don't know who you are."

"I hope you don't feel the need to stand on ceremony and demand an introduction. This case is rather heavy . . ."

"No, of course not. Yes. Please. Come in. You can put it—"

But he was already through the door past the hall, into the parlor, setting the case down on my desk.

"I would prefer if you could put it somewhere else. Although that is a rather extraordinary . . . What is it exactly?" From a swath of strap-like leaves a cylinder of golden flowers protruded. Reminiscent of a hyacinth, our cook might have taken it for a bottle brush. It was wholly unexpected.

He bent beside me to look at the flower I was examining. "It's a lily."

"A lily? It can't be. But it's quite stunning."

A smile tipped up the corner of his mouth. "Quite."

I went round the other side in order to see it from the back.

"I found it on a visit to one of those subantarctic islands Mr. Withersby has written me so much about. Dreadful weather. Went to terrible lengths to get it, and then nearly broke my neck on the way out of the valley in which I found it."

The flower was like nothing I'd ever seen before.

". . . can see that my exploits impress you very little."

I straightened. "Pardon me. What was it you were saying?"

He was regarding me with a rueful smile. "Nothing. I was wondering if Mr. Andrew Withersby happens to be in. I should very much like to see him, if it's at all possible. I feel as if I already know him through our correspondence."

Something he'd said worked its way to my consciousness. "*You* found this specimen?"

"Yes."

That changed everything. "I took you for a delivery man, and . . . I'm very sorry."

"I take no offense. But if Mr. Withersby is in, might you tell him Mr. Edward Trim—" He bit off the end of his sentence. "That is, I suppose you might recall me to him by the name of Mr. Edward Trimble."

"*You* are Mr. E. Trimble?"

"Yes. Is he here, then? I should truly like to see him."

"You can't be Mr. Trimble."

One of those thick black brows of his rose. "I can assure you he knows me by that name. We've undertaken the most marvelous correspondence about—"

"But you're not . . ." *Of middling years or wiry or . . . or anything like Mr. Trimble was at all.* "You just can't be." He didn't look at all like a sheep farmer.

At that moment, my father came in from the lane, tin vasculum slung over his shoulder.

"Ah! My fine young fellow." My father never forgot a face, though he could never remember a name.

The fine young fellow, who seemed in fact both fine and young, strode over to my father and offered his hand. "It's so good to see you again, sir."

My father took up the hand Mr. E. Trimble offered. "How long has it been, then?"

"Three years since I met you in Liverpool."

"Three years." Father transferred his gaze to me. "Imagine, Charlotte."

I was. I was remembering all of the correspondence that had passed between Mr. Trimble and me. And all of those times I had imagined him a thin, nondescript sort of man. All of those times I'd written to him of my hopes and dreams, the times I'd argued with him about one botanical theory or another. With any sort of luck it would never become known that it was me with whom he had corresponded.

Going to the sofa, my father began to empty his vasculum of

specimens, placing them atop the stacks of papers. Indicating a chair with his chin, he spoke to our guest. "Come over here, young man, and tell me about New Zealand."

Mr. Trimble tried to do just that, but soon my father was interrupting with questions about lilies and whether he had gotten to Australia yet and if the Alps of the colony were as barren of flora as had been written up in the journals.

I ought to have been gratified that my father's questions echoed those I had already asked in my letters. I couldn't help but feel a pinch of unease, however, when Mr. Trimble seemed puzzled by my father's failure to recollect those things of which he'd written in great detail. Feeling the need to cover for my subterfuge, I interjected. "You must remember, Father. He did indeed journey to Campbell Island. And he wrote of it to us, to *you*, in great detail."

Father had installed himself in a chair, and now his brow furrowed as he looked toward our guest. "I suppose I should just read your letter, then."

Our visitor had screwed round in his chair to look at me. "Father? Mr. Withersby is your *father*? I had assumed from the way . . . well, from the way you . . ." He closed his mouth with a frown and then tried again. "I don't believe we were ever formally introduced."

The way in which he said it made me wonder why he seemed to think that was my fault. "I'm Charlotte." The one who had sympathized through that first hard year he'd had in establishing his farm. The one who had consoled him when he had lost his first ewe. The one who knew he hoped to one day add thousands more sheep to his flock and a textile manufactory for the benefit of the colony to his holdings. But, of course, he attributed all that correspondence to my father.

"I seem to have gotten everything wrong. I beg your pardon, Miss Withersby."

Father had been watching us, and now he gestured to the piles of paper mounded on the floor beside his feet. "Where is that letter to which he was referring, Charlotte? That one about Campbell Island?"

I went to retrieve it from its place in the cupboard, where it was still filed among old tax notices and discourses on taxonomy.

Mr. Trimble raised a hand. "Please don't trouble yourself. There's no need. I'm sure you must get reports from your correspondents by the dozens. And I'm happy to speak of my journey to the island. I've never seen anything like it."

They went on to speak of the topic at length, and it was with some relief that I worked on my illustration, consulting my microscope once or twice to be certain of the structures I was coloring. I had almost finished with it when I realized their conversation had stopped. I glanced up to find the pair of them staring at me.

"Don't you agree, Charlotte?" My father asked the question in such a way that I was quite sure I was to answer in the affirmative.

"I should think so, yes."

"Good!" A healthy color suffused his cheeks, and he looked quite content. "It's settled, then. We'll have this fine young man stay for supper."

I wished I had not been so hasty in answering, for I feared our cook would have an entirely different opinion of the matter. "I'm not certain Mrs. Harvey will allow it."

Father took a big bite of his mustache, nearly pulling it into his mouth. "Will you please . . . could you warn her while I show this fine fellow the proofs of my first volume?"

I nodded in agreement. But still, I paused as I approached the kitchen door.

I could hear Mrs. Harvey humming some tuneless song.

Really, I wished I didn't have to consult with her. She considered the kitchen her private domain, and since the time she had caught me plumping up my dried specimens in one of her kettles, I had earned myself no favors.

As I entered, she was pulling a tray of blackened biscuits from the oven. When she turned to place them on the sideboard, she saw me.

I nodded. "Mrs. Harvey."

"I suppose you'll be telling me you want fancies like butter with your biscuits. And after I've already cooked up your supper!"

"No. I wanted no such thing."

She speared me with a look as though she didn't quite believe me. "Then you'll be after a cake or hot tea for your breakfast."

"No. The tea you leave on the stove at night is quite adequate." I'd become almost used to drinking it cold in the morning. I found the bracing chill of it refreshing. In the summer months, at least.

"Heaven knows you plague me with demands!"

"It's just that . . . you see, one of father's correspondents is come, and we were hoping . . . That is, Father is wanting to know . . . if it is at all possible, could the man stay for supper?"

She took the biscuits from the tray, one by one, and slammed them down into a bread bowl. Then she threw up her ash-blackened hands. "Isn't it enough that I work my fingers to the bone?" She stomped over to the cupboard, pulled forth some salt pork and hacked off several pieces of it with the big knife she liked to stow in the waistband of her apron. "But to be put upon like this? An honest outrage is what it is!"

"I'm truly very sorry. We didn't know the man was coming."

"And that's supposed to make it all fine? I suppose you'll be wanting to invite the whole town over next!"

"Of course we won't. It will be just this one man." I took up the bread bowl and went with it through the other door into the dining room.

The conversation between the men had moved from the parlor to the dining room table, and Mr. Trimble was seated in my chair, with Father across from him. They were still discussing father's book.

Mr. Trimble stood when he saw me.

I nodded as I put the biscuits down on the table, and then I moved a stack of specimens from a chair and began to draw it toward the table. Mr. Trimble took it from me and set it into place. "Pardon me. I ought to have done that for you."

I would have replied, but Mrs. Harvey stalked out just then and banged the tray of salt pork and a dish filled with what could only be spinach onto the table. I waited until she left before I sat and helped myself to a biscuit and a piece of pork.

Father took some food as well, and then Mr. Trimble did the same. He brushed a bit of ash from his biscuit and took a bite. When it failed to yield, he looked at it with no little astonishment.

I made a point of lifting my cup of tea and dunking my biscuit into it.

He followed my example, though I noticed he took only one bite before he put it back down on his plate. He didn't eat his salt pork either.

"Does the food not suit you, Mr. Trimble?"

"The last time I had such fare was on my voyage to New Zealand three years ago. We were blown off course and had to make do with our provisions for an extra month."

Father smiled broadly. "Mrs. Harvey, our cook, was married to a navy man. She'll be glad you find the food so authentic."

"Indeed, I do." But contrary to his words, he had set his fork down and did not seem as if he intended to use it anytime soon.

I dunked my biscuit into my tea again and ground it against the bottom of the cup to soften it. "New Zealand. What an astonishing land that is. You must miss your sheep. I hope Emilia survived her lambing?"

Mr. Trimble blinked. "Had I known you would be reading my letters, Miss Withersby, I might have phrased things a bit differently. Or written of other things entirely. My stories of life in the colony cannot have interested you much."

My father choked on a mouthful of biscuit. "It's *sheep* that you have, then?"

Mr. Trimble looked at him in surprise. "A good hundred of them."

"Is that considered a large flock?"

Perhaps I had erred by introducing the topic. "He told us, Father, that he's starting with a small flock since he's just begun to establish himself, but he has plans to own many more. The countryside can be quite treacherous, if you recall."

"You sound almost as if you know it, Miss Withersby."

"I do not. Of course I do not. But I do read the journals. And an occasional letter from you that Father shares with me."

My explanation seemed to satisfy him, and he talked at length of that fair land in a way that almost made me wish to forsake my own gentle hills and open glades for the high mountains and steep valleys he described. I had always yearned to see the specimens he'd collected for us *in situ*. And if the colony inspired such passion in a man who had seemed so philosophical in his letters, then it must truly be extraordinary.

We repaired to the parlor after supper, and father went in search of the brandy he kept under a domed glass. It had displayed an orchid before the unfortunate plant had died. He rousted about for his pair of cups before I reminded him that I had last seen them on the mantel. After retrieving and filling them, he gave one to Mr. Trimble. "You must stop talking, young fellow. If you say any more, Charlotte is likely to send you right back to where you came from with a list of new specimens to collect."

I felt the need to protest. "I would not. Mr. Trimble has already shown us he is incapable of following our directions. It would be pointless to send him back for more."

Those distinguished brows of his collapsed and he began to bluster. "Incapable of following directions? I've sent half a dozen chests filled with specimens in the last three years! Every chance I had, I beat about the brush in search of those you asked for, Mr. Withersby."

Mr. Trimble's outrage had little effect on Father, but why should it? It was I who had posted those lists to New Zealand. And I who had dealt with the consequence of his poor preservation and mislabeling. His carelessness seemed quite out of character for a man who had once proudly described to me the system he had devised for shearing his sheep.

"If I may be so bold as to ask . . . what was wrong with them?"

Though the appeal was to my father, I answered in his stead. "They weren't labeled. They weren't attached to your sheets. They weren't even properly pressed. If you had used the drying-paper we sent to you, then—"

"Paper? I never got any paper! I dried all the specimens I sent you with packing paper I begged from the butcher."

That explained the unfortunate result. "Most of your early specimens arrived half-decayed, covered in mildew."

"I'm sorry to hear it. If you make a list of those that were discarded, I will renew my efforts upon my return."

"I would if I could, but I hardly know what the plants were meant to be. The least you might have done was record what they were and the environs in which you found them."

"I did for those I collected, but some of the natives gathered specimens for me, and I couldn't very well write down where they'd come from." He had given up speaking to my father, who had taken off his boots and was looking forlornly at a hole in one of his stockings. Mr. Trimble instead spoke directly to me.

"And why not?"

"Because a description 'found down by the great river in the place where the water turns back upon itself opposite the tree that smells of lemons' wouldn't fit on those tiny labels I was meant to use."

"Such an intimate description is not required, but it would have been useful to know if the specimen were found in a woodland or a meadow. In moist soil or dry. The requirements of taxonomy are quite specific and to receive the specimens all jumbled about—"

"Jumbled about! That hardly seems fair. I put great care into the packing of them."

I rose and went to the chest that had arrived that morning. By a combination of pushing and tugging, I brought it to his side. "We got this one just today, and—"

"Today? But . . . I sent it eight months ago!"

"That only goes to prove my point. If this cannot be called a jumble, then I do not know what can be."

He leaned over and looked inside. Then he reached in and pulled out a dried stem of something that could not, unfortunately, be easily identified. "When I sent this it was secured to a card." He picked out another. "And this one. They all were." He sounded quite surprised.

"Perhaps the paper disintegrated during the voyage."

He was digging through them in earnest now. "And all of my notations with them? I must apologize. If I had ever imagined that they would arrive in this condition after so long a delay, then I would have kept them all to bring back with me. I cannot fault you for your outrage, Miss Withersby."

I didn't know whether I should thank him for agreeing with me or continue to air my grievances. He seemed to expect some sort of reply—indeed it sounded as if he wanted to fault me for something, which would be absurd.

My father had peeled his stockings off and draped them over the back of his chair. Now he slumped, feet toward the hearth. "In fact, the Admiral and I have been discussing Charlotte of late." He spoke in such a placid manner, of such an incongruous topic, I wondered if he'd heard my conversation with Mr. Trimble at all. "As much as I have appreciated her assistance, it seems I have been remiss in not allowing her to partake of society."

The Admiral's words still rankled, and I had no desire to hear them repeated. "I wish you wouldn't speak of me as if I were some specimen to be fixed to a sheet of paper and admired."

"But you are. At least according to your uncle." He shifted to speak to Mr. Trimble directly. "She's a specimen in her finest flower in need of a young man. Wouldn't you agree?"

Mr. Trimble looked me over as if I were a species of noxious weed. "I couldn't say, really."

My father returned his gaze to the fireplace. "That's what the Admiral thinks, and as I've pondered the thought, I realize that I've been too selfish, keeping her closeted here with me. She's nearly twenty-two."

"I *am* twenty-two. And I am *not* closeted."

Mr. Trimble flashed a smile. "For my own part, I could think of nothing finer than to be shut up with the renowned Andrew Withersby."

"Good. I see you agree with me." Father sighed as if in great

31

relief and leaned his head back against the chair, closing his eyes. "It's settled, then."

Mr. Trimble looked at me as if expecting me to say something. I shrugged.

He turned back to my father. "What, exactly, is settled?"

"You will be my assistant so that Charlotte can go find herself a husband."

3

M r. Trimble blinked his eyes wide.
  I heard myself gasp. "You . . . you cannot just *command* me to marry! I have illustrations to finish for your book. And there are papers to write and notes to transcribe. And mother's old publisher just asked me to write a book on how to make wax flowers. There's no end to the—"

Father opened his eyes. "But you don't make wax flowers. Do you?"

"I can learn. And we need the money. You're months away from turning in the manuscript for your next volume."

Father turned to Mr. Trimble. "Can you make wax flowers?"

"I've never made one in my life."

Father was frowning again. "Why would anyone want to make a *wax* flower? Why wouldn't they just go and pick a real one?"

I didn't know. I didn't care. I'd already written books on crafting dolls from flower blossoms and making flower-scented footbath salts. I'd even done a compilation of rose-themed poetry. "You can't just expect this man to drop his plans when he's only just returned from the colony. I'm sure he has other things to do—don't you, Mr. Trimble?"

"Not really. Nothing that I'm anxious to do, in any case."

"You must have family. Friends. Someone, somewhere, must be expecting you."

"The voyage from New Zealand can take unexpectedly long, as you've seen. . . ." He nodded toward the chest of moldering specimens. "So I didn't warn any of them of my coming. In truth, I'm not so certain anyone I know would want to see me again."

He was no help. I appealed to my father instead. "You never, in fact, asked him, and he never actually agreed."

"He just did."

"He didn't. He said he wasn't expected anywhere else and that no one ever wanted to see him again." Which seemed to beg the question that, if the people who knew him didn't want to see him, why in heaven's name should we want him either? Perhaps he wasn't a fine fellow after all.

My father straightened as he turned to look at our guest. "Will you?"

"I can think of no greater honor than to work beside you, Mr. Withersby."

He'd done it again! "He didn't actually say yes, and—"

The man sent me a dark look. "Yes. I'll do it. And thank you, kindly, for the offer."

"But we can't pay you." I gave my father a stern look. "We can't pay him."

"I'm a . . . well . . . it would be an honor to work beside you, Mr. Withersby, for the simple pleasure of it."

But I didn't want him to say yes. He couldn't. I didn't want to find a husband, and I didn't want to go out into what the Admiral called *society*. I saw all those people at church on Sunday. Wasn't that good enough? I didn't want to do anything other than what I was already doing.

Mr. Trimble put up a hand. "I would like to assist you, but

I don't wish to cause a family argument. I've been involved in quite enough of those already." He stood. "Why don't I look through this chest and see if there is anything in it I can salvage?" He picked it up as if it didn't weigh four stone and carried it off to a clear spot in the center of the room while Father followed behind him.

Knowing that Mrs. Harvey would likely ignore our dishes until morning, I returned to the dining room and piled the utensils on the plates and put the plates atop the serving bowls and the bowls atop the platter before taking them to the kitchen. Afterward, I returned to the parlor to experiment with forming petals from accumulated dribs and drabs of candle wax as Father and our guest worked through the chest of specimens. Mr. Trimble finally begged off work in order to be allowed to search for a room to engage for the night. "I was so intent upon renewing our acquaintance that I came here straightaway from Liverpool."

"And why shouldn't you have?" Father seemed to take the very suggestion as an offense. "But you'll stay here, with us, of course." He extended the invitation as if he didn't know that the spare room had been taken over by our stores of gum arabic and sulphur and quires of drying-paper.

I finally gave up on wax flowers, squeezing all my drooping, misshapen petals into a ball. "I don't actually think that we have the—"

But Mr. Trimble was already refusing. "I wouldn't wish to inconvenience you."

Unfortunately Father wouldn't hear of it. "How could it be an inconvenience? If you'll be working with me, you ought to stay with me. Charlotte can take you up to the room."

Mr. Trimble hesitated as he looked at me, and then he squared his shoulders and nodded. "Then I accept your kind offer."

With great resignation and no little frustration, I took up a lamp and led him toward the stairs. "You'll need to skip the fourth one because there's a leak just above it in the ceiling. Water comes in through the roof, and it's fairly rotted the stair right through."

Mr. Trimble paused and put a hand to the doorframe, as if testing its sturdiness. "Forgive me for asking, but what do you do when it rains?"

I pushed at the edge of a tin pail with the toe of my boot. "That's the purpose for this."

He made no reply but simply stepped over the pail and then waited in the hall upstairs as I took the drying-paper off the bed, pulled some specimens out from underneath the mattress where they had been drying, shoved the chemicals into the corner, and fluffed up the pillow a bit.

He took a step into the room. "Are you certain this isn't a bother?"

"Having you stay here or having you take up my position?" I took a look in the pitcher sitting atop a wash basin and realized it had long since gone dry. I lifted it. "I'll get you some water."

As I moved toward the door, he failed to step aside. "I didn't mean to be the cause of trouble, though sometimes it seems I do nothing else."

His tone was glib, but I didn't think he spoke an untruth. "It's not you who caused it. I have my uncle to thank for that, although I can't understand why a man so recently returned from the colony would wish to seclude himself here with us."

A corner of his mouth rose. "You would if you knew my family."

After filling Mr. Trimble's pitcher with water from my own, I left it in front of his door and returned to the parlor. My father was bent over Mr. Trimble's specimens, although he straightened when he heard me. "Such a shame there aren't more here we can use."

I joined him, feeling quite angry that so many of them would have to be discarded and rather testy at his discarding me like some improperly pressed plant. Had I not taken up where my mother had left off? Had I not kept us on our feet? And now he'd asked a stranger to take over for me as if anyone could do all those things that I had done. "You can't just steal the man away from his life. I'm sure he didn't come all the way from New Zealand intending to stay here and take up my position."

"He volunteered."

"He did not. You volunteered him."

Father blinked. "He agreed to it. If he had something else to do, I'm sure he would have said so. He's a fine young fellow."

"But the man's just returned. There must be some reason he's come home, and it can't have been to stay here with us and write books about wax flowers."

"I don't know that I'll ask him to do *that* exactly."

"If he doesn't do it, then you'll have to. I already signed the contract, and we've been given the advance." I hated to press my point, considering the dark circles under his eyes, but I had to make him see that such a hasty, ill-thought decision would have grave consequences.

"Perhaps I can write to them and return the money."

"It's already been spent."

He sighed as he chewed on his mustache. "*Wax* flowers? I just don't see why—"

"It shouldn't be very difficult to write. If I can do it, anyone can do it. Isn't that what you've meant to say?"

"Charlotte, you've done so much for me these past few years. I simply wish to relieve you of—"

"I'll say good-night now. Good night."

"Charlotte, I didn't mean—"

I neglected to hear what it was he didn't mean because I was already on my way up the stairs.

I vowed not to give up my position as easily as that and endeavored to press my case the following morning on our ramble. Our habit was to be out of the house and down the road some distance by the time the church bells rang six. There was no reason why a good day's worth of specimens could not be collected before the sun rose high enough to burn off the dew.

We stepped from the pot-holed road onto a rutted country lane and then wandered through a field into the wood. I held a branch aside so he could pass without trouble, and then I warned him about a patch of churned-up mud that lay ahead. His rheumatism was decidedly worse this year. Normally I would not have been quite so concerned about it, but the hunters and stalkers had descended upon our countryside from London and everything was in upheaval.

As we walked out of the wood and into a meadow, I spied a rosebay willow herb, its wine-colored stem and purple spike of blossoms bent from a horse's passing. Stooping, I propped it up between two twigs. "I still don't think it right that a complete stranger should be welcomed into our work while I am put out into society as some bloom in full flower, ready for the plucking."

"I rather think we should advertise you as a girl ready for marriage."

"I've no *time* to get married. And we're only five pounds away from the poorhouse! Unless . . . have you solicited any new subscribers for your volumes on orchids?"

His sudden attention to the top of his cane let me know that he had not.

"At least I have that wax flower book contracted. And you have a memoir on lilies due to the Society, which you might use to gain some more subscriptions for your books. But you still need to write it and I still need to finish illustrating it."

"I'll ask Mr. Trimble to write the memoir. Maybe he can do the illustrations as well. And if he could manage to write about wax flowers—"

"It's not an easy thing to write a book."

"But neither of you knows how to make wax flowers, so whether you write it or he writes it, I fail to see how it could matter."

"But there are so many things that must be done, and—"

"And now he can be about the doing of them instead of you."

"But I've helped you for years, and you've only just met *him*. He doesn't even know how to press a proper specimen!"

"He's a fine young fellow. I'm sure he can learn."

"Well, you can't expect him to transcribe your notes for you." My father's handwriting was atrocious, but besides that, if he did, Mr. Trimble would soon discover my secret.

"I suppose I shall have to do that myself. But how difficult can all the rest of it be? If you were able to do them for all those years, then . . ."

I felt my mouth drop open. Even now after eight years, if I wasn't very careful, if I wasn't extremely diligent, everything was liable to come crashing down upon our heads. "If that's the way you feel, then I suppose you'll be happy to be rid of me."

It would serve him right if Mr. Trimble bumbled it all.

"The Admiral said most girls your age are engaged by now, if not married. I honestly didn't realize you are as old as you are. I can't think how . . ." He let out a great long sigh. "I ought to have let you go years ago." He gave me a keen-eyed glance. "How did you get to be so old? And why haven't I noticed before now?"

He hadn't noticed much of anything, not for a long time, after my mother had died. But what point was there in recalling to him such misery? I held another branch for him and helped him over a fallen log.

"You're certain you'd rather have him than me?"

"Of course I am. Consider yourself freed of all your responsibilities. You shouldn't give us a second thought."

I shouldn't? Well then, I wouldn't. I'd let them muddle about on their own for a while. And when the first bill went unpaid, and his correspondents' specimens stopped being delivered, and that bucket on the stair overflowed, it wouldn't take long for Father to show Mr. Trimble the door and beg me to return.

We found a few good specimens of lace-capped ground elder and rust-colored *Achillea*, and then, with the sun fully risen and carriages and carts already raising dust along the road, we made our way back to the house. As we turned from the road, onto our lane, Father suddenly stopped, raising his walking stick and pointing it up into the air.

"What do you think that young fellow is doing up there?"

"Up where?" I followed the direction of his stick and was astonished to see Mr. Trimble bending over the pitch of the roof. "I'm sure I have no idea."

Father cupped a hand to his mouth and shouted up at the man.

Mr. Trimble stood and lifted a hand in reply, though he did not speak until we drew nearer. "I think I've found the leak."

"The what?" Father glanced at me, puzzlement turning his brow.

"The leak. The one that's come down through the roof to rot that stair."

"Oh. Oh! Carry on, then." Father kicked at the front stoop to knock the dirt off his boots and then went on into the house.

A call from Mr. Trimble wafted down to me. "Miss Withersby?"

I walked back into the yard so that I could see him.

"There you are! Do you know, have you got a hammer? Can you ask the boy to bring it?"

"We haven't got a boy." We had me.

"Well then, do you know if you've got a hammer?"

"I have no idea."

"Your roof has rotted to a great extent, although someone's put a row of buckets in the attic just below here to catch the worst of it."

That had been me. I'd done it when we had first moved in. It was quite enormous, that gaping hole in the roof. "Do we need to find some more buckets, then? Is that what you're saying?"

"No. I'm saying, why don't you fix it?"

"Me? I suppose I'd need some more wood and a large amount of nails for that, Mr. Trimble." And seeing as how I didn't have them, pails seemed to work well enough. Shaking my head, I finished scraping my boots and then went inside.

Mr. Trimble soon came in as well, though he must have done it through an upstairs window, for he did not come in the front door. "That hole in the roof really should be patched."

Father was shuffling through my illustrations, and now he looked up. "Do you think so? Those pails seem to have worked well enough."

"If you don't patch it, it will just get worse."

He'd already returned his attention to my illustrations. "I suppose it will. . . ."

"It's generally preferable to repair these sorts of things right away. And there's no telling when we'll be in for a rain. It would probably be worth the time and trouble to do it today."

If one didn't know better, one might think my father was Mr. Trimble's assistant. I wondered if all sheep farmers were so overbearing.

But Father was nodding. "Of course, you're right. By all means, do what you must."

"I'll just . . . I'll go look to see if you've got a hammer any-where about."

Not long after Mr. Trimble disappeared, the sound of pounding rose from the roof. And before long, it descended into the stairs.

I put down my paints and went to find him. "Could you stop that beating about?"

He set his hammer down and looked up at me. "I'm replac-ing your rotting stair."

"Could you do it more quietly?"

"No. I'm afraid it would be quite impossible to use a hammer without hammering."

I returned to my illustration, determined to ignore him. I did wish I could remember all those things that I had divulged about my research and hopes for publishing papers. It was one thing to take advantage of our correspondence to convey my secret hopes, knowing that I would never have to meet the man. But it was another thing entirely to have him take up residence in my house.

Late that afternoon, Mr. Trimble set a stack of pails at my feet with a great flourish.

I shoved them aside with my foot as I finished the coloring of a petal. "What are those for?"

"They're your pails. There's no need for them anymore in the attic, or on the stair, so I'm returning them. The roof is repaired."

As I thanked him, Father called across the room. "You say you've done the roof?"

"I have. It was very—"

"Then come right over here. We've still got time to speak of that memoir on lilies I'm to write."

As they were consulting, I heard Mrs. Harvey drop our supper onto the dining room table. I did wish she would warn us so that we could move things out of the way. Going into the dining room, I set the food on the floor, gathered the specimen sheets and put them atop the others that rested on the burled-wood sideboard. Then I took Mother's china plates from the shelves and passed them about, saving for myself the one decorated with a bouquet of strawberries and buttercups. Only, Mr. Trimble sat down in front of it.

With a frown, I switched my buttercups for his tulips. "Watch your foot!"

He seemed startled to observe a serving bowl sitting beside his chair, but at least he picked it up for me and put it on the table.

We sat down together, the three of us. Father blessed the food. I picked up a biscuit and dunked it into my tea.

Mr. Trimble did the same and then gnawed at a corner. "This tastes remarkably similar to the meal Mrs. . . . . What did you say her name was?"

"Harvey."

"—to the meal Mrs. Harvey served us last night."

"There's not much variety to her meals—it's true—but I've always supposed that sailors must not care very much what they eat."

"Not having a choice is different than not caring."

Upon reflection, I agreed that it was. I dipped my biscuit into my tea again. "She does cook us a roast for Christmas." At least she had done the previous year.

We ate in silence for several minutes before Father spoke. "You should give the notes regarding your work on Ranunculaceae to this young man, Charlotte."

"Why?"

"So that he can finish the study for you and write it up."

But it was my work. It had been my work for nearly a year. And if he read my notes, then he'd recognize my handwriting! "Why shouldn't *I* be the one to finish it?"

"Because you're to marry soon. You've put so much work into it, it would be a shame for all your effort to go to waste."

"If the choice is between finding a husband or continuing my work, then I must say I'd rather—"

"Are you familiar with Ranunculaceae, Mr. Trimble?"

Why were neither of them listening to me?

"I know what they are."

Know what they—! Clearly, I had let this plan of theirs progress too far. "Have you done any extensive studies on the Ranunculaceae family, Mr. Trimble?"

"I know what buttercups look like."

"Buttercups are only one member of a family that numbers over one thousand species." I sent a look of protest toward my father. "And are you proficient with use of the compound microscope?"

"I've used a single lens. Does a compound microscope have two of them?"

I appealed to my father. "It's impossible for him to do it. I'll just have to complete the work myself." And that way, I could avoid giving him access to my notes and he would never realize that it was me, and not my father, with whom he had corresponded.

"We can discuss it later." Father's face brightened. "I was going to ask you, Charlotte, if you've heard back from the Botanical Society of London about the letter I submitted to the editor."

"I believe I did. I received something in the post just the other day." I'd put it where I always put Father's letters, even though he never remembered where that was. I had to practically place his mail into his hands, and even then I had to watch where he set it down to make sure I could later retrieve it. "I'm sure Mr. Trimble will be happy to assist you in finding it."

Mr. Trimble was already protesting. "I really don't know if—"

"Because that's what assistants do. They assist." If they were determined to push me out of my research, then I was determined not to help them in any way. I'd finished my biscuit and eaten as much salt pork as I intended to, so I pushed my plate away and rose.

Mr. Trimble stood as well. Not for the first time, I wished he were the Mr. Trimble of my imaginings. That way he wouldn't be so . . . present. Or intimidating. He would be entirely manageable. "I'll leave you to your work, then."

Father held up a finger. "Before you retire, Charlotte, I was hoping you could—"

"I'm sure Mr. Trimble will help you with whatever you need."

I went into the parlor and gathered my papers from my desk, as well as the illustrations I had been working on, before going upstairs. I nudged open the door to my room with a shoulder. Once there, I took my books from their shelf and stacked them on the floor. Then I replaced them with my illustrations. My mother's children's books kept their place of honor atop my chest of drawers.

Emptying out a hatbox, I shoved my papers into it and pushed it under my bed, knowing it would not be long before I could work on them again. The couple days I would have to spend waiting for Father to realize his mistake should enable me to take up my work once more with a renewed vigor.

4

I got up at half past five the next morning, dressed, and went downstairs—only to realize that I no longer had to. Assisting father on his rambles wasn't my responsibility anymore. And neither was doling out cold tea or praying Mrs. Harvey had remembered to leave out something for breakfast. Since I was up and awake, however, I determined to put the time to good use. I started writing up my notes on those suspicious yellow flowers Mr. Trimble had sent but soon remembered I ought not be doing that either. So I began writing a letter to our publisher, proposing that I write on something other than wax flowers, because really, I couldn't conceive of how to create one. But then I stopped midsentence. This, too, was something Mr. Trimble would now be doing. I stood and moved toward my father's study but halted halfway, walked toward the bookshelf but then gave it up. Finally I sat down again and wondered what there was to do if I wasn't supposed to be assisting my father.

I'd never done anything else.

The sun rose, and a ray of light illuminated the desks and shelves and floors with their fuzzy coatings of dust. I *could* do some dusting . . . but wouldn't that better fall under the juris-diction of father's assistant?

If I read the latest issue of *Magazine of Natural History*, it couldn't quite be called assisting could it? It wasn't truly pertinent to anything I was currently working on. As I settled myself into a chair, there came the sound of footsteps on the floor above, and soon Mr. Trimble appeared. Was he . . . was he just now waking? "If you're here, then who is with my father?"

"I don't know. Is he not here?"

I stood. "No, Mr. Withersby, he is not. He's out there some-where!" I gestured toward the window. "Out there by himself, wandering around." I dropped the magazine to the floor and hurried out into the hall. "Really, Mr. Trimble, he's not as young as he used to be, and he has dreadful rheumatism. I confess that I am disappointed to be put aside in favor of you and much in-clined to resentment, but I will not simply stand by and watch my father suffer under your tenure."

"He seems in perfect health, and I didn't know that—"

"He's much inclined to melancholia and distraction. If you don't look after him and I'm not *allowed* to look after him, then who will?"

"I had no idea, Miss Withersby. Please, forgive me. I will take the utmost care of him in the future. You can depend upon it."

"That's all very well and good, but who is going to take the utmost care of him now, this morning?"

"If you could point me in the right direction, I would be happy to undertake a search for him."

"There are a thousand right directions for a morning's ramble. I'll just have to go find him myself." I wrenched open the door and started down the lane toward the road. Thank-fully, I happened upon Father not long after. "I thought I'd lost you!"

He held up his vasculum. "I found some interesting specimens."

"You can't just leave without saying anything!"

He blinked in surprise. "What was there to say? You were
sleeping. And besides, I only went on my ramble."

"By yourself! Anything might have happened."

"I did just fine."

"But it's not safe. You're not to be left alone, and you're not
to be disturbed by anything. That's what the doctor said."

"What doctor?"

"The doctor. After Mother died."

"After Mother died, I was indeed quite . . . I was quite unlike myself. But really, Charlotte, that was many years ago. I'm
fine now."

I could not keep my chin from trembling. My mother had
been fine too, up until the day she wasn't.

Mr. Trimble met us at the door and helped Father off with
his coat. Father went into his study to work, and Mr. Trimble
sat himself down at my desk.

I took Father's vasculum into the parlor and began to sort
out the specimens, though I was quite clumsy in the doing of
it. It took a while for my hands to stop shaking.

There was nothing to do and no one to speak to. Finally, I
took my mother's Bible across the front hall and into the sitting
room, with its mismatched tufted blue chairs, vowing to read
it from start to finish. This room wasn't as cold as the parlor,
owing to its thick Turkish carpet and the stacks of papers that
lined the windowsills.

The house had gone silent and I ought to have been able to
read quite peacefully, but I couldn't quite get over the idea that
something about Mr. Trimble just didn't make sense. After having read through the same three verses in Leviticus four times,

I closed the Bible and went into the parlor. Mr. Trimble looked up and then stood as I entered.

I nodded and he sat. "I wonder, don't you miss New Zealand and those sheep of yours?"

"I do. Yes."

"May I ask why you undertook to return to England?"

He lifted a brow as he tilted his head. "There are things one does, not so much because one wishes to but because one must."

I mirrored his brow lift.

"Promises made must, at some point, become promises kept. I am the victim, Miss Withersby, of an injudicious past."

"So you intend to stay here, with us until . . . ?"

"Your father says I'm to stay until you marry. If you wish to be rid of me, might I suggest that the quickest way to do so would be to find a husband?"

I sniffed. There was something odd about his answers to my questions. "If you made a promise that would bring you back to England, then why go to New Zealand at all?" He'd never really said, not in all the time we'd been corresponding.

"Because there were opportunities there in sheep."

Sheep. Sheep and my *imagined* Mr. Trimble went quite nicely together. This Mr. Trimble I would have paired much more sat-isfactorily with a hound or a horse. I could quite easily imagine him joining the season's hunting-and-stalking crowd from Lon-don. "In all truth, I find that idea so completely preposterous—"

"So does my mother. She would much rather I—" He bit off the words so quickly he nearly choked over them.

"Would much rather you what?"

"Nothing."

"If you have a mother still living, I should think you'd much rather stay with her instead of us."

"But you don't know my mother, do you?"

"No."

"Then I would advise you to reserve your opinion." He picked up his pen, as if marking an end to the conversation.

"I should think your mother would want you to come home, now that you're back in England."

"I assure you, my mother wishes to see me just as much as I wish to see her. If she never knew I have set foot in England, then I would be happy."

"She doesn't have anything to do with that promise you made?" It was all so mysterious. "One would think that after . . . How old are you, Mr. Trimble?"

"I've four and twenty years."

"One would think that after so many years you might have figured out how to get along with her."

"Or she with me?" He smiled, but it was a stretching of the lips more than a sign of pleasure or of mirth. "One would think."

I repaired to the parlor after our midday meal, determined to keep an eye on Mr. Trimble. Again I had trouble concentrating on my Bible reading. The thought of marriage kept intruding. I found I could not object to the idea of *pretending* to look for a husband if the result would have Father returning me to my position. I did not, of course, actually want to marry. That would be taking things a bit too far. I reminded myself not to worry over things unlikely to happen. At the rate Mr. Trimble was disrupting the household, my reinstatement was only a few short days away.

Someone pulled at the doorbell, and I rose before remembering I wasn't to do things like that anymore. I returned myself to the sofa.

The bell sounded again.

I coughed. "Aren't you going to get that?"

Mr. Trimble started. "Get what?"

"The door. It's something I used to do that I'm not to do anymore."

"Surely getting the door won't interfere with your finding a husband."

"It might. I've never sought a husband before, so I'm sure I don't know."

He sighed, put down his pocket glass, and stalked to the hall. He yanked the door open with no apparent trouble, spoke for a moment with someone, and then shut the door. As he returned to his task, he pitched a letter into my lap.

"Tsk, tsk." I tossed it back at him. "I've been relieved of all responsibility for correspondence. Have you not heard?"

He gritted his teeth, broke the seal, and began to read. "'My dear Charlotte, it is with a gladdened heart that I hear of your decision to take up your Christian duty and turn your attentions to securing a suitable marriage. Being somewhat familiar with the way the boat rolls—'"

I snatched the letter and continued on with the reading of it. In silence. I recognized the Admiral's handwriting.

> *. . . may I be allowed the honor of providing you an escort on those occasions when your father may not be available?*

Knowing how little my father involved himself in drawing-room affairs, even when my mother was still living, I suspected those occasions would be many.

> *I have taken the liberty of securing for you an invitation to a dinner party this evening, and it is with great hope that I await your reply.*

Reply? I lifted my gaze from the letter. "Who delivered this?"

Mr. Trimble blinked at my inquiry. "I have no idea."

I waved the letter. "It's from the Admiral. He's requesting a reply."

"Then I suggest you make one."

I might as well agree to go. It was vital that I pretend to take this seriously if I wanted to prove to my father how invaluable my assistance had been.

Motioning for Mr. Trimble to move from the desk, I rummaged through my drawers for a sheet of stationery. I could not find any. In fact, I could not have found anything I was used to finding there.

Mr. Trimble shut up one of the drawers I had opened. "May I offer my assistance?"

"You've been enough help already." I went to the sofa, where a stack of father's notes was tidily stowed beneath a cushion, awaiting the day when I would find someplace to file them. Flipping through the pages I found a sheet of paper that recorded a line of investigation he had recently abandoned. Taking it back to the desk, I marked a diagonal line across his musings, then turned it over and wrote out an acceptance of my uncle's invitation and his offer to escort me.

"You can't send *that*."

I raised my head to see Mr. Trimble standing over me. I don't know why he felt the need to insert himself into my business. Hadn't he enough to keep himself busy? "I don't see why not. The Admiral asked for a reply."

"Haven't you got a clean sheet on which to do it?"

"Not at the moment. And I can't see how it very much matters."

"It shows an appalling lack of taste. And the man, you say, is an admiral?"

"He's also my uncle. And it's a good thing this reply is to him and not to you."

He snorted and went back to his work, while I stepped out into the lane in my stockinged feet to see if the messenger might have waited for a reply.

He had—and my begrudging answer was soon on its way to the Admiral.

That afternoon I nearly forgot about the Admiral's dinner entirely in my attempt to pretend as if I did not realize a bill was going unpaid for want of notice, father's notes were rapidly multiplying as they waited to be transcribed, and a draft of his latest memoir was in danger of arriving late to the Botanical Society—that is, if it ever happened to be posted at all.

When I found myself once again picking up a pen with the intention of writing to the butcher, I finally decided to take a good long ramble out toward Gavel Green. For simple pleasure, of course, rather than for any particular purpose. I dug my elastic-sided boots out from the cupboard and donned one of the Admiral's old shooting jackets. To the costume, I added my cylindrical vasculum in which I could store any specimens worthy of further investigation. Not, of course, that I would actively search for them, but if I happened upon one, it would be a pity not to collect it.

I occupied my thoughts with questions of the distribution of the earth's flora as I walked, and then I spent some time over the puzzle of exactly what a dinner party entailed. In the midst of my pondering, I realized I did not know what time the Admiral would be coming for me.

Being closer to the Admiral's abode than our own, I determined to put the matter directly to him. He lived at Woodside, a dignified sandstone house with a gabled roof. There was a window on either side of the central door and three on the second story. It was entirely respectable and quite unlike our own timber-framed house, which had three chimneys and hipped roofs that sprouted from all sides of the structure in all directions.

The butler answered the door, after which he showed me into my uncle's study. Though several books lay open upon his desk and he was in the process of writing, there were none of the stacks of opened books or scattered papers among which I was used to working.

He glanced up and then stood, putting down his pen with a grunt. "My dear girl."

I greeted him in return.

"I congratulate you upon coming to your senses where the topic of matrimony is concerned. What can I do for you?"

"I've come to learn what time I'm to go to that dinner you mentioned in your letter."

"Why, it starts at eight! I'll come for you at half past seven. I know you're used to dining rather earlier than is fashionable, but you'll soon become used to it."

By the hour of eight, I was usually climbing the stairs to my bedroom.

His glance took in my shooting jacket and the vasculum slung across my shoulder. He half rose from his chair and looked over his desk toward my feet. "May I make a suggestion, my dear?" He cleared his throat and at my nod continued, "There is no way in which to be delicate about this matter, so I shall simply say it."

"Please do."

"Eccentricities aren't well tolerated in society. Do you have anything more . . . stylish that you can wear this evening?"

"I've something I wore to London just last year, when Father went to address the Botanical Association. Remember, you urged me to get something new?"

"Splendid. These things require uniforms of a sort, and I do not wish to see you falter upon your first foray."

"I do not intend to. As you've said, it's long past time that I should venture out into society."

I was gratified to see that he almost smiled. "Quite right. I've high hopes for this campaign!"

Having concluded my visit to the Admiral, I walked back by way of Cats Clough. For good reason *clough* rhymed with *rough*. The term designated a steep valley that was rugged enough to require some care in traversing, though there was always something there of interest for the finding. I was accompanied on my ramble by the sounds of hunting horns and dogs barking away off in the distance. As long as they did not seem to be approaching, I typically paid them no mind. What the stalkers and hunters did was their own business, though it was a shame they always seemed to leave a trail of destruction in their passing.

I was astonished how very clearly one could see by the day's full sun. Without putting much thought into it, I soon collected an arm's worth of corn daisies. Their yellow, white-tipped petals always cheered me, and aside from that, my father had asked for some just several days before.

But oughtn't Mr. Trimble be the one to provide what was needed? It seemed a waste to simply discard them all, so I settled on the idea that I would place them in a jug on the mantel, and if Mr. Trimble took that to mean he should bring them to my father's attention, so much the better.

But *that*, I vowed, would be the last bit of aid I would give him! I climbed up the clough and had just started off on the road

56

toward home when I saw some cream-colored, trumpet-shaped greater bindweed in bloom. The name made one think there ought to be a lesser bindweed somewhere, but if there was, I had never heard of it. Pausing, I considered whether I ought to pick some when I heard the scuff of a footstep on the road.

Glancing up, I saw a stranger approach. Though he carried a vasculum, I did not recognize him. As he came abreast of me, he took care to pass to the other side of the road, but once there, he did not walk on past. That is, he seemed to want to, but each time he took a step or two in that direction, he ended in coming right back. He opened his mouth twice, as if he meant to say something, but both times, he swallowed his words instead. Just when I thought him determined to continue with his walk, he pivoted to face me. "You must think me terribly rude . . . or dreadfully forward." His gaze was darting everywhere but toward my face.

"I can't say what I think of you. I don't even know you." Though, from his earnest, even features and open manner, I presumed him to be a decent man.

"I am the new rector, Mr. Hopkins-Whyte, come to you from Northumberland."

The new rector? Perhaps that accounted for the way his fair hair had been swept straight away from his brow . . . though it had relaxed a bit into a wave as it approached his ears and curled altogether where it touched the collar of his coat.

I nodded. "Miss Charlotte Withersby."

"Perhaps I ought to have waited to have someone introduce us properly, but then might you not have thought the new rector a bit pretentious if he did not wish to meet one of his parishioners?" He patted the vasculum that hung from his shoulder the wrong way around. "I see that you are a botanist, and I like to think that I am one too. But then I considered that perhaps you wished to accomplish your ramble in peace, and an intrusion upon your privacy would be quite impolite . . ."

His pause seemed to offer a sort of apology, although I could not quite decipher what he meant to apologize for. "I can see now that I ought to have passed on by as I meant to do at first. Only . . . I was hoping to add some specimens to my collections, and I wonder if that is not hawkweed you have there in your arms?"

"Hawkweed?"

"They have yellow, tightly-packed flower heads." He was staring pointedly at my daisies.

"Yes . . . but these"—I lifted my blossoms toward him—"are corn daisies."

He fumbled with the opening of his vasculum. From it he pulled a well-worn copy of Hooker's *British Flora*. "I can't quite seem to work out how to use these tables. . . ."

"Perhaps an illustrated guide would be more useful." If he had one, he could never have mistaken a corn daisy for hawkweed.

"Perhaps. But I'm a rector. I ought to be an expert in botany by now. Least that's what everyone thinks. People seem to assume that being a clergyman necessitates an interest in God's creation. Not that I have no interest. I do. I can assure you that I do. But I can't tell you the trouble I had back in my old parish for not being keener on this sort of thing."

"In spite of what everyone seems to think, this sort of thing takes some time to master."

He sighed. "So I've gathered." A ghost of a smile seemed to curl his lips. "Gathered. Look there: I've gone and made a joke."

A full-fledged smile swept his face, and I could not help but return it. "How long have you been on your ramble?"

"An hour."

An hour with nothing to show for it. His vasculum was empty.

"Why don't you take some of these, then?" I separated out several of the better corn daisy specimens and placed them into his vasculum.

"That's quite generous of you. What did you say they were again?"

I told him once more.

"I ought to have known, I suppose. I assure you I'm much better at sermons than I am at botany."

I hoped so.

"Maybe I should try to find some actual hawkweed since that's what started me off on this ramble."

"If there are any yet still in bloom, you might find some over near Salterswall."

His face brightened. "Perhaps I'll be better at this than I had feared! Would you . . . I hesitate to ask this since I've only just met you, but you seem to know quite a bit about the area's flora . . . Would you ever consider coming to the rectory to view my collection?"

"I would." I had not seen many specimens from Northumberland.

"You would? You would! Well, that's . . . that's very kind. Thank you. I suppose . . ." He glanced down the road. "I suppose I should try to find that hawkweed of which you spoke. Good day. I hope to see you Sunday."

5

It was only after I had returned home and put my flowers into a jug that I turned my thoughts to the evening ahead. I decided I might as well change into my London attire and so be ready for my uncle when he came. I had not worn it since the previous year and was dismayed by how much dust had accumulated on it in the interim. I took my hairbrush to it and soon found that, through a combination of beating and brushing, most of it came off.

I'd forgotten how very little I had liked wearing it, the collar being too stiff and the arms being too tight, but I had told my uncle I would, so I vowed to withstand the suffering. My room, with its northern exposure, was becoming quite gloomy, so I went downstairs to wait, a treatise on British brambles in hand.

While I wished to avoid Father and Mr. Trimble, the sitting room had been entirely taken over by quires of drying-paper and plant presses. In order to sit anywhere I would have had to have found alternate locations for it all. I went into the parlor instead.

Father was nowhere to be seen, but Mr. Trimble was bent over a specimen, knife in hand. He stood as I entered. "Your father is taking a bit of a lie down at my suggestion, but he offers his best wishes for tonight. On my own behalf, I had hoped that I would see you before you left."

"I am afraid I cannot return the sentiment."

He stared at me for a moment as if rendered speechless, and then he laughed. "At least you're honest. A man would always know where he stood with you." He resumed his seat. "Your father told me I should speak with you, first, about a discourse on the classification of bog orchids and, second, on where to find a bill from . . ." He consulted a sheet of paper on his desk. "A bill from a Mr. Denton."

The butcher. "Father has been quite clear about his wishes. Both those items have now fallen under your purview."

"If you could just tell me where I might find the bill and the discourse, I would be happy to search them out."

I surveyed the various piles that covered all the flat surfaces in the room. "I should think it would become quite clear if you simply looked for them."

"I *have* looked for them. What I've found are—" he looked about and then grabbed at a pile that had been accumulating atop an overstuffed footstool—"piles of papers just like this one. They're everywhere!"

I gestured for the papers he held, and he placed them into my hand. I took a glance at them. "These are the Fs."

"The . . . ?"

"The Fs. Those things like extra foolscap and bulletins from the National Fern Society and letters from Mr. Fuller, one of my father's correspondents."

"But the one is for writing, the other is a society, and the third is a person."

"Exactly."

"So . . . should I happen upon a treatment of foxgloves, you would have placed it here as well?"

"Don't be ridiculous. They'd be under D."

"For?"

"Their proper name, Mr. Trimble. *Digitalis*." I peered more closely at him. "Did you not sleep well? You look rather pale."

"Tell me, Miss Withersby, should I expect to find twenty-six of these sorts of piles? One for each letter of the alphabet?"

"It's entirely possible."

"And where would you suggest that I look for that bill?"

"In the B pile."

"B for . . ."

"Or perhaps might it be under D for *Denton*?" I could not resist needling him. Maybe because my collar was so tight.

"I think it would help me a great deal if you would sketch me a map of your filing scheme."

"I could, but that would be assisting you, wouldn't it? And that's something I've been told I'm not to do. So I hope you'll understand when I say that I won't." I made a point of flipping through the pages of my treatise.

He took my measure through those blue eyes of his. "Have I done something to offend you?"

"You? Not at all, Mr. Trimble."

"I'm so glad because it seemed as if—"

"It's just that I find it extraordinary and quite patronizing to be told to give over to you—a man with whom we have just become acquainted—my life's work and that of my father and then be expected to *help* you in the doing of it. As if all that I've done, all the letters I've written, all the pennies I've pinched, all the . . . all the . . . all the *pails* I've placed beneath all the leaks in the roof didn't matter at all."

"I can assure you—"

"And not only that, but I've been writing nearly all of his—"
I stopped myself.

"His?"

"I've been writing . . . writing . . . *books* and such to pay our
bills. He's working on an illustrated series, for which I've been
doing the illustrations as well, but it's a large undertaking and
is being financed by subscription, and though it's quite com-
prehensive, I don't expect that it will provide any more money
than his previous works have. And I don't suppose that you are
proficient in the drawing of orchids?"

"I can't say that I've ever—"

"So I'm to leave my illustrations half-finished and my work
half-done in order to find someone to marry?"

"I never said—"

"And leave all of my father's work in the hands of someone
who doesn't even know the proper name for a foxglove?"

"It was just a joke, I assure you."

"Yes. Exactly. That's exactly how I feel. As if all that I've done
and all that I've accomplished are to be set aside for some more
suitable assistant simply because I've got *pistils*!"

"Pistils . . . ?"

"As if they're somehow considered less worthy than *stamens*!"

"Stamens . . . ?"

"Can you see how this is quite enraging?"

"I can see that you're highly incensed."

"Extremely."

He stood once more and then bowed. "Extremely incensed.
I think it more accurate, perhaps, to say that it is you whom I
am ultimately assisting."

If he hadn't usurped my position then I might have appreciated the sentiment. "Thank you, Mr. Trimble." At long last, I

had seen a glimpse of the man I had come to know through our correspondence.

"So . . . would you do it, then? Make a map of your piles?"

I felt my face flush. "Have you not understood a word I've said? My answer is no!"

For once, someone pulled at the bell at a most opportune time. Mr. Trimble nodded toward the front hall. "Shall I . . . ?"

"Please." I picked up the treatise once more, with the intention of actually reading it this time, but the Admiral strode into the room. He came to a dead stop as he took my measure from head to toe. "I had hoped you would be ready by now, my dear."

I stood. "I am."

"I rather thought . . . That is, I had hoped . . . Didn't we speak of the subject of uniforms just this afternoon?"

"This is what I wore to London last year."

"Yes . . . but haven't you something that you wore while you were *in* London? Something that . . . glitters or shines?"

Glitters or shines? Were the two rows of brass buttons on my bodice not shiny enough? "I've just this. But it's only a year old and very sturdy."

Mr. Trimble broke into our conversation. And rather rudely, in my opinion. "What your uncle means to say is that you're wearing a traveling dress, Miss Withersby, when what is expected at this time of the day is an evening gown."

"Quite right, young man. Thank you."

"I don't see why this can't serve that purpose. If I wear it in the evening, then it must, by definition, be an evening gown, mustn't it?"

Mr. Trimble was shaking his head. "I think you'll find your definition is rather more literal than what is generally accepted."

"It serves its purpose, does it not?"

My uncle was scowling now. "The proper uniform for the proper job, dear Charlotte. You can't steer the ship if you're dressed as a midshipman."

"Proper or not, this is the most recent addition to my wardrobe."

Mr. Trimble inserted himself again. "And . . . what about . . . What would you wear to church for instance?"

"Just a . . . just a dress."

"Perhaps your 'just a dress' would be a better choice."

"If you say so."

"I do."

I directed my gaze toward my uncle. "Then you'll have to allow me a few more minutes."

Really, I couldn't see what all the fuss was about. The Admiral had asked for something stylish, and the London outfit was the most recent purchase I had made. Not that I had wanted it, but it had been he himself who had insisted upon a new dress when he'd found out we were going. What's more, he'd taken it upon himself to have it made. But I took it off with a sigh and debated my remaining choices.

The first, a green striped gown, was embroidered with primroses and trimmed with ribbon. The second, in light blue, looked as if it had a jacket though it had been sewn to the bodice and wouldn't even open. It was really quite infuriating.

Being that it was rather chill, I settled on the one with the useless jacket, though it took some time to fasten, seeing as how I had to turn my back to the mirror and do up the hooks with my hook holder in one hand and the hook fastener in the other. It had taken me quite some time to devise the method, but I'd been left without recourse after Mother had died. The hooks done up, I took out my bonnet, which looked very much like an open-ended vasculum, and tied the ribbons at my chin.

If I had expected smiles or congratulations upon my return to the parlor, I would have been sorely disappointed.

The Admiral frowned. "You've got nothing then with . . . more . . . material? Or spangles?"

"Spangles? I should think not."

"Perhaps . . . perhaps we should stay in tonight, my dear. I could have a note sent and—"

"That will never do." Mr. Trimble had been staring at me, and now he stepped forward as he nodded toward my skirt. "That's a day dress, not an evening dress. You need something with more . . . Are you wearing *any* petticoats beneath that?"

I didn't see why he should be lecturing me on fashion, considering he, himself, was a sheep farmer. With his height and those broad shoulders of his, one might have accused him of looming over me. It made me feel distinctly . . . odd. "Petticoats? Why?"

"Because that's what's done. Least it was when I left for New Zealand, and I haven't noticed that fashion is much changed."

I wasn't wearing any petticoats. I detested them. They always got caught up round my ankles, unless, of course, I wore those I'd used when I was much younger, but they were too tight about the waist. "How am I to do anything if I wear all those skirts?"

"The point is not to do something, the point is to—"

"I'm to do *nothing*? Then why am I even going?"

"That's beside the . . ." He was peering with great interest at a place just below my bosom. "Is that a . . . What *is* that exactly? That splotch on your bodice?"

I peered down to try to see it, but my sight was blocked by my bosom. "I couldn't say for certain."

I took up the pocket glass Mr. Trimble had left on the desk and held up a black book behind it. Aiming it at my bosom, I recognized the stain immediately in the reflection. "It's a bit of India ink. As a rule, I wear a smock when I work on my illustrations, but there was that day last month—"

"India ink?" Mr. Trimble's words were indignant. "The gown is ruined."

I scoffed. "It's not so bad as that. I only got it several years ago. It's still quite serviceable."

"If the spot can't be got out, then it's ruined."

"Well, it won't be got out tonight, and it's just a small spot." I looked into the pocket glass again. "It's hardly longer than my thumb. Just a smear, really, and I don't see why—"

"Then at least do us all the favor of wearing some sort of mantle. You do have one of those, don't you?"

"I do. Of course I do."

The Admiral cleared his throat. His face had gone flush. "If we do not hurry we will be late, and punctuality is the duty of subjects."

I ran up the stairs and grabbed my mantle from its hook. And I put on a petticoat as well.

In the front hall, Mr. Trimble stopped me with a hand to my arm. Untying the ribbons that bound my hat to my head, he took it off. "This is a carriage bonnet."

"It can't be. Why, I ask you, would I have purchased a carriage bonnet when we have no carriage? The very idea is ridiculous."

"It's just that it's meant for a daylight excursion instead of . . . Never mind. Better to go without one. Perhaps . . ." He drew me into the parlor and dashed toward the Wardian case in which I was growing moth orchids. Lifting the lid, he broke one off its stem.

"But that's . . . that's my orchid! I'll thank you not to concern yourself with things that aren't any of your . . . your . . . *concern!*" I'd worked for months to grow it so that I'd have a living specimen from which to draw. But I suppose it didn't matter anymore if I wasn't to be allowed to draw anything ever again.

He pushed it into my hair just above my ear. "As we decided earlier in the evening, Miss Withersby, it is you whom I am ultimately assisting."

The advantage of wearing a flower in one's hair is that it was much lighter in weight than a bonnet. But even so, I could not quite bring myself to forgive Mr. Trimble for ruining my orchid.

The Admiral got himself into a sort of stew as we drove to the dinner party. It seemed to be that general kind of foul mood that usually presaged some launch upon the waters of the empire's politics, or some policy of which he considered the government in grave danger of doing *the wrong thing*. But as we turned from the road onto an estate's lane, he made a rather unexpected pronouncement. "There is just one rule, that which we call golden in polite society, my dear. Treat others as you would like to be treated."

Just one? I felt myself begin to relax. "I shall endeavor to keep it in mind."

We were greeted by a footman, and I was shown to a room where I could leave my mantle. Considering Mr. Trimble's opinion of my India ink stain, I decided to keep mine with me. The attendant did not seem to understand my wishes, so a momentary scuffle over my mantle ensued, but I emerged victorious.

After rejoining the Admiral, we were bid to ascend the stairs, and soon we found ourselves at the entrance to a large open room. It was lined on both sides with windows festooned with red curtains. They were held back to reveal the night by thick golden ropes that ended in tassels. From the coffered ceiling hung three chandeliers that must have counted a hundred candles between them. The room was filled with people milling about, conversing in groups.

As we crossed the room, the Admiral pointed out our hosts, the Bickwiths. Perhaps a decade younger than the Admiral, they looked a pair, being rather short with florid faces. He introduced me to various guests in turn, and I noted that his demands for a dress with more material or spangles were not quite as unmerited as I had earlier thought. My skirts looked like a wilted flower compared to those of the other women. Although most of them had bared their shoulders, I was glad of my long sleeves and covered bosom. I was quite thankful as well for the mantle I had refused to surrender, since the windows had been thrown open to the night.

By the time we crossed the room, Mr. Bickwith was conversing about dogs and their keeping with quite a number of those gentlemen who had come from London for the hunt. I had just determined to speak to one of them about the possibility of their taking more care with the flora in the area when the Admiral took me by the arm and introduced me to Mrs. Bickwith.

"*Miss* Withersby?"

I had never thought my name difficult to pronounce . . . although her difficulty might be explained if she were hard of hearing. I raised my voice when I answered. "That is correct."

"I don't believe I have ever met anyone so secure in their expectations that they can afford to flout convention."

I smiled. "Thank you."

She sniffed and walked away, leaving me quite pleased with the encounter.

6

The Admiral led me over toward an older man and a girl. As we approached, he identified them as Sir Templeton and his daughter, Miss Templeton. With no little trepidation, I understood somehow that she was the ideal specimen by which the rest of us in the room must be judged. What was a generally accepted practice in botany suddenly seemed most unfair.

The blond hair that had not been twisted into a profusion of curls above her ears had been gathered at the back of her head into a knot and then covered in a mass of ribbons. She was wearing a dress in a shade of pink that was common to hollyhocks but the fabric was embroidered with all manner of strawberry blossoms and strawberry fruit attached to twining vines. As I peered more closely at the pattern, however, I began to suspect that the depiction of the flower petals was faulty. If only she would stop moving, I would be able to tell.

She smiled while the Admiral made the introductions. As he embarked upon a conversation with her father, she turned to me. "It's very nice to meet you, Miss Withersby. I must confess that I feel quite certain I've seen you before."

"Perhaps out in the field."

"The field? What field would that be?"

"It's difficult to say exactly. I've visited so many of them." It looked as if some of her strawberry flowers had five petals and some of them had six! I could see it quite clearly now. "I take a ramble every morning to look for specimens."

"I do as well! That is, not every morning. And if truth be told, not very often, but I have done. Once or twice. Botany is all the rage at the moment, you know, and I do so like to keep up with rages!"

I heard myself sigh. "My rambles are finished though. At least for the time being. My father has decided I should marry. He's afraid I've nearly become too old to do so."

"Mine too. But . . . how old are you, then?"

"I just turned twenty-two."

Her brow crimped in concern. "You *are* old! However did you manage to stay out of society for so long?"

"No one ever seemed to notice that I wasn't in it." And it hadn't ever mattered before.

"I wish no one would notice me sometimes!"

"It's the Admiral's fault. He convinced my father that it's my duty to marry."

"My father says the very same thing. Duty is rather a heavy responsibility, isn't it?"

"I'm not against marriage in the case of other people. I might not even be against it for myself one day, but I've got papers to proof and books to write and bills to pay and . . . and what no one seems to understand is, if I'm not there, then none of the work will get done."

She was nodding as if she understood exactly. "Someone is bound to realize soon enough."

"That is my hope. My father took on someone to replace me. But the man knows nothing about nearly everything, so it shouldn't take long. Until then, however, it's necessary to continue pretending that marriage is in fact my intention. That should make my absence even more dire."

"That's brilliant, Miss Withersby! You've such lovely hair to go with those brown eyes of yours. And such pretty ears—I daresay you've the ankles to match? With your fashionable figure, you could attract even the most confirmed of bachelors. Do let me help!"

I wondered . . . should I tell her about the flowers on her dress? Would it be considered impolite? My uncle had said that I must treat others as I would like to be treated, and *I* would certainly wish to know that the embroidery on my dress was a gross misrepresentation of nature.

She looked at me with a keen-eyed gaze. "You miss your rambles, don't you."

"I do. I cannot lie."

She linked an arm through mine. "Then we should go on a ramble ourselves, you and I."

"Perhaps we could go tomorrow." I eyed her dress again. Really, the mistake was quite glaring.

"Tomorrow!" She seemed rather startled with the idea, even though it had been her own. But then she smiled again. "I would look forward to it if it weren't Sunday."

"I don't see why it should matter. I could meet you at half-past five, I should think. Depending upon where you live and how long it will take me to walk there, of course."

"Half past five? I'm quite a lazy creature, Miss Withersby— you can ask anyone who knows me—but isn't that rather late for a ramble?"

"I suppose I could meet you a bit earlier, at four, perhaps, but with the sun not rising until six, I don't quite know what we'll be able to accomplish."

"You meant in the *morning*? Oh!" Her laughter rang through the room. "To have the pleasure of my company, on most days you'll have to wait until at least ten. I'm really quite decadent, I must warn you."

"Ten . . . ?" By ten I would normally be investigating the specimens I'd collected, but nothing was as it normally had been, and I wasn't to be working. I was supposed to be engaged in finding a husband. "I suppose ten would be fine. On Monday, then?"

"I'll feel ever so industrious! But not on Monday. I'll need a day to contemplate this and work up to the endeavor. Shall we say Tuesday?"

I agreed. "I wonder, Miss Templeton, may I tell you something?"

Her brows peaked. "Please do."

"Do you know that the flowers on your dress haven't got the right number of petals?"

She glanced down at it. "I had no idea."

"Some of them have five petals and some have six, and although that's possible considering that different varieties of the strawberry have different numbers of petals, I would assume that your dress is meant to depict just one variety, wouldn't you?"

"Why, I'd never given it a thought!"

"I wouldn't have mentioned it, except that I thought you might want to be made aware of it."

She grasped my hand. "I'm sure I wouldn't have noticed if you hadn't told me, but now that I know, I can't think that I'll be able to wear this again with a clear conscience." She paused and glanced about the room. When she spoke again, it was in a whisper. "Do you think anyone else has noticed?"

I didn't see how they could have failed to, the omission was rather glaring, but if she hadn't noticed, then maybe . . . "Has anyone else mentioned it?"

"No . . . no, they have not."

"Then perhaps they haven't. You can hope so in any case."

"I do hope you're right. I am certain that, if Mrs. Bickwith has seen the fault, she would have found some way to tell me by now. She's really quite spiteful."

She'd been nice to me. She'd even given me a compliment. "The man my father took on in my place is like that. He never ceases to tell me of the mistakes I've made. Or those I'm about to make."

"Is he one of those pompous sorts, with a loud voice and a barreled chest, who goes about with his nose in the air?"

"He *is* rather large. And he does make a very many pronouncements and hasn't ever once listened to any of my suggestions."

"Say no more, Miss Withersby. I detested him on principle before, hearing how he had taken up your position, but now I shall detest him upon your evidence as well."

"That's quite kind of you."

"Think nothing of it. We must stick together, you and I."

I glanced around the room. "I haven't been to any of these dinner parties before. I'm astonished by how many people I truly don't know." Even those I recognized from church, I couldn't say I was actually acquainted with, for normally we happened into the service late and sat in the back pew, ducking out at the opening notes of the postlude.

"Many of them are just here for the hunt. It's best to ignore them. I assure you, they're none of them interested in country folk. Not even a baronet's daughter like me. Now, I shall point out all the rest. Over there is Mr. Stansbury."

I looked in the direction she was nodding and saw a man of middling years speaking to Mr. Bickwith.

"He's an industrialist come from Liverpool who has bought

Overwich Hall. And as if he doesn't have enough money already, he's leasing out the rights to his hunting park. I'm afraid I've heard his taste is somewhat vulgar." She tipped her head as she considered him. "But I have to consider that there must be some hope for him, otherwise he would never have chosen to wear that waistcoat. I'm sure it must be velvet. At least, that is, mostly velvet. It's quite stunning, don't you think?"

I didn't know what to think, but I nodded anyway.

"He's very keen on his glasshouse and the development of the grounds of his estate but seems to have little interest in marrying, though I doubt very many people know that. It's just that I might as well not exist for all the attention he pays me, and I don't mind telling you I'm considered quite the catch in Cheshire. He might be just the man for you, Miss Withersby. He's quite handsome, in his way, don't you think?"

I could only agree.

"Knowing him to be disinterested in matrimony, you could safely be seen to pursue him without putting yourself in danger of receiving a proposal."

"I will keep that in mind."

"Although, as I said, he made his own money, so he's most definitely not a gentleman. Oh! That could be a point we can use in your favor. Might your father not be even more alarmed if you're thought to be drawn to a man like him?"

"I—"

"Now. Enough of Mr. Stansbury. Just to his left, beyond Mr. Bickwith, is Mr. Robinson, also a bachelor, who might be . . ." She paused as she frowned. "No. No, I've changed my mind. You definitely wouldn't wish to marry him, and perhaps it's best not even to encourage him. He's proposed to almost every female in Overwich over the age of fourteen." She leaned toward me. "And it's rumored he even proposed to Miss Fletcher."

"Miss Fletcher?" I hadn't met her. At least if I had, I couldn't remember. "I don't think I know who—"

She pointed out a woman across the room with a flick of her fan. "She must be forty, if she's a day." Her eyes swept the room. "Across the floor, over there, is our new rector—"

"Mr. Hopkins-Whyte. I have already met him."

She studied my face for a moment. "And it wasn't a pleasure. Is that what you mean to say?"

"He was very apologetic about the whole thing."

"Apologetic! Whatever did he do?"

I explained our way of meeting, and she considered him from behind the sweep of her fan. "On the whole, I would have to say such behavior does not bode well. A rector ought to be quite sure of himself, otherwise one would find it very difficult to put much confidence in his sermons, would one not?"

"I suppose one—"

"And you say he *apologized*?"

"He did."

"For meeting a lady such as yourself?"

I nodded.

"When he has eight children to find a mother for . . . that seems rather odd to me, does it not to you?"

"I suppose it—"

"Then he also would be safe for you to encourage." She gave a decided nod as she snapped her fan shut. "I daresay he's not sufficiently recovered from his wife's death to propose marriage to anyone yet. Otherwise, he would already have done so."

"What about that man over there?" He looked to be about my age.

"Heavens no! His mother is as mad as a hatter. As soon as you talk to him, he'd offer for your hand, and before you could say, 'God, please save me!' you'd be married and chasing the old woman through the streets, trying to make sure she didn't stick someone with her pair of shears the way she's always threatening to do."

I shuddered.

"Of course, if she suddenly died, I'm sure you would be quite comfortable as mistress of his house. But all in all, I don't think it's worth the risk, considering that you don't really wish to marry."

"I don't. I really don't."

"There's Mr. Hobbes's son." She nodded toward another man. "Don't let those ears of his frighten you. He's got some cousins who come to town now and then and they're all really quite dashingly good-looking. You wouldn't know it to see *him*, but *they* take after his father's side of the family. They bring their dogs and run them in the hunt, and it's all quite marvelous, really, but I suppose they wouldn't help you any since the point is to have someone be *seen* to have an interest in you and that would be rather difficult since all they seem to care about is the hunt."

"And what about that man?" I indicated him with a nod of my chin.

"He has his cap set for Miss Atkinson over there. It's quite tragic, really. He won't propose marriage because he hasn't the means and even if he did, her father would never agree because he's not from Cheshire, not originally in any case, and so they just keep gazing at each other."

"Is there no one else?"

"No one worth your time or trouble. Of course, I might answer differently if you actually *wished* to marry. In that case you could even consider old Mr. Carew, but the goal is to provoke a man into paying you attention enough to raise alarm, but not enough to propose. You've issued quite a challenge, Miss

Withersby, but I've both talent and time, and if you leave it to my capable hands, you'll soon be back to your life's work."

"I'm so grateful for—"

She patted my arm. "No gratitude is necessary. It will be ever so entertaining to make you the belle of the ballroom, and it will take some of the pressure off of me. Now then, who shall we start with? Mr. Stansbury or the rector?"

I'd already suffered through an introduction to the rector, so I chose the other man instead.

"A wise choice. Now then, just leave everything to me."

She pulled me along to the Admiral who had wandered off toward the windows and was staring out into the darkness of the night as a stiff breeze flattened his hair. She tugged at his sleeve.

He turned with a start and bowed. "Miss Templeton."

She curtseyed. "I had the most engaging conversation with your niece, Miss Withersby, and I was struck by inspiration! Mr. Stansbury has the best glasshouse in the county. I was telling her all about it, wondering if she hadn't happened yet to see it. He sometimes gives tours to visitors, but she told me she'd never had the pleasure of an introduction."

The Admiral was regarding the man in question through narrowed eyes. "He's not quite a gentleman, to my way of understanding. Didn't he have an interest in shoe black?"

The tiniest of frowns marred her brow. "Something to do with the railways, I rather thought, but considering Miss Withersby's interest in botany, perhaps an introduction might be merited."

The Admiral sniffed.

"*Warranted*. Perhaps an introduction might be *warranted* is what I meant to say."

He peered at her, lips pursed for a moment. "Perhaps it is. I haven't been introduced myself, but I daresay if I can convince China to open her ports, then I can introduce myself to an industrialist from Liverpool."

He marched out across the ballroom floor as Miss Templeton and I struggled to keep up with his long strides.

She clutched at my arm. "This is going quite perfectly! How alarmed your Admiral will be if he thinks Mr. Stansbury's interest in you surpasses his interests in plants and is, in fact, genuine. You'll be recalled to your father's side in an instant!"

For the first time in several days, my spirits began to lift. "I've so longed for my microscope and—"

"You really must try to smile, Miss Withersby. You look frightfully dour the way you are just now."

I fixed a smile to my face.

Mr. Stansbury glanced toward us, and when his gaze fixed upon the Admiral, his eyes widened. He bent at the waist in a short, choppy bow.

The Admiral nodded. "Stansbury, is it?"

"Indeed, sir. It's a very great honor to make your acquaintance."

"I've been told you have an interest in botany."

"I do. A very great interest."

"May I present my niece, Miss Withersby. Her father is a botanist. The entire family has an ancient affinity for the topic."

"Miss Withersby." He bowed, and I curtseyed in return. "I am pleased to make your acquaintance. Do you share your family's interest?"

"I do."

"Perhaps, then, you would do me the favor of viewing my collections?"

I needed to know what they were before deciding. "What is it that you've collected?"

"Orchids. Ferns. Palms. Anything my correspondents can get for me."

Palms weren't my favorites. I considered them altogether too expansive for my taste, and they didn't much flower, but it did not seem an appropriate time to quibble. "Yes. I will."

"Tuesday perhaps? At two o'clock?"

I looked at my uncle.

He replied on my behalf. "Very well. We shall see you then." He nodded at the man as one would in taking leave, but he continued to stand exactly where he was.

After a glance at Miss Templeton and me, Mr. Stansbury nodded and moved off.

The Admiral harrumphed, took out a handkerchief, and patted his brow.

Miss Templeton took me by the hand and pulled me close. "Now we just have to get you introduced to the rector."

"I've already met him."

"Nobody knows you've met him, and if your uncle didn't see it . . . ?"

"No."

"So the first time might have been for nothing for all the good it does us now."

"Then what shall I do?"

"We must obtain another introduction by way of the Admiral. That's the way it's done." She pushed me toward him.

"Uncle?"

He glanced over at me. "My dear?"

"I wonder . . ."

Miss Templeton was nodding as if to encourage me.

"Have you met the new rector yet?"

"I have. Though he seems a likeable fellow, I have decided to withhold my judgment until I hear him preach a sermon. Let's hope he's one of those who has sense enough to dispense with politics and satisfy himself with the Word of God."

I lifted a brow at Miss Templeton.

She stepped forward. "I hear he brought an excellent collection of . . . of plants with him from . . . wherever it was that he came. Where *did* he come from?"

"Northumberland." At least that's what he'd told me.

"I am entirely besotted with the idea of the north! And I'm sure Miss Withersby would love to see his collections. I was wondering, since my father is otherwise occupied at the moment, could you make an introduction for me?"

"I would be happy to do so."

The Admiral marched over to the rector, and once again Miss Templeton and I were left to follow in his wake. There were bows and nods and altogether too much of a fuss made of my uncle's sordid past.

The Admiral pinned Mr. Hopkins-Whyte with a glance. "I've heard that you haven't met Miss Templeton or my niece, Miss Withersby."

The rector bowed once more. As he straightened he looked at me. "Your . . . your niece?"

"My sister's daughter."

The rector was beginning to look apoplectic.

"We're ever so happy to have you here, Mr. Hopkins-Whyte." Miss Templeton's words were spoken with a smile.

"Thank you?"

"I've heard you've come to us from Northumberland."

"I . . . I have done so. Yes. From Northumberland."

"I've also heard there are ever so many beautiful . . ." She was kicking me in the shins. "So very many beautiful flowers such as . . ." She gave me another kick. "Oh, do help me, Miss Withersby. You're so much better at flowers than I am."

"I'm sure you must have seen many specimens of privet, Mr. Hopkins-Whyte."

His brow furrowed. "I've rather . . . an uncollected collection at the moment, you see, but yes. I did collect many specimens during my time in Northumberland. I'm sure privet must be among them."

Miss Templeton sighed. "I do so love the exotic. Don't you, Miss Withersby?"

"Certain exotics." Others I found entirely too foreign.

"I was thinking of local exotics. Specifically the sorts of flowers from the north that we don't often get to see here."

Mr. Hopkins-Whyte was trying not to smile. "Northumberland being in the north, I must say . . . Rather, I suppose one might *wish* to say, that altogether it would be expected that you would have a much greater variety of flowers here in Cheshire."

"But you seem to be saying your collection isn't worth seeing!" Miss Templeton was practically chiding the poor man. "Your modesty becomes you, but Miss Withersby and I consider ourselves devotées of flowers, and we're avid collectors ourselves, and I do hope that you might someday be persuaded to share your own collection."

"Of course, I would be happy—"

"How generous you are! We wouldn't want to interrupt your sermon writing, but could we possibly prevail upon you to entertain us Tuesday afternoon? Around four o'clock?"

"Tuesday? Well, of course, Tuesday is—"

"How perfectly splendid! We'll see you then."

We both dropped curtseys, and as the rector stared with wide eyes at my uncle standing beside him, Miss Templeton took me by the hand and pulled me away. "Good gracious! And the man has eight children. It's a wonder he ever gathered his thoughts long enough to get married."

"He's not so bad as all that." In fact, he was better than I had remembered. "And really, he was quite right about there being so many more flowers here in the south than he had access to in the north."

"I don't care about his flowers, Miss Withersby!"

"Then why did you provoke him into showing us his collection?"

"So that you can be seen going to the rectory. No one will suspect that he has any designs on *me*. Papa would never entertain his suit! But you, Miss Withersby, are a different matter entirely. I shall let it slip that we are going to visit Mr. Stansbury *and* Mr. Hopkins-Whyte on Tuesday and we'll just see how long it takes for tongues to start wagging!"

7

Mrs. Bickwith came up to us not twenty minutes later. "I hear the new rector has *eight children*." The tops of her cheeks had gone red, and now they matched her gown.

Since she seemed to be speaking to me, I answered. "I've heard the same."

"I suppose it wouldn't make any difference to you, however."

"To me? Why would it?"

"It doesn't pay to be discriminating at your age."

"Discriminating? I suppose it depends upon what the question is. In terms of microscopes, for instance, I should think it most definitely pays to be discriminating. My father and I have always held that German lenses, though they're terribly expensive, are a better purchase because—"

"Microscopes?" She turned to Miss Templeton. "What do microscopes have to do with—"

Miss Templeton smiled at her. "Miss Withersby is enamored of flowers. Her father is quite well-known in botany."

"Oh?" Her gaze fluttered back to me. "Then you must become a member of the King's Head Field Club."

"I don't think so. I—"

"You *must* join us. There's nothing more uplifting than flowers. We meet on Sunday afternoon."

As the woman left, I confided my objections to Miss Templeton. "I don't want to become a member of a field club."

"But why not? I'm a member of the field club."

"I object to the very idea of field clubs, because most of the time they destroy the very fields they're meant to be viewing, and by the time a true botanist comes along, there's nothing left to pick!"

"Hush now. You shouldn't speak so loudly. People are beginning to notice." She deployed her fan and began to sweep it back and forth.

"They ought to notice!"

"My gracious, Miss Withersby, it won't do to hold such strong opinions. Not when you're supposed to be bent on marriage." She patted my hand as she looked around the room. "I wonder who we'll be seated next to at dinner. I'm going to be very bold and hope you're a pair for Mr. Stansbury. I daresay he has the *makings* of a gentleman. It's such a shame he made his fortune in railways. There's just no way for that to sound appealing. Pity."

By the time we arrived at the table, I was famished. The assembly as a whole was quite colorful. It resembled nothing so much as a field of wild flowers in July.

At dinner, I was seated across from the Admiral and next to both Mr. Stansbury and Mr. Hopkins-Whyte.

I must confess that at first I paid much more attention to the food being served than to my dining companions. The bread was like nothing Mrs. Harvey had ever made for us. I didn't even have to dunk it into my tea to be able to eat it. There were oysters, which I didn't eat, and transparent soup, which I did.

There was a boiled fish of some sort and stewed cardoons and then some collared pig, which wasn't at all dry or even tough. It was enough to make me wonder why it was that father and I had to eat like sailors when some people appeared to eat like kings.

As I ate, Mr. Hopkins-Whyte kept apologizing for the state of his collections, while Mr. Stansbury attempted to persuade me to the merits of something he called a stumpery.

It wasn't until the cheese was served that I could devote my attentions to a reply. As a rule, I didn't really much care for cheese. "When you say *stumpery*, Mr. Stansbury, what is it exactly?"

"Finally! Some interest in my undertaking." I liked the way he smiled as if he really meant to. "I can tell you, Miss Withersby, that the rest of the county's population considers it a folly."

"I know what it is to have your life's work discounted. Or dismissed and considered a hobby." Or treated as nothing at all.

"You do understand." Mr. Stansbury had a very frank way of gazing at me through moss-colored eyes. His hair was dark, and he had combed it back to reveal a triangular point. His face had been fashioned with a firm hand, which had left behind a decided chin and a broad brow. Something about him reminded me of an invasive weed that has crept its way into a flower garden, trying to insinuate itself among the other plants. He looked harmless enough, he probably was harmless enough, but somehow he didn't quite belong.

"To answer your question," he said, "a stumpery is simply a collection of stumps."

"Stumps. As in . . . ?"

"Tree stumps."

"So you've taken a parcel of woodlands and cut down all the trees? Is that what you mean?"

His bark of laughter rolled across the table, making me almost wish I could understand the humor of my words.

"Excuse me, Miss Withersby, for laughing. Anyone will tell you I'm not the most couth of men. I've simply had tree stumps brought in and planted, stump down, in one of my gardens."

"So . . . the roots are exposed?"

"Exactly."

"You've a garden of tree roots, then?"

"Precisely."

"I've never heard of such a thing."

The Admiral drove me home and accompanied me to the door. When I bid him good-night, instead of returning to his carriage, he came into the house with me.

Although Father must long ago have gone to bed, at least I hoped he had, Mr. Trimble was still hunched over my desk, working. He stood when he saw us.

The Admiral nodded and then proceeded to pace in front of the fireplace for several long minutes. "I don't know how to put this to you delicately, Charlotte," he finally said, "so I shall simply come right out and say it."

"Please do."

"Mrs. Bickwith inquired as to whether your trunks had not yet arrived."

"My trunks? We've been here for nearly four years now. Of course they've come!"

"That's not what she meant to say. What she meant was . . . Well, I think . . . That is . . . I think . . . you should pay a visit to a dressmaker."

"Why?"

Mr. Trimble cleared his throat.

The Admiral transferred his gaze to him.

It took me a moment to realize my uncle was waiting for an

introduction. "Admiral Williams, this is Mr. Trimble, a corre-spondent from New Zealand, come to work for my father. You might remember him from before we left for the dinner. He was speaking of petticoats and . . . and other things."

Mr. Trimble stepped forward, hand extended. "Admiral *Williams*?" He spoke the words almost reverently.

My uncle nodded. "Her Majesty's Navy."

"I consider it a very great honor, Admiral. Though I may not be the first, I wish to offer you my congratulations on the reopening of China to trade."

My uncle took his measure from head to toe and finally nod-ded. "So noted."

"Forgive me for intruding upon your conversation with Miss Withersby, but may I offer my observations?"

"If you think them relevant."

Mr. Trimble addressed himself to me. "You are lacking the appropriate attire in which to find yourself a husband, Miss Withersby."

"Why would it matter what I'm wearing? Are we not taught from the cradle to look beyond appearances?"

"Appearance does matter, and quite a bit to some people, I assure you."

I considered his words for a moment. "I suppose . . . I put on my shooting jacket and boots when I go for a ramble in order to better facilitate the collection of specimens . . ."

Mr. Trimble raised a brow as if waiting for me to go on.

"So the corollary is that I must put on some other sort of costume when I go to these dinner parties in order to better facilitate the collection of a husband?"

The Admiral let out a breath in a great *whoosh* of air. "Quite so, quite so. The right uniform for the job. Just like I always say."

"I've got to have one of those gowns? One of those with all

the . . ." I moved my hands about my skirts to try to gather the words to describe those massive dresses I'd seen.

"I daresay you'll need more than one." Mr. Trimble spoke in the most benign way, but his eyes made me think him quite serious.

"*More* than one?"

"They're like day lilies, Miss Withersby. A new bloom, a new gown, each day."

This pretending to find a husband was going to require an extravagant amount of money. It's a good thing I had never done it in earnest before. But that didn't get me out of the bind I was in at the moment. "Surely I can make do with what I have." It should only take a few more days for Father to realize my worth and after that no one would care about my gowns any longer. "We've hardly money enough to pay Mrs. Harvey, and if I'm not going to write that book on wax flowers, I don't see where we'll get the funds for—"

The Admiral harrumphed. "You can tell the dressmaker I'm good for it. Haven't got the expense of children because I left it too long and now I can't live with anyone but myself."

I blinked. Had he . . . had he just offered to pay for new gowns? He'd never done anything of the sort before. He'd always seemed almost as embarrassed on our account as we were on his. I wanted to tell him to save his money, that new gowns were hardly required, but I'd perpetuated a deception and had no choice but to continue in it. "Thank you. When shall we go, then?"

"Go where?"

"To the dressmaker."

His brows rose in apparent alarm. "You're asking *me* to go with you? I don't know anything about frills and furbelows."

It was apparent to me that he knew more about the subject

than I did. "I suppose I shall go by myself, then. Although . . . I don't really know what to ask for."

"I can write it all down for you." Mr. Trimble returned to the desk, which had formerly been mine, seeming intent upon doing just that.

I followed him. "I can't think how it is, being just a sheep farmer from New Zealand, that you know about this sort of thing."

"A general knowledge of this and that comes in handy even in the wilds of the empire, Miss Withersby. And when you're raised with sisters, you can't help but come by a knowledge of fashion and its modes."

The Admiral snorted. "I had my own sister." He glanced over at me. "Your mother always hated this sort of thing. Said it took too much time away from what was important." He frowned. "Though I can't go with you, my dear, you must go with someone—otherwise, they'll talk you into all sorts of fripperies that aren't needed. You'll want what's appropriate and useful, but no more than that. No point in putting a mast on a dory. I could send a message to Mrs. Bickwith and ask her to accompany you."

Not Mrs. Bickwith. She reminded me too much of broad-leaved dock. Some admired its flowers, but I had always found them to be too drooping and waxy for my taste. "What about Miss Templeton?"

"Brilliant idea," the Admiral said. "I ought to have thought of her myself. I'll write out a note and have it delivered tomorrow. Ask her to accompany you on Monday."

"Could you make it on Tuesday morning?" Miss Templeton seemed to have a need for contemplation. "But don't make it for any earlier than ten."

Mr. Trimble passed him a sheet of paper. The Admiral cleared a place atop the mantel and composed his message.

"There!" He signed it with a flourish and slid it into his pocket. "I've asked her to accompany you on Tuesday morning. I'll send my carriage for you both."

As I sat in church the next day, I realized the rector had not lied. His true calling was to the pulpit. I had never heard a finer sermon. One point followed upon the other in such an orderly manner and with such clear logic that his thesis could not be called into question. And far from the wandering, dubious conclusions of the previous rector, this rector's sermon called for moral courage and immediate action.

I fairly pledged myself to clean and virtuous living.

The next day after I had woken far too early with nothing to do, after wandering about the house and refraining from all things related to flowers, I took myself off on a ramble. Again I encountered the rector around the region of Cats Clough.

"Miss Withersby." He tore his hat from his head and clasped it to his chest.

"I must say, Mr. Hopkins-Whyte, that I quite enjoyed your sermon yesterday."

His shoulders eased. "Thank you."

"I had no idea that you were so . . . that you . . ."

"That I could speak so eloquently?" He smiled as I began to laugh. "That's what my wife always says. Said. She claimed I courted her through psalms and visions of heaven instead of bouquets of flowers, with the stuff of paradise rather than earthly jewels."

He was holding onto the strap of his vasculum, gripping it so tightly that his knuckles gleamed and his fingers trembled. "She never asked me for anything, but I told her I would make her proud, that I would become a proper clergyman. And I have tried." He held up his metal cylinder. "You can see that I have tried."

"Indeed you have."

"But I must tell you that it's very tiring tramping about the countryside in search of flowers you've never seen before. I suppose I don't have to tell you that. Your father has made a career of it. And, as you said, you're a devotée of flowers yourself."

"Indeed, I am."

He sighed. "I am getting better at it. And I do have quite a collection at the rectory. Quite a large, fine, big collection." He blinked his eyes open wide as if he'd just startled himself. "A collection you are coming to see tomorrow!"

I nodded. "Miss Templeton and I, both."

"I must . . . I really should . . . I think it best if I go now."

"Please don't trouble yourself on our account, Mr. Hopkins-Whyte. I wouldn't want you to set aside your sermon for—"

"Sermons come easy, Miss Withersby. It's the flowers that have proved to be so confoundingly difficult. But I do try."

"Flowers come easy to me. I suppose that's why I like them so. They sprout and bloom and die, but they never prevaricate. A violet is always a violet. It's very reassuring."

"It's the way I feel about God's Word. It always remains the same. Little wonder, I suppose that His creations are constructed in a similar manner. I feel, like so many others, that I ought to be inspired to higher thoughts by botany, but I must confess I normally feel very . . . confused." He looked sadly down at his vasculum and then glanced up at me. "I suppose I had better get back. To the children." He nodded and then replaced his hat. "I'll see you tomorrow."

When I returned, Father was closeted in his study and Mr. Trimble was sifting through a stack of journals.

"Enjoying your work?"

He had stood absentmindedly as I'd entered. Now he glanced up at me and then sat back down, continuing his work.

"I would offer to help you, but I can't." I sat in a chair and pulled off my boots.

"Your father has given me the task of compiling recent writings on the classification of orchids. Do you have any idea where the rest of the *Botanic Gazette* magazines would be?"

"No."

"Because there's a previous article referenced in this one"—he held up an issue—"that I cannot find."

"By whom?"

He squinted as he consulted the issue. "Mr. Allen."

"That sounds familiar, and he did publish a monograph on monopodial orchids last year, didn't he?" Mr. Trimble began to reply, but I continued. "No. Forgive me. I believe it was the year before. But I wouldn't wish to say that I was certain. It caused quite a stir, though you probably wouldn't have heard of it, being halfway across the world as you were. Which leads me to wonder just how much you actually know about the current state of botany."

He smiled, but I could tell there was no humor in it.

"May I ask, why didn't you tell me your uncle was Admiral Williams?"

"Why would it have mattered?"

"He's the finest seaman to ever sail in Her Majesty's Navy! If he were related to me, I would make certain everyone knew it. To have such an honorable man share my family name . . . I tell you, Miss Withersby, it would be a vast improvement upon the family I was born into. I must confess that I don't understand your lack of family pride."

"My family—my father's and my mother's both—are botanists, Mr. Trimble. They always have been, back as long as anyone can remember. Can you imagine the scandal the Admiral caused by insisting upon going into sailing?"

"I would hardly call it *sailing*."

"But surely you can see what a disappointment my uncle was."

"I hardly call being the hero of the Opium War a disappointment."

"In a family with such longstanding botanical roots, his insistence upon eccentricities—"

"Such as?"

"Such as . . . what?"

"That's what I'm wondering. What were his supposed eccentricities?"

"*Supposed*? Are you mocking me?"

"I'm merely trying to understand you."

I sighed. "He and my mother were raised in Essex. From what I have been told, he had a near constant need to be out upon the river."

"That hardly qualifies him as an eccentric."

"And he built himself a boat."

"How very devilish of him."

"Upon which he sailed far and wide."

"As a proper sailor should."

"And when he won a bursary at his entrance to university, he turned it down for a commission in the navy instead."

"I see. For which provocation he was . . . ?"

"My grandfather didn't speak to him for many years, and my grandmother never wrote to him, and he was off sailing about when my parents married."

"And I suppose when he was knighted by Queen Victoria for the valiant service he had offered his country, then . . . ?"

"Then we couldn't hide our relation to him any longer."

He burst out laughing.

"I fail to see any humor in the situation." I reached over and tapped on the lid of a Wardian case, and a droplet of condensation fell onto an orchid's leaf.

"Perhaps you ought to consider past events from his point of view. It's not a pleasant thing to be the bane of someone's existence. I can tell you, from experience."

"I wish someone would consider things from my point of view. I am being forced to abandon my life's work. Does no one understand that? If my father and the Admiral have their way, my generation of Williamses will contribute nothing to the record of botany."

I had been speaking rather more loudly than I meant to and revealing more about my sentiments than I had wanted to. *Confound it!* I took a deep breath. "I never said the Admiral was a bane."

Mr. Trimble opened his mouth to speak and then closed it up. A look of indecision crossed his face. "Didn't you?"

"He has done much for my father since my mother died, and I won't have him disparaged."

"I never meant to."

The Admiral *had* done quite a bit for us. Until that moment, I hadn't quite realized how very much he'd done. He'd gotten my father out of bed, and he'd moved us to Overwich. He'd been . . . he'd been our saving grace. Which made me feel rather mean and very small about my opinions of him. "He simply doesn't fit. He failed to meet the family's expectations."

"Don't we all? From time to time?"

"Perhaps you have, but I haven't. I never have. I have done precisely as was expected."

"But why must expectations always become obligations?

Imagine if he had done as your family expected. Then who would have won Hong Kong for the queen? It's a well-established fact that he was the naval genius of his generation."

Could it be that I had been looking at the Admiral all wrong?

Mr. Trimble cleared his throat and continued, "I should confess that I have no great love for my family. And I've been wondering what my obligation is to them when I can't abide by their strictures. So I find your opinion of the Admiral quite illuminating. And rather alarming, if I may be frank. He's the hero of the realm, and yet you seem to hardly tolerate him."

"You sound as if you don't quite fit with your family either."

"No, I do not. So I must ask myself, if I prefer the woodlands to the meadows, if I prefer sunlight to shade, if my habit inclines to the upright instead of climbing, then why must I live my life twisting and coiling about a tree's trunk? Why can I not just live as a tree?"

"It's impossible to change one's genus, Mr. Trimble. Is that what you're trying to do? You might as well try to hide your roots and declare yourself to be an owl." I tucked my feet up on the chair, beneath me. "Your family are not inclined to sheep, then?"

"No."

"Are they inclined toward botany?"

"No. They are more inclined to excess and dissolution than pursuits such as this." He shuffled through the pages of one of the journals for a while before he gave up with a sigh. "Do you think it possible to change what one is, Miss Withersby? Fundamentally? At the core?"

"Are you asking again whether a vine could ever become a tree?"

"I suppose that I am." He looked at me, a crease lining his brow.

"It would seem to be impossible, would it not? Even those plants some believe to be new species are often simply varieties of the old and are prone to reversion."

"Yes . . . I suppose, in my darkest thoughts, I have often feared the same."

M r. Trimble's strange words stayed with me throughout the afternoon, and I pondered his question.
Was it possible to change one's habit? To modify
one's very nature? God created each corn daisy, each stem of
hawkweed, each flower, for His purposes to serve at His good
pleasure. Did that mean each creation of His was lovely?

It did not.

There were flowers that gave off the most putrid of smells
and twining leaves that could cause a most maddening itch. It
did not mean, however, that those creations were any less.

They had to have been made by God. Everything was. And what
was the alternative, in any case? To not believe in God? To believe
in . . . in simple chance? Or magic? The idea seemed preposterous.

I had to believe that even the meanest of creations served
God's purposes. And yet anyone could see there was a great
difference between a thorn and a flower and no hope at all of
one becoming the other.

If Mr. Trimble's family was dissolute, as he had said, did it
not stand to reason, that he would eventually become the same?

It was a confounding sort of puzzle.

I supposed I must remember that people could make choices that plants could not. Or . . . perhaps Mr. Trimble was the true representation of his family and the others the aberrations. I rather liked the idea that *they* were the exception rather than him, for—in spite of his taking up my position and his annoying tendency to lecture—the author of all those letters, the possessor of all those hopes and dreams of which he'd written, couldn't be all bad.

But for how long could one hope to defy one's own nature? What if *I* was ignoring God's divine plan? What if my true calling, my one purpose, was, in fact, to marry and bear offspring? What if my botanical investigations were simply self-serving?

I had never before pursued such lines of reasoning, and the whole idea and the unsatisfactory nature of my conclusions unsettled me. Would it not be wonderful if mankind were more like plants? If their habit was plain and they always did those things for which they were intended?

At ten o'clock the next day, the Admiral sent his carriage round for me, and then I went to fetch Miss Templeton at Dodsley Manor. With many columns and pilasters, arches and parapets decorating its substantial façade, it was equally as decorative as she.

After the footman helped her up, she settled into her seat, shook out the sides of her blue many-caped mantle, and then clasped her gloved hands in seeming glee. "I have never ridden in a Berlin carriage before. Can you believe it? But it's so spacious, so stately; I wonder why it was ever scorned for the Clarence?"

Indeed it seemed as if she did wonder, for she was looking around the interior as if in amazement. But then she turned her cornflower-blue gaze on me. "In any case, I was ever so excited to read the Admiral's request. I hadn't planned on visiting the dressmaker for another month—at least! So what is it you need, Miss Withersby? And how am I to be put to use?"

"I need everything."

"*Everything?*"

"Everything. Apparently I'm not suitable."

"How shockingly delightful! We must make sure my father never finds out. He was so certain, considering how old you are, that you would be an appropriate companion. It's the only way I could get him to let me go round without an escort—to promise that you would provide the escort for me!"

"You must remember that I'm only doing this to make my father get rid of Mr. Trimble and take me back. With any luck, it should only take a couple more days. You can understand, then, my reluctance to visit the dressmaker."

"You must never be reluctant to visit a dressmaker."

"I fear it will be a waste of her time and my uncle's money."

"But that's no reason not to take your wardrobe seriously."

"What I really need is a new shooting jacket."

"A new *shooting* jacket! You say the most extraordinary things. I am going to like being your friend very much."

"Well, you see, the pockets of my current jacket have the worst holes in them, and just last week, I lost a perfectly good specimen because it dropped right through the seam."

"Then we'll add a new shooting jacket to the list."

"I really don't know what's required. Although . . ." I reached down into my reticule for the list. "Mr. Trimble wrote down a few things."

"Mr. Trimble . . . your father's new assistant? As if *he* could know anything at all about the matter!" She sniffed and reached a hand toward me. "The list, if you please."

I gave it to her.

She tore it in two and let it flutter to the floor. "*That's* what I think of Mr. Trimble and his lists! If you have any doubts or questions, just ask me. I will not allow you to go astray. You can depend upon it."

The dressmaker gestured me over to a velvet-draped corner and said something about cutting my gowns to my stays and for that reason she had better see them, hadn't she? So she undid my dress, helped me off with it, and turned me round.

"I can't possibly cut a gown to those!"

I looked down at them and didn't see anything very objectionable.

"Those stays aren't even fit to you!"

The dressmaker I'd seen for my London clothes hadn't objected. "They were fit to my mother, but since she hasn't any use for them anymore, I didn't see why—"

"You're going to have to get new stays before I can do anything with you." She helped me back on with my dress and then put us both back out onto the street.

I turned to Miss Templeton, who was blinking from our abrupt departure. "I don't suppose there's a staymaker in Overwich?"

She nodded and started off. We took care to avoid the channels of foul-smelling brine that ran in rivulets through the streets. I wished I could have avoided the clouds of soot as well, but they seemed to sink toward the ground, filtering the sun's rays and leaving sooty smudges on the buildings. The town ought to have displayed itself in the sunny golden tones of its sandstone, but thanks to the saltworks, it looked as if it had been doused with dirty dishwater. I always felt as if I ought to bathe whenever I returned from town. Only one of many reasons I avoided Overwich.

Miss Templeton's disposition, however, did not suffer from the setting. She seemed to know everyone and stopped often to talk. In between her conversations, we visited the staymaker and the glover. It seemed everything required a visit to everywhere. She also extracted a promise from me that we would visit the milliner once we'd ordered my gowns so that we could purchase some hats to match. After two hours had passed, I found myself quite exhausted by the ordeal. I threw myself upon her mercy, hoping to be allowed to go home for a rest before our afternoon visits, but Miss Templeton forbade it. She would not even parole me to a pub.

"We can't possibly take refreshment while there are still gowns to be ordered. If they aren't started soonest, you'll have nothing to wear!"

Back we went to the dressmaker. The woman undressed me once more and sniffed at my new stays when she saw them. "I don't know if I could call those an improvement."

"I've others on order."

"At least I've something to work with now." She took my measure and then set about compiling my order. "It's late in the season, but I assure you we can still provide for your needs. What is it that you desire?"

"I need a dress to make me look like a moonflower." Remembering the dresses, like Miss Templeton's, that had been covered in blooms and twisting vines, I thought it best to be specific. "It probably ought to be embroidered with them as well."

"You want to look like a moonflower . . . ?"

"Exactly, except that the dress should have lots more petals."

"Petals?"

Miss Templeton was beset by a spasm of coughing. I pounded her on the back until she recovered.

She waved my hand away and then took in a great breath

of air. "Miss Withersby means the gown ought to have a great many flounces."

"But no sepals." At least not like the kind that my blue dress had.

The dressmaker was peering at me from beneath a furrowed brow. "No . . . ? Have you lately come from the Continent? I haven't heard these terms you're using . . ."

"I just don't like sepals. At least, not on a dress."

"Sepals? I still don't quite understand your meaning."

"Have you got a piece of paper and a pen? I can show you what I mean."

I made short work of sketching the sort of gowns the women at the dinner party had been wearing.

"Oh! Yes. Of course I can make you a gown in the style of Louis XV, Miss Withersby."

"But remember, no sepals."

She made an appeal to Miss Templeton. "Whatever can she mean?"

I took up the pen to sketch in what I didn't want. "You see most flowers have sepals. Right here, where they join the stem. But I don't want any."

"Oh! You mean a redingote. Of course you wouldn't want that for an evening gown." She took up the sketch. "Just leave this all to me. I'll see you're well taken care of."

"Mr. Trimble had said that ordering just one dress wouldn't do. I'm supposed to be like a day lily."

"A day lily!" The dressmaker muttered the words to herself.

"A different bloom each day."

"I don't quite—"

"What Miss Withersby means is that she'll need five evening gowns, five day gowns, three visiting dresses, a mantle, a cloak, and . . . and a promenade dress."

The woman wrote up the order, shaking her head all the while. "And I suppose you'll want all of these tomorrow."

"I would be much obliged."

Miss Templeton laid a hand on my arm. "By the end of the week she'll need two of the evening gowns, and really, she ought to have one of the visiting dresses tomorrow."

The woman's brow rose. "We will proceed as quickly as we can, but even I cannot perform miracles."

I couldn't let my most urgent request go unmet, however. "I hate to add one more thing to the list, but I'll also need a new shooting jacket."

Miss Templeton grasped my arm. "Oh! And do order a new skirt as well to go with it!"

"I don't think I really need—"

She smiled. "We'll just add it to the list."

After leaving the dressmaker, we went to Woodside to get the Admiral and then presented ourselves to Mr. Stansbury at Overwich Hall.

Miss Templeton looked round the front hall with great excitement. She took hold of my arm and stepped close. "I've never been here before!"

"Neither have I."

"It's just like a setting for an opera." Her eyes were full of wonder.

I'd never been to an opera before, but if the setting consisted of vivid reds and gleaming wood, colonnaded balconies and ivory-colored plasterwork, then she was right.

"Would you like to see my glasshouse?"

The Admiral grunted while Miss Templeton clapped her hands. "Oh, yes!"

Mr. Stansbury showed us the way with a sweep of his arm.

We walked through a series of twisting hallways and then the house seemed to leave off and give way to a green-tinted, light-filled paradise of soaring heights, copious plants, and . . . were those *parrots?*

"I started out collecting orchids." He showed us several baize-lined shelves of orchids. "And then I decided to add some orange trees." They lined the long central aisle on both sides. "And then some ferns." These made up an enormous mountain reaching nearly to the roof, from which cascaded a waterfall in miniature. "And then I started on palms."

"How clever you are! How delightful this is!" Miss Templeton leaned over to sniff at an orchid.

"It has no fragrance." Mr. Stansbury and I cautioned her at the same moment.

His lips turned up in a smile as he met my glance. He took her by the elbow and gestured across the path toward an orange tree. "But these do." As they wandered down the aisle together, I left the Admiral admiring a fountain and walked down the path in the opposite direction toward some more orchids. It was there that Mr. Stansbury rejoined me.

I fingered an orchid's leaves. "Are you quite sure this is an *aloifolium?*"

"That's what my correspondent said. See there? He wrote it on the label."

"Because it looks rather more like a *dayanum* to me." I considered myself more knowledgeable than most, since my father and I had spent so many hours dissecting those species.

He pointed to a third plant. "I've a *dayanum* just there, though it's hardly budded."

"I wonder if your correspondent got the two confused . . ." I read the label on another in his collection and stroked its long pointed leaves. "And are you certain this one isn't just a grass?"

"I should hope not. I paid thirty pounds for it!"

"Has it bloomed yet?"

He frowned. "Not that I can remember."

"It can be quite difficult to identify a plant if you haven't seen its flower. It could be almost anything."

"I've been told I have the finest collection of orchids in the realm."

Miss Templeton had rejoined us by that point. "Miss Withersby knows ever so much about plants. She's practically a genius. Her father is working on some volumes about orchids."

"Withersby! I knew I'd heard that name before. Your father is the author of *A Complete Account of the Orchid in the Empire*? And its companion volume, *Ranunculaceae in Britain*?"

"He is . . . although it wasn't quite as complete as he had hoped, so he's writing another volume." I, in fact, had written most of the *Ranunculaceae* book. And I had illustrated all of it.

"You're one of *those* Withersbys? I have those books! Both of them." He gave me a keen-eyed glance. "Forgive me for saying this: I thought your criticisms just now ill-founded, but perhaps you're correct. Could I trouble you to return when my orchid has bloomed? Then you can view it for yourself. If my correspondent turns out to have been unreliable, then I'll need to find myself another one." His cheeks flushed. "If there's one thing I can't abide, it's being made a fool of."

"I should hardly think it would make you a fool. Misled, perhaps, and thirty pounds the poorer, but not everyone knows what to look for."

He seemed little consoled.

Miss Templeton had wandered from us, and now she called

from the far corner of the glasshouse. "You must come look at this!"

Mr. Stansbury cocked a brow at me and nodded in that direction. We found her with my uncle. "Look at this palm. Can you believe it? It's growing flat, just like a fan!"

"It's not a palm." Again Mr. Stansbury and I spoke the words together. As I began to laugh, he joined me.

The Admiral glowered at us and then spoke to Miss Templeton, whose face had turned quite red. "A common mistake. It certainly looks like a palm."

She hardly seemed mollified. "It's not polite to laugh at a girl, just because she doesn't know a palm from a . . . whatever it is. And it *is* quite something."

Mr. Stansbury nodded. "I agree." He turned on me. "Shame on you, Miss Withersby."

"I hardly think . . ." I let my words die, when I perceived that he was joking.

He bent toward Miss Templeton. "Have you ever seen a palm with a beard?"

"A beard? Don't tease, Mr. Stansbury."

"Let me show it to you." With a wink at me, he led her off through the palms, leaving me with the Admiral.

Several minutes later, her voice floated toward me over the squawking of the parrots. "Oh! Miss Withersby! You *must* come and see this. It has the beard of an old man."

"Must be a *Coccothrinax crinita.*" The Admiral mumbled the words as he strode toward them, hands clasped behind his back.

"How . . . how do you know about that palm?"

"Any fool who's put in to Havana has seen one. Can't say I've ever gotten used to the sight of it though."

I hurried up the path behind him, wondering that he, who had forsaken botany for boats, would have known a thing like that.

We spent some time admiring a grouping of ribbon ferns and a display of maidenhairs, and then Miss Templeton put a hand to her bosom and sighed. "Thank you ever so much for your kindness, Mr. Stansbury. Your collections are magnificent."

He bowed.

"I so hate to leave, but we must be off. Mustn't we, Miss Withersby?"

"But we haven't yet seen the—"

"Perhaps we will be honored with an invitation to visit some other time." She was looking at Mr. Stansbury quite hopefully.

"Yes! Please do come back. Any time you'd like."

Why was she so determined to leave? "I don't see why we can't stay here for just—"

"We're expected elsewhere." Miss Templeton whispered the words through her smile.

We were?

She grabbed my arm and turned me round and then pulled me right down the path. "The rector!" She whispered the words into my ear.

The rector! I don't know how I had managed to forget him.

We arranged ourselves in the Admiral's carriage and set off in the direction of the rectory. Miss Templeton rhapsodized about the glasshouse all the way.

"I adored his ferns! And his orchids! And his palms!"

"One might venture to say that you adored *him*."

"Miss Withersby! How you shock me. I hardly know the man."

The Admiral was watching us through a narrow-eyed gaze.

She saw him watching too. "I think the more accurate statement might be that he seemed to adore you."

"Do you think so? I hadn't really noticed." Though I was hopeful. I did want to see whether his orchids turned out to be incorrectly labeled.

"If you didn't notice, it's because you were so intent on criticizing him and his orchids."

"I wasn't criticizing him. I was criticizing his correspondent."

"You'll never find a husband if you go about disparaging people's collections."

"I wasn't disparaging anything. It was a very nice specimen. In any case, if I were him, I'd want to identify it correctly. Wouldn't you?"

"It doesn't matter what I would want; it matters what he wants. Although I have to admit that it seemed he was quite taken with your knowledge of plants."

"I don't suppose the rector has a glasshouse, so I daresay I shall be saved from making any more mistakes."

9

He may not have had a glasshouse, but he did have children. There were a bunch of them running wild through the yard as we alighted from the carriage. One of them ran into me and almost knocked me to the ground.

The Admiral reached for the boy's collar but missed. "In my day boys knew how to behave!"

I could sympathize with their plight, but I couldn't approve of their antics. In my experience, being bereft of a parent meant more work and less leisure. I wondered that they had time for such aimless pursuits.

"Good gracious but those children need a mother!" Miss Templeton took up my arm and hauled me toward the front door.

The rector answered the door, a baby cradled in his arm. "Yes?" He seemed not to be expecting us.

Miss Templeton smiled at him. "We've come."

He stood there blinking at us. "May I assist you in some way?"

"You asked us to view your collections."

"My . . . *collections!*" A pallor swept his face, then was immediately replaced by a flush. "I don't know that . . . they're not quite . . ." He pulled the door open wider, stood aside, and flapped his arm toward the interior. "Please. Come in."

We entered, Miss Templeton clutching my arm as we did so. The Admiral gestured to the yard. "I'll stay out here."

The rector was continuing to speak. "I had remembered about your visit earlier in the day and I put Peter and Elizabeth to work sorting through things. But then the baby needed to be put down and then he needed to be got back up and the children insisted they were hungry and the nurse had gone out and I had an inspiration for a series of sermons and started reading the Bible and I just . . ." He paused to survey a parlor that was in such disorder that it was difficult to know where to walk. "I could make some tea."

"Oh no. No, thank you." Miss Templeton answered on my behalf as well. "Perhaps Miss Withersby could take up where the children left off."

He looked at me with surprise. "You're hungry? I think they were having some bread and cheese." He picked up a plate holding a half-eaten meal and offered it to me.

Miss Templeton intercepted it. "That's so very kind of you." She put it back down. "But I'm sure the children will still be hungry once they've realized they haven't yet eaten. I had thought instead that Miss Withersby could help you with your collections. I'm sure she's very interested to see them." She took the baby from him and made her way to a sofa, where she sat and dandled him on her knee.

His ears turned red at the tips. "Of course. So sorry. I just . . . I'm not quite certain where to begin." He put a hand to a tottering pile that sat atop a desk. "I have these." He then bent to lift a coal hod and dumped a pile of dried plants onto the floor along with a stream of sooty ashes. "And then there are more in there." He gestured toward a bookshelf, but I didn't see any.

"There?"

He nodded quite vociferously.

"*Where* there?"

He pulled a book from the shelf. "Between the leaves."

"You mean to say that all of these books have specimens inside them?"

"Most of them. Not all of them. At least, I don't think . . ." He took another book and opened it, spilling a treasure of dried plants from its pages. "Perhaps, yes."

I felt my brow lift in amazement. "But you can't dry specimens in books. You need a press."

"I just thought that since most of them are so thick and heavy . . . to spare the expense of a flower press . . . "

"You'll ruin the books as well as the plants." I took up a particularly thick book and opened it. "You see?" The pages were marked and wrinkled where they had absorbed the plant's moisture, and the plant itself was discolored.

"I hadn't realized."

"Moisture mildews the book and the paper eats at the plant."

"Good gracious!" He began pulling books from the shelves, holding them by the spine and shaking them. Flattened specimens drifted to the ground like falling snow.

"Wait!" I closed a hand about a book. "You'll lose all your field notes if you keep on like that."

"I've got them all in a notebook that I keep in my desk."

"But if the specimens are here and your notebook is there . . . how do you know which belongs to which?" I stooped to the floor and grabbed up a specimen. "This, for instance. How would you know on which ramble you found it and on which date and where it was growing?"

"Oh." Comprehension dawned in his eyes. "I . . . don't." He took the specimen from me and looked at it as if hoping it might tell him. "So you mean to say all that time and all those walks are for . . ." He looked up at me. "Were they for nothing?"

Most probably yes. But somehow when I opened my mouth to respond, I just couldn't find it within myself to tell him. "Why don't we see what you have first, and then I'll better know how to advise you."

He shook the rest of the specimens from the books and then brought over the pile from the desk. As he pushed them toward my feet, I was left with more specimens than I knew what to do with. It was one thing to be at home in a mess of my own making and another thing entirely to try to navigate someone else's.

He brought over a footstool and bade me sit.

As I gazed at the specimens, my hopes sank in just the same manner they did when father and I had opened Mr. Trimble's latest crate.

As I sifted through the plants, I separated them out and placed them into a pile. "These speedwell specimens all seem to be of the flowering stage. Did you not pick buds?"

He gasped. "Buds? No. It seemed too cruel to pick them and keep the plants from flowering."

"Why don't we make a list of what you need and a list of what you can offer, and we can write the Botanical Society of London to see if an exchange might be made."

"I didn't know there was such a thing as an exchange."

"It's quite extensive, with a great many correspondents. I'd be happy to write the letter for you."

"Would you . . . You would?"

"Correspondence is one of my specialties."

"Unfortunately, it's one of my great deficiencies." He grabbed up a pen and inkwell.

"Perhaps you can do the writing." I decided to start with the speedwell, since he'd collected so much of it. "So you need specimens in bud, in fruit, and with seedpods." I glanced at the pressed specimens in my lap. "Do you not pick your flowers by the roots?"

"Lavinia always says . . . That is . . . she used to say . . . She's my wife you see. Or she was. But she says it made an awful mess when I brought the roots home with the flowers."

"If you wash the dirt off before you bring them inside, it keeps everything tidy."

"I never thought of that."

"You really should include roots in the future."

"I shall make a note of it."

After finishing with the speedwell, I took up several specimens that appeared to be of the same plant. "And these? Are they lady's-mantle?"

"Lady's-mantle? I had looked for them but thought I'd never found one. Are those . . . are those really them?"

"I should think so." I looked at them more closely. "If we boil them up, I would be able to tell."

"Boil them?"

"In order to revive them. Plump them up a bit."

Miss Templeton had been entertaining the baby, but she now rose from the sofa and held it out toward the rector. "I don't know that we have time for boiling at the moment, but I'm sure we could return, Mr. Hopkins-Whyte."

"We haven't any more time?"

"I'm afraid not." She said it with a smile, but it didn't truly look as if she were happy.

From outside there came a great bellow.

"Is that the Admiral?" I lifted the specimens from my lap and stood, trying to get a look out the window.

The rector strained to see as well. "Are the children—?"

Miss Templeton offered a hand to assist me in the negotiation of the great piles of specimens that lay around me. "I believe the poor Admiral is quite beside himself. Next time perhaps he'll be content to come inside."

We opened the door to find the Admiral sitting inside his carriage and the children pelting it with pebbles. Miss Templeton stood beside me, eyes wide, hands clasped to her bosom. "Whatever are they doing?"

The rector had come out behind us and shouted at his children. "Look here! Where is Miss Lytton?"

One of the brood, a tall girl, turned to address him. "She's cooking supper. She sent us outside to play."

"Yes, well, it's not polite to throw things at people."

She was joined by one of the boys. "But he said he was an Admiral. We were just shooting cannonballs at him."

The rector stepped around us to gather the children up, taking the younger ones by the hand and then dropping them almost immediately in order to open the carriage door for us.

He called through the window to the Admiral. "I am so sorry!"

The Admiral mumbled something as the rector helped us into the carriage.

As we pulled away, Miss Templeton leaned out the window. "Good-bye! We'll see you soon."

The Admiral was scowling. "I didn't get treated so rudely by the Chinese. I've never seen a more insufferable group of children. And their father a rector!"

Miss Templeton sighed. "The poor darlings. And without a

mother. I suppose that's why he's so interested in your niece. I shouldn't be surprised if he proposes marriage before a fortnight is over."

I shuddered to think of owning children like those.

She continued with a bright smile. "I daresay it would be such a blessing to have a ready-made family. Don't you think so, Miss Withersby?"

"A *blessing*!"

She frowned. "What girl wouldn't want a family like his?"

Me. I wouldn't.

She cocked her head as she looked at the Admiral. "I can't help but wonder if Mr. Withersby counted on his daughter being snatched up so quickly."

"What's that?"

"Miss Withersby's attracted the attentions of two of the most eligible bachelors in the county! Don't you worry, Admiral Williams. We'll have her married off in no time." She winked at me when the Admiral wasn't looking.

We returned Miss Templeton to Dodsley Manor. She did not make us come in, for which mercy I was heartily thankful. When I returned home and walked into the parlor, Father and Mr. Trimble were conversing about the classification of some flower or other.

"I think you'll find Linnaeus's system works quite as well as any other," my father was saying.

"But what about the benefits of a natural system?"

"What benefits?"

"I simply think that reducing the entirety of a plant to its sexual system is an unjust simplification of a wondrously complex creation, and de Jussieu's system—"

"De Jussieu? Bah, he's a Frenchman!"

I collapsed into a chair and levered off my shoes.

My father looked surprised to see me. "Back already?"

"I've been gone all morning. And the afternoon as well."

"I hadn't realized."

"It looks as if I'm to be proposed to soon."

"What's that?" My father had come round the table to stand in front of me.

"It looks as if I'm to be proposed to soon."

"Why that's . . . that's . . ."

Mr. Trimble joined him, staring down at me, hands at hips. "You'll never be proposed to if you insist upon traipsing about in gowns like that."

I glanced down at it. "What's wrong with it? Neither Mr. Stansbury nor the rector voiced any objections." With primroses embroidered upon the material and green trim circling the hem, it had been a favorite of mine for years.

"It's meant for a summer season."

"I like primroses at any time of the year." However, it was, perhaps, a bit light in weight for just sitting about in. The parlor really was quite drafty. I went into the hall, took up the Admiral's old shooting jacket and buttoned myself into it, turning up the cuffs. That was better. I turned around, only to find that Mr. Trimble had followed me.

He stood staring at me, his expression indecipherable. I moved to pass him, but finally he spoke. "Did you give the dressmaker the list I made for you?"

"Miss Templeton said you couldn't possibly know what you were talking about, and she tore up your list."

"She *what*?"

"Tore it up." I pantomimed her doing it. "In two." And then I returned to the parlor.

"I don't think I like your Miss Templeton." He spoke from the doorway.

Settling myself in the chair, I sighed with satisfaction. "The feeling is decidedly mutual."

He strode into the parlor. "But I've never met the girl."

"And she's never met you, and you both assure me that it makes no difference."

"Whatever you do, don't go out until the dressmaker sends your new gowns." He gave me a long look and then took a seat behind my old desk.

"But we've agreed to go visit the rector again, and the dressmaker made no promises of a speedy delivery." I looked past Mr. Trimble to my father, who had not spoken for quite some time. "The rector has requested my help with his collections. I don't see why I should be kept shut away here when there are plenty of men in society who seem interested to marry me even if I am not properly adorned. Isn't that the point of all of this? To find a husband?"

Mr. Trimble scowled at me.

I scowled back.

My father gave me a teary glance.

I had to steel myself against a tug of emotions. He was doing entirely too much work. But he had made his choice; he had cast me aside. The sooner he realized the error of his ways, the better it would go for both of us. I must remain firm.

My father picked up a pen and returned to the table where they had been conversing when I'd returned home. "Come back here, young man, and leave Charlotte alone. She's only doing what she's been asked."

Perhaps I was, but Mr. Trimble's comments worried at me. I composed a letter to Miss Templeton asking for her advice. If it really was such a grave offense to wear a summer dress in the autumn or to go about with a smear of ink on my bodice, then perhaps it would be wise to refrain from visiting the rector until I received my new gowns. Besides, after the dinner party the previous week and the afternoon's calls, it seemed reasonable to me that I might have earned a bit of a break from society.

Miss Templeton's reply came the next afternoon. It was accompanied by a package done up in string.

My dear Miss Withersby,

Please don't mistake my reply for an endorsement of Mr. Trimble's point of view. You know that I can't approve of him. However, I do think there is some merit in your going about in gowns appropriate to the season. In that spirit, please accept the loan of this gown, and don't worry too terribly much about its return, since I wore it last year. You're a bit taller, perhaps, than I, but if you can manage to wear it with slippers instead of dancing boots, it shouldn't matter.

Yrs etc.

Postscript: I shall send a note to the rector to tell him to expect us next Monday at two.

Post-postscript: Please wear this gown on that occasion. As well as to our next dinner party.

Post-post-postscript: Mr. Trimble will probably try to convince you that you cannot possibly wear the same gown twice in a row.

Post-post-post-postscript: Don't believe him.

Post-post-post-post-postscript: I really, truly detest that man!

Post-post-post-post-post-postscript: Don't worry. Before long Mr. Trimble will be but a distant, and very bad, memory. Rather like a nightmare.

I turned the paper over, but there were no more postscripts. Untying the string on the package, I undid the paper to find a dress in a lovely, almost larkspur shade of blue.

Holding it up by the shoulders, I tried to view it in my mirror, but my room, being on the north side of the house, was gloomy so late in the afternoon.

I tiptoed across the hall to Mr. Trimble's room and opened the door.

There was hardly anything out of place, the bed being made in an uncomfortable-looking perfect sort of way and his clothes tidily hung on pegs. The mirror was fixed to the wall above the dresser. I moved his pitcher and basin from the dresser to the floor so that I could see myself and then held the dress up to my chin.

It was quite pretty, although . . . I fixed the shoulders to my own and stuck out my foot. She was right. It seemed a bit shorter than those I was used to wearing. But why should anyone be staring at my feet? They probably wouldn't even notice. As I turned away, the dress brushed against the corner of the dresser, and a letter fluttered to the floor.

I picked it up, meaning to set it back down, but the regular, elegant script caught my eye. It was quite unlike the rounded letters of Miss Templeton's hand.

The letter was dated three years before and written from a place called Eastleigh.

My dearest Edward,
    I so wish that

I stepped toward the window with the intention of moving into more direct light so that I could read it more easily. But . . . was someone coming up the stair?

I returned the letter to the dresser, drew the door shut behind me, and returned to my room wondering how Mr. Trimble could ever be anyone's "dearest" anything.

10

By the time I ventured downstairs, Mrs. Harvey was banging about the kitchen in a clatter of pots and pans. With autumn come, I was hopeful that one day soon she might sauce some apples or mince some quince for a pie, but the less said to the woman about expectations the better.

Several hours later we were, in fact, served apples, although they came from the kitchen whole, with stem and leaves still attached.

Mr. Trimble stared at them for a moment before he twisted one from its stem, stabbed it with a fork, and began to peel it with his knife.

I grabbed mine, brushed off the dried leaves on my napkin, and took a bite.

Mr. Trimble gave me a glance. "Tut, tut, Miss Withersby. Eating an apple that way is fine when you're alone, but in the company of polite society, one should always—"

"On the whole I've always thought manners are for people who have more time and opinions than good sense. Why should anyone care how I eat an apple? I don't impose my views on others. For instance, I don't insist that you should just pick yours up and take a bite, now, do I?"

My father sat watching us, rubbing his own apple against his shirt.

"I'm only trying to assist you. I should think you'd find a husband more quickly if you could be depended upon not to humiliate yourself."

"And I should think I liked you much better when you were on the other side of the world and all I knew about you was that you adored your sheep and that you called your horse Archibald."

He flushed a bit from the neck and glanced up at me before taking a vicious swipe at his apple's peel.

How the man did annoy me! I continued on. "When I was, I will confess, quite taken by your descriptions of the country-side."

Done with his peeling, he cored the apple and sliced it into eight even parts before he replied. "Had I known you were going to read your father's correspondence, I might have spared you both those sordid details."

While I reminded myself I must not let on that I was the one with whom he had been corresponding, he took up one of the pieces. Then he put it down. "But forgive me for waxing a bit sentimental whilst I was in the wilds of the colony without another farm for miles. Sometimes I felt as if that exchange of letters with your father was the only thing that kept me sane. There were times it felt as if he was the only one on God's green earth who truly understood me."

My father's brow dipped, and he opened his mouth to reply, but I picked up the tray of dried sausage and handed it to him. "You haven't had any yet, Father."

"Haven't I?" He slid several slices off the tray with his fork and onto his plate.

Ignoring Mr. Trimble's finer feelings, I continued. "I have been wondering, whatever happened to your ewe Emilia?" I felt a twinge of shame at that last bit, but truly, the man had galled me.

"Is nothing sacred?" He stood and nodded at me and then at my father. "Please excuse me. I find I'm no longer hungry."

Father turned round in his chair to watch Mr. Trimble stalk out of the dining room. "What was that he was saying? About letters? And what were you saying? Who are all those people you mentioned?"

I reached over, picked up Mr. Trimble's plate, and handed it to my father. Why should all his hard work in peeling that apple go to waste? And why was I feeling so mean and small when he was the one who had displaced me, going about as if he owned my work? If anyone ought to be feeling betrayed, it was I.

"It's just that I feel rather sorry for him, really."

Miss Templeton had invited me to meet her at Dodsley Manor for a ramble the next afternoon and I found myself explaining my bad behavior from the night before.

She took my hands within her own. "Don't!"

"I can't help but feel that—"

She squeezed them before letting them go. "This is just like a man—to make you feel as if it's your fault he's gone and usurped your place at your own house and that you should be the one to apologize for his intrusion. Does that make any sense to you?"

I was trying to follow her reasoning, and when I finally worked it out, I had to agree with her. "No, it does not."

"Exactly. So what you must do is put Mr. Trimble out of your mind and concentrate on Mr. Stansbury. Or the rector." Her eyes narrowed as she looked at me. "Which one do you prefer, by the by? I haven't thought to ask."

"Prefer for what?"

"Prefer to give your attentions to."

"I don't see that it really matters. We've made it known I've visited both men. My father ought to begin displaying alarm at any moment."

"I hope, for your sake, that will happen. Although, for my own sake, I must admit that I will sorely miss you. It's been ever so diverting to have something to do besides pretend an interest in stalking and the hunt and make it look as if I'm trying to catch the eye of some London dandy. I shudder to think of having to do it on my own again. Such a dire existence."

"Why don't you take the season off?"

"You *are* good for me. How you make me smile!" But as soon as she said it her smile disappeared. "I've already eighteen years, you know. If I don't settle on someone soon my choices will be slim indeed. No, Papa has told me that I *will* become engaged this year. He wants to see me settled, wants to know that I'll be taken care of once he's gone. His title cannot pass to me, of course, so I've got to find my own way, as it were. I've only got to get myself used to the idea. Once I do, then I'll be as fine a fiancée as you've ever seen. I shall practice with you first and then—"

"But I don't want to be anyone's fiancée. That's the whole idea of this plan."

"Of course you don't. But you want everyone to *think* that you do. Therein lies the genius of our efforts."

I just wished the genius would soon begin working.

She reached over and patted my hand. "Don't worry. It will all come out in the end. I just know it! Now then, shall we be off on our ramble?"

We might have done, only she couldn't find her gloves, and then she didn't want to wear the boots her maid brought, and finally she decided that perhaps a different dress might be better, so she changed her outfit entirely.

An hour later, we had just gotten to the road when horns sounded, and several moments later, a pack of dogs raced by.

She shook her fist at them. "Would you look at that!"

I was. And as I did so, I mourned the certain destruction of the fields that would follow in the riders' wake.

"After all that! And now my gown is ruined."

"It is?"

She held out her skirt. "Just *look* at it!" She was quite indignant about it, although the skirt looked fine to me. "There's no point in going out now. We might as well have tea."

"We're only going to get more soiled as we go." Especially if we were going to walk, as I had intended, to where the bracken were growing. "And we can have tea out in the field." I lifted my vasculum. "I brought a flask."

"*More* soiled! You astonish me, Miss Withersby. And having tea out in the wilderness? You must be truly dedicated to your work to endure such hardship." She shook her head sadly. "I'm afraid I'm not made of such stern stuff as you."

I took a sort of ramble by myself as I walked back to our house after tea with Miss Templeton. I had forgotten just how delectable it tasted when it was hot. And there was something to be said for those tiny sandwiches and biscuits we had been served. Pity that Mrs. Harvey never seemed to have time to do any of that.

That evening the Admiral was to take me to a concert, so I changed into the dress Miss Templeton had sent. I was quite taken with it once I put it on. The bodice dipped ever so slightly between my shoulders and was filled in with several rows of white lace. The sleeves were made of that same blue as the skirt and put me in mind of a draped shawl, though they didn't have to keep being pulled up. All in all, it was quite satisfactory and seemed to have the effect of adding a kind of glint to my brown eyes.

As I entered the parlor, Mr. Trimble was working with the dual-view microscope, but he stood when he saw me, and his gaze traveled the length of the gown. He nodded and then resumed his work. He hadn't said anything to me since the night before, which I took to be a sign that he was still cross with me. In spite of Miss Templeton's admonitions, I was still ashamed of myself. If any amends were to be made, it appeared that it was my responsibility to make them.

"It seems to me, if I remember correctly, that your Emilia ought to have a lamb by now. That was what I had meant to ask about last night at supper."

He glanced up from adjusting a lens with a rather blank look. "Yes."

"You must miss your home. And your sheep."

He didn't bother to look at me this time but instead bent his head to the eyepiece. "I do." He made another adjustment and then looked up toward me. "Would you . . . I mean, might you, come over and take a look at this? I don't quite understand what I'm seeing."

I considered refusing on principle, but the Admiral hadn't yet arrived and I had nothing else to do. I set my mantle on a chair and went over to the table and put my eye to the second eyepiece. "What is it?"

"A *Ranunculus*."

"From?"

He lifted his head from the eyepiece and consulted a sheet of notes. *My* notes. "Your father called the place Way's Green."

Relief swept over me. He'd attributed the writing to my father. Of course he would attribute it to my father. "So my father is interested in this for what purpose?" I refocused the lens and saw that Mr. Trimble had dissected the flower's stigma.

"It's not for his interest. It's for mine."

"Yours? Why?"

"I came across what I assume must be your R pile. What I can't understand is why this is classified as a *Ranunculus*. They're supposed to have more than twenty stamens, though I can't find anything anywhere that says how many more than twenty they're to have."

"It doesn't matter how many. More than twenty is sufficient."

"Then this must not be one because—"

"I assure you that it is."

"It only has sixteen stamens."

"Yes, but they're all located on the receptacle, so it doesn't matter."

"It ought to matter if it's supposed to have more than twenty, because sixteen is less than twenty."

"But they're not on the calyx, are they?"

"No. But sixteen is still less than twenty."

I found the rest of the specimen, took a dissection that included several stamens, and put them onto a slide. After mounting it on the stage, I went round to his side and bent to look at it from his point of view. Putting a hand to the slide, I turned it a bit. "There." I straightened so he could have a look.

He bent to look but soon sighed. "I confess, I just don't—"

Pressing my temple to his, so that I could share his view, I began to explain the placement of the stamens to him. "Do you see them now?"

"Yes, but—"

I put my arm across his shoulders and drew him closer, so that we were looking at it cheek to cheek.

"I . . . I . . ." He cleared his throat as he tried to pull away. "That is, I still don't understand why the placement is . . ."

I turned my head from the eyepiece toward him and found us nose to nose. His eyes were so much bluer up close. "Why it's what?"

He blinked. "Why is the placement more important than the number?" He swallowed. "That's what I meant to say."

"Because."

"Because?"

"Because it is." His lashes were quite extraordinarily long. "It is because it is."

He was still staring at me, his face so close I could feel his breath. "I . . . I . . ." He seemed troubled, as if he was relying upon me to tell him what it was he meant to say.

"You've become quite incomprehensible, Mr. Trimble."

"I feel quite incomprehensible, Miss Withersby. In fact, I've never quite felt . . ." He blinked, and when he opened his eyes they seemed to fill with comprehension, leading me to think that he had indeed finally come to understand.

He stood up from the microscope so abruptly that I staggered backward. Though he grabbed me by the elbow and pulled me upright, he let go almost immediately and then clapped that hand to the back of his neck. "Pardon me."

I sat down in the chair he had just vacated. It seemed the safest thing to do. Talking to him so closely had set my stomach into an odd sort of spin. Probably because we had been speaking at a tilt.

"So it . . . erm . . ." He was squinting at the slide as if he didn't know what it was. "What you were saying was . . . what you were saying was that it doesn't have to meet the definition of Ranunculaceae in order to be one."

"Yes. That's right."

I let him ponder the thought in silence for several long moments as I looked into the lens, admiring the view. "I wonder if I might be frank, Mr. Trimble."

"No."

No?

"That is, I mean yes. Of course you may be frank." He closed his eyes and shook his head. "Are you ever anything but frank?"

I rose and gestured toward the seat. "I've taken your place."

He sat and bent his head toward the eyepiece, though he threw a disapproving sort of glance at me as he did it.

Walking round the table, I took the seat opposite and bent to the other eyepiece to look at the slide as well. "If you were so happy in New Zealand with all those sheep, why did you come back here?" I lifted my head.

He did the same. As he looked at me he seemed quite miserable. "Because I once made a promise, and a gentleman always keeps his word."

"Then it's a good thing you aren't a gentleman, isn't it?"

That seemed to rouse him from his strange mood. He raised a brow. "I like to consider myself—"

"I meant in the strictest sense. It's not as if you were born into nobility or carry a title. According to Miss Templeton, those of us who are not can't ever quite hope to attain so lofty a status. I don't know that anyone would expect a man like you to be bound by his word. So if your promise has become such a burden, then surely the other party will understand if you explain your second thoughts about it."

"It would be nice to think so."

"In any case, if you came back to fulfill a promise, I can't think that you could do it from here."

"I'm beginning to agree with you, Miss Withersby. The thing

of it is, I'm quite certain the anticipation of the promise will turn out to be much more satisfying than its fulfillment. Especially for the other party."

"If that's the case, then why fulfill it at all? I must return to my earlier statement. Why not simply explain the circumstance and see if the other party will release you from your word?"

"If only it were so easy as that. . . ." He was staring at me with a queer sort of desolation. "If only all people were as understanding as you."

"I didn't mean to be understanding, I simply thought that, perhaps . . . Shouldn't you be on your way back home? Sometime soon?"

He had been staring at my lips as if they might help interpret my words. "Yes. I mean . . . I mean no."

"Which is it?"

"Which is what?"

"Charlotte? Are you there?" My uncle strode into the room. "Why does no one answer the door anymore?"

11

As the Admiral and I made our way into the concert hall, Mrs. Bickwith hurried over. She surveyed my dress with a stern eye. "I would hurry if I were you, Miss Withersby. That Miss Templeton is liable to take all your beaux." As soon as she said the words, she bustled away.

Indeed, Miss Templeton was besieged by many admirers. She pulled me into her circle, however, and introduced me around. Then, with a smile and a nod, she pulled me away to a quiet corner.

"They all seem to be quite enamored of you, Miss Templeton."

She dismissed my words with a wave of her fan. "As soon as they go back to the city, they'll forget me." She smiled at a pair of them, however, as she said it.

"What about that one over there?" I indicated a man across the room with a nod of my head. "He's a handsome specimen."

"I cannot disagree. But he's from London, like the rest of them."

"It seems as if they're all from London. And if you won't

have any of them, and if you must be married, then who are you going to choose?"

"Papa has a friend coming to visit in the spring. He has a son who will do in a pinch if I don't happen upon anyone better before then." Her lips twisted in a rueful smile. "I don't know the first thing about him, but they do live in Kent, and I've always thought the sea so terribly romantic."

We surveyed the ballroom for some moments together, and my gaze fixed upon Mrs. Bickwith. "I'm not so sure I like her."

"Mrs. Bickwith? I don't. And I'm quite certain of my opinion, for which I have my reason. . . . Shall I tell it to you?"

"Only if you—"

"I hate to speak of it, I really do, but it was just so spiteful what she did to me! I suppose you have a perfectly lovely name, don't you?"

"It's—"

"Don't tell me what it is. Please don't! Or maybe . . . just say it very quietly."

I leaned close so that I could whisper. "It's Charlotte."

"Charlotte? Oh! I could just about weep." Indeed, she looked as if she might. "It's such a lovely name. I hope you won't mind that I never intend to use it. Doing so would just make me feel so much worse about my own."

"What is it?"

"What is what?"

"What is your name?"

"It's so dreadfully old-fashioned that I can only attribute it to my mother dying as I was born. She was quite a stylish woman, so it couldn't have been her idea. I just know it wasn't. And Mrs. Bickwith was the only other person in her room when she expired. I feel for that woman the closest thing I can to hate without it actually being a sin."

I didn't know what to say.

"You may be quite certain that I shall always think of you as Charlotte, though you'll know now why I can never bring myself to say it. You will have to remain Miss Withersby so that I can remain Miss Templeton. That's why I despise the woman, but why do you?"

"I wouldn't say that I despise her, exactly, but she seems to think we ought to be rivals, competing for the same men. Of course, she doesn't know I don't have any intention of marrying, but—"

"How I wish I didn't have to either. But it's time I accepted my fate, which is not an easy thing to do, I assure you. It's difficult to admit to myself that I shan't be here much longer."

"Are you going away, then?" Who would I talk to at these parties and dinners and concerts if she wasn't in town?

"Quite soon I imagine. Least it will be soon once I marry, for I am not long for this world. I am going to die."

"Pardon me? Perhaps I didn't hear you correctly, but it sounded as if . . . did you . . . did you say *die*?"

"I cannot help it. I am the picture of my mother who was the picture of her mother who was the picture of . . . Well, I'm sure you understand. The point being that they all died in childbirth. It's our hips, you see."

"Your *hips*?"

She nodded quite decidedly. "Our hips. They may look round and full with all the petticoats I'm wearing, but I must tell you the shame of my existence: I might as well be a boy for all the good they'll do me. They're not meant for having children."

But she was a vision of health and vigor. "You must be mistaken."

She shook her head gravely. "I may be young, Miss Withersby, but I am not stupid. I'm simply not destined to be long-lived."

"That's . . . that's dreadful knowledge to live with!"

"I can, perhaps, put off the inevitable for several more months—your example has given me great hope. Perhaps longer if I could manage to work myself into some sort of scandal. But scandals are tricky sorts of things. I've noticed that sometimes they seem to *require* marriage instead of prohibiting it."

"I just . . . I don't . . . I really don't know what to say."

"That's truly the best thing about you, Miss Withersby. I can always count on you not to know what to say. And I can't tell you how much it's lifted my spirits since I've known you."

"I'm glad." I was beginning to suspect that most people thought quite the opposite.

"If I can find someone completely besotted with me to marry, someone who can truly mourn for me after I am gone, then it won't be so bad, will it? If I'm not going to live long, then I really want to do it in style. Do you think that very dreadful of me?"

"I wish you didn't have to marry at all."

"My father insists upon it. He can't bear to think that I would have no one to take care of me once he's gone. And what else am I to do? I'm not like you. I have no talents and no passions, and I find it so difficult to interest myself in causes." She sighed. "It is my burden, and I shall bear it."

"But—"

She squeezed my hand as she looked into my eyes, and then she turned her head away as she put a smile on her face. "I rather think our new rector *has* taken a fancy to you."

"He's taken a fancy to my illustrated field guide."

"Come!" She gave me a chiding look. "You must do a better job at pretending if you're going to be convincing. And just think of being a mother to eight children. I must confess that, when I think of our visit to the rectory, I'm rather glad I won't be given the chance to look after any for myself."

"I hardly think——"

"Oh, look. He's coming to speak to us, and he's hardly spared me a glance in his approach. Really, I think it's to *you* he's coming to speak." She patted my hand. "So I'll leave you alone to enjoy the benefit of his exclusive attention."

"Miss Templeton, don't——!" But she'd already flitted away.

"Miss Withersby." The rector bowed.

"Mr. Hopkins-Whyte."

"I hope you don't mind entertaining a question of botany, but I happened upon a curious plant during my rambles."

The hitch in my stomach settled as I realized he was only interested in my knowledge of plants. I had Miss Templeton to thank for putting the thought of matrimony in my head.

Upon our return, my father asked, "And how did it go, Charlotte?" as if he were afraid of my answer.

"Splendidly, if you judge such things on the music. Appallingly, if you wish to judge on the true merits of the conversations before and after and in-between."

My father looked to the Admiral.

He sighed as he put a hand to his neck and loosened his cravat. "There is not much scope for conversation when Charlotte seems to take great pains to say things nobody expects to hear."

"I don't understand the purpose for conversation if no one wants to hear anything unexpected. Isn't that the reason for conversing?"

The Admiral took my father's flask from beneath its glass dome. "These things are so scripted, my dear. That's what everyone takes pleasure in—the idea that at a dinner or a dance or a tea, everything goes according to plan."

"Then I wish they would share what the plan is."

Mr. Trimble put down my favorite pen with a sigh. "If I may?"

My father and the Admiral both nodded.

Mr. Trimble drew out a chair and motioned me to it.

I sank into it, and immediately picked up a foot and pried it out of one of the flat-bottomed blue-kid shoes Miss Templeton had lent me.

"The plan, Miss Withersby, is to do exactly the thing people expect in exactly the way they expect you to do it."

I wriggled my toes. It was heaven, being freed from that shoe! "I believe it's safe to say that I have no idea what is expected of me. Perhaps that's the problem."

He pursed his lips as he stared into my eyes, seeming to search for something to say. "Perhaps we should discuss instead what people do *not* expect you to do."

"You mean to say what I ought not do instead of those things that I should be doing? Yes . . . yes, that might be best." I picked up my other foot and peeled the shoe from it.

"You are *not* expected, for instance, to show your ankles." He yanked down my skirts, took the shoe from my hand, and set it quite firmly on the floor.

"Why not?"

"Because you're not meant to have them."

That seemed a silly sort of rule to me—everyone had ankles. People would not be able to walk if we did not. "My feet wouldn't work if I didn't."

"Then perhaps the better way to phrase it is: I'm not meant to notice them."

"Then don't."

"Believe me, I am trying my best not to."

For some reason his tone made me feel as if I ought to apologize.

He turned his back on me. "You are *not* expected to make

allusions to wearing anything but gowns and bonnets and you are *not* expected to speak of botany as if you know anything at all beyond, perhaps, acknowledging a pretty flower when you come across one."

"Here, I must protest! You cannot—"

He held up a finger. "And you are *not* expected to protest. Anything!"

"You mean I'm to say *nothing* if—"

"If it is an objection or a complaint, then no, you must not say it."

"In short, I am to say nothing of my life before this autumn? Or what I truly think about anything?"

He turned round to face me, with a nod. "Exactly."

"One might go so far as to think it would be better for me not to speak at all."

"One might."

"Which would lead me to ask what I am doing in society in the first place."

"I don't know. Why don't you tell us?"

Who knew it would be such an unbearably bothersome business to pretend to find a husband? But I had to keep up the fiction that I was trying to do so. Otherwise, I would never be rid of Mr. Trimble. I smiled, but not overly so, as I folded my hands atop my lap. "I am trying to find myself a husband as I ought to have done long ago. It is only right and fitting that I should do so."

Mr. Trimble was looking at me with a suspicious slant to his brow.

"You wouldn't fault me for trying to maintain the natural order of things, would you?"

The Admiral gave me a stiff pat on the shoulder. "There now. Exactly so. That's the way to do it. I knew you could make a good go of it."

Mr. Trimble didn't look convinced. I wondered anew where he had come by all that knowledge he loved to spout. His familiarity with fashion could be explained away by his sisters, but what of his command of dinner parties? A dissolute family couldn't be credited with partaking in such amusements, could they? I rather thought not. And neither could a sheep farmer in the wilds of the colony.

I had tired of speaking of my failings, so I addressed myself to Mr. Trimble. It was time for *his* failings to be made plain. "I don't suppose you've heard from the Botanical Society about Father's memoir yet?"

Though I had been hoping for prevarication and the look of anxiety that comes from a project forgotten, Mr. Trimble did not oblige me. "As a matter of fact, we have."

I constrained myself from asking what their response had been. I could search for it after he and Father had gone to bed.

"But let us not be swayed from our lesson, Miss Withersby. You must learn not to directly say what you're thinking."

"To first determine what it is I want to say and then try to find the best way not to say it requires quite a bit of effort, Mr. Trimble. I find it dreadfully inefficient."

"Inefficiency is just another word for *politesse*, Miss Withersby. Now then, pretend I am wearing . . ." He glanced about the room and then reached for a cushion and set it atop his head. "Pretend you have just been introduced to me and I am wearing this cushion on my head."

"Are you quite mad?"

"Tut, tut. That will never do. I've just said you must not say those things you first think."

"Even I would never do such a thing."

"You're an intelligent woman, Miss Withersby. I'm sure you can come up with a more clever retort than that."

"And now I must be clever too? You ask too much."

The Admiral and Father were looking on with much concern.

"To survive in Overwich's dining rooms and ballrooms, you must sharpen your wits. Elsewise, you are bound to become fodder for the town's gossips."

"Perhaps. But what is it to me if you decide to walk around with a cushion on your head?"

"I am defying all expectations of polite society, Miss Withersby, and I cannot be tolerated. You must not comment directly, but you must put me in my place at once or you will suffer all season from my impertinence."

"I would think your stupidity in doing so provides its own sort of reward." Then, as if a gift from above, Mrs. Bickwith's words from the first party I'd attended came back to me. "I don't believe I have ever met anyone so secure in their expectations that they can afford to flout convention, Mr. Trimble."

The Admiral sniffed.

Mr. Trimble clapped. "*Very* good, Miss Withersby! You might just do after all."

When I had first heard those words, I had thought them a compliment, but now I realized that they had been an insult. Perhaps I did in fact despise Mrs. Bickwith.

"Are you quite well, Miss Withersby?"

"What?"

"Is something wrong?" He took the cushion from his head and returned it to the sofa.

"No. I think it safe to say I've learned this lesson. I shall endeavor to remember it."

12

When I came downstairs the next morning and peeked into the parlor, I opened my mouth in astonishment. Gone were my piles. Gone were the scattered manuscripts and proofs. There weren't even any specimens on my desk!

Mr. Trimble had looked up at my approach. Now he was standing. "May I help you?"

"What . . . what . . ."

"What?"

"What happened?" And how had we come by a red rug? And that blue chair over in the corner? I nodded toward it. "Is that new?"

"No, I simply uncovered it. It's quite nice, really. A Robert Adam, if I am not mistaken." He walked over to the cupboard and opened the door. "I also found this." He offered me a tin of biscuits. "And this." He showed me a lacquered box I recognized as my mother's.

"I'd forgotten all about that!" I took it from him.

"And I found a desiccated mouse in that ceramic jug by the

sofa. It must have fallen in and become trapped by the journals set atop it.

I couldn't keep myself from shuddering.

"And now, as you've just observed, you have a chair that can be put to good use."

"But where did everything go?"

"If by *everything* you mean the bills and receipts and drafts of papers and illustrations, they've been put into their rightful places."

"Where?"

He looked at me as if he thought I'd made some joke. "In drawers and cabinets, where things like those are usually placed."

"But . . . but . . . how will I ever find them?"

He bowed. "Just leave it to me. Let me know what you need and I'll retrieve it for you."

A swirl of panic overtook me as I glanced around that tidy room. I sat down on a chair. Hard.

Mr. Trimble winced.

"It's all very well and good for you to put things where *you* can find them, but how am I to know that the bills are being paid and the correspondence is being conducted and—"

"How did you know all those things before?"

"I just . . . I just *knew*. I knew what had to be done." I had kept up with all of those things in the way that one keeps up with a spinning top. At just the right second, before it topples, a little push is supplied. I had kept a sort of running tally in my head about it all, and now and then my mind would prompt me to tend to something. "And then I did it."

"Now, it's quite easy to tell what's been done and what hasn't been. So you don't have to worry yourself about it anymore."

How could I not worry when I couldn't see what there was to worry about?

"Besides, as you never tire of telling me, it's my responsibility now."

"Yes, but, that doesn't mean you can just upend everything and—"

"I'd hardly say that I upended anything. I simply put away all those things that had already been upended. By you."

"That's hardly fair!"

My father wandered in and over toward his study, but when he got there, he stood in the doorway for a long moment and then turned toward us, blinking rapidly behind his spectacles. "I wonder . . . I thought . . . I could have sworn that I had been working right there just yesterday." He was pointing at his desk.

"You were indeed." Mr. Trimble entered the study and strode over to my father's desk. He opened one of the drawers and took from it a sheaf of papers. "Here you are. Just as you left them."

"I thought . . . I was really quite certain I had left them just there." He gestured toward the window ledge with an open palm. Then he glanced at the room anew. "Has there . . . was there . . . Do you think a thief came in the night?"

"Not a thief. It was Mr. Trimble. He tidied up."

"*Tidied up?*" My father looked at him, aghast. "Why?"

"I couldn't find anything."

"What was there to find? It was all right . . . here." He said the words sadly as if mourning the loss of the papers and all of the specimens he was used to seeing.

"But I . . . I needed to know what was there. In order to assist you. And I thought I might as well put it all away so that I could find it when you needed it."

"But Charlotte always knows where everything is."

"Yes, but she isn't assisting you anymore."

"But I don't . . . I fail to see how . . . How can I work?" His appeal to me was heartrending, but I steeled myself against it. He'd wanted Mr. Trimble instead of me, so now he had to learn to live with the consequences of his decision. "Couldn't Charlotte have told you where things were?"

Here, I felt the need to intervene. "No, Father, I couldn't. Because I'm meant to be finding a husband, remember? That's what you said you wanted. So now you'll have to try to fit your work to Mr. Trimble's new housekeeping scheme." Victory was close at hand. I could feel it.

Mr. Trimble scoffed. "It's hardly a scheme. It's an accepted way of doing business: putting things into the drawers they're meant to be in in the first place."

"Be careful, Father. Next he'll probably be wanting to organize your stockings."

"My stockings!" Father was looking at the man in horror. "I plan to do nothing of the sort."

Father was patting his desk as if to assure himself that it was still there. "You can't . . . I don't know . . ."

Mr. Trimble took him by the elbow and helped him into a chair. "It's just that I can't assist you when I don't understand what it is I'm meant to assist with. I think I'm in a much better position to be able to . . ." He kept talking as I left the room. I needed to go on a ramble. To be out in the tangle of the fields. In the natural order of—!

I stopped in the front hall, turned around, and went back into my father's study. "Even God himself didn't find it necessary to put fences round His meadows or plant His flowers in geometrical arrangements!" Once done, I exchanged my shoes for my sturdy boots and went out into the wilds of Cheshire.

But when I reached my favorite field, I stood gazing at it, wondering what there was to do. I'd left so quickly that I hadn't grabbed my vasculum, but even had I done so, there wouldn't be any point in picking anything. I wasn't to do fieldwork anymore.

I felt as if I ought to give Mr. Trimble a good cursing, only it wouldn't have been very charitable of me, and he'd taken up enough of my thoughts as it was.

Several miles away, I could see the tips of Dodsley Manor's towers, so I decided to visit Miss Templeton. She would sympathize with me. She would support me. And then she would help me decide how to move our plan along.

"It's quite simple, really." She sounded surprised that I had even put the question to her.

"What is?"

"You've only to start undermining his organizing scheme, and then it will be sure to fail."

"*Under*mine it?"

"It's like when I leave my fan in the music room or my bonnet in the parlor. The next time I ask for it, my maid can't find it and then she goes into a panic and then I go into a panic and then we're both in quite a state of hysterics until I can remember what I've done with it."

"So you're saying that I should . . . do . . . what, exactly?"

"I'm saying that his arrangement works only so long as things stay wherever it is that he's decided they're supposed to. So the quickest way to ensure his failure would be to make sure things *don't* stay where they're supposed to."

"And how am I to do that? When I'm not supposed to be sorting through the papers?"

"I don't know. You asked for my advice, and I've given it. So now you must return the favor."

I squared my shoulders. "I'll do what I can."

"Good!" She lifted a bell from the table beside her and began to ring it. Soon a maid appeared at the door, bobbing a curtsey.

"I'd like you to dress my hair in the ways we spoke of." She turned to me. "And you can help me decide which style I'll wear to Lord Harriwick's ball."

"I'm not very proficient in the dressing of hair. I don't think I'm qualified to judge."

"Which is specifically why I want you to tell me what you think is most becoming. Since you have no idea what you ought to think, then it seems to me that I'll be able to trust what you say. You'll give me your complete and utterly honest opinion, won't you?"

"What else would I give you?"

"Exactly." She seated herself in front of a table that had a mirror attached to it. Beyond it stretched the rest of her bedchamber. A large floral rug in pale greens and golden yellows lay on the floor. Atop it were placed a half-dozen chairs and a sofa with scrolled arms, all upholstered in a deep red that had since faded to a rosy pink. Her bed was every bit as magnificent as the house and had been hung with brocade curtains. My own room was a plain and simple buttercup to her frilly, multilayered peony.

It seemed to take a terribly long time just to comb through the length of her hair and then to pin it all up again and attach something she called a fall that had curls stuck to it. Frankly, it didn't look much different than when I had first come. Finally, the maid stepped back and Miss Templeton turned to face me. "Now. Here is the first one."

"How many of them are there going to be?"

"Just two."

"Two? That's three all together if I count the way you were wearing it when I first came in?"

She nodded.

"Why don't you just wear it the way you always do?"

"Why should I when there are so many ways to dress it? Don't you ever change your style?"

"No. I just pin it back and then put things on top of it."

She broke out into gales of laughter. "Things! Like lace, for instance? Or ribbons?"

"Both. And of course that flower that Mr. Trimble pushed behind my ear."

"He put a flower in your hair? That's rather bold of him, don't you think?"

"He had to do something since he took away my bonnet."

"He *took it away* from you? The beast! He's quite in danger of overstepping his place, in my opinion."

"He's far past overstepping."

"Ha! He's leaped right over it, hasn't he. All right. Now then. You'll have to tell me what you think of this next one."

For that one, her hair was once more combed through, and arranged to fall toward her jaw in great swoops that reminded me of a hound's ears before being gathered into a knot at the back. "I like the first one better."

"The first? Truly? How disappointing. I was really quite hoping for this one." She looked at me expectantly as if I might say something further.

"Be that as it may, I like the way you normally wear it."

She sighed. "There's no help for it, then. I'll just wear it the same old way." She looked at me through the mirror. "Don't you ever get tired of doing things the same way you've always done them?"

"I find particular comfort in routine."

"Not me. I want to do everything and see everything and experience everything."

"Then maybe you should try the last one, even though it makes you look like a hound."

"It makes me look like a hound? I don't think I've ever looked like a hound before. At least not on purpose. I'll have to think on it." She turned and leveled a most direct look at me. "Now then, why don't we see about you."

"Me?"

An hour later I was sitting in front of her mirror with my hair twisted and pulled and curled into what I could only call a torturous departure from my normal style.

"It's magnificent!"

"It feels rather . . . tight."

"Don't worry. It's supposed to."

"Are you sure? Because I'm quite afraid it might give me a headache."

"I hope so. Then you'll know it's been gathered securely enough."

I couldn't imagine going about all night with my head pounding.

She frowned. "Oh, don't look like that. Please don't. It ruins the effect."

"But the effect is meant, it seems, to ruin me."

She clapped her hands. "It looks so very stylish. Promise me you'll try it out tomorrow night."

"Of course I will." And I would. I would have to now that I promised. I just wouldn't try very hard.

"Oh, Miss Withersby!" Miss Templeton came close to kiss me the next evening at Lord Harriwick's ball. "What happened to your hair! I thought we had agreed that you would do it up in side ringlets with the plait at the back."

"I couldn't seem to put it up the way your maid did."

"Then you'll have to get yourself a new maid."

"That would be possible if I had an old one, but I don't."

"You don't have a lady's maid?"

"I don't know what I'd do with one, and in any case, we can't afford—"

"Why, I don't know what I'd do without mine! Oh, look! There's Mr. Fulwell come for Lord Harriwick's hunt. He's not from London, he's from Worcestershire, and Papa wants me to make a good impression, although you understand, of course, that I can't make *too* good of an impression. Least not right away. So make sure you stay close to me tonight."

That suited me just fine. Her attentions wouldn't be monopolized by any man in particular, and I wouldn't have to pretend an affection for anyone in particular, and we could both be happy together. Her father made the introduction to Mr. Fulwell, and she and the man spoke at great length about the hunt and London and the holidays and then he bowed and left us.

Miss Templeton seized my hand. "What did you think of him?"

"He seemed rather nice."

"He is, isn't he? Quite nice. Although . . ." She brought my hand up to her heart in a gesture of desperation. "I just don't think I can become besotted with him on account of he has no chin. Oh! That's terribly unkind of me, isn't it?"

"I wouldn't say he has no chin. It's practicably impossible for a man not to have one. Or a woman either, for that matter."

"Then where, I ask you, would it be?"

I glanced over, across the room at him. "Well it's . . . I mean, it must be . . . Well, I suppose it is rather small."

"Exactly. Which is why I just don't think he will work."

"I find that rather unjust."

"I don't think I would need it to be pronounced, it just has to declare itself a very tiny bit."

"We can't all have pronounced chins."

"Why?"

"Because that would be an aberration, and aberrations, by definition, are uncommon."

"Miss Withersby, please don't think me rude, but I don't think I can abide a lecture at this particular moment in time. My short period of happiness depends upon my finding a man with a chin. I will not be moved from that expectation."

Mr. Stansbury came by, and Miss Templeton engaged him in conversation. She was so very good at that. I tried to study her, as I would a specimen, but I soon became caught up in the story she was telling Mr. Stansbury. I wondered if I was gazing at her with the same fascination that he was. He was quite swept up in the tale, his eyes fixed on hers and his lips curved in an admiring sort of smile. It was a shame she wouldn't be among us much longer, but I could not say that she was mistaken in her beliefs. As any good botanist knows, offspring almost always manifest the characteristics of their parents.

Mr. Stansbury gave off one of his hearty laughs, and I joined him in it, willing to do as Miss Templeton herself had vowed to do: endeavor to enjoy the time she had left.

The next morning, Mr. Trimble made us even later for church than was our habit. First, he tried to bully me into a different dress, and then he objected to my wearing elastic-sided boots. I pointed out that we had a rather long walk ahead of us and suggested that if I wore my thin-soled slippers he would have to carry me.

One might even have accused him of dragging his heels on

the way, and especially down the central aisle during Communion, but he was quick enough in bolting from the pew once the rector finished with the benediction. Once clear of the church, he started out for home at such a fast pace that Father and I struggled to keep up with him.

"Mr. Trimble!" I called out to him, for by that time he was nearly ten paces ahead of us. "If you would be so kind as to slow down?"

He broke his stride and seemed surprised to see us so far behind. "Please, forgive me." He adjusted his pace to our own.

"I don't find conversations regarding the state of my health or of the weather particularly illuminating, but you have nothing to fear from the people of Overwich. They've been quite kind to us."

He pulled his hat down over his ears as we stepped off the road to let some of the carriages from London pass. "It's not the people of Overwich I worry about."

That begged the question of what exactly did worry him, but he and Father had embarked upon a discussion of printer's proofs, and I kept my ponderings to myself.

Monday dawned, and I woke with a sort of dread. I was tired of going about in dresses so tight that I could hardly breathe. My feet were aching from the snugness of my slippers, and I'd had entirely enough of spending my time among people I really didn't know and couldn't talk to.

After breakfast, I found myself poking about in Mr. Trimble's desk drawers.

He paused as he entered the parlor. "May I help you find something?"

"I was just . . . just looking."

"My offer to assist you still stands."

"I am used to finding our correspondence here." I put a hand to the table where I had always placed my C pile of letters and missives, with the oldest at the bottom.

"Ah. Yes. I found it rather difficult to tell what had, in fact, been replied to and what was still waiting for a response, so I placed those to which some reply had been made on that shelf just there." He nodded toward the cupboard. "And those which needed some response—that is, the most recent missives—I placed over there." He nodded toward a wire basket on the table.

"I see." I drifted toward the basket and tried, in a subtle way, to sift through the pile.

"Is there any piece in particular for which you are looking?"

"No. I'm just . . . just looking."

"I can assure you that, if anything had come for you, I would have brought it to your attention."

Right after he'd read it, most probably. "I suppose you're rather behind in keeping up with my father's notes."

"Not especially."

"No?"

"No. We've found it to be most efficient if he reads his notes to me at the end of the day. That way, he can keep his copy and I can place a perfectly readable copy into his file."

"He has a file?"

"You mean other than the W pile?"

I gave him a sour look.

"I've extracted all of his papers and placed them into a cabinet."

"Does he know you're doing that? I can't imagine that he would have let you touch his notes, let alone move them." And if he'd seen them, he knew my father could not have written him all those letters!

"We agreed that since I am the keeper of his papers, he must allow me the privilege of keeping them. But perhaps . . . if it wouldn't be too great an inconvenience, you wouldn't mind offering me your assistance, Miss Withersby."

"What is it that you need?"

"If you could just . . ." He pulled a paper from the shelf labeled *Correspondence Already Replied To* and spread it out on the table before me. "What I really need is some sort of aid in the transcription of this paper."

"Transcription? Of what?"

"Of your father's handwriting."

The bottom fell from my stomach as I realized he had indeed divined my secret.

"Is there some sort of code he uses when he makes these notations? I didn't have this sort of trouble when we corresponded."

"Notations?" I bent over the paper and felt my spirits lift as I read through my father's observations on the research he was undertaking. "I suppose you might say this is written in a sort of Withersby family shorthand."

"Then I wasn't mistaken in thinking it perfectly incomprehensible."

I pushed it back toward him. "Not at all."

"Would you mind, terribly, providing an interpretation?"

"This is not a sort of word-for-word code. It's not even a shortened form of anything really. These markings represent theories and thoughts fully formed that have taken the Family Withersby over four generations to perfect."

"I see."

"I don't know that you do, Mr. Trimble. I really don't see how you can do much good here."

"I believe I did, in fact, understand your meaning. But until your father tells me otherwise, I will continue to assist him."

He stalked over to the desk and made a great show of putting pen to paper.

Which gave me an idea. I made my way over to the wire basket containing the most recent missives and flipped through the correspondence. Among them were a letter from the University of Edinburgh, a letter from a missionary correspondent in Ceylon, and a plea from the butcher for payment of last month's bill. After checking to make sure Mr. Trimble wasn't looking, I concealed them all in a plant press. When he went into the study to confer with father, I traded them out for the correspondence already replied to. That should put a snarl in his system!

13

Late that morning, some of my new dresses were finally delivered. I chose what Miss Templeton had called my promenade gown for the call we would make on the rector later in the day. It had a great many rows of what I now knew were called flounces. They filled out both the skirt and the sleeves.

When the Admiral and I arrived to collect Miss Templeton, she came out to us along with a maid carrying three hampers filled with food. After exclaiming quite vigorously over my new gown, she said, "It's such fine weather, I thought we could all go on a picnic for our tea."

The Admiral agreed most heartily. "Perhaps we could find a place on the river."

She smiled at him. "Yes. That was my thought exactly!"

There were many carts and wagons and carriages on the road, so we were slow in reaching the rectory. When we arrived, the children seemed to be everywhere at once. When Miss Templeton declared we were to have a picnic, they cheered as a whole and raced off down the lane toward the river and then dug into the hampers at once when we sat down to eat.

As we ate, I spied some flowering stems of autumn lady's tresses, and when we finished I convinced them to go off and pick me some.

It kept them occupied, though not for long. They soon returned, running their hands up and down the soft, hairy stems. One of the younger boys, however, was wrenching off the small white flowers that grew around the stem in a spiral.

I took the specimen from him. "See here! Those flowers are like babies. How would you like it if someone came along and snapped off your little brother's head?"

The children's eyes widened as they turned to the mite, who was sucking at his thumb as he lay in Miss Templeton's lap. She put a protective hand to his head. "I'm sure Miss Withersby was only teasing."

"Is this a good flower?" The oldest of the girls had come back cupping what looked to be some sort of bog orchid in her hand.

"It might be, but I can't really see it very well. Why don't you lay it down and we'll have a look at it."

She dropped it onto my lap.

I knelt and placed it on the ground before me, straightening out the stems and separating the leaves. "It does have some promise, but to be very certain, I would need to see its roots as well."

"I can go get them." She was nearly a dozen paces gone before I called her back.

"There's no use digging them out now. The thing about specimens is that they need to be as close to perfect as possible. Do you see this?" I pointed out a place where the tiny stem had been bruised and bent. "There might have been something important here, but it would be hard to tell in this state, wouldn't it?"

Several of the other children had gathered round as I was speaking.

"A botanist is always very careful to take up a plant, roots and all, without harming any of it."

The girl's chin was trembling.

"Do you think you can find another of these? Because I would be very interested in having one." Or I would have been, had I still been illustrating my father's volumes.

She nodded. "There were ever so many by the pond over there." She pointed off behind her.

"A pond?" The rector's brow rose. "Do be careful. Those can be very deep. Perhaps I should go with—"

But she was off before he could say anything else.

He looked at me with a worried frown. "Do you think it's safe? Encouraging them to go digging near the water?"

"Around the meres? Just think of them as lakes in miniature. It's really quite fascinating to see what's grown up around them. The children will get used to them. You can't ramble anywhere around Cheshire without almost falling into one." My words didn't seem to reassure him. "I was looking for specimens much rarer than those at their ages. If you teach them what to look for, you'd have a wonderfully complete collection in no time."

"With more time to write my sermons, I daresay." He smiled. "They've been at loose ends since Lavinia died."

"I was too when my own mother died. My interest in botany is what got me through. And the fact that I needed to finish up her contracts."

"Her *contracts*? How old were you?"

"Fourteen."

"That's quite a burden."

"We needed the income. To dedicate one's life to science isn't the most profitable of undertakings."

"Much like the ministry, I suppose."

I supposed it was. "My mother wrote children's books to contribute to the family coffers. I write my own now, though they're meant for an older reader."

"You do very well with the children. Few people could handle so many at one time."

"They're a bit like plants in a glasshouse."

His brow rose.

"The very number of them seems overwhelming until you put each in its place and determine to give it the things that it needs to thrive. After that, they practically care for themselves."

"Erm . . . I suppose it is . . . rather . . . perhaps . . ."

The children returned to us in a group, trailing plants and carrying rocks and all manner of other things, which they proceeded to drop into my lap.

"Well . . . this is . . . What is this?" I pulled a brown, shriveled stem from the pile and held it up for inspection. It looked as if it might be a *Pseudorchis albida*. I hadn't known there were any in the area. "Who found this one?"

"Me."

"Which *me* is that?"

"*Me*, me." One of the boys pushed his way forward to stand in front of the others.

"Where did you find this?"

"In a pasture over there."

He had pointed out beyond us, and I turned to follow his gesture. "Do you think you could show me the location?"

One of the girls grabbed up my hand. "And then can I show you where I found mine?"

Another of the girls grabbed my other hand. "And I'll show you where I found mine!"

"But what about me?" One of the smallest of them was stamping her foot right atop the pile of specimens.

The rector took her up in his arms, set her on his shoulder, and we started off for the pasture.

We had quite a good ramble while the Admiral drifted about in a boat and Miss Templeton played pat-a-cake with the younger children. At length, the rector declared the hour late and herded the children back down the lane in the direction of the rectory. The Admiral and I deposited Miss Templeton and her hampers at Dodsley Manor and turned toward home.

When we arrived, my uncle persuaded my father from his work and sat him in a chair in front of the fire. Father stretched his stockinged feet out toward the fireplace.

"Young man?" The Admiral was looking in Mr. Trimble's direction.

"Sir?"

"You may join this war council as well."

War council?

Mr. Trimble wasted no time in pulling up a chair.

I drew up a chair too, wondering if I might safely pester Mrs. Harvey for a biscuit. The scent wafting from the kitchen was unusually tantalizing, and despite the picnic, the outing had left me ravenous.

"Now then." The Admiral was pacing in front of the hearth. "We must first address tactics."

"Tactics?" Mr. Trimble exchanged a glance with my father.

"The way the battle is shaping up, it's going to be between the rector and that industrialist, what's-his-name."

I supplied it. "Mr. Stansbury." Now we appeared to be getting somewhere! And at just a little over a week since I had joined society. It had taken, perhaps, a bit longer than I had expected, but victory was now at hand.

Father raised a brow. "The rector?" He said it with a dubious sort of lift to his voice.

Now my father would call a halt to this nonsense, send Mr. Trimble off, and let me resume my work. All that was needed was an underscoring of the current situation. "The rector has grown quite fond of me, I believe."

Father chewed on his mustache for a moment as the Admiral turned on his heel and started back by the hearth in the opposite direction. "I don't think—I don't believe I've ever met the industrialist fellow."

Which ought to make his trepidation all the greater. "It's said he's the wealthiest man in the county. And if I marry him, I shouldn't have to work another day in my life. *Ever*." That should put the fear of God into him. "Miss Templeton seems to think both of them are quite taken with me." Which is not to say that I agreed with her, but she had said so, and it would cause no little anxiety if they thought it was true.

"Which one do you favor?" my father asked the Admiral.

"I am always on the side of the Almighty. However, I must point out that He is not the most generous of paymasters. With the rector, however, she would have the added benefit of children."

Or the added nuisance. "None of them even knows how to select a proper specimen!"

The Admiral sent me a keen-eyed look. "They've been left without a mother, adrift on the sea of life. You could teach them. And besides, I've heard he has a very interesting collection."

"Of which he comprehends very little."

He gave me a perplexed sort of glance that reminded me I was to pretend as if I was actually trying to find a husband. "But I suppose that too could be righted."

My father was frowning. "Well . . . what of Mr. What Did You Call Him?"

"Stansbury." Mr. Trimble and I both answered at the same moment.

The Admiral turned on his heel again and started back in the other direction. "He seems devoted to the study of botany." He threw a glance at my father. "He has quite a fine glasshouse filled with orchids and palms and ferns."

"But he's quite mad for something he insists upon calling a stumpery." I couldn't keep myself from saying it. I really couldn't.

"A stumpery?" My father's brow rose. "I've never heard of such a thing."

"It's like a fernery, only it's filled with stumps."

"*Stumps?*"

"With the trunks buried so the roots twist about in the air. Or so he says."

Father's eyes widened. "It sounds . . . indecent. Surely his interests could be turned to something more traditional."

I could not agree. "Not at present. On that point, he is quite firm."

The Admiral started back again. "But there cannot be any fault found with his glasshouse collections. They're the finest in the county. Some say the best in the realm."

There, too, I had to object. "But it's filled with specimens that appear to be quite badly mislabeled and poorly cited."

Father turned in his chair to look at me. "Well, then he needs someone like you, Charlotte, to guide him."

Mr. Trimble regarded me through those piercing blue eyes of his. "Who do you favor, Miss Withersby?"

"I . . . can't really say."

Father rose and came over to pat my hand. "You need more time." He turned to address the Admiral. "She needs more time."

The Admiral pshawed. "My vote goes for Stansbury, even if he is prone to fanciful ideas."

Father frowned. "I'd rather decided I preferred the clergyman. He seems to be a decent sort." My father stared at the toe of his stocking for a long moment and then looked up to Mr. Trimble. "What about you, young man? You're closer to a marrying age than either of us. Who do you favor?"

"My vote is with Miss Withersby."

With me?

"With Charlotte?"

Was that . . . was that a choice?

"She'll be the one to live with the decision. As long as you don't disapprove of either, I say leave her to make the choice. I don't think there's much to gain by making decisions on another's behalf."

I would have thanked him if I had any intention of marrying.

The Admiral grunted. "In my day, children were told what to do; they weren't asked for their opinion."

I'd had quite enough of the discussion. "I'm sure I'll come to a decision very soon. In either case, once I marry, I plan to be very busy attending to the needs of my new household. I'll probably never see any of you except on Sundays at church."

The Admiral came over and leaned down to kiss me on the cheek. "Won't be the same without you, but it's all for the best."

Best for whom? I walked toward the front hall. "I believe I will retire now."

My father put out a hand as I passed. "Won't you stay and have supper with us, Charlotte? Mr. Trimble's gone and got us a new—"

I had tired of hearing of Mr. Trimble and his irritating habit of changing everything. "I don't think so, no."

I went upstairs quite perplexed. It seemed as if talk of an impending marriage hadn't bothered anyone, except me, very much at all. Nothing was working as I had planned.

I determined to lie abed the next morning as Miss Templeton habitually did, until the hour of ten, but to my great frustration, I could only manage to stay prone until seven. When I could stand it no longer, I dressed and descended the stair for breakfast, hoping to sneak into the kitchen before Mrs. Harvey bestirred herself. From the sound of activity in the kitchen, however, it seemed I was too late. Now I would have to content myself with whatever it was she threw at me.

The idea that I would have to survive until the evening hours on a diet of stale bread and cold tea filled me with despair. Perhaps I could walk over to Dodsley Manor and cast myself upon Miss Templeton's mercy. As I stood in the front hall contemplating doing just that, I heard Mr. Trimble conversing with someone in the parlor.

"And what is it you would say that you're doing now?" he was asking.

"Now?" a female voice answered him. "Well . . . I've melted the wax to make a sheet, haven't I? So now I have to add the color and then I'll have to pour it into the mold, won't I?"

"I wonder how I ought to write that up. . . ."

As I stood there listening, a young woman came out from the kitchen carrying a tea tray filled with delectably browned buns, a bowl of glossy hard-boiled eggs, and a steaming teapot. She could not have been any older than I. Her ginger-colored hair was caught up in the back with pins. Freckles mottled her high, flat cheeks and thin nose.

She dropped a curtsey.

Could it be *hot* tea she was carrying? She proceeded into the parlor and must have deposited it there, for when she returned, she was not carrying it. I followed her down the hall to the kitchen and looked inside. Mrs. Harvey was nowhere to be seen.

Returning to the front hall, I peeked round the corner and tried to catch Mr. Trimble's eye.

At length, he spied me and promptly came to his feet. "Miss Withersby?"

I gestured him over.

He excused himself from his guest and stepped out into the hall to join me. "How may I be of assistance?"

I stepped closer to him so I could whisper.

He took a hasty step backward.

"Who is that woman?"

He turned and cast a glance toward the visitor. "Her name is Mrs. Gribble."

"And what is she doing here?"

"She's telling me how to make a wax flower."

"Why?"

"So that I can write the book you promised to your publisher. Really, Miss Withersby, is that the reason you asked me to come out here? Because I've rather a lot of work to be accomplished and it's already—"

"No, I'm sorry, it's not."

"It's not what?"

"It's not the only reason. What I really wanted to know was who is that girl? The one with the tea tray? And where is Mrs. Harvey?"

"That is Miss Hansford. I took the liberty of firing your Mrs. Harvey."

"You . . . you *fired* her? Are you allowed to do that? She came with the house."

"She wasn't a box hedge or a window shutter. And her cooking was abominable! No one should have to suffer such food. It's a wonder you and your father survived as long as you did." He was glaring at me as if she were my fault. "And I would not say that's to your credit. Most people eat genuine food at their meals."

"But the leasing agent—"

"The leasing agent was quite accommodating when I told him that it was either Mrs. Harvey or you."

He must have read incomprehension in my eyes. "I told him that if she did not go, then we would."

I heard myself gasp. "But that . . . that was a lie! We never would have—"

"*I* would have. As much as I feel fortunate to be working with your father, I would not much longer have stood for that dreadful food."

He didn't have to be so adamant about it. "The new girl seems pleasant."

"She ought to be. She's being paid quite well."

"But there's no money to—"

"There was plenty of money after I realized the butcher was billing you for meat you never saw. Didn't you wonder why you were always being served salt pork when you were billed every week for sausages and roasts and chops?"

"Well . . . no." I hadn't. "Are you saying that we paid for real meat? But . . . where did it all go?" And why had I never noticed?

"I expect they went to some friend of Mrs. Harvey's."

I felt my mouth drop open.

The bell sounded at the front door, and the girl in question came out from the kitchen, hurrying past us.

"She answers the door too?"

"She'd better if she wishes to keep her position. I've tired of doing it myself."

She came back to us and dropped another curtsey. "A package for Miss Withersby."

I took it from her, nodded to them both, and went to the study to find my father. "Did you know Mr. Trimble has fired Mrs. Harvey?"

"I was going to tell you last night, but you retired before I had the chance." He was actually smiling. "I told you he was a fine young fellow."

"You approve?"

"Why shouldn't I?"

"You mean . . . I could have fired her months ago?"

"Of course you could have."

"But . . . why didn't *you* fire her?"

"I hadn't noticed just how bad things had gotten."

"But wouldn't you have been upset if I had done it?"

"If *you* had done it, that would have been fine. *I* wouldn't have wanted to though. That woman frightened me."

She'd frightened me too. The question was, why hadn't she frightened Mr. Trimble?

I took the package upstairs to my room and found it to be an eglantine-colored silk dress and other bits from the dressmaker. I took up a piece of lacey . . . something that had fallen to the floor. It looked as if it ought to be a cape, but it was too short to serve that purpose, and the sides ended in points. If it was too small to be a cape and too large to be a handkerchief, whatever could it be for? There must be some purpose for those pointed ends. They were meant to be tied around something. Perhaps on my head in place of my flowered fall? I made several attempts to secure it there, but it didn't want to stay.

Holding it up, I tried to envision where else it might go. Around my waist?

I tried it, but it seemed rather awkward, and I hadn't noticed any other women wearing lace tied about their waists.

The only place left was my neck, so I tied it on. The ends weren't long enough to make into a bow, so I left it knotted and then looked at the effect in the mirror. It wasn't what I would have thought of as stylish, but my taste in fashion appeared to be eccentric in the extreme.

Untying the lace, I left it on my dresser top and the dress spread upon my bed and went downstairs. I was able to get a cup of tea and two whole slices of bread from the kitchen and I didn't even have to beg for them!

By the time the Admiral came that evening, I was ready and waiting for him. In order to avoid another vexing conversation with Mr. Trimble, I descended only when I heard my uncle's carriage arrive. But I did feel the need to venture into the parlor to bid farewell to my father and urge him to retire earlier rather than later.

Mr. Trimble spared me a long glance. And then another. "That's a rather novel . . . What *is* that there about your neck?"

"I've no idea. But it was meant to be tied around something. It has two long points to it."

"Points? Can you . . . ? May I see it for a moment?"

He didn't wait for an answer but simply stepped forward to dismantle my knot himself, and then he pulled the lace from my neck. As he held it up, I saw his jaw twitch. "It's a pelerine, Miss Withersby, but you were not far off. It's meant to be placed about your shoulders." He leaned round me, brushing my nose with his cravat, and drew the fabric about my shoulders, leaving the pointed ends to dangle down the front of my gown.

I picked one of them up and waved it under his nose. "And what about these?"

"I'm afraid they're meant for no purpose."

"None?"

"Unlike in nature, you will soon discover that there seems to be no purpose to fashion."

"But . . . why are they there, then?"

He took up the other and tickled my nose with it. "To be dipped in your soup, perhaps. Or to catch the wind and fly away."

I reached for it, my fingers tussling with his as I did so. "I asked for a mantle, not some useless bit of lace."

He let the ends drop, and they fluttered back to my gown. His teasing manner had disappeared and he had stepped away from me with an abrupt bow. "There. You are the picture of perfection. So keep your mouth closed as long as you possibly can, and perhaps you will manage to avoid persuading your companions otherwise."

His tone was so reasonable that I was out the door and settled in the carriage beside the Admiral before I realized I had been insulted.

14

I returned from the dinner with a headache and woke up
with it as well. A piping hot cup of tea didn't really help
matters, but it tasted heavenly. After eating a bun and a
soft-boiled egg, I strayed into the parlor. Mr. Trimble was bent
over a table, my pen in his hand. So rapt was his attention that
he gave no sign of hearing me, and I was able to observe his work
unnoticed. He seemed to be drawing a spider orchid, though if
so, he must have been drawing it from memory. It didn't correlate
with the established type. "What are you doing?"

He blinked as he lifted his gaze from the paper before him.
Then he stood. "Forgive me. I'm trying to do up a spider orchid
for your father's book."

"You can't." I was the one who illustrated my father's books.

"I'm inclined to agree with you. It's been quite some time
since I've seen the actual flower, and I think it would be much
easier if I actually had one to draw from. But I've looked everywhere and can't find the specimen."

"There isn't one."

"Then how were you meant to draw it?" He gave me a keener
glance. "And where have *you* seen a spider orchid?"

"I haven't."

"Ever?"

"Never. But I know that the variety you're working on is nearly black in color, and its sepals are lateral. There should be a botanical plate illustrating the ideal of its type in the sitting room. That's what I would have drawn it from."

"I found that plate and was astounded by how little it looks like the actual flower."

"It's not supposed to."

"Then perhaps we're speaking of two different plants. On the specimens I observed in New Zealand, the flower blooms below the leaves, not above them, and the petals actually droop. It looks nothing like the one in the illustration."

"It's not supposed to look like anything you'd find in the field. It's the *type*—the *ideal* specimen."

"I assure you that one could look forever along the streams of the colony and never find a single plant that looks like *the type*."

"You're being too literal, Mr. Trimble. And the plate is not meant to offend you. It's . . . it's a simple compilation, if you will."

"In that Wardian case I brought you, there *is* a spider orchid. A real one. When it blooms, I promise, you will find it looks nothing like that type of yours."

"Be that as it may, the important thing is the type, not the individual specimen."

His neck had gone flush, and he was drumming his fingers on the table. "You're asking me to submit some idealized lie of an illustration instead of the truth?" He spoke the words quite carefully.

"If we illustrate an actual specimen, it's possible that we may have chosen an aberration, and then people might walk through a field expecting to find one, and—"

"Beside a stream would be a more likely place to find—"

"They might walk beside a stream, then, expecting to see something that can never be duplicated."

"That's better than expecting to see something that never was." He took up his pen and started drawing once more. "Is your father going to put a notation in his book? Warning to the reader: The flowers illustrated within have no basis in reality and exist only in the artist's imagination?"

"I'm simply requesting that you do the work the way my father expects you to. Otherwise, I would be happy to do it myself."

There was no reply save a tightening of his jaw.

I took my indignation over to Miss Templeton's, feeling certain that she would understand. I was led into a sitting room where I found her drawing by aid of a camera lucida.

"Miss Withersby! You are heaven-sent. Please come and tell me what I'm doing wrong." She was looking through a prism at her paper and attempting to draw a crested buckler fern that sat on a table in front of her. Its image was reflected down upon her paper. "I'm afraid it doesn't look like a fern at all, but I can't say why, for all I should have to do is sketch the form on the paper. That's why I begged Papa to get me one." She adjusted the prism. "I'm beginning to think it's defective!"

Looking down at her penciled lines, I had to disagree. "You've done admirably well in copying the outline."

"Then why does it look so flat? As if it hasn't got any life in it?"

"Because it hasn't. I daresay it looks the way it does because you're only drawing what you see."

"But that's the genius of this contraption! It shows me, more clearly, what it is that I'm seeing."

"But if you don't know what parts make up the plant, then how can you correctly interpret it? This for instance." I pointed to the base of the plant, where the few fronds seemed to rise from a single source. "Each of these fronds comes from a different branch of the rhizome." I took her pencil and emphasized the distance between them. "And here you must be very precise." I pointed to the places where her leaves joined the stems. "They alternate."

"They what?"

"The leaves alternate. They aren't directly opposite each other. And see here: this bare portion of the stem isn't smooth. It's covered with scales."

"Well, of course it is, but I only wanted to draw the outline."

"The fern is nothing without its parts."

She pushed the paper aside with a sigh. "And I so wanted to have something to show the watercolor society on Friday!"

"You can. If you have a sharp knife, I can show you what's inside and—"

She took the plant and set it in a Wardian case by the window. "No good can come from poking about at things that weren't meant to be seen. I'll just go empty-handed, the way I always do. One good thing about me: I can admire the handiwork of everyone else. I never stint on praise where praise is due." She took her pencil from me and deposited it in a drawer along with her drawing paper. "Oh! Why don't *you* join the society? We'd have ever so much fun. And I'm sure that any painting of yours could beat out Mrs. Archer's. It wouldn't even have to be a very big one. That way someone else could win artist of the month and I could take all the credit for recruiting you."

"But I'm not an artist. I'm a botanist. I don't paint. I illustrate."

"Don't worry. No one will care. They really won't. And in

any case, illustrations and paintings are very nearly the same thing. Do come! We're having a genuine drawing tutor come to give us lessons. And he's going to be the judge of our contest."

"I think it highly probable that I'll be back to assisting my father in just a few days."

"If you are, then think nothing of it, but if you aren't, you must promise me you'll come. And that you'll bring the biggest painting you've done."

By Friday, Mr. Trimble was still ensconced in my position, so I leafed through my most recent illustrations, selected a particularly finely detailed drawing of a potato orchid and put it into a portfolio. I added several sheets of additional paper for drawing, and then took up my box of brushes and paints—which, upon further investigation, I found that Mr. Trimble had ruined. For an exceptionally tidy person, he was remarkably careless with other people's paints. "I'm going out to a watercolor society meeting."

I might have simply spoken to myself for all the attention I received. It would serve them right if I did win artist of the month. Then maybe the society would insist upon keeping the illustration and Mr. Trimble would go mad trying to determine what had become of it.

I felt myself smile.

Perhaps I would enjoy this meeting after all.

The group met at the society president's house. Just inside the door, I saw Miss Templeton. She waved. "There you are! I had worried you'd gotten your position back and I'd be left on my own."

"Not yet."

"Good!" She took my portfolio from me and wielded it like a

shield as she cut a path through the gathering men and women, heading down the hall toward an open door.

I hurried to follow before the path closed up again.

"Now . . ." She surveyed the various chairs and sofas placed in a semicircle about the room. It was a sort of glass-sided conservatory that appeared an ideal location for growing specimens, though there were only a half-dozen potted ferns placed about the room. "We'll just put ourselves here." She moved a pile of papers and brushes that was already sitting atop a chair.

"Isn't someone already sitting here?"

"If they were sitting here, then really, they ought to be sitting here." She leaned closer and dropped her voice to a whisper. "Besides, it's Mrs. Shandlin, and she's so tall that whenever she sits in the front, I can never see through her. If she were at all courteous, she'd sit in the back." She deposited the afore-mentioned Mrs. Shandlin's things two rows back. "There." She turned to me. "Where is your painting?"

"My *illustration* is just there." I nodded toward the portfolio.

Miss Templeton tore into the portfolio and pulled the illustration out like a prize. The beginnings of a smile had limned her face, but as she looked at the plant, her brow fell. "I had hoped for something a bit more . . . flowery . . . Although I suppose it's very well drawn. It looks quite detailed."

"It's a potato orchid from New Zealand. A specimen Mr. Trimble sent us last year. I'm quite proud of it, actually, because it's a challenging plant to draw and paint. They're naturally brown, so it's difficult to portray them without the flowers looking withered and dead."

"Yes. I can see that it is. And this . . . ?" She was gesturing toward the bottom of the paper, where I had illustrated the root system. "Is that an actual potato?"

"It's the root structure. Have you ever seen anything so un-usual?"

"In a painting? I have not. Are you certain you want to display this? If it's the only potato drawing you have, don't you think you'd rather keep it for yourself?"

"I'm quite happy to have it displayed."

We left our chairs and went back into the front hall, where some paintings had been propped against the hallstand.

Miss Templeton moved several smaller ones out of the way, set mine against the hallstand, and then put the others back in place in front of it.

"But you can't really see it that way."

"I would hate to seem too forward about it. You *are* quite nearly a professional."

Among the amateur paintings of flowers and insipid land-scapes, mine stood out for its detail and clarity. Miss Templeton was right. Why call extra attention to it when my skill was plain for all to see?

The meeting started with a reading of the previous meeting's minutes and reports from the president, the four vice presi-dents, the treasurer, the secretary, the correspondence secretary, the chair of membership, and each of the six council members present, as well as written reports from the two council mem-bers absent. That accounted for about half of the people in the room. The president then stood once again, in her capacity as hostess, and welcomed us to her home and then went back to being president to welcome guests to the society, and finally, the drawing tutor was introduced.

He talked at great length about the holding of a drawing pencil and the proper ratio of water to paint and a great many other things that had nothing to do with actual drawing or paint-ing at all. But as I looked around the room, I saw the men and women sitting around me were listening with rapt attention. At last, he set a pot of anemone with vibrant purple flowers atop a table with instructions to paint not its form but its essence.

I set to work sketching with ink, and then—

"Better to do it in pencil."

I looked up to find the tutor frowning at my drawing. "I prefer not to have to retrace my pencil lines in pen. It's more efficient that way."

"Be that as it may . . ." He lifted the sheet from me, revealing a clean one. "It's much better to start in pencil, trace over it in ink, and then color your final drawing."

Miss Templeton was glancing at me with a worried pull to her brow.

"Once you accomplish the correct method, believe me, you will never wish to draw any other way." He tapped the paper with his knuckle. "Back to work, then."

I tried to brush away the mark his knuckles had made, but I only succeeded in turning it into a greasy smear. Clenching my jaw, I discarded the paper for a second fresh page and hurriedly redrew what I had just done. There. I felt my shoulders relax as I started filling in the details.

But then he came back round again and took my pen from me.

"If you insist upon sketching with a pen, then I suggest that you draw the stem thusly." He grasped it with a firm hand. Such a firm hand that his stem had no suggestion of its natural suppleness. He offered my pen back to me, and I took it from him.

Paying no attention to his suggestions, I went on drawing the flower's leaflets, sepals—which so many mistook for petals—pistils, and stamens. Some of the society members went up to the front to consult the plant but, as it was an anemone, and since anemones were classified as Ranunculaceae, I had drawn a good several dozen of this variety over the years, so I accomplished my illustration nearly from memory. After not having picked up a pen in two weeks, I found myself exhilarated by the experience.

As I worked, the tutor came back along our row. I might have been tempted to hide my work from him, but even he could not fail to be impressed with my illustration.

As he passed behind me, however, I heard him gasp. "Oh no! No, no, no! We do *not* do that here."

Do what? I screwed myself around in my chair to try to see him.

He bent so that he could speak into my ear. "We don't draw *those*."

"Don't draw what?"

"*Those!*" He was pointing to my illustration as if it were some plague-infested rat.

"You mean the pistils and stamens? But that's what it has. It's an anemone. It has numerous pistils and stamens."

A tremulous shriek sounded from behind me. There was a rustling of skirts and then a soft thud.

Miss Templeton turned round, eyes wide. "Oh dear! Mrs. Shandlin's fainted."

"Just look what you've done!" The tutor's cheeks had gone red at their tops.

"What? What have I done? I drew an anemone with its pistils and stamens."

Miss Templeton leaned close as well. "It's not done, Miss Withersby."

"What's not done?"

"You're not supposed to draw those."

"But anyone can see that they have them. Why shouldn't I draw them? If I can't draw those, then I can't draw their ovaries and then they might as well not be plants!"

There was another rustle and second thud.

"Oh dear. That was Lady Harriwick."

The tutor took my illustration from me, grabbed me by the arm, and pulled me along up to the front. "I don't know what you're trying to do here, but everyone knows those *things* aren't discussed in polite society."

"One can't just ignore them!"

"If we must refer to them, we call them *the man and his wives*."

And that was less scandalizing? "Well, then each one has a multitude of them. They are running a veritable harem in that flower."

"For your purposes, they don't exist."

"Then I might as well not draw the sepals or the leaves."

"Perhaps that would be best." He took a sheet of his own paper and gave it to me, looking pointedly toward my seat.

I took it from him and sat back down. I tried to start anew, but my zeal for the task had entirely disappeared.

Eventually, he called for our attention and pulled a book from his satchel. "Now. It's always helpful to compare your work with that of a true professional, therefore, I have brought along a volume to which I often refer." He presented us with the cover of the book. "Mr. Withersby's *Ranunculaceae in Britain*."

Miss Templeton prodded me with an elbow and flashed me a smile.

"There is quite a nice illustration here of an anemone, just like ours." He flipped through the pages and then proceeded to show the society *my* illustration. He walked slowly about, up and down the rows so that the society's members could compare their drawings to my own. I held my breath as I waited for the women to gasp and faint at the sight of those pistils

SIRI MITCHELL

and stamens, but they only leaned forward to peer at the page more closely.

When he came to me, he paused. "I will admit that your work shows some promise. If you could just bring yourself to follow the correct process, and if you're willing to practice, I think you might be able to produce a fine little painting one day."

15

Church was quite agreeable that Sunday. I nodded to several people that I had met earlier in the week and when church ended, I even spoke to some of them before Mr. Trimble dragged us back to the house.

I saw Miss Templeton on Monday evening at a dramatic reading I attended with the Admiral. There was an air of resolution in her manner as she approached me. She took me by the arm and pulled me back toward the wall. "I confess that before the watercolor society meeting, I didn't understand that there was a difference between a painting and an illustration. Upon reflection, I admit that you were quite right to think that a watercolor society is not the right place for your work." She was watching me quite carefully.

"I thought so as well, but I didn't want to seem pedantic about it. You seemed so badly to want me to attend."

She smiled. "So let us try to speed you back to your work. Now then . . ." She glanced about the room. "Mr. Stansbury is here, and I think it an ideal time for you to speak to him. Shall I go with you?"

I sighed. "Every time I see him, I think of that dreadful stumpery of his, and I just can't pretend an interest in a man so immune to good taste in nature."

"Try thinking instead of that terrible Mr. Trimble and his taking over your job."

"I try. I do try."

"Then you must try harder, because Mr. Stansbury is an eccentric. He's liable to do just about anything. It's quite startling, really, the number of odd things he's done since he moved here, so if the Admiral can be convinced that he's set his cap for you, then your father cannot afford to hesitate any longer."

"I do understand, but if you consider that I will have to hear him talk about that dreadful stumpery—and probably have to go see it—then you would not ask me to be kind to him."

"Then I shall approach him for you and declare myself mad to see it and I daresay he will invite us for a tour. And if I let it slip that you've been invited to Overwich Hall twice now, just imagine what people will think!"

"I hope they won't think I approve of his stumpery."

"They shall think that he begins to favor you."

"They will?"

"Indeed. And then I shall be able to see it too! I've been dying to do so, you know. He really is quite extraordinary. Perhaps he'll even give us a tour of his house. He didn't last time, and I've heard there's an entire room given over to swords and sabers and another to a collection of clocks and watches. I've half a mind to tell him that to really have a respectable estate he needs a menagerie, just to see what he'd do. I've always wanted to see one of those what-do-you-call-thems with the long necks." She sighed. "It's such a pity you don't want to marry him. I should think it ever so amusing to be married to a man like that."

"Perhaps you should have him, then."

She frowned. "My father would never approve. Although he hasn't approved of half the things I've said and done, so in the end, that would probably be no obstacle." Snapping her fan open, she fluttered it as she pondered Mr. Stansbury for a long moment. "The problem is that he seems quite incapable of falling in love with anything but his glasshouse and that stumpery. And my express wish is to marry someone completely besotted with me. Remember? No, I shall stand by my original decision: I think he's best left to you."

Between the readings, Miss Templeton took my hand in hers and walked the length of the room as she conversed with me about hair falls and gowns. When she paused to open her fan and look about, I was quite surprised to find that we had come to a stop in front of Mr. Stansbury.

He bowed.

We curtseyed.

She squeezed my hand. "Miss Withersby has told me such stories of your . . . your . . . ?" Her brow puckered.

I mouthed the word *stumpery.*

"Sumpery."

"My *stump*ery?"

"That's it! You see, it's such a fantastical idea that I really can't quite conceive the picture of it."

"It's a garden of sorts set with tree stumps placed upside down so their roots show. Does that give you a better idea?"

"Not really."

"There are twenty-three such stumps. I just began to cultivate it last spring, and I—"

Really, I'd had enough of such foolishness. "What I've always wondered is how one *cultivates* a stump." It defied the definition of the word *cultivate*, did it not, when the thing was dead to begin with? "Perhaps caretaking would be a better way to explain it."

Miss Templeton's smile was fixed to her face, although her eyes looked quite vexed. "I really have *so* little imagination, Mr. Stansbury. I'm afraid it's one of my most grievous faults."

He smiled down at her as if he considered her fault a virtue. "I've always been a man more inclined to the practical than the fanciful myself, Miss Templeton. I see no reason for you to apologize."

"That's so kind. So very kind. Isn't it, Miss Withersby?"

I felt my brow wrinkle as she looked at me.

Her brows sunk into a curve. "You're so very kind, Mr. Stansbury, that I wonder if you would consider doing me a favor?"

"For you I would descend into the salt mines, Miss Templeton; I would brave even those steaming, malodorous salt pans."

Her cheeks colored. "I'm such a dreadfully curious creature. My father is forever saying so. I've always supposed it the consequence of having been left motherless—"

The levity left Mr. Stansbury's eyes in an instant. "I'm so sorry. I had no idea that your mother—"

"There's no reason you ought to be sorry, but in any case, I *do* so wish I could see your stumpery."

He searched her eyes for a moment before answering. When he did, his smile had returned. "I would consider it an honor. Why don't you come tomorrow? I will show it to you myself."

She linked her arm with mine. "You're too generous! You're so thoughtful! We'd be delighted to come. Wouldn't we, Miss Withersby?"

"Tomorrow? I'm not certain I can—"

She jabbed me in the ribs with her elbow.

"Yes. That would be fine."

"Is anything wrong, Miss Withersby?" Mr. Trimble asked the next day as we sat across from each other at our midday meal.

"Wrong? No. Why would you think so?"

"You're attacking that veal quite violently."

I looked down to find I'd been shredding the meat with my knife. "It's just . . ."

Father looked over at me, pushing his spectacles back up his nose.

"It's just that . . . I am contemplating Mr. Stansbury and how dreadful it would make me feel to leave this place for his."

"Dreadful? You sound as if you don't care for the man."

"Did I say that? No. I did not. I've actually become quite . . . quite . . . fixed to the idea that I could improve his taste."

Mr. Trimble was frowning at me. Again. "It seems to me one ought to marry a person of whose taste one already approves."

I smiled. "They say love is blind. I daresay it must be true."

He was looking at me as though he held my words suspect. "Perhaps. In any case, we received a missive yesterday from the butcher demanding last month's payment. He said he had sent the bill, and I know that I saw it, but it's quite gone missing."

Father sighed. "I searched for it half the night." He stifled a yawn. "I can't imagine what happened to it. Mr. Trimble has quite the system, you know, for managing . . . for managing . . . everything."

He'd stayed up half the night? Looking for a bill I'd hidden? Guilt pinched my conscience.

"Might you have come across it, Miss Withersby?" Mr. Trimble's gaze seemed to peer deep down into my soul.

I meant for *him* to be the victim of my perfidy, not my father.

My father spoke again. "I suppose . . . there must be some-place I didn't look. Perhaps I'll just start again and look through everything once more."

"No!" Heaven help me, I was no good at deception. "Let me look. Maybe I'll find it." And the letters from Ceylon and the University of Edinburgh as well.

Once the men began their discussions after lunch, I made quick work of undoing my deceit. I couldn't leave fast enough once the Admiral arrived with his carriage. We fetched Miss Templeton, who chattered the entire way.

Once arrived, we exchanged our carriage for Mr. Stansbury's open landau, and he proceeded to take us through his stum-pery at an excruciatingly slow pace. I have to think that several hours passed before we reached the middle of it, and there—in a pagoda up on a rise where we could view the stumpery in its entirety—we found tea waiting along with a tray of biscuits and some tiny little sandwiches. The Admiral took up several.

"So what do you think of my stumpery, Miss Templeton?"

"If you must know, I think it completely appalling!"

I very nearly choked at her words.

Mr. Stansbury blinked, and a flush began to rise up around his ears. "You . . . you do? I rather thought it the height of fashion."

"I do hope you're not finished with it yet."

"Well, no. In fact, I'm not. I had thought that—"

"What's needed are some ferns and some vines." She had left us at the table and was walking around the pagoda, look-ing at the views.

Mr. Stansbury had half risen from his chair in order to keep her in sight.

"And I do hope you're thinking of adding some birds?"

"Well, I hadn't thought that—"

"Because I find birds are so necessary to creating a natural sort of garden. I should think they'd find these roots the perfect place to build their nests."

"I'm sure they—"

"You *will* have some vines, won't you?" She was walking back to us now. "I'm sure Miss Withersby knows exactly which ones would grow best. You'd want some really vicious ones that like to climb." She was looking at me as if I ought to say something. "You know the ones, Miss Withersby, don't you?"

"Perhaps some ivy. Or wild lilac."

"A wild lilac! Those flower, don't they?"

I nodded.

"They'd like it here ever so much."

Mr. Stansbury was spluttering. "But it's meant to look like a ruin!"

"Yes, but ruins are only a means to a romantic vista. When I visited Tintern Abbey last year, I was delighted to find it overgrown. It was so picturesque. You do approve of the picturesque, don't you?"

"I'd never considered—"

"Yes. I think the picturesque is what's lacking here." She paused and turned to survey the stumpery once more. "I'm sure Miss Withersby could have it looking perfectly decrepit in a matter of days. She's an expert in botany, you know."

"I certainly agree with—"

"A veritable genius." She came forward and took me by the arm, propelling me from my seat toward his. "I'm sure it will take some time to get it to look respectably overgrown, so you and Miss Withersby have much to talk about. I don't mind taking a bit of a ramble while you speak. If, that is, you don't mind my going about here and there to look around?"

"Of course not. Please, feel free . . ."

The Admiral had already offered up his arm to her. They turned to stroll down the steps and then ambled off along a pebble-strewn path toward a particularly monstrous specimen of an upturned stump.

Mr. Stansbury watched them for a moment and then slid a glance in my direction before looking once more toward Miss Templeton. "I hadn't quite realized before how bare this all is. But if she says it needs to be more picturesque . . ."

"In my experience, Miss Templeton is quite knowledgeable where fashion is concerned. If she says a thing is stylish—or not—you can be certain it's true."

"She's rather formidable for one so young."

"I quite agree."

He threw back his head and laughed. "I haven't been so entertained, nor so thoroughly scolded, in ages." He left off looking at Miss Templeton and turned his green-eyed gaze upon me. "Now then, Miss Withersby, I throw myself entirely upon your genius. What would be the quickest, most fashionable way to make my stumpery more suitably picturesque?"

We spoke for quite some time about ivy and honeysuckle, dog roses and wild clematis. While I didn't generally approve of invasive plants, I laid aside my prejudices for the greater good of covering up Mr. Stansbury's stumps.

Miss Templeton and the Admiral took quite a long walk, so after conversing about the stumpery, my conversation with Mr. Stansbury turned toward his other plants, and I asked whether his orchid had not yet bloomed. We had got into quite a discussion about the perils of entrusting our work to colonial correspondents when they returned.

During the drive back to Overwich Hall, I noticed Miss Templeton glancing wistfully at the house. Why didn't she just ask him for a tour? Perhaps I could help her.

"Miss Templeton said you've not been long at Overwich Hall. Have you changed things very much inside?"

"Not much. I must confess that my attentions have been devoted almost entirely to my glasshouse and the stumpery." He smiled and the conversation ended.

If I had been Miss Templeton, he would not have missed my meaning. She made it seem so easy to ask for something she wanted, and yet it was, in actuality, quite difficult. I supposed the only thing to do was to put the question to him quite plainly. "May we see it?"

A look of mystification swept his features. "We just . . . we just did."

"I meant the house."

"Oh! Of course." By that time we had pulled up in front of it. "Please." He gestured to the entrance. "Please come in."

He showed us about the ground floor and led us through his collection of swords and sabers, and then he showed us his clocks and explained to us the inner workings of the gears about which he seemed singularly fascinated. He took a positively gigantic gold watch from a shelf and held it out to Miss Templeton. "What do you say of this one? Do you favor it?"

She was already shaking her head, curls swinging back and forth. "I can't say I do." She gestured to a second watch, which had been displayed next to the first. "That one is much better."

"It only has half the shine."

"Yes, but it probably cost three times as much, didn't it?"

He nodded.

"It's not the shine; it's the quality that counts."

He bowed. "I'll have to remember that."

The Admiral became rather absorbed by a clock Mr. Stansbury said was fashioned from ormolu. I stayed with him while Miss Templeton and Mr. Stansbury wandered on into the front hall. Eventually, we met up and toured all three stories before Mr. Stansbury walked with us out to the drive.

Miss Templeton waved gaily to him as we drove away, and then she sat back against the cushions, a satisfied smile upon her face. "So, how did I do?"

"How did you do what?"

"I took care of your problem."

The Admiral was looking at her with alarm. "What problem was that?"

"The stumpery!"

He hmphed and then leaned back against his seat. Folding his hands over his stomach, he closed his eyes.

She continued on. "Mr. Stansbury is a very stubborn man, but at least he's consented to having it grown over by vines. All in all, I consider the outcome quite satisfactory. Oh! And I convinced him to invite the watercolor society to draw in his glasshouse Friday next. Don't you think that kind of him? He's agreed to consider our drawings for inclusion in the publication of a guidebook. He intends to offer tours of the glasshouse once his collections have been completed."

"You mean he's to be the editor? I suppose he'll be paying for the illustrations he selects, then?" If that were the case, perhaps I would reconsider my opinion of the watercolor society.

"*Paying*? For a drawing?" Her laugh burst forth and bubbled out over the gloved hand she had clasped to her mouth. "I hardly think so! The honor is in being invited, and the payment is in the pleasure of being chosen."

"For which such work, I have been accustomed to being paid by a publisher in the past."

"Oh, it's not meant to be a published work."

"It won't be printed then? Or bound?"

"I'm quite sure that it won't be." She didn't sound so certain.

"Will it not be sold?"

"Only to visitors. As a limited edition, perhaps. Or maybe on a subscription basis."

"For which work I am normally given a premium."

"Don't be so dour, Miss Withersby. It's all in fun. And in spite of our agreement about your not coming to the watercolor society meetings, I do think you should come to this one." We had reached Dodsley Manor. She clasped my hand, however, as she descended and would not let it go. She leaned close to my ear. "It will be just the thing to make your father think your attentions have been captivated. Say you'll come."

"I will."

"You'll be so glad!"

16

After a week's worth of card parties, teas, church committee meetings, and other events to which Miss Templeton had subscribed me, not to mention those evening obligations to which the Admiral insisted upon taking me, I found myself longing for the solitary pleasure of contemplating a species heretofore unknown to science. But Friday found me packing up my drawing paper, my pen and brushes, as well as my pocket glass and colors for the drawing party at Mr. Stansbury's glasshouse. I decided to take the microscope as well. That way I would be able to really see what I was drawing.

"What are you doing there?" Mr. Trimble was looking at me, his brow furrowed in what I took to be disapproval.

"I'm gathering my tools for the drawing expedition."

"Expedition? What expedition?"

"The one to Mr. Stansbury's glasshouse."

"You can't take the microscope."

"I don't see why not. It's not that heavy."

"It's not a matter of weight; it's a matter of propriety."

"If I'm going to draw, then I need to understand what it is that I'm seeing."

"Most women just look at a flower to draw it. They don't feel the need to examine it."

"Which may be why most drawings I've been shown are regrettably lacking in accuracy. Do you know Miss Templeton has a dress that is embroidered with strawberry flowers that are missing some of their petals?" Or perhaps it was the case that they had too many petals. It was difficult to decide since I didn't know what variety they were meant to be.

"And I suppose you told her so."

"I most certainly did. Who would want to wear a dress with inaccurate flowers?"

"Really, you are the most . . . most . . ." He gave up and simply shook his head.

I clutched the microscope to my chest and left the house before he could say anything further.

As the expedition was to be undertaken by the watercolor society as a whole, the Admiral had begged off going, although he did allow me the use of his carriage. Miss Templeton was already engaged in the sketching of a palm when I arrived. Rather than joining her, I turned my attentions to some orange blossoms. I was well on my way to completing a sketch when Mr. Stansbury approached. He tipped his chin in the direction of Miss Templeton, who was nibbling on her lip as she drew.

"She's a marvelous girl, isn't she?"

"Charming?" That was one of those words Mr. Trimble was so fond of using.

"Yes. Most charming!" He went on for several minutes about the virtues of Miss Templeton, but I confess that I hardly heard a word because I was endeavoring to determine the relationship between the calyx and the corolla of the orange flower. From glancing at the sketches of the society members around me, I saw that most of them failed to grasp that the relationship was fixed in each species. Some of the drawings had a ridiculous number of teeth to corolla.

I was beginning to realize, however, that the Admiral's golden rule must not be taken too literally. After my argument with the drawing tutor about the presence, or lack thereof, of pistils and stamens, I had concluded that my information about teeth and corolla might not be welcomed as much as I would have expected.

Mr. Stansbury moved on to speak to Miss Templeton, and I was left alone to my work for quite some time, until he moved on from her to speak to his other guests. At that point, she began to gesture for me. Laying down my brush, I went to talk to her.

"You let him escape!"

"I what?"

"Mr. Stansbury. You let him escape! How is word going to get around that he's flirting with you if you don't flirt with him?"

"*Flirt* with him? We were invited here to draw. And that's what I'm doing. That is, I *was* drawing, but now I'm ready to begin coloring. I was just about to start mixing my paints when—"

She reached out and grabbed my arm, drawing me close. "We were invited here under the *pretext* of drawing, but the whole point was for you to be seen monopolizing his attentions. Really, Miss Withersby, I cannot help you if you will not try to help yourself!" Her words broke off in a hiss.

I glanced off down the aisle where I could see him speaking to Mrs. Bickwith, who was drawing one of his ferns. "I don't see what I can do about it now . . . unless you want me to color from memory at home." I supposed I could do that, but it wouldn't be half so satisfactory. Though the petals were white, there was a sheen to the leaves that was difficult to capture.

Miss Templeton let out a great sigh. "It's no good pretending that you wish to marry since your heart just doesn't seem to be in it. No one—not your father, and most definitely not Mr. Trimble—will be alarmed if it doesn't seem as if anyone will *ever* ask for your hand."

She did have a point. "It's just that it has been so long since I've drawn anything at all, save that anemone at the previous society meeting, and—"

"Miss Withersby, I begin to have serious doubts as to the efficacy of our plan."

She was right. I nodded. "I'll just . . . I'll go and . . . What should I say to him?"

She gave me a long, hard look for a moment, and I felt as if I were eight years old again. "Never you mind. I'll get him and bring him back for you. Just stay right here so I'll be able to find you." She squared her shoulders as she slipped her reticule over her wrist. "Oh! I just remembered." She reached into it and drew out a book, which she thrust into my hand. "You might consider giving this a read sometime soon."

I held it up to view the title. *"Etiquette?"*

"Not, of course, that you don't already know all of those things, but I always reread the manual myself in preparation for shooting season. Or . . . I used to in any case." She patted the cover. "Keep it as long as you like! Now then, I'm off to waylay Mr. Stansbury."

Better her than me. I picked up her drawing pencil and completed her sketch of the palm illustration.

Miss Templeton never did get around to coming back with Mr. Stansbury, although they seemed to have quite a good conversation between them. I had time enough to finish her sketch and then return to my own illustration.

Once home, I made short work of reading the manual Miss Templeton had passed on to me. It began pleasantly enough, with the topic of conversation, by posing the question of how one could aim to be conversant without first having spent the time to consider politics and the travails of men and other questions of philosophy. As I had dedicated my life's work to becoming ever more philosophical, I very nearly quit reading. Reflecting, however, that Miss Templeton might ask what I thought of the book, I decided I had better read it through.

It soon ventured into the requirements of having an appreciation of the arts and the reading of poetry. From there I began to think myself quite inadequate to the task when it proposed that cheerfulness and bonhomie could overcome nearly any failing. Having never been accused of being particularly cheerful, I read on with growing dread.

I was informed of the social trap of the laugh. Of the virtues of the truly graceful smile, which the author seemed to think no one adept enough to achieve. It went on to consider whether it was, in fact, rude to contradict. In short, it seemed nothing about conversation was truly sanctioned and yet everything was permissible.

There was nothing to be gained by continuing to read such equivocation and so I turned to the chapter on dinner parties and balls. It began by urging that the reader ought to go into such endeavors by banishing all thoughts of what he ought and ought not do. Which made me wonder why the author felt the need to write the book in the first place! It was truly a very unsatisfactory instruction, if instruction it could even be called.

Reading further, I found the information for which I had been looking: actual rules that might be followed. Eat peas with a fork. Curry and desserts must be eaten with a dessert spoon. If there is a sauce, it must be poured to the side of the plate. Help fish onto your fork not with a knife but with a piece of bread. Only fingers ought to be dipped into finger-glasses. Never gargle at the table.

Thank heaven I had never thought of doing such a thing.

At private concerts, ladies are seated in the front, with the gentlemen behind them. Finding fault is never acceptable—which seemed to contradict the previous discussion of contradiction. Never offer a person the chair from which you have just risen. Do not drum on the table with your fingers.

Ha! I knew Mr. Trimble was not the gentleman he wished so badly to seem.

The next evening, I attended a musical recital and took particular care to avoid doing any of those things prohibited in the manual. When Miss Templeton waved her fan at me from across the room, I started toward her . . . but then remembered that no polite person would use a fan in such a manner. So I started back . . . but then recalled that generosity of spirit and the forgiveness of foibles was required of those who consider themselves mannered. Caught between coming and going, I stood there for some moments. Miss Templeton came to my rescue by crossing the room to meet me.

"How did you find the music?"

"Quite nice."

She smiled. "I did too! Ever so nice. And I saw that Mr. Stansbury took a seat next to you."

He had. But, really, he ought not have. If he were a true

gentleman, he would have left that first row to the ladies. But he could not truly be considered a gentleman, could he? He'd made his money; he hadn't inherited it. So . . . that rule could not apply to him, could it?

Miss Templeton was looking at me as if she were expecting some sort of reply. "Yes. Yes, he did sit next to me." Did this conversation fall under the sort of thing that was too trifling to speak of?

"And what are you doing tomorrow after church, if I may be so rude as to inquire?"

I sighed. "I shall probably do nothing worthwhile even as I am thinking the whole time of all the things Mr. Trimble is doing that I would like to do instead."

"That will never do! If your father sees you at home all the time, then he's not likely to imagine that you will ever not be there. The King's Head Field Club meets on Sunday afternoons. A person so impassioned of plants as you are ought to go. I go. We should go together. I think it will be much more success-ful than the watercolor society. It's a much better fit for your talents."

"My general opinion of field clubs is that they're composed of people who don't know anything at all about the plants they claim to love." I clapped my hand over my mouth. I should not have said that. Being polite was so very difficult.

"Well, then you must certainly go—and I must beg to differ as I consider myself quite above the average field club member. And would your father not fear for himself if you cease working on his behalf and instead begin to seek the company of those you had formerly chosen to scorn?"

I didn't quite follow her logic, but as she was the expert in this sort of thing, I found myself agreeing.

"So you'll meet me at the King's Head, then?"

"At the King's Head? Isn't that a pub?"

"It is. It's where the club meets. At the pub. Hence its name: The King's Head Field Club. The meeting starts at one o'clock. And don't be late!"

I returned home that night to find Mr. Trimble sitting at his desk, letter in hand, looking right past me at . . . I turned to look, but there was nothing of any interest behind me in the hall. "Mr. Trimble?"

He blinked. "Miss Withersby." He stood so quickly his chair almost tipped over.

"May I help you?" I hated to say the words. In fact, I had vowed never to offer my help to him in any way, but his manner was so odd. He looked ill.

As I spoke, he shoved the letter into his coat pocket. Now he was staring at me with a guilty sort of look. "No. Thank you. Just some correspondence that has caught up to me. Does your hunt for a husband progress, Miss Withersby?"

"Yes. Quite well, thank you."

He nodded rather absentmindedly. "You don't find society too demanding?"

"I find it inscrutable."

He squinted. "Pardon me?"

"I don't understand the rules. Miss Templeton gave me a book on etiquette, and I was hoping it would educate me on those things I haven't understood, but it has only confused me more. If I'm to believe what I read, I should hardly be allowed to speak. Miss Templeton speaks all the time, however, and I noticed the same of nearly all of the women in town. There must be some method to it, but even upon examination, I have not been able to discover it."

"It's quite simple, really. You must stop thinking of conversation as a sort of examination and start thinking of it as a game. The point is not to be the person at whom it stops. It's rather like a game of twirling the trencher."

"I've never heard of it."

"Come. You must have played it in your youth."

"I have not. I never have."

He said nothing.

I said nothing.

A great and familiar silence fell over the room. "See, this is what always happens to me."

"Conversation, my dear Miss Withersby, is a very fragile creature. You must nourish it if you would have it survive. Its favorite food is a question. When I mentioned twirling the trencher do you remember what you said?"

"I said I had never played it."

"And I said?"

What had he said? "You said I must have played it in my youth."

"And what did you reply?"

"That I had not."

"And then?"

"The conversation stopped."

"You made a statement. Could you think of a question you might have asked instead?"

"About what?"

"In answer to my saying you must have played it in your youth."

"Was there something questionable in that? If there was, I fail to see it."

"Miss Withersby! You are the most exasperating—!" He took a deep breath. "Forgive me. You are one of the most *intelligent* women I know. You have not learned your science by giving statements, have you? Isn't all your progress in botany made by asking questions?"

"Of course it is."

"And why?"

"Because there's so much to be discovered. If I don't ask questions, then how will I learn anything?"

"Exactly. You're approaching conversation all wrong. The point is to learn something."

"About what?"

"About anything! About the person to whom you're speaking. About the topic they're speaking on. You're missing fascinating bits of information because you're failing to ask questions. You're simply waiting to be asked them. Waiting to give answers."

Perhaps he was right.

"Shall we try again?"

I tried to think of something else to say, but what other remark could I make about a game I had never played? "I . . . I have never played the game but . . . perhaps I might like to." I paused as I reconsidered. "That's not strictly true, Mr. Trimble. As a general rule, I don't like to play games, but—"

He was laughing.

"I fail to see anything amusing in—"

"I'm sorry, Miss Withersby, but you've never said a truer thing. The whole problem is that you don't like to play games. I cannot tell you how much I admire that, but I will tell you a secret. Most people say things they don't mean all the time."

I felt my mouth drop open. "You mean to say they lie? On *purpose*?"

"I wouldn't call it lying. In any case, you were telling me you'd never played twirling the trencher . . . ?"

"Perhaps . . . perhaps you could explain to me how to play that game since I've never played it before?"

200

He clapped. "*Brava*, Miss Withersby. Well done! And because you asked a question, now we can have a conversation." He proceeded to explain to me how to play it. Something about spinning a trencher or tray on its end and someone having to pick it up before it falls. But when he was finished he looked at me as if expecting something.

"Now I suppose I am to ask you some other question."

"That would be quite agreeable."

I didn't care about spinning trenchers and I could see he was going to be quite obstinate about this whole thing, so I tried to think of something else I didn't know that I could discover. That's when I began to see how I could use this exercise to my advantage. To get him to leave, it might be useful to determine from where it was that he'd come. "Where, in fact, are you from, Mr. Trimble? I don't believe you've ever said."

"The east."

"As in . . . Kent? Or India?"

"I wish I could say I was from the subcontinent. I hope one day to journey there."

"I do as well. I dream of seeing a lotus in its natural state. Do your interests there lie in botany?"

"Partially. I've also heard there is a good living to be made in that colony from tea."

"You are quite unexpected: a sheep farmer with an interest in flowers and a passion for tea."

"I would say you are quite unexpected as well, Miss Withersby, with your unnerving combination of highly developed intellect and unspoilt beauty. Your appeal is the same as that of a Scottish heath."

". . . I . . . can't think that any of those things go together."

A flush had crept up around his ears. "Forgive me. It was meant to be poetical."

He saw me as a Scottish heath? How was I to respond to that? The etiquette book didn't cover how one should reply to poetical men.

When I next saw Miss Templeton, at the field club meeting, I kept Mr. Trimble's words about conversing foremost in my mind. He had told me that a question answered begs a question in return, so when she asked if I was well, I told her I had the most pernicious crick at the base of my neck. I then asked a question in turn. "But how is your scandal coming?"

We dropped a curtsey at Mr. Shandlin, but before he could acknowledge us, she drew me past him over to a secluded pair of chairs toward the back of the room. As we passed by people who were eating and drinking, I wondered if we might not be served refreshments during the course of the meeting. I hoped so.

"How clever of you to remember my scandal! I've taken my maid into my confidence on little things now and then, such as my suspicions that I look much better in pink than in green. Quite soon I feel I'll be able to ask her outright how one goes about such things. Papa is getting quite anxious that I marry, so I feel as if my time runs short. And you? Does our plan seem to be succeeding?"

I considered the question for a moment before I answered. "On the whole, I rather think it does. Mr. Trimble, at least, seems very set on the best ways to improve me, but don't you think that—"

"*Improve* you? What a beast! I like you quite well the way you are. If he succeeds in changing you, he shall have to answer for it. Besides, what could a man from a family like his have to say about improving you?"

"Rather a lot."

She laughed. "I can just imagine him, going on about . . . What has he gone on about?"

"He . . . taught me a parlor game. And he saved me from going out with a pelerine knotted about my neck, and—"

"Why would you have knotted a pelerine about your neck?"

"I thought it was . . . That is to say, I was mistaken about what it was. In any case, he's been quite helpful."

"Don't for a minute begin to trust him! He's only trying to gain your sympathy, and I *won't have it*. You must be strong, Miss Withersby. Remember: the whole purpose of our plan is to make him return to whence he came."

"New Zealand. And before that, from the east."

"What?"

"He came here from New Zealand. He's a sheep farmer."

She sniffed. "Perhaps that's why he smells of sheep."

"He doesn't."

"Doesn't what?"

"Smell of sheep. He smells of something quite wonderful really. I've been trying to place it . . . something almost like cinnamon. Or cloves."

"Well, it's not to be borne!"

"What isn't?"

"I won't have you going around sniffing him. You must not forget that he's old and rude and . . . and *mean*!"

"He's not very old in fact, and he's not rude. At least not all of the time."

She was glaring at me.

"I do, however, understand what you are saying, and I'll try to be more circumspect about him in the future."

"All in all, I think that's wise."

The room fell quiet as a man began to speak at the front of the room. He introduced himself as the president of the field club and said a few words of welcome before someone rose to read the minutes of the previous meeting. A woman sat down next to Miss Templeton. As the man spoke, the room began to get quite stuffy, and I wondered when the field club would actually move out to a field. Glancing about the room, I saw that I was the only person who had brought a vasculum.

Some other man replaced the reader of the minutes and talked about the schedule of events for the coming year and the party that was to take place in December, along with several other items that didn't really seem to be of much importance. It was followed by a general discussion about a spring excursion to Chester on the train.

When he sat down, no one took his place and everyone seemed determined to order drinks all at once, and . . . "Is that all there is to the meeting?"

Miss Templeton leaned toward me. "What's that?"

"Are we not going out to the field?"

"Not this week. Next week. Perhaps. Depending upon the hunters and stalkers."

"But what is the purpose of a field club if it doesn't venture out into the field?"

"We do venture . . . sometimes. Next week, perhaps, but mostly in the spring and summer, when the weather is better. We went to Ravenhead once. It was delightful!"

The woman sitting next to Miss Templeton began to rhapsodize about the trip. Mostly she recounted how the village was quite unlike what she had expected and how the train they'd taken was so comfortable.

I could not keep myself from interrupting them. "What about the flowers?"

"What flowers?" The woman looked at me as if I were quite mad.

"Was there nothing of distinction that you found?"

"Not really." She giggled with Miss Templeton. "Unless you count Mr. Leighton."

"Mr. Leighton? Is that a colloquial name for a flower? I've never heard of it before."

Miss Templeton laughed outright. "It's the name of her husband. It wasn't long after our Ravenhead excursion that they were betrothed."

A swath of light swept across our table, and we turned to see the door had opened.

"Oh, it's Mr. Stansbury!" Miss Templeton stood and waved him over as Mrs. Leighton left.

He bowed as he greeted us.

"Do pull up a chair and join us." She scooted hers away from mine. "You can sit just here, between us."

He soon returned with a chair.

"You missed the meeting!" Miss Templeton chided him, though she did it with a smile.

"I'm so sorry to hear it."

"We're to go out toward Comber Mere, if weather permits. I daresay if you are late for that meeting, you'll miss the outing."

"Then I will try to be punctual." He turned toward me. "Are you going to scold me as well, Miss Withersby?"

"I couldn't say. Have you done something about which you'd rather I not hear?"

He laughed. "I've done a good many things I'd rather you not hear about, but I can't say I've done anything scandalous lately."

"Perhaps you could give Miss Templeton some advice then. She's trying to work up a scandal of her own."

Miss Templeton's mouth dropped open, and then she snapped it shut as her cheeks grew pink. "Miss Withersby! I . . . I . . ."

17

For the first time since I'd met her, Miss Templeton had nothing to say.

Mr. Stansbury was looking at her with great disappointment. "I'm shocked, Miss Templeton, and I would advise you that scandals are nothing to play at. They are never as amusing as expected to those who are scandalized in the process."

Now her eyes were watering, and she was blinking quite rapidly. "I assure you, Mr. Stansbury, that upon further reflection, I think myself quite incapable of doing anything of which you'd disapprove. And so is Miss Withersby."

He gave me a speculative look. "I accept your word on your own behalf, but I would have to ask Miss Withersby for hers. What say you, Miss Withersby? Are you incapable of scandal?"

"I suppose it would depend on what sort of scandal it might be. So . . . what sort of scandal would it be?"

Miss Templeton gasped.

"Because if you are speaking of the type in which the great minds of botany air their grievances between the pages of our societies' journals, then I must tell you that I have, from time to time, been tempted."

"But would you?" A corner of his mouth was lifting.

"I think so. On the whole, I would hope so. Some things are worth speaking up for, are they not?"

"Well said. Indeed they are."

I returned from the field club meeting much dissatisfied. Miss Templeton seemed a bit put out, and I could not work out why. She had at first seemed so glad to see me. She had pulled me away from the others to speak to me, but when I left, she hardly acknowledged my leaving. I didn't know what to think of it.

I remembered that she had cautioned the less I said to Mr. Trimble, the better, but I did not know who else to ask about the matter and so I simply put it to him plainly.

He took his time in replying. "So . . . you think she's angry with you?"

"I do think so. But I don't know why."

"Is it something you said?"

I thought about our conversation and could hardly credit it. "No . . . no. I can't think so."

"Of what did you speak?"

"Of field club excursions and Mrs. Leighton. And then I mentioned to Mr. Stansbury that perhaps he could help Miss Templeton with a scandal she's planning, and—"

"Wait. Right there. What was it you said about scandals?"

"Well, it was a . . ." How had that happened exactly? "Mr. Stansbury made some comment about having done some things that were better not mentioned, though he hadn't done anything scandalous lately, so I offered that since he apparently has intimate knowledge of scandals, he might offer some advice to Miss Templeton, who has been planning one."

"I think I understand where things went wrong." There was

a curious gleam in his eyes, and he was clenching his jaw quite tightly.

"Truly? I don't. I still don't. I was making conversation. I was asking questions, just as you said I should, and—"

"The thing about scandals, Miss Withersby, is that they're scandalous to speak of, which is why polite people don't." He was enunciating the words quite clearly.

"Ever?"

"Never."

I thought about that for a long moment. "But if scandals should not be spoken of, then no one would know something scandalous had taken place." There was something about this that didn't make any sense. "Someone, somewhere, must be speaking of scandals or there wouldn't be any."

"Perhaps I should say that you may speak of scandals, but not with the general public."

"I wasn't with the general public. I was with Miss Templeton and Mr. Stansbury."

"You may speak of scandals, but not in mixed company."

"So . . . if I had been with Miss Templeton, and another woman had come to sit with us, or perhaps if Mrs. Leighton had stayed with us, I might have asked her about helping Miss Templeton with her scandal?"

"At this point in your conversational progress, I think it best not to speak of scandals at all. In any form. In any company."

"I was only trying to help."

"I suspect that you only succeeded in embarrassing your friend."

"Oh. Oh! But I hadn't meant to. What should I do? Should I tell Mr. Stansbury his help isn't needed?"

"I rather think you should apologize to Miss Templeton for airing news of her hoped-for scandal and leave off speaking of it to Mr. Stansbury ever again."

"I do feel badly. I didn't mean to humiliate her."

"She's spent quite a bit of time with you of late, so I'm sure she understands."

I hoped she did. I was rather worried now that she might not. That etiquette book she had lent to me must have a section on scandals. Although if it did, I had managed to miss it.

Turning toward the hall, I determined to atone for my error. As I did, Mr. Trimble spoke. "I wonder . . . what was that scandal Miss Templeton is trying to perpetuate?"

"It's—" I stopped myself from speaking. "You are very sly, Mr. Trimble. You're trying to test me, aren't you? Please be assured that I have learned my lesson. You are mixed company, and I shall not make the same mistake twice."

"It's not that. It's just that I was curious what a girl like Miss Templeton might—"

"My lips are, as they say, sealed."

"You couldn't just—?"

I shook my head and ascended to my room, where I soon discovered, to my great disappointment while paging through the etiquette book, that there was no section on scandals.

The next evening, I decided to wait for the Admiral in the front hall. The number of petticoats I was expected to wear made sitting more of a chore than a pleasure, and in any case, Miss Templeton was always decrying my wrinkled skirts. Mr. Trimble soon joined me. He regarded me for a moment, taking in my dress with one long glance. "Isn't it a dance you're attending this evening?"

"It is. At the Leweses."

"You might, perhaps then, wish to wear a costume more accommodating than that."

The gown, a wine-colored brocade, was a late delivery from
the dressmaker and the last of those I had ordered. I liked it
for the most part, except for the sleeves, which were quite tight
from my elbows to my wrists. They closed with at least two
dozen buttons, which had taken me almost half an hour to fasten. I didn't know how fashionable people ever had time to get
anything done. "If I change, I risk committing the mortal sin of
being seen in public wearing the same thing twice—a vice, says
Miss Templeton, that only the truly gauche would commit."

"I can guarantee that *she* won't be dancing in cashmere."
He leaned against the doorframe as he crossed his arms over
his chest. "Pardon my asking, but do you know how to dance?"

"I know several country dances. I find them quite stimulating.
My mother used to make us pause now and then in our work
and perform them. She said vigorous movement was good for
the soul."

"Do you know the polka, then?"

I pulled up my skirts and began performing the steps that I
knew, turning this way and that, kicking my feet. "I know this
one, though I don't know what it's called."

His smile had a strained look at the edges.

I jumped and whirled down the hall.

As I passed, he put a hand to my arm. "Yes, well, although
the polka is rather vigorous, polite society doesn't hold with
the idea of leaping about *quite* so strenuously. They're more
inclined to genteel dances like the varsovienne and the waltz."

"I don't know either of those."

"And I don't much believe you've left yourself the time to
learn. Really, did the Admiral not warn you that you'd been
invited to a dance?"

"Of course he said it was a dance, but I didn't understand it
to mean that anyone would expect *me* to dance."

"That's what is generally done at dances, Miss Withersby. One . . . dances."

"I suppose I shall just sit them out, then. You don't suppose the dancing will last long, do you?"

"If you sit them out, you'll be sitting all night."

"All night?" In all of these petticoats? I heard myself sigh. "I suppose it won't be so bad if I can sit near the refreshments table. Last time I was at the Leweses, for a concert, they served a truly delicious punch."

"Sitting out will never do. I'll teach you what I can before the Admiral arrives." He extended a hand. "Here. Let me show you."

I put my hand into his.

"I'll teach you an older dance first, to a song they're sure to play. The most important thing, of course, will be to watch everyone else and simply do as they do."

I nodded.

He bowed and then began to hum.

I bowed.

"No, no, no. I bow. You curtsey."

"But you said to do as everyone else did. It's quite unfair for you to berate me for simply following your instructions."

"I did not—" He took a deep breath. When he spoke again it was in a softer tone. "I did not berate you. So . . . I bow." He bowed. "And you . . . ?"

I curtseyed. "I really don't see why I have to curtsey if I've already curtseyed to half the room upon entering. It strikes me as highly redundant."

"What you call redundant, the rest of society calls a dance step."

He started humming once more, taking me by the hand, and made as if he intended to take a tour of the hall, but that seemed a strange sort of dance, so I was slow in following.

"Miss Withersby, I think it best if you just hold yourself loosely and allow yourself to be led about."

I bent my knees and my elbows and tried to make them go wobbly.

"I said, hold yourself loosely, not go about like someone's granny."

"This is very confusing. First you tell me to relax, and then you tell me to stiffen up."

"You're to dance. Not talk, not object, but dance."

"I would like to, but you keep interrupting me. Please be so kind as to continue."

I think he may have gnashed his teeth, but he did take up my hand once more and pulled me forward toward the front door. "Now, a series of chassés is needed, and once we reach the end of the hall, we turn."

"What have sachets to do with dancing?"

"A chassé. A . . ." He released my hand and took another sliding sort of step.

"You mean you want me to slide across the floor? Then you ought to have said so. The Admiral will be here any moment and I'd like to learn as much as I can."

He looked at me for a long moment. "Perhaps we should concentrate on the waltz then. There's really nothing to it." Again he extended his hand. But this time when I put mine into it, he pulled me quite close.

"I . . . I wonder, Mr. Trimble, is this really necessary?" I was so close to him that I was speaking into his throat. His cravat had come loose, and that wonderfully spicy scent was wafting up from beneath his collar.

"The waltz is all the rage, Miss Withersby, and I'm quite sure you will be asked to dance at least one." He tightened his grip on me and put his other hand to the back of my waist. It was then that I understood what he meant about cashmere being unsuitable for dancing. Of a sudden, my face felt flushed and my bosom constricted.

"The waltz is a three-count dance."

"Could you hurry, please? I am beginning to feel quite overcome with heat."

"I start out stepping forward with my right foot, so you must step back with your left."

I stepped back and opened up a chasm between us.

"At the same time. We must both do it at the same time."

"Well, I can hardly read your mind, can I?"

"One-two-three. One-two-three." He directed me backward with a slight push on my hand.

I took a few hurried steps back so that he wouldn't bump into me.

"Just *one*, Miss Withersby. I take one step and you take one step."

We tried again, with the same result.

"Would it help you to look at my feet, perhaps? Just for the moment, while you're learning?"

"Yes. I believe it would." I glanced down toward his feet at the same time he did, and our heads met in an unfortunate collision. "I'm so sorry!"

"It's nothing." He said it in a dismissive sort of way, but not until I'd seen him wince. "Shall we try again?"

I looked down once more, but not quite so pointedly, and in doing so, I was able to step at the same moment he did.

"Mr. Trimble, I wonder . . . ?"

"What is it?"

"Would you mind terribly if we traded sides? It's just that I'd like to know where it is that I'm going."

"Traditionally the waltz is danced with the woman facing backwards."

"Which is a contradiction in terms because one can't face anything when one's back is toward it. But you're the one who is steering. Since you know where it is you want to go, it seems quite mean to keep me from that knowledge."

"It's not a question of malice—it's an assumption of trust. You must trust that I will lead you."

"I do. In principle. However, this hall isn't the largest, and I keep thinking I'm going to run into the stairs, and I just don't see how . . . Frankly, I just don't see at all."

He stopped dancing, dropped my hand, and stepped back with a bow. "I think I've done all that I can for you, Miss Withersby."

"But . . . that can't be it. I don't feel as if I've learned anything yet."

He nodded toward the door.

I turned to see the Admiral standing there regarding us, a frown marring his face.

"She doesn't know how to dance." Mr. Trimble said the words in a tone that made me wish I could deny the accusation.

My uncle's eyebrows shot toward his head. "Doesn't know how? Why not?" He was glaring at me as if it were somehow my fault.

"Mother taught me several country dances, but otherwise, I never learned." I was struck by inspiration. "But you don't dance much, do you, Uncle? So I'll just do what you do when the music starts playing."

"Generally, I smoke my pipe. And try to get up a game of cards."

That wouldn't do. "Perhaps I could wander the gardens."

Both their brows spiked. "In the dark? In this weather? Without an escort?"

"Or perhaps not. Maybe I shouldn't go at all."

Mr. Trimble handed me my reticule and fairly pushed me out the door.

The ballroom looked like a grotto with candles shimmering on their sconces and evergreens draping the windowsills. The band was playing a lively melody, and my feet itched to join in, but once the couples assembled and began their steps, I saw that it was nothing I knew how to do.

Miss Templeton was standing in a corner conversing with her father. I excused myself from the Admiral and went to speak to her.

I made my apologies for announcing her intended scandal, and she graciously forgave me. As we were speaking, the song came to an end, but after a slight pause, the orchestra struck up another. A man came by to ask Miss Templeton to dance, and she whirled out onto the dance floor with him. After that song came yet another. And then the musicians stopped playing.

Miss Templeton came by, her cheeks bright and eyes sparkling. "This is ever so amusing, Miss Withersby. I don't see how you feel satisfied just standing there not dancing. We must find you a partner!"

"I don't know how to dance."

"But surely you don't mean—?" Her mouth dropped open, and her eyes grew round. "I've never heard anything more tragic! You don't know how to dance?"

I shook my head.

"At *all*?"

"Not dances of this sort."

"Oh! I wish I could blame this on that terrible Mr. Trimble, but I suppose I can't . . . can I?"

She looked so hopeful that I wished I could oblige her. "No." I wanted to blame it on him too. How was it that I hadn't realized just how important dancing could be?

She went off to the refreshments table with her dancing partner, and I was left standing next to the Admiral. He stood stiffly, arms clasped behind his back, looking quite stern. It occurred to me then that perhaps the trouble with my lack of beaux wasn't me. Perhaps it was him.

"You could dance, Uncle, if you'd like. Or go smoke your pipe. Please don't feel you have to stay here beside me."

"I couldn't leave a likely lass like you unattended."

The dances were quite wondrous to behold. I wouldn't have minded being taught how to do them. But there were so terribly many of them, it seemed as if it would be difficult to keep them all straight.

During one of them, Mr. Stansbury approached. He bowed and then crooked his arm. "Would you care to dance, Miss Withersby?"

"I don't think so. No."

He blinked.

18

O h dear. I've said the wrong thing again, haven't I?"
       "Not if you don't want to dance with me. A girl
       ought to have a say in the matter." He spoke the words
rather stiffly.

"It's not that I don't want to dance with you. I might. Or I
might not. It's difficult to say, really, because I don't know how
and it looks quite complicated."

His shoulders relaxed and he moved to stand beside me,
hands clasped behind his back. "To tell the truth, it *is* rather
complicated. And I didn't know how to dance either until I hired
an instructor to teach me at the grand old age of thirty years."

"Mr. Trimble warned me not to try. He seemed to think I
would make a fool of myself."

"Do you always listen to this Mr. Trimble? He seems to have
a rather poor opinion of your skills."

"There's really no one else to listen to. He's my father's assistant, you see, and he's the only one who knows anything
about any of this." I paused to slide a look toward the Admiral
and leaned closer. "Except for my uncle. He's been wonderful

about it all but rather lacking in conveying many of the practical suggestions on how to actually get on in society."

Mr. Stansbury smiled. "I'd say you're getting on quite well."

"I don't think that's strictly true, but I do appreciate your kindness."

"Then perhaps you would reconsider your answer."

"I don't think I ought to. Mr. Trimble was rather definite in his pronouncement."

"Miss Withersby, if by some slight chance you were to make a mess of things on the dance floor, it would be entirely your partner's fault. Any man worth the name should be able to cover for his partner's mistakes."

"Should he?"

"He should. And I suspect your Mr. Trimble is not quite the man he'd like to be." Mr. Stansbury adjusted his gloves and extended his hand toward me.

I placed mine into it. "If you're quite sure . . ."

"I am." He pulled me close and placed his hand to my waist. "And I happen to know that this next dance is a waltz."

Oh dear. What was it Mr. Trimble had said? To hold myself rather loosely.

I tried, but it had the effect of making my knees quiver.

Alarm spread across Mr. Stansbury's face. "Are you feeling well?"

"Yes. I think I am. That is, I expect to be feeling much better once this dance is over."

"Just allow me to lead and we'll be fine."

I tried. I really did. He swung me about the room, and I started to understand what was meant by the music having a three-count. At one point, however, I stepped quite firmly on his foot. "I'm so very sorry."

"Don't mention it, and neither will I. I can't think that anyone noticed. Do you see? They're all concentrating on their own dancing."

He was right. They were.

Mr. Stansbury was quite encouraging. More than Mr. Trimble had been. Perhaps we weren't as graceful as Miss Templeton and her dancing partner, but by the time the song ended, I was enjoying myself.

I curtseyed. "Thank you, Mr. Stansbury. And I apologize for my lack of grace."

He bowed. "Never apologize for being courageous, Miss Withersby."

Miss Templeton danced with Mr. Stansbury next. It was a dance I would have liked to have known how to do, as it was quite vigorous. It seemed there *were* some things Mr. Trimble didn't know!

"I wonder, Miss Withersby, would you care to dance?"

I was startled from my thoughts by the rector. As I found him a thoroughly agreeable man, I was loath to refuse him, but I didn't see what else could be done. "I don't suppose I ought to lie to you, Mr. Hopkins-Whyte. I barely survived a waltz with Mr. Stansbury. To be entirely truthful, I suppose you might say that he just barely survived a waltz with me. I don't think it possible that I could tempt fate twice in a night. And I'm afraid I don't know any of the other dances."

"Pity. I've always found dancing a wholesome amusement."

"Perhaps one day I'll learn."

He smiled at me.

I smiled at him.

There was silence . . . except for the musicians, of course. And the sound of the dancers' feet. There must be *something* I could say to him. Mr. Trimble's words came back to me. I must ask a question, make some sort of discovery. What I really wanted to know, of course, was how his wife died, but I supposed it wouldn't be polite to ask. "Are . . . the children doing well?"

"Yes. Very well. Thank you."

So much for the children.

"And the rectory? Do you find it agreeable?"

"Quite."

Fiddlesticks. That hadn't gotten me very far. "Because . . . the old rector thought it quite drafty. He was always going about with a muffler around his throat. But you don't find it so?"

"No."

"Well . . . good. That's good then."

There must be something about the man that was worth discovering. Something that I could ask him. No questions about flowers, though, for he was bound to speak of his collections, and all in all I didn't think I could bear it this evening. What else was there? . . . His preaching? "Have you prepared the sermon for this week?"

"I prepared my sermon weeks ago. I like to do them all in one go, you see. At least I do once I've settled on a theme. Or a book. Books are easy." He'd become quite animated. "Not perhaps, Leviticus, of course. I don't know if I've ever heard anyone preach on Leviticus, but James, for example, is easy. Easier. That's what I ought to have said. Because James is emphatically not easy. There's hardly a more challenging book in the Bible. Would you not agree?"

"Me?"

"Is there a book you find more challenging?"

"Than James?"

He was looking at me as if he really wanted to know.

"I suppose . . . I always found it rather difficult to understand Job. God speaking through storms, and Job's friends saying such terrible things and him being in such dire straits and . . . all in all . . . I'm not quite certain what to think of it exactly."

"Job is one of my very favorites. I like to think that I specialize in the difficult. And possibilities. I don't think there's anything finer than trying to understand the mind of God."

"I'd always thought He'd said it was beyond understanding."

"It is, of course, but that doesn't mean we shouldn't try. Or at least try to discern the patterns of it."

"Patterns. I specialize in patterns myself." Or at least I had done. Until Mr. Trimble had come. Now *he* was specializing in *my* patterns.

"So you do understand, then. If we think of the juxtaposition of God's grace and mercy."

"His wrath and love?"

"Yes. Exactly! Grace and mercy. Wrath and love. It's difficult sometimes to think of them as part of the same pattern."

"Yes. I suppose it would be. Rather like honeybees and oak trees."

He blinked. "Honeybees and oak trees?" He fell silent for a moment. His eyes narrowed. And then they widened in surprise. "Honeybees and oak trees! Yes. I see it now! Honeybees can be quite a nuisance, especially if they make a nest in a tree, and yet they're quite beneficial, aren't they? Without bees, how would anything get on?"

"And how would we have any more oak trees if the bees didn't—" I broke off, remembering what had happened the last time I spoke of the reproductive organs of flora. "That is . . ."

He was patting about at his pocket and ended by pulling out the nub of a pencil and a small notebook. "Do you mind if I write that down? It might come in handy sometime."

"Please do."

"You wouldn't mind if you heard me mention that phrase

from the pulpit sometime?" He was waiting for my answer, pencil poised above the paper.

"Not at all."

"Marvelous!"

"You ought to join the King's Head Field Club. I'm told they speak of flowers in platitudes all the time."

"Do they really?" He looked as if he was torn between accepting or refusing the invitation. "I think not. I've troubles enough with my collections already. I don't need to add any more to their number. Although . . . people would probably expect me there, wouldn't they?"

"I've been told the old rector was quite faithful in attending."

"He probably was." He said it quite miserably. "When do they meet?"

"On Sunday afternoons, at the King's Head Pub. They didn't take an excursion last week, but Miss Templeton thought they might at the next meeting."

"I had meant to ask you, Miss Withersby . . . You said one time that you also specialized in correspondence . . . ?"

"You might say writing letters is a significant part of my life's work."

"I wonder if I might be able to convince you to help me with some of mine."

"I'm sure they couldn't be any more difficult than those I'm used to writing."

Miss Templeton came up with Mr. Stansbury in tow. "What a splendid dance this has been! And I've heard they're going to start serving dinner now!" She let go of Mr. Stansbury's arm and took up my hand. "Let's go. I want to see the dining room when the doors are opened."

She positioned us just to the side of the doors so that when they opened we were given a grand view.

"Oh!" She gasped the word. "It looks just like a dream."

It did. With bowers of palms and potted ferns in abundance and silver candelabras twinkling on the tables.

I was seated, as before, between Mr. Stansbury and the rector. As we began to eat, I recognized a fault in Mr. Stansbury, but remembering the words in Miss Templeton's book, I tried my very best to be polite. Formerly, I would have told him of his mistake, but the etiquette book advised silence on such matters. Although, if no one spoke of poor manners it was a wonder anyone knew how to correct their flaws.

Perhaps the idea was to learn by observation. That made sense, since it was the way I'd progressed in botany. But then I realized a person like me who knew nothing at all about etiquette might learn exactly the wrong thing by observing a person like Mr. Stansbury. That put me into a muddle again. It was quite exhausting eating dinner now that I knew how it ought to be done. On the whole, I confirmed that I would rather spend my time alone, at home.

Mr. Stansbury sent me a glance. "Is anything wrong, Miss Withersby? You seem quite unlike your normal self tonight."

"I'm just trying to do the right thing."

"That's very admirable."

"I only hope that I succeed in actually doing it."

"As we all should."

"Do you ever fear, Mr. Stansbury, that you'll never remember all the things you're supposed to be doing at these kind of events?"

"I used to, but then I decided I could spend my time worrying about doing the right thing in the eyes of people who were just waiting for me to do the wrong thing, or I could please myself instead."

I met his gaze. "Thank you. I'll have to remember that."

Miss Templeton and I met the next morning to walk to the rectory. From there, we would continue with the rector on a ramble to The Hollies.

As we walked along, I couldn't help feeling a bit saddened by the night's hard frost. It was expected, of course, in mid-October, but as far as the eye could see, grasses lay bent and browned. Since it was only Miss Templeton accompanying me, I felt that I could speak freely. "Is there any news on your scandal?"

She colored like a rose. "No. Not really, no. Once my maid told me what that sort of thing entails, I decided I had better come up with a different plan."

"Have you, then?"

"I must tell you, Miss Withersby, that I have not. I am completely stumped and must confess my spirits to be miserably low. I feel as if I hover at death's door. Not even the thought of a dinner party can cheer my soul."

"I suppose I shouldn't bother you for advice in dressing my hair in a new style?"

"Oh! Please do. It is probably the one thing guaranteed to restore my zest for living."

She spoke of the gown she planned to wear to the next dinner party and of my gown, and by then we were in sight of the rectory.

"Now is when you must begin to look infatuated with the very idea that all of that could one day be yours." She gestured toward the house.

All of that? All of the children and all of those poorly preserved specimens? I could hardly bear the thought.

She waved a handkerchief. "I think that must be the rector!" She waved it again. "Can you not put down your vasculum? You should be waving too."

We waved as we approached, and the rector came across the

yard to meet us. At least he had his vasculum thrown across his shoulder in the right direction today.

"It's rather cold for this sort of thing, isn't it?" He had a muffler wrapped round his head and mitts on his hands. He gave a glance toward the rectory. "The nurse has charge of the children and I've a parishioner coming to visit at noon, so shall we be off?"

I gestured down the lane in the direction of The Hollies.

"What is it we're meant to find?" Miss Templeton had stopped in the middle of the lane. "Everything's dead, Miss Withersby. Maybe we ought to just repair back to the rectory for a nice cup of tea."

"Not everything has died, I assure you."

We passed several groups of cyclamen on the way, and then I led them out into a meadow, taking care to walk around some goldilocks asters that were still in flower. When I turned back to check their progress, what I saw alarmed me. "Stop!" My cry rang out across the field.

The rector threw up his hands to help maintain his balance, and Miss Templeton shrieked. "What! What is it?"

"Asters." I bent to finger a fragile stem. "And you were both about to step on them!"

"I never noticed." The rector bent beside me. "Pretty, aren't they?"

I glanced up and met his gaze. "They are. And rather unusual for this time in the season."

Miss Templeton spoke from above us, hands clasped to her chest. "It just goes to show that even in the darkest, dreariest cold, beauty can still be found."

The rector looked up as if startled. "Oh. Oh! Oh my. That's very good. The cold and a killing frost needn't keep a flower from blooming. That speaks to Job, you know, Miss Withersby.

It speaks to a good many things, in fact. Do you mind if I write that down, Miss Templeton?"

"Of course not. I heard it from the president of the field club. He has a great many phrases just like it. You really ought to attend, Rector. It might do wonders for your inspiration."

"It's not inspiration I'm usually after. Illustration is what I need."

"Then you won't want to attend a watercolor society meeting. That's for painters, not for illustrators, as Miss Withersby was kind enough to explain. But the field club might be just the thing for you."

"I wouldn't have to come with my collection, would I?"

"No. Oh no. And mostly you don't really need to come with a vasculum either."

The brisk ramble cleared the worries from my thoughts, and it was with renewed determination to pretend an interest in marriage that I returned to the house.

Mr. Trimble stood as I entered the parlor.

I sat in a chair and removed my shoes, extending my feet toward the fire. If he didn't want to see my ankles, then he'd just have to keep his eyes closed.

"Miss Withersby? I've come across a paper I'd like your opinion on."

"If it's help you're looking for, I can't—"

"I know you can't assist me, but perhaps you could simply listen. And if you agree with my summary, then you could simply nod." He looked at me, as if challenging me to defy his suggestion.

I said nothing.

He sat at the desk that had formerly been mine, picked up

the paper he'd been working on, and read about the distribution of Ranunculaceae in the subantarctic islands. When he had finished, he looked at me. "Do you agree?"

I nodded. What else could I do? Apparently he had found my notes, for he had summarized my own thoughts on the matter quite nicely. And rather more succinctly than I might have done. "Are you going to submit it?"

"Of course. To the British Association for the Advancement of Science."

Under his own name probably. And no doubt it would be accepted for publication. "If it's that short, they might not consider if for a discourse. It might only get printed as a letter to the editor."

"But it would be printed, in any case."

I shrugged. I had never been printed in the journal in any format whatsoever, so what was it to me if his submission went in as a letter or into columned space?

He folded his hands atop the paper. "So you do agree, then?"

"Of course I agree. You have to know that I agree." I twisted in order to see him. "Most of those words are my own! And I don't doubt that you'll find a way to have them published. Goodness knows that I have not. But it's not for lack of trying. I've come to believe that nothing I write will ever be published and that my uncle is right: Girls aren't fit for anything other than marriage and motherhood."

"I admire your frankness. One always knows where they stand with you."

It was the second time he'd said that. "And why shouldn't one? I am amazed that you seem to have gone about with persons who continually lie to you, prevaricate, or fail to show you the honesty inherent in friendship. I have to tell you that I wouldn't consider such people friends, Mr. Trimble."

"Neither would I."

"Then why do you maintain the friendships? You seem surprised at me. Perhaps it would be more useful to be surprised by *them*."

He laughed. "Perhaps it would be. I will tell you something, Miss Withersby. There is nothing like a voyage halfway round the world to show you who your true friends are."

"These friends of yours, did they not write to you?"

"They did not. In fact, there was only one person with whom I carried on a regular correspondence."

"Then I would say *that* person ought to be accorded the honor of your friendship." I turned back to face the fire.

"That person, Miss Withersby, was you."

19

I twisted again to face him. "Me! Why would you ever think that—"

"Come. I am not blind. And I have been tasked with organizing your father's papers. With everything in such disarray, it was only a matter of time before I happened upon your papers and recognized your handwriting. I had wondered why your father seemed nothing like I had imagined."

"But . . . to consider me a friend? I hardly think I count as one. It was a correspondence of business, was it not?"

"It started out that way, perhaps, but to whom else did I write of my travels? And my sheep?"

My secret was out. I turned, placing my elbows on the back of the chair and pulling up my feet to hide them beneath my skirts. "You never answered about Emilia's lambing. How many did she have?"

"Two. And who else but you knows how many sheep I lost in that snowstorm last—"

"Forty-nine."

" . . . year, but you?"

"Then I confess: I have been the one maintaining my father's correspondence. If I hadn't done it, he never would have."

"He's been doing quite nicely these past few weeks. I simply give him a list of those things that need his attention, letters that need to be written, and he does them."

"He's writing his own letters?"

"Dictating them, in any case."

That wasn't fair. How many hours had I spent laboring to make his point, working to plead his case, when he might have done those things himself?

"He's not some young boy who needs you to do everything for him."

"He used to do all those things himself, when my mother was still living. But after she died he just . . . he just . . . stopped." He'd stopped doing everything. He'd done nothing. Nothing but lie abed and stare at the ceiling. "It was frightening and . . . and dreadful."

Mr. Trimble left the desk to squat beside me, his arm stretched around the back of the chair.

"I didn't know what to do, so I just started doing what needed to be done." I didn't dare to meet his gaze. "I wrote the letters that needed to be written and I paid the bills that needed to be paid and I just kept going . . . kept hoping . . ."

He put his hand on my elbow. "Charlotte . . ."

As I glanced up, his gaze fled from mine.

He cleared his throat. "Miss Withersby . . . he's a man grown. His work is not your responsibility."

Not my responsibility? It felt as if somewhere deep inside my heart was breaking. As if the pieces I had bound together when Mother died were inexorably coming apart. What would I do if I didn't take care of my father? I drew my elbow away from him, turned in my chair, and placed my feet on the floor.

"No. That responsibility is no longer mine. It's yours now. Perhaps you count me as your friend, but I hope you understand why I can never consider you one of mine." I rose and went upstairs.

Miss Templeton had convinced me to attend a parish function on behalf of the poorhouse the next afternoon. Though I had grudgingly agreed to do so at the time, now that I knew Mr. Trimble had discovered my secret, I was happy for the chance to leave the house. Shut away up in my bedroom, I had begun to feel as if I were a prisoner.

After making my escape, with no option of bypassing town, I picked my way past the channels of brine and dodged salt wagons on my walk, but I also stopped to greet several women whose acquaintance I had made over the previous weeks. I even involved myself—mostly by declining to offer my opinion—in their conversation as to whether the shade Blue de France could ever compare to Blue de Roi.

As I approached the parish function, Miss Templeton hurried to my side. "I've come up with a way to advance your plan."

"I'm afraid it's not going to advance at all unless I actually find myself married, in which case it will be too late."

"Come, Miss Withersby, such glumness isn't like you, and it mars your pretty features."

I tried to make those pretty features more agreeable. "I fear Mr. Trimble is here to stay."

"I was going to say that you need to mention either Mr. Stansbury or the rector every time you speak to your father, but now I'm beginning to think that it's time for me to meet him." Her mouth was set in a way that made me think she actually meant it.

"Meet my father?"

"No. Mr. Trimble!"

"You aren't going to do anything to him, are you?"

"Not initially, in any case. So how shall we proceed? I don't suppose you could get him to escort you to a dance or a dinner, could you?"

"I don't see how. The Admiral has taken on that responsibility. And I don't wish to spend any more time with him than I have to."

She sighed. "Then—oh! I know. The lecture by that mesmerizer!"

"What about it?"

"I'll come by tomorrow morning and persuade him to join us."

"How?"

"Just leave that to me."

The next morning, as I waited for Miss Templeton to come, Mr. Trimble and Father consulted on a letter to the editor of some journal as I sat on my hands so I wouldn't be tempted to push away from my chair, walk over, and join them. I thought once, or twice, of warning Mr. Trimble—such as one might offer warning of storm clouds gathering on the horizon—but on the whole I considered that an encounter with Miss Templeton might do him some good. At eleven o'clock precisely, I heard a carriage come down the lane.

Moments later, Miss Hansford curtseyed as our visitor entered the room. "Miss Templeton for Miss Withersby."

Miss Templeton came at me smiling, hands extended, reticule swinging from her wrist. "My dear Miss Withersby! How charming this place is. How cozy your situation. I see now why

I always have to coax you out into society." She stood in the middle of the room, smile bright, brow lifted.

"It's . . . it's so good to see you. Whatever brings you out our way?"

She tilted her head toward my father and Mr. Trimble several times, and then she came over and took my hands up in her own, leaning forward to kiss me on the cheek. "Introduce me." She whispered.

"What?"

"Introduce me to Mr. Trimble!" The words came out in a hiss.

I turned toward them. "Miss Templeton, may I introduce you to my father and his assistant, Mr. Trimble?" I gestured toward them, but they were still discussing the letter.

She frowned. Taking up my arm, she pulled me forward until we were opposite the desk, and then she jabbed at me with her fan as she tilted her head toward them once more.

"Miss Templeton, may I introduce you to my father?" I made the introduction. "And to my father's assistant?"

By this time, Mr. Trimble had stood. Now he bowed as I made that introduction as well.

Miss Templeton smiled. "I don't believe I've seen you before, Mr. Trimble. You must be hiding from us all."

"I've been engaged in work for Mr. Withersby."

"Which must be quite fascinating, but we've a lecture by a mesmerizer on Monday, and I've decided that you ought to come with us."

A corner of his mouth lifted. "But what of my work?"

"I must warn you, I am quite ruthless in pursuit of what I want, and I won't be put off by refusal or naysaying. You might as well agree."

He glanced at my father, who shrugged.

Mr. Trimble actually seemed to be considering it. "It's just a lecture? By one of those fool mesmerizers?"

Miss Templeton's smile vanished. "I wouldn't call them fools. They're delightful! But yes, it's just a lecture."

Mr. Trimble bowed. "Then I agree."

She clapped her hands. "It's all arranged, then!"

Linking her arm about mine, she drew me out into the hall with her. "Are you quite sure that was Mr. Trimble? Because he's not at all like you described. He's not ill-tempered and he's not old. He's decidedly handsome! If he didn't come from such a humble family and if he weren't clerking for your father, I'd say he would be quite a catch! Now I don't know *what* to think of him." She gave her fan a few twists. "Quite honestly, he isn't gruesome at all! He's really rather extraordinary. On the whole I'd say he's something quite different from what I expected, but I'll reserve final judgment until the lecture."

"I wouldn't go so far as to say he's extraordinary."

"And you say he's a sheep farmer?"

"From New Zealand."

"That's rather a shame, for I can imagine myself quite besotted with him."

For some reason that annoyed me. I had thought she was on my side. Was she going to abandon me for him, in the same way my father had done? "Well, I can't imagine him ever besotted with anyone. And that was your goal—to marry someone entirely besotted with you."

"That's true. That *is* true. But I wonder now whether I haven't miscalculated."

"He isn't worth *any* calculation. Believe me."

"Do you know anything about his family?"

"They come from somewhere in the east, and they're complete dissolutes."

"That's a wretched bit of luck. I might have worked up an interest in him. Now I can see why you so fervently wish to be home and why you're so difficult to budge once you're here."

"He has nothing to do with it. He's the reason I was pushed out the door in the first place. If you'll remember, my primary aim is to make my father release him."

"Are you sure?"

"Am I sure of what?"

"Are you sure you wish to do that?"

"Why wouldn't I?"

She gestured toward the parlor with her fan. "Have you not *looked* at him?"

"Of course I've looked at him. I have to look at him every day. Every morning and every evening too."

"I begin to see how we might use him to your advantage."

"My *advantage*? The only advantage he can offer me is through his departure."

"He's quite handsome. And he *looks* as if he comes from a good family . . . if no one knew any better, they might think, if they saw you with him, that he was also competing for your hand. People will think what they want. They always do. But better than what people might *think* is what Mr. Stansbury and the rector might *do*."

"What might they do?"

"They might begin to be more serious, more pronounced, in their devotion to you."

"Truly?"

"Trust me." She patted my hand. "What we have to do next is figure out how to drag your Mr. Trimble into society."

"You've already badgered him into attending the lecture."

"We need to figure out how to drag him *permanently* into society. He must see and be seen."

So it wasn't enough that I had to put up with him at home? I now had to suffer the misfortune of having him out and about with me as well?

"Don't look so gloomy. With a little bit of a push, and Mr. Trimble's help, you should be back to your work by next week. And it will be all the better, won't it, knowing that Mr. Trimble helped himself out the door?"

20

As I was surveying the yard that afternoon, the Admiral came by. I gathered up the purple asters I had just picked, welcomed him, and led him inside. After taking his coat, I accompanied him to the parlor. While he greeted Mr. Trimble, I set to work finding a vase. When Father voiced a welcome from the study, the Admiral entered and shut the door. They conversed for some while as I tried to ignore Mr. Trimble. But after Miss Templeton's approval of his person, it was rather difficult. I snuck another look at him. I supposed, all in all, he was rather handsome. For a sheep farmer.

He caught me looking at him. "May I help you, Miss Withersby? Did you need something?"

Why had I never noticed him in this way before? "No. No! No, thank you."

When the study door opened, both the Admiral and my father stepped out. The Admiral waved an envelope at me. "For you, my dear. An invitation to a rowing party to be held down by the river next Saturday, although—"

Mr. Trimble rudely interrupted. "A rowing party? This late in the season?"

Must everything be subject to his scrutiny? "It's not really that late here in Cheshire. It's still fine weather for a river outing."

He shot me a dubious glance.

Remembering Miss Templeton's plan, I took advantage of the opportunity he'd provided. As Miss Templeton had said, what could be better than to watch him work himself out of his position? I put on my best smile. "Why do you not come with us? That way you'll be able to experience our temperate clime for yourself." I smiled again for good measure.

"Your Miss Templeton already talked me into the lecture on Monday night. Don't begin to count on me for such things. If you do, I warn you now, you will be bound for disappointment."

But my uncle was clapping him on the back. "Yes. Yes! A brilliant idea, my dear. I've been called to London next week and I had despaired of having to let your father escort you."

"I don't see why you ought to have *despaired* of such a possibility." My father looked up as he was tying on a pair of viewing spectacles he'd made from two pocket glasses fixed into holes in an old stocking.

The Admiral stepped forward, pulled them from Father's head, and laid them on the table. "If you can provide the escort, young man, then Charlotte can still go."

He shook his head. "I don't think that's such a good idea."

Miss Templeton would be so proud of me if I could get him to agree. "And why not? You've words enough about what I'm not doing and saying that it seems to me you would fit admirably into such a milieu."

"I haven't been invited."

238

The Admiral waved a hand. "Nothing that a note would not take care of. So it's set. You'll provide the escort."

"I don't see how I can, really. There's too much work to be done."

Not so easy to do everything at once, was it? Perhaps they *were* beginning to understand. I laid a hand on his arm. "I'll say not one word about your background, Mr. Trimble. And the way you hold yourself, no one will believe you haven't been born to a family just like theirs."

"I can't go. It wouldn't be wise."

"But if you attend, you can criticize my taste and appalling lack of good manners as we go along instead of afterward. It would be much more efficient that way and save you the trouble of doing it later. I daresay you might even have a good time."

Mr. Trimble came upon me in the sitting room the next morning. I was using one of the plant presses as a sort of portable desk. "And what have you there?" He was eying my pen and paper rather suspiciously.

"I'm just undertaking a bit of correspondence for the rector. Some business with his old parish."

"Is he incapable of doing that as well?"

"As well as what?"

"As well as managing a simple collection."

I laid my pen down. "I don't see why you should denigrate him so. Do you hold something against him?"

"Only that he seems to have delegated to you all those tasks he prefers not to do."

"If you would bother to listen to him preach on Sundays instead of glancing round the church like a crazed lunatic, you would never dare to insult him again." I could not say that his suspicions about the collection were unfounded, but Mr. Hopkins-Whyte did not deserve Mr. Trimble's disdain. "If it wasn't him, it would be my father delegating tasks to me, wouldn't it?" Had I just . . . had I just said that?

"Or that other fellow."

Other fellow? "That other fellow's name is Mr. Stansbury."

"And you know vastly more on the subject of flowers than he could ever hope to learn."

"I'm sure he's seen more exotic species than I have. His glasshouse collections are really quite admirable."

"And I've seen more of New Zealand's flowers in the field than you have, and still I recognize that I know nothing compared to you."

"He has asked me to help him round out his collections."

"Does he know that you wrote *Ranunculaceae in Britain*?"

"I wouldn't say that I wrote it. Not exactly."

"I would." He gave me a long look. "You disappoint me."

"I disappoint you? I don't see why you should be so set against my doing what God and nature have apparently ordained me to do."

"And what is that?"

"I'm to be a helper. I believe that's what Eve was called."

"A helper? Is that what you think you're being? God calls himself our helper too, if I recall, but no one makes *Him* engage in correspondence or keep track of labels or leave His name off books He's toiled to write. We ask Him to lend His strength to ours. I don't think you're being helpful, Miss Withersby. I think you're being taken advantage of."

"And why should you care what it is that I'm doing with my time? You've waltzed in here and taken up my position, so why object to the ways in which I must now occupy myself? Why should it matter to you?"

"It matters because you're made of better stuff than this. Believe me, Miss Withersby, I've seen much of society, and what passes for obligation most of the time is stuff and nonsense."

For a moment, his words shamed me as I remembered the sort of family from which he'd come, and then I became quite exasperated and endeavored to ignore him.

My vow held until Monday evening when Mr. Trimble appeared in the parlor, dressed for the lecture. It was then that I began to think better of Miss Templeton's plans. I wasn't quite sure what had changed, but in evening dress, he made an altogether different impression than he had while working at his desk in his shirt sleeves. Formerly, I would have believed quite willingly that he was a sheep farmer. But in his pleated shirtfront and gloves, he looked every bit a peer of the realm. It was really quite as vexing, as if I had misclassified a colchicum as a crocus.

He bowed. "Miss Withersby."

I curtseyed.

I was used to seeing him bent over a microscope or sitting at my desk. I had forgotten he was so tall. Or that the scent of him held such intrigue. I still couldn't place what it was. Maybe I could ask Miss Templeton to take a sniff of him so she could help me to decipher it.

We travelled to the lecture with nary a word spoken between us, and as we entered the ballroom, he peered around furtively.

I put a hand to his arm. "Have no fear. As I've told you before, the people of Overwich are quite kind." Excepting the Family Bickwith.

Miss Templeton introduced him around. I suppose I ought to have done it, but I still hadn't gotten down who I was to introduce to whom. Whether I was meant to say, for instance,

Mrs. Such-and-So, this is Mr. Trimble or if it should be the other way around.

At the reception after the lecture, I saw Lord Harriwick's son lounging against the wall opposite. He and his friends normally didn't have much to do with *country folk*, as Miss Templeton called us, but he stumbled over, raising a glass in our direction.

"Hail, Saxon! Haven't seen you for ages. Not since Eton." He slapped Mr. Trimble on the back and offered him a drink.

Mr. Trimble stepped back as I stepped forward. We stood there, together, shoulder to shoulder.

Miss Templeton smiled and stepped out in front of us both. "You can't have met him. Mr. Trimble farms sheep in New Zealand. He's only just come back for a visit."

The man leaned around Miss Templeton to peer at Mr. Trimble through narrowed eyes. "Funny. He's a familiar look about him, but I can't say I've ever visited the colony." He raised his glass again and seemingly swallowed a belch with a great grimace. "I'll have to take your word for it."

A strained sort of smile bent Mr. Trimble's lips. "I suppose you'll have to."

As the man left, Mr. Trimble drew a shaking hand up to his brow.

Poor man. If he had not usurped my position, I might have felt sorry for him. "I have to say, you look the part of a gentleman, even if you do work for your living."

He turned to me with a slight bow. "I would say the same to you."

The same to me? That I looked the part of . . . ? "Was that a compliment?" I did quite like the raspberry-colored dress I was wearing. It was woven with blue threads, and the color changed whenever I moved. Miss Hansford had aided me, dressing my hair into ringlets, and I felt that on the whole I fit in with the milieu rather admirably.

"I think, perhaps, it was." The look in his eyes seemed to be a kind of peace offering.

I accepted it with a nod.

At that moment, Mr. Stansbury approached and greeted me with a bow.

I curtseyed.

"You look as pretty as a pansy, this evening, Miss Withersby." Mr. Trimble raised a brow as if to press his point.

I concentrated all my attentions on Mr. Stansbury. "Thank you, Mr. Stansbury."

"Speaking of which, my orchid has bloomed."

"And?"

"And you were right." He said it with a twinkle in his eye. "I never would have thought to question that label, but I am glad that you did. I was hoping you might come take a look at it and tell me whether—"

"She'd be delighted to." Miss Templeton joined our conversation with a smile.

"Wednesday, then?"

"It would be our pleasure."

Mr. Stansbury smiled back at her. Smiled at Mr. Trimble. Smiled at me.

He was such an interesting man. Most of the other men in the room seemed painted from the same palette of muted greys and browns, but he always displayed a surprising bit of color. Miss Templeton assured me that really should not be done, but I thought it enlivened his ruddy cheeks and set off the gleam of his precisely combed hair.

Compared to Mr. Trimble, he was positively dazzling, and yet there was something established, something settled, about Mr.

Trimble that was lacking in the industrialist. Miss Templeton's words about the shiniest watches echoed in my thoughts.

Miss Templeton jabbed me with her elbow and tilted a brow toward Mr. Trimble.

I raised my own brow in response.

She smiled at Mr. Stansbury. "May we introduce you to Miss Withersby's father's assistant?"

That's what I'd forgotten. The introduction. What a pleasure it was to work with flowers. They never begged an introduction from anyone, and if you misidentified them as Mr. Stansbury had, they never took offense and one could still appreciate their beauty.

Mr. Trimble nodded at me. "I would be delighted to make a new acquaintance."

I still couldn't remember which way introductions went but embarked upon it just the same.

The two men nodded at each other.

Mr. Stansbury glanced at me. "Is Admiral Williams not here?"

"He's been—"

Miss Templeton placed a hand to my arm. "He asked Mr. Trimble to escort Miss Withersby this evening."

Mr. Stansbury gave him another, longer, look.

Mr. Trimble smiled.

Mr. Stansbury did not return it. He gave him a cool glance and then continued in conversation with me. "I received an Italian orchid today from a correspondent. Remind me to show it to you when you visit on Wednesday."

"I should very much like to see it."

He crooked an arm for me, and I threaded mine through it the way I had seen other women do.

He walked us off down toward the end of the room, although there seemed to be nothing there worth seeing. "I take such pleasure in your interest, Miss Withersby. Most people would see my passion as a waste of time."

"If that's so, then I've wasted my entire life, haven't I? In any case, I would love to draw your new orchid, if you would allow it."

"Why should you bother about such things? I'll have a sketch made for you, if you would accept the gift."

"It would not be a bother." I could not fault him for his generosity, but I must confess my fingers itched to take up a pen and a brush and try to match the flower's subtle shadings, to try and capture the essence of a plant I'd never before drawn.

I turned and saw Mr. Trimble was looking at me as if . . . there must be something, then, that I'd failed to do. Or something I'd done for which I now must apologize. But I could not determine what grievous sin I'd committed. "Forgive me. Thank you." I hoped that would cover my offense.

"It would give me pleasure to offer it to you. A woman like you shouldn't have to draw it herself."

Perhaps not. But what if she wanted to?

Eventually, Mr. Stansbury returned me to Mr. Trimble. After the industrialist had gone, Miss Templeton turned to him. "So what do you think of our Mr. Stansbury?"

"A self-made man, I believe."

"You say it as if it were a slur!"

"Do I? Then I must amend my tone, for there are some in New Zealand who would call me the same."

A smile animated Miss Templeton's lips. "He seems to have developed a distinct fondness for our Miss Withersby."

He slid a look in my direction. "I must agree with you."

I wished they wouldn't speak as if I were not present. "He is very kind. And quite forthright. More so than most, I would say."

Miss Templeton arched a brow. "I should think he would

do quite nicely, Mr. Trimble, don't you?" She winked at me behind her fan.

"Do for what?"

"Why, for a husband, of course."

Mr. Trimble's eyes were scanning the room. "He might do for some, I suppose, but I hardly think him the man for Miss Withersby."

Miss Templeton snapped her fan shut. "Why ever not?"

"He might do, but would he do very well? *That* is the better question to ask."

What gave him the right to concern himself in my affairs? Whatever Mr. Trimble might have thought of Mr. Stansbury, he could not deny the man was impassioned of flowers. If he mixed up his species from time to time or assigned plants to the wrong genus, could that not be forgiven for his ardor? And if the rector's collections were somewhat haphazardly put together, might that not be forgotten for the absolute kindness with which he treated everyone? Even the objectionable Mrs. Bickwith?

Now that I considered it, I really was quite proud to call the men my friends. Or . . . perhaps not friends. Would that be too forward? Maybe they were just acquaintances. But then again, they were supposed by many to be courting me, so friendship could probably be assumed without objection. They were friends. And as such, they deserved my defense. "I would thank you to keep yourself out of it."

"But is that not why I'm here? To help with your husband finding?"

He was involving himself much more in the process than my uncle had. On the whole, I much preferred the Admiral's presence to his. My uncle didn't seem to care who I spoke to so long as I was speaking to someone. And that was the goal, was it not? To solicit the interest of someone? Why should I care who that man was? "I can hardly see why it matters to you whom I choose to spend my time with."

"Because it pains me, Miss Withersby, to think that years from now, I might be imagining you as some man's glorified assistant instead of knowing that you're using that brilliant mind of yours for your own purposes."

Miss Templeton looked as if she wanted to rap him on the head with her fan. "I suspect Miss Withersby would thrive wherever she might be. I think you do her an injustice, Mr. Trimble."

"I think she does herself an injustice, Miss Templeton. She aims far too low."

Miss Templeton's eyes seemed to darken for a moment and then she put a smile on her face. "Come." She linked an arm through both of ours, securing herself a place in the middle. "Let's be friends, shall we? I've always loved intellectual stimulation, and I would hate for it to be spoiled by such a sour face as yours, Miss Withersby."

She pulled us towards the punch bowl and then left us there as she tipped her head in greeting to someone and started back across the room.

I crossed my arms. I never knew what to do with them. Nor with my hands. There was nothing normal about holding them naturally when most often I was employing them for some purpose. Upon reflection, perhaps it wasn't my arms that were the problem. Perhaps it was standing about doing nothing. There was no point to it. I glanced over at Mr. Trimble. "You made it seem, back there, as if you don't approve of me."

"I don't."

"It might interest you to know that I don't approve of you."

He didn't seem very distraught by my pronouncement. "You're hardly the first."

"I don't see how you can just go round disapproving of people you don't even know."

"But I *do* know you."

"In just five short weeks, you've earned the right to meddle in my affairs? I find that rather presumptuous."

"You forget . . . I've earned that right over three long years. So the question I must ask myself, and which you should ask yourself too is, why in God's name would you wish to spend your life as some man's transcriptionist or secretary when you've a mind of your own between those pretty ears of yours?"

Why did he take my search for a husband as a personal affront? "Because apparently all the research I've done, all those papers I've written hold no value. Why else would my father offer me up to the general population like some ceremonial lamb?"

"Perhaps because he feels it is his duty. Perhaps because he wishes to see you happy. *Are* you happy, Miss Withersby?"

Happy? How dare he ask me that! "Only a man who has forced himself into my family and then usurped my position would think to ask me that."

"Because if you aren't—"

"Make no mistake about it, Mr. Trimble. My first responsibility is to my father's work."

"And what of your own work?"

"*My* work? I've already told you. No one in a position to judge seems to think that my work matters."

"I think it matters."

"And who are you? Do you sit on the board of the BAAS? Are you in a position to decide which papers to publish?"

He said nothing.

"I thank you for your concern, but I'm very nearly beginning to think none of it matters." The more I pretended an interest in marriage, the more trapped by my efforts I had become. I wasn't thinking of papers or books anymore. I was thinking of dinner parties and dances. "Perhaps a marriage to a regular, unphilosophical man is best. It's worked for so many others. And as the Admiral says, it's what I was made for."

But if that was true, then why did the thought of that very thing make me want to cry?

21

One would have thought I had earned a several day reprieve from social obligations, but Mr. Stansbury's orchids awaited.

After that visit, however, I had one glorious day to lose myself in the doing of nothing in particular. After that I was subjected to a series of card parties and a round of calls—and then the morning of the rowing party dawned. At least it began early in the day. I was hoping that meant I would be able to spend a pleasant evening at home.

Down at the river's edge, there were boats for rowing and pony carts for the children. Rugs had been laid out along the riverbank, and sofas and chairs had been arranged atop them. Mr. Trimble proved himself to be an able and attentive escort. Too attentive, perhaps.

"Is there something wrong, Mr. Trimble? You've been staring at me for nearly an hour."

"I apologize. I was just trying to determine . . . There's something . . . about the way you walk."

"The way I *walk*?"

"Yes. It's all wrong."

"Pray tell, how else ought I to do it?"

"It's not the action; it's the motivation. You move as if you're inclined to be going somewhere."

"Generally speaking, I believe, that is the case. If I'm walking, I wish to get from where I am to where I am going."

"Must you try so hard, though?"

"Must I try so . . . ? I don't know any other way to do it. Do you mean that I should give up going to wherever it is that I'm going?"

"I'm simply suggesting that you might not want to be so pointed in wishing to be elsewhere."

"You want me to slow my pace?"

"That might help the problem."

"But then it would waste my time. And your own as well, since you insist upon going everywhere that I do."

"It's just that you have a way of making people think you'd rather be somewhere else."

"We have, in fact, already established, that is the case."

"But you ought to be making your companions think the only place you want to be is with them."

"Why do people have to be so demanding? Is it not bad enough that I can't say what I want to? Now I can't even go where I wish to?"

"You can. It's just that you ought not be so obvious about it. I don't mean to offend you, Miss Withersby. I simply wanted to relay my observations so that you might be able to incorporate them into your efforts." He caught me by the arm. "Look there, at Miss Templeton. Where do you think she's going?"

I watched her for a moment as she walked with Mr. Stansbury. I was quite sure that they were headed for the river, but then she stopped to listen to him speak. After toying with her fan for a moment, she took his arm when he offered it and headed out in the opposite direction. And even then I couldn't say for sure where they were going. "I have no idea."

"What do you think her reason is for walking about, then?"

"It looks as if she's . . . I confess I don't know."

"It looks as if she's simply enjoying conversing with her companion, doesn't it? What is his name again?"

"Mr. Stansbury. The one you deem unworthy of me." It did appear, however, that he had a point about Miss Templeton. "It does look that way, doesn't it?" But as I watched . . . "Good gracious, now they've gone and changed directions again!"

"And what's so terrible about that? We've done the same, you and I, haven't we just now?"

To my great astonishment, we had.

Mr. Trimble burst into laughter. "There's no good in glaring at me like that. It's hardly my fault you've been talked into not paying attention."

"Is that what you mean? That I ought not pay attention to where I'm going? For I assure you that on lanes like ours and roads like Cheshire's, I'm liable to end up wrenching my ankle if I don't watch where I'm going."

"Perhaps you could think of it as going for a ramble. You're out for a walk, not certain of what you'll find or where your observations will take you. You're simply . . . enjoying yourself."

"Enjoying myself?"

"Enjoying yourself. In the same way that I am enjoying being with you."

"You . . . you are?"

The corner of his mouth twitched. "Strange as it might seem, I am."

Mrs. Bickwith came toward us on the path. She stopped and simpered at Mr. Trimble. "I can't say that I remember a more delightful autumn."

I could. "I can. There was October two years past."

"But it was so dreadfully wet!"

"Admirably so, I thought. It kept the flowers in bloom and then the fruits came in quite full."

"I hardly think that compensated for the difficulties it caused in getting about."

"If you wear sturdy boots and tie your skirts up a bit, they don't get quite so damp and it keeps the mud from clinging to the hems."

Mrs. Bickwith's mouth fell open and stayed that way for several seconds before she shut it up with a harrumph and then took herself off.

I felt Mr. Trimble's arm shake and looked up to find him trying not to laugh.

"I suppose I've said something I shouldn't have again."

"Most women, most people, don't talk about rain and mud with quite the same fervor that you do."

"I wasn't talking about mud or rain. I made quite deliberate references to clothing, just as you said I should. Didn't you hear them?"

He laughed outright. "Is that what you were doing?"

"I don't see why you should laugh. Miss Templeton is always talking about dresses or hats or . . . other things."

He steered me about in the opposite direction. "Why don't we walk over this way for a while?"

Miss Templeton and Mr. Stansbury soon joined us. She and I sat on a bench while the men stood beside us.

Mr. Trimble pulled a small sketchbook and pen from his pocket and began to draw. I peered up at it, but he pulled it away, toward his chest. "Tsk, tsk. Not until I am finished."

He worked at it for a few moments longer, pen dashing across the page, and then tore it from the binding and presented it to Miss Templeton with a flourish.

"Oh!" She put a hand to her mouth as she gasped with pleasure. "But it's charming! And so clever. How cunning you are, Mr. Trimble. What skill!"

Mr. Stansbury didn't look nearly as impressed as she was.

"Do look, Miss Withersby!" She handed it to me. Mr. Trimble had depicted her as a laughing nasturtium. Though it was not colored, I could immediately picture her, cheerfully golden. It was altogether fanciful and quite charming, actually. Her cries drew a crowd of ladies, who soon clamored for Mr. Trimble's attentions.

He did Mrs. Shandlin as a foxglove, the bloom cleverly turned into a bonnet; one of the party from London, he turned into a dahlia with a multitude of flounces to her skirt; and Mrs. Bickwith, he drew as an overdone carnation, though she seemed to like it well enough.

Miss Templeton clapped her hands in delight. "Now do Miss Withersby."

"No." Although I was quite fascinated with his matching of flowers to personalities, I couldn't think what he must make of me. And in a strange fit of sentiment, I didn't wish to know.

She laid her fan across my lips to keep me from speaking as she appealed to him. "Yes. Do, Mr. Trimble. You must! It's only polite. You've already done everyone else, so now you must do her as well."

He scrutinized my face, as if considering what flower best represented me.

I decided to be firm. "Please, no. I've spent my life in flowers— I hardly need to be depicted as one."

He ran a hand over his book. "All the more reason to sketch you." He drew a pen from his pocket and put the nib to the page, but I put a hand over his to stop him. "How do you—? What sort of pen is that?"

He held it up. "This? It's a rather amazing mechanism. Doesn't need an inkwell. It has a cartridge just here." He tapped a finger to the shaft.

"A cartridge? Inside?" I'd never heard of such a thing. "Where did you get it?" If I didn't have to take an inkwell about with me to draw, I could draw just about anywhere.

"I had it sent from New York City."

"New York. As in . . . America?"

He nodded, having already begun his drawing.

New York? That sounded . . . Well . . . frankly, it sounded odd for a sheep farmer to have contacts in New York City. It sounded altogether like the sort of thing Mr. Stansbury might say. Or Miss Templeton. I considered how that might fit with what I knew of his family and could come up with no explanation.

He spent several minutes swiping his hand this way and that over the page. And then he raised his head to look at me.

"You don't have to continue this foolishness."

"Foolishness? Are you denigrating my talents, Miss Withersby?"

I felt my face flush. "No. I only meant that—"

"Don't worry yourself. I know what you meant."

He was quite adamant about my not seeing the drawing until he was finished, but Miss Templeton stood beside him, sighing now and then at what she was seeing. He made one last grand sweep of his pen and then passed it to me.

He had sketched Miss Templeton with the sort of wholesome exuberance she exuded like a perfume. Mrs. Shandlin, he had sketched as a foxglove, just as tall and slender as she. Me, however, he had drawn as a common bluebell. The petals formed an unfashionably narrow skirt, and one of its pointed bracts he had made into a bonnet. Plain, though somehow elegant. Sturdy, yet delicate. It was altogether unlike me. And yet, it somehow made me wish to be one.

Miss Templeton snatched it from my hand. "Oh, you've gone and drawn her exactly, Mr. Trimble." She gave him a knowing look. "But our Miss Withersby is quite tenacious, and bluebells wilt at the slightest provocation." She spoke the words as if chiding him.

"Only when they are wrenched from their home. If left to their own, they're quite the hardiest wildflower in the land."

"Yes, but if we are not to collect them, then how are we meant to admire them?" She left him with a puzzled frown as she took Mr. Stansbury and went to show my sketch to the gathered women.

I had to give credit where credit was due. "You have a rare talent."

"For parlor tricks, perhaps."

We had been abandoned by the others.

He studied my face for a moment and then glanced down at his empty sketchbook. "You don't approve of my choice?"

"May I remind you of the bluebell, Mr. Trimble? It's a very common flower. One might even say it's the commonest."

"I have never thought so. Indeed, most consider it the kingdom's favorite flower. And what would our lives be—how would we ever make it through a barren winter—without the hope of our bluebell woods come spring?"

"But bluebells droop under the weight of their own blossoms, of their own expectations. They're much too fragile for the realities of life."

"Bend, Miss Withersby. Bluebells don't droop, they bend. They offer their strength to the needs of the moment."

I wished it were so. "They're destined to live their lives in the shadows of others, sinking their roots into the litter of plants long dead. If they spread at all, they do it under cover of those flowers that have gone before them."

"That's a sad indictment."

"It's a sad state of existence. And . . . don't think me dismissive of your talents, but I don't . . . I don't want to be a bluebell."

He thought I was a bluebell? Truly? I blinked at the tears that had formed in my eyes.

"How can you be other than you are? And why would you wish to be? Surely you know that bluebells don't have to grow only in the woodlands. They can grow almost anywhere. And some say they do much better in sunlight than in the shade." He took ahold of my chin with a gentle hand and wiped away a tear with his thumb.

"I suppose you mean to say that . . . although bluebells might not like to be picked, they don't mind being . . . transplanted?"

"I mean to say that there's no end to what you might accomplish, Miss Withersby, if you would stop trying to be a nasturtium."

I knew I shouldn't have started talking to him again! "I can be anything I want."

"Can you?"

The next afternoon, after church, I tried out Mr. Trimble's method of turning people into flowers. If I could draw flowers, didn't it follow that I could draw flowers as people in the same way that Mr. Trimble had? I looked at my drawing of Lady Harriwick, who I was trying to make into a pansy.

I sighed.

Mr. Trimble pulled up a chair and came to sit beside me. He took hold of my paper and turned it round. "You mustn't keep such tight control of your pen. It's all in the recording of an impression. It doesn't have to so rigorously adhere to the actual lines of the flower." He took a clean sheet and sketched out a quick cartoon.

"How do you do that?"

He tilted his head as he looked at what he'd just drawn. "I don't know exactly."

"The proportions are all wrong but . . ."

"But you recognize it as a pansy, don't you?"

"Yes." As incredible as it seemed, I did.

"And you know it's Lady Harriwick."

"Yes." The resemblance was unmistakable. I took hold of my own drawing and began to crumple it.

He laid his hand across mine.

I protested. "It's no use. I can't do it like you can."

"Here." He took it from my hand, spread it out on the table, and added a flurry of strokes to my outlines, softening the edges of my sepals and rounding it about the petals. It seemed as if he were adding movement, if that were possible. "There. See?"

I did see. I saw that even a colonial sheep farmer was better at my job, and was a more talented illustrator than I. In five minutes' work he could create a drawing, perhaps not more accurate, but more evocative than one that took me hours to complete. "You really are quite good at this."

"As I said, it's nothing. Just a parlor trick meant to amuse ladies."

He had done that too. Even Miss Templeton, always so cheerful and winsome, had shone even brighter in his presence.

I wondered what it would be like to be Miss Templeton and have everyone leap to fulfill my demands. It would be quite nice, probably. There was something about her that made one hesitate to disappoint her. Could that sort of nature be cultivated? Could I, perhaps, turn myself into a Miss Templeton?

No.

That is, I could. Isn't that what I had been trying to do? But I felt as if I were playing at something.

"Please don't think this a slur on your friend's good name, but the repartee we shared was a simple amusement."

"An amusement?"

"Of the most effortless sort. I said what was expected, she said what was expected, and we carried on in good fashion. It was rather like being handed the script to a play I had already memorized. I had forgotten how easy it is to speak without having first to think."

I looked directly into his blue eyes. "I find it troubling that you don't always do so."

"When I speak to you, it's completely different. I have to think what I mean and mean what I say, and it's both exhilarating and utterly exhausting."

I glanced back down at the drawing. "If you don't like it, then you don't have to converse with me anymore." I took the paper from him. "I'm sure I won't mind." It would be much less annoying on my part.

"But that's just it. I think you enjoy this as much as I do, Miss Withersby."

"Enjoy what?"

"Talking."

I had to think on that a moment. Most of the relationships I had consisted, primarily, of me listening. I was always the writer, taking notes. With my father. With the rector. With Miss Templeton. Perhaps I didn't write notes for her, but as I observed her, I registered my observations just the same. "I suppose I do enjoy it, Mr. Trimble. Upon reflection, I have just discovered that most of the time, I only listen."

"That, my dear Miss Withersby, is a very great shame, for I have found that most of the time, quiet people have more to offer."

"Do we?" At his words it felt as if something deep within my heart had taken wing.

"I believe so. I might go to Miss Templeton for amusement, but I would come to you for thoughtful commentary. And for observation."

I found myself ridiculously pleased with the compliment.

He had been leaning toward me, but now he sat back with such abruptness that I might have said he scrambled to do so. "How is your campaign for marriage coming?" he asked. "Do you anticipate receiving any proposals?"

I blinked. "Proposals? I . . . don't think so. . . ." Proposals? Proposals! "I mean, yes. Yes, I do think so. Soon." And then Mr. Trimble could go away. That was the whole idea. To make him go away.

He smiled one of those bland, perfunctory smiles that I had come to realize meant nothing at all. "All men should be so lucky."

"Why?"

He froze under my gaze as if trapped. "Why what?"

"Why should they be so lucky?"

He blinked. "It's uh . . . It's just a saying. Just . . . something one says."

"You mean without thinking? But hadn't you just got done saying that when you talk to me you *do* think about what you're saying?"

He was looking at me with an odd sort of curve to his brow, as if I were a weed that had begun choking out his prized plants. "I really should get back to your father's notes."

"But I don't understand. You—"

"Some things are not worth understanding, Miss Withersby." He had taken on the manner of a lecturer once more. "In polite society when one is paid a compliment, one generally accepts it without peering beneath it."

I followed him to his desk. "You mean you simply said something because . . . because *why*? I didn't ask you for a compliment."

"No."

"I wasn't expecting one."

"I never thought you were."

"So then why did you feel the need to give me one? And a compliment that was so obviously ill-thought at that? Why didn't you say something you actually meant?"

"I did mean it."

"But . . ." My head was starting to hurt. "But what did you mean by it?"

"I . . . I do not have the right to say."

"But I thought . . . I mean I thought we . . ." I thought we knew each other better than that.

"If you would . . ." He gestured me over to the other side of the desk. "You're blocking my light."

Blocking his light? I might like to block his head instead. I decided I didn't like polite society. There was something mercenary and decidedly lacking in it. I took his hand intending to move the pile of papers beneath it into the light. "I think you might find it easier if you—"

He snatched it from my grasp. "I think I might find it easier if you left."

22

I decided to speak of my confusion to Miss Templeton the
next day when we saw each other at another parish function. "Why would someone pay you a compliment they
didn't mean?"

"To be polite."

"But Mr. Trimble and I have been quite impolite to each
other since we first met." There really was something I wasn't
understanding about what he'd said the previous afternoon.

"Mr. Trimble? He paid you a compliment?"

"He did. At least, I think he did. And I think he might have
meant it, only I suspect he didn't want me figuring out exactly
what he meant by it."

"I think you'd better tell me what he said." She squared
her shoulders as though she expected to hear something dis-
tasteful.

"He said . . . Well . . . we were talking about proposals and
whether I thought I might be getting any, and I said—"

"Of course you said that you would be."

"I said that I would be, and then he said that all men should
be so lucky."

"And . . . ?"

"And that was it."

"Well . . ." She hesitated as if she sensed some sort of trick, and then she frowned. "That was actually quite kind of him. I hope you thanked him."

"I . . . well . . . I didn't. I asked him why."

"Why what?"

"Why all men should be so lucky."

"And he said . . . ?"

"He said he didn't have the right to tell me."

"Didn't have the right . . . ?" Her mouth pursed as she gave Mr. Trimble's words some thought. "Perhaps . . ." She gasped. "Oh! Perhaps he's married!"

"But why, then, would he have gone to New Zealand by himself?"

She thought some more. "Well . . . perhaps he's gotten himself engaged."

"In New Zealand? Then why did he come back here by himself?"

She sighed. "That doesn't make any sense either. What do you know about him?"

Nearly everything. At least everything about his life in New Zealand. "He's a sheep farmer who—"

"I know that. What else?"

"There really isn't anything else. He's got that terrible family. That's all I know."

"That's it then. He doesn't have the right to tell you because of his terrible family."

"Why should they matter?"

"They *must* matter, otherwise . . . why would he have gone to New Zealand?"

"Because he likes sheep?"

"Miss Withersby!" She was shaking her head. "The only

reason he would have gone abroad was to run away from something."

"So . . . ?" I still didn't quite understand.

"So the only reasonable conclusion to draw is that he was running away from his family, trying to establish a new life for himself. It's best not to look too far into these things."

"That's what he said."

"It's enough to know that he thinks quite highly of you even though he's in such a humble position that even you could not deign to consider him at all."

"Consider him as what?"

"As a *suitor*! Really, Miss Withersby, haven't you been paying attention? Poor man. I should think he might make something of himself if he didn't have that dreadful family of his hanging about his neck like a millstone. The sooner we can get him out of the way, the better. For everyone concerned."

I didn't quite know what to make of Mr. Trimble's sentiments or Miss Templeton's explanation, so I finally decided that what I needed was an hour or so to ramble over God's green earth . . . though it was looking rather brown this late in the year. Collecting my bonnet, the shooting jacket, and my vasculum, I took myself straight out the back door and out towards Cats Clough. As I went, I wondered why father hadn't yet called a halt to my search for a husband. Perhaps it was because I hadn't been speaking enough about the rector and Mr. Stansbury. Maybe he wasn't acting with any urgency because *I* hadn't been displaying any sense of urgency.

Clapping my mitts together to warm my hands, I stooped to look at some thistle seedpods that were standing near a fence. *They* were displaying the proper sense of urgency. The seeds had already allowed themselves to be blown away against winter's coming. I stood and looked about the field for specimens. But, I reminded myself, I wasn't to be looking for flowers. I wasn't to be thinking of my research or of writing papers. What I really needed was the exclusive attentions of a suitor.

Off in the distance came a chorus of hunting horns.

It was difficult to locate flowers at this time of year when their seedpods tended to blend in with the dead grasses. And now, with the tootling of horns and the barking of dogs, I found myself distracted.

A fox darted beneath the fence, past my feet. I saw them often in the fields, but they weren't usually on the run. So panicked did he seem that I doubted he even noticed me. Hardly a moment later, the fence was beset by a pack of hounds that brayed in their mournful voices as they dug frantically to widen the gap between the ground and the fence. If it wasn't enough that the fields were regularly being trampled by amateurs and hunters, now they were being dug up by dogs!

The thud of horses' hooves came up the lane. A hunter. He left the path for the field in which I was standing. Aiming his horse for the fence, he yelled at me. "Get out of the way, you daft woman!"

"I am not daft!" In fact, I suspected I was probably much smarter than he.

Behind him came a thundering of hooves, and horses began to jump the fence in an unceasing procession.

I sunk to the ground and threw my arms up over my head as they bounded past. "I must protest!" But I made my complaint to no one in particular, as the riders had already passed, leaving a mess of torn and muddied grasses in their wake.

I did manage to locate some lady's tresses, only they had been mashed into the mud by a horse. Or perhaps by the paws of one of those hunting dogs. As I was bent over them, mourning their destruction, I heard the sound of another horse approaching and turned my head toward the noise.

"Get out of the way!" Its rider was gesturing wildly for me to move.

Was he yelling at me? I straightened, putting a hand to my waist as I looked around. He *was* yelling at me. There was nothing but grasses and open fields about, and the rest of the pack of horses had already thundered by. I didn't see why I had to move when he could just as easily go some other way. I turned round to say so and was surprised to find that he was already quite close.

"I said, *move!*"

The last thing I remember was thinking that horses were quite extraordinarily large when you got up right next to them.

It was the pounding in my head that woke me—that and the cadence of Mr. Trimble's voice. I put a hand to my temple and gasped as my touch set off a new sort of throbbing. "Do be quiet. My head hurts insufferably." I cracked open an eye.

Miss Templeton came into view. She had a handkerchief pressed to her nose, and tears were streaming down her cheeks. She gasped. "Oh! We didn't know if you'd ever wake."

Mr. Trimble appeared beside her. "Of course we knew you'd wake." His tone was faintly disapproving. "The only question was when."

"But the doctor said that she might not—"

Mr. Trimble knelt beside me and put his fingertips to my jaw as he searched my eyes. "He said that you'd taken a good blow to your head and a thump to your ribs and the best thing to do is to rest." His hand had moved to my hair, which he stroked away from my face.

Rest. That was a good idea. If I slept, then maybe I wouldn't feel the ache in my head, and if he kept stroking my hair, then maybe I would be able to breathe easier as well.

When I next woke, the room had gone dark, save for a fire in the hearth. I could smell the scent of it and I could see its glow. But the it didn't seem to be in the right place. Where was I?

I put an elbow to the . . . What *was* I lying upon? I tried to peer around, but the effort made my vision go hazy, so I decided the best thing to do would be to try again for another look in a little while. But . . . was that Mr. Trimble? Why was he . . . wherever it was that we were? And why had he fallen asleep in his chair?

I closed my eyes to rest for a moment. The next time I opened them, there were five people looking back at me.

My father, Mr. Trimble, Miss Templeton, the rector, and Mr. Stansbury.

I tried to smile, but the effort made me wince.

Mr. Trimble held up a hand. "Don't move."

I hadn't been planning to.

Miss Templeton blinked her eyes wide. "You're not . . . you're not going back to sleep, are you?"

Had I been sleeping?

My father stepped close and knelt as he picked up my hand. "You were knocked over on your ramble by one of those . . . those . . . ." He was trembling with something quite like rage.

"Those asinine, self-absorbed, pitiful progeny of our kingdom's finest families." Mr. Trimble supplied the words.

"I was?"

"But don't worry." Miss Templeton was smiling as if that alone might cure me. I was more interested, however, in the idea that she thought I ought to be worried. If that was the case, then why . . . ? "The doctor said you *should* be fine."

The rector passed her a handkerchief as her smile was overcome by tears. "We've all been praying for you."

They had? I closed my eyes as I tried to remember if anyone had done that for me before.

"Is she . . . ?"

Miss Templeton's whisper made my eyes fly open. "Is who, what?"

"Oh! I was worried you were going to sleep some more."

"Sleep if you want to." Mr. Trimble's words were more like a command than a suggestion.

Mr. Stansbury was a holding a . . . "Is that an Italian orchid?"

He glanced down toward his hands as if surprised to find himself holding it. "Yes. It is. For you. I'll just . . ." He held it out before him, glancing about the room.

I sought my father's gaze. "Why am I in the parlor?"

He brushed my cheek with his mustache as he pressed a kiss to my forehead. "It's because you were run into by that horrid man—Lord Harriwick's son. And do you know what he did?"

"He ran into me?"

Miss Templeton took over the narrative from my father. "He left you there—in the field!—until after the hunt. You were so long in coming back from your ramble and—"

My father wrested the dialogue back. "And I knew you didn't like to be out when the bats start flitting around."

Mr. Trimble cleared his throat and took over the telling of the tale. "We were worried about you but had no idea where to start searching until Lord Harriwick's son finally thought to send a messenger round to apologize for knocking you off your feet."

Miss Templeton gave a tremulous cry as her brow collapsed. "And that's when Mr. Trimble rode out to the Harriwick estate and—"

"And I demanded to be taken to the place he'd run you over."

Miss Templeton gave Mr. Trimble a pat upon his arm. "And he carried you back here and then went for the doctor and—" She threw herself into Mr. Stansbury's arms and began to weep, which was just as well, for I'd become quite dizzy from keeping up with the conversation.

Mr. Trimble came to kneel before me, tucking a corner of the blanket back underneath me. "The doctor said you shouldn't be moved, so we've kept you here. And now you'll have to rest for a while."

A while. "How long would that be?"

"Three weeks? A month?"

"No dancing?"

"No dancing. No fieldwork. In fact, very little walking."

"But what about . . ." What about all the things I was supposed to be doing?

The rector reached down to pat my hand. "I won't do anything with my collections until you're recovered."

Mr. Stansbury scuffed a boot against the floorboards. "And I'm still waiting to hear from my correspondent about those plants you suspected were mislabeled, so don't worry yourself about that."

Miss Templeton had ceased her crying, and now she was trying to smile again. "It will be fine. Everything will be fine."

Mr. Trimble's hand slid from my temple down to my cheek. "Don't worry. I have everything taken care of." As much as I had been trying to rid myself of Mr. Trimble, somehow his words gave me great comfort. So I let my head sink down into the pillow, and I willed myself back to sleep.

Mr. Stansbury and Miss Templeton returned the following day. As my father hovered about, she drew a chair over and sat beside me while Mr. Stansbury put an arm around the back of the chair and bent to squat beside her. He smiled at me, and I was pleased to find I could smile back without inducing too much pain.

"I spoke with Lord Harriwick, and he's agreed to pay the doctor's bill as well as send over a side of beef for scraping and the making of beef tea."

Miss Templeton twisted to look at him. "How marvelous you are, Mr. Stansbury! Don't you agree, Miss Withersby?"

"A whole side? Where ever are we expected to put it?"

"While you've got him feeling guilty, why don't you get him to subscribe to Mr. Withersby's volumes as well?" That bit was from Mr. Trimble, who from the sound of him was sitting somewhere behind me. "He and all those indolent friends of his."

Mr. Stansbury lifted a brow. "I'll see what I can do."

"Threaten them with a termination of hunting rights to your park. That will make the bunch of them listen."

Miss Templeton reached out and touched my hand. "Mr. Stansbury has convinced Lord Harriwick to invite you to his Christmas ball as well."

Did that mean I would have to go? My head was throbbing again. If I didn't know my visitors were hoping to cheer me, I would have asked Mr. Trimble to help me up to my bed. Unfortunately, they stayed until he chased them out at half past three.

As father held some tea for me to drink, Mr. Trimble appeared beside him. "Could they not see that you are exhausted?" He lifted my head with a gentle hand, took my pillow and beat it against his thigh, and then slipped it back beneath me. "Perhaps . . . should you like to be taken to your bed?"

"Just leave me here and let me be. My head hurts too much to move."

"And here I was thinking it was my company you relished."

"If that's one of your jokes, I don't have it within me to attempt a smile."

"You must be feeling poorly. You haven't once shouted at me all day."

"Don't tease. I feel too wretched to be made to feel more wretched. Let me nurse my misery in peace."

My peace was to be short-lived. The rector arrived at four, Bible in hand.

Mr. Trimble and my father stood as Miss Hansford announced him. My father excused himself and headed toward his study, leaving Mr. Trimble as my self-declared defender. "I don't know that Miss Withersby is up to—"

"Let him stay." Though I wasn't, in fact, up to his visit, I had tired of doing nothing.

The rector sat in the chair Miss Templeton had only recently vacated and proceeded to read about meaninglessness and drudgery.

"Is that Ecclesiastes?"

"It is indeed."

"Could you not find something more uplifting?"

Across the room, Mr. Trimble coughed. "The Song of Songs, perhaps?"

A flush burned across the rector's face.

I reached out a hand toward him. "I was thinking more in the way of Psalms."

"Of course, you're right. I naturally incline towards the melancholy, so I must remind myself that not everyone appreciates the same." He flipped to Psalms. So eloquent were the words, so emphatic was his diction, that I was swept up by the vision of heavenly realms and right into a dreamless sleep.

Much of the week passed in the same way. Mr. Trimble was ever present, though rarely seen. By me, in any case. On Monday I was recovered enough to push myself to sitting. When Mr. Stansbury visited that day, he declared me much improved. "It must be tiresome, shut up here with your father's assistant. Won't you come for a drive with me?" He slid a glance toward Mr. Trimble. "There's something I would like to show you."

"I may look recovered, but my head still aches much of the time."

"If you would allow it, I would be happy to carry you to the carriage. And once settled, there would be no need for you to move."

I heard the scraping of a chair, and Mr. Trimble propelled himself into my view. "I don't know if that's wise. I've been told head injuries take a surprisingly long time to heal, and—"

"I would be delighted." Tired of being bullied about by Mr. Trimble, I smiled at Mr. Stansbury.

He took me up in his arms.

"I don't really think she should—"

Mr. Stansbury stepped right past him. "Has she a mantle? And a bonnet?"

Mr. Trimble hurried past us to collect them from the hall and flung them at me. "Why don't you allow me to—"

Mr. Stansbury held me tight. "It's no trouble at all. I'll return her to you within the hour."

Mr. Trimble hurried ahead of us and vaulted into the carriage. "I'll provide the escort."

"It's really not necessary."

"I insist."

As we began to pull away from the house the carriage dipped

into a hole, and I began to think that Mr. Trimble had been right. My head was not yet properly healed, and the sun seemed to be especially shiny for November. But it was too late to amend my decision. And Mr. Trimble and Mr. Stansbury were already glaring at each other.

I felt every bump of the road, and once we reached Overwich Hall, Mr. Stansbury had the carriage pass by the house and drive into his . . . Not his stumpery!

My misery gave way to despair.

"I had the last stump placed just yesterday." He signaled the carriage to stop and then bent to push the door open. "What do you think?"

I thought it not nearly worth the effort I had expended to see it. Really, it was all so tiring. "I . . . I truly don't have the words."

"I knew that seeing it would cheer you!"

Once we got back to the house, I felt like tying a ribbon round my head to keep it from cracking in two. But I did not wish to admit to Mr. Trimble that he had been right, so I asked him for some tea instead. He went into the kitchen and then came back to sit in the chair beside me while Father continued on with his work for which he was using Mr. Trimble's desk.

"Really, Miss Withersby, a man can hardly hear himself think with all the suitors flocking about."

"Does it bother you?"

His gaze met mine. "Only insofar as it keeps me from my work."

"I suspect one of them will propose quite soon and put you out of your misery." If I couldn't do anything else, at least I could try to help my cause. I turned toward father. "You've had a chance now to acquaint yourself with the rector and Mr. Stansbury. Do you have any opinion on the matter?"

He looked up from his microscope, squinting. "Which matter is that?"

"The matter of my finding a husband. I'm certain one of the men will soon be asking for my hand. Do you have a preference?"

If I had hoped to see alarm in his eyes, I was mistaken. It looked more like resignation. "I suppose it will be for the best. You'll be much happier married."

"But you don't have an opinion about it?"

"I'm sure your uncle will tell me what he thinks of the pair of them. He usually does."

The ache in my head was so pronounced that I feared my tone was rather sharp when I replied. "They aren't a pair. They're quite different, really. If I marry the rector, I won't have any spare time to come help you, what with the children and all the work that I would have to do. And if I marry Mr. Stansbury, who is to say that he won't suddenly decide he's tired of Cheshire and wishes to live in London instead. Or somewhere on the continent even!"

Father looked up sharply. "I hadn't realized he was so prone to the whims of fancy."

Had I said the wrong thing? "But even if he decides to stay on here in Overwich, I won't have that much opportunity to come see you what with helping him with his glasshouse. He has plans to expand it."

"I suppose that's to be expected. Undertakings of that sort are never truly finished."

"But what I mean is that I'll no longer be available to help you."

"Mr. Trimble seems quite capable. His assistance is sufficient."

I appealed to Mr. Trimble. "Don't you have family to see to, Mr. Trimble?"

"I assure you, the less seen of them, the better."

"But your sheep must be in need of you."

"I left my flock in very capable hands. I am at your father's leisure."

"But, Father, you must need someone to decipher your notes, and I'm sure Mr. Trimble can't—"

"That's something I do myself these days. I've found that it forces me to be more disciplined in the expression of my ideas."

"But . . . but . . . Mr. Trimble *can't* be keeping up with your correspondence."

"Isn't he? I've been signing quite a few letters and writing some of my own. At least it seems as if I have been."

Was that alarm I read in Mr. Trimble's eyes? "If you care to look over my files, Miss Withersby, I'm sure you'll agree that I haven't fallen behind."

"But . . . the bills! The lease!" There must be something Mr. Trimble had been leaving undone. Something my father must need me for.

Miss Hansford came in with a tea tray and placed it on a table between Mr. Trimble and me.

He handed me a cup. "The lease has been paid. In advance."

"Advance? But where did—"

"I persuaded your father to argue for a discount."

I didn't even know that could be done. "You must . . . There must be something . . ." Father had to miss me, didn't he? There had to be some point at which he would tire of Mr. Trimble and ask me back.

After our discussion, I fell into a troubled, restless sleep. When I woke, I lay there for some time, trying to work up the impetus to sit. I heard someone come down the stairs and pushed myself up on an elbow. Mr. Trimble crept into the room. His arms were filled with . . . "Are those *my* papers?"

"These?" He looked down at the papers as if astonished to find them there.

23

I swung my legs over the side of the sofa and pushed to sitting. "They *are* mine! What are you doing with those?"

"I need them for a paper—"

"You can't use them. They're mine!"

"—and I couldn't find them anywhere. The only place I hadn't looked was your room, and . . ." He looked down at the pile and shrugged.

"But you can't—"

He disappeared into my father's study, leaving me fuming on the sofa. As many papers and discourses as I'd written in my father's name, as many times as I'd signed his signature instead of my own, I would not have predicted the absolute rage that encompassed me as I contemplated Mr. Trimble's plan to use my work as his own.

I pushed to my feet. With a hand to my head, I took one step and then another. I wouldn't be dancing anytime soon, and thank heaven for that, but I didn't doubt that I could walk to the study.

If I didn't proceed too quickly.

I sat down on a chair and rested for a moment as I waited for my head to stop throbbing.

It took me several minutes to make it to the study, but when I did, I was greeted with all the shock one would welcome a ghost.

It was quite satisfying.

I approached the desk where Father and Mr. Trimble were consulting . . . about my papers if I read the situation correctly. "I must insist that I be given back the papers which were taken from my bedroom."

Father frowned. "You mean the notes about your subantarctic islands?"

"Yes. My notes. The timing for writing up a paper on them is perfect really . . ." I hobbled over toward Mr. Trimble and had almost reached him when he swept my papers up in his arms. "It's perfect, because now I have the time to work on them."

My father dismissed my words with a sweep of his hand. "No, no. You can't. That's why I have Mr. Trimble. So that you can concentrate on finding a husband. And it's even more important for you not to be taxed with your work, now that you have to recover from your injury as well."

"I am recovered. I'm standing before you, aren't I?"

Mr. Trimble stood looking at me, as if daring me to say the words again. "Then perhaps we should send word over to the Admiral that you can attend the band concert with him tonight."

"That won't be necessary. I'm still a bit fatigued, and—"

"Perhaps you should retire to your bedroom, then?"

The room began to sway, and I grabbed onto the corner of the desk for fear I might faint. "I don't want to retire."

"It will do you good."

"But I don't *wish* to retire. At all. In any way."

My father was looking on with great concern. "You're exhausted, Charlotte. And you're—"

"And I don't want to marry, and I don't like being pushed into—"

Father had come round the desk to take up my hand. "You're overcome by your injuries. If you would just go back into the parlor and rest . . ."

But I couldn't. I wouldn't. Words were pouring from my soul in great sobs. "I've been pushed into something I don't want, when what I really want is just to be wanted!" A large teardrop splatted onto Father's desk. "I just want it all to be the same. Like before. But different."

Mr. Trimble picked me up in his arms and carried me out of the room and up the stairs. I threw my arm about his neck and buried my head in his shoulder. "I want my work to matter. And I want it to be my own." Why did it seem as if everything had gone wrong? Why did it feel as if I were being flattened in a flower press? As if all the vitality and life were being forced out of me?

"If it were up to me, you would want for nothing at all."

"But that's just it. I don't want to be taken care of, and I don't want to take care of someone else's collections. I just . . . I don't . . . I don't know why no one ever wants to know what *I* want. They just make me do what they want."

The next morning I woke to a knock at my door.

I pulled the blanket up over my head, for I planned on never speaking to my father or Mr. Trimble, face-to-face, again. "Who is it?"

I heard the door creak open. "Miss Withersby?"

Was that Miss Templeton? I lifted a corner of the blanket to look. It was. I threw the blanket off and sat up.

"Are you . . . are you worse?"

"No. That is, yes."

"Which is it?" She was standing there in the doorway, wringing her hands.

"I'm never going downstairs again. Ever."

"Why? What's happened?" She strode over to my windows, thrust back my curtains, and secured them.

I winced from the sudden light. "It's all too humiliating."

She took off her bonnet and looked around for a place to put it. Finding no space, she simply held it in her lap as she sat on the edge of my bed beside me.

"I gave myself over to hysteria and crying last night. It was dreadful."

"I'm beginning to wonder . . . why don't you just ask for your position back if it means so much to you?"

"After Mr. Trimble's done it even better than I? And look as if I'm begging? Wouldn't I risk being told I'm not needed anymore?"

"You're right. You can't. So you do still need your suitors."

"I suppose I do. But that still doesn't take care of Mr. Trimble. It's not a question now of my being asked back and him being shown the door. It's quite clear that he's got to leave first if I'm ever to reclaim my place. And I don't even know if my father would give it back to me! Not after I went and sobbed about everything last night."

"So you're just going to let him stay here?"

I fell back against my pillow. "He doesn't seem to care much about his family, and he's left all those sheep of his in someone else's hands. *Capable* hands is what he said. He'll probably work here and die here and have himself buried in Cheshire and I've only myself to thank for it."

"You've the Admiral, in fact, to thank for it, don't you? Wasn't it his idea to find you a husband?"

"It *was* his idea!"

"In any case, the thing to do is to get Mr. Trimble to go away voluntarily. But you say his sheep don't need him."

"No."

"What about his family?"

"They're some despicable, degenerate sort of people. Remember?"

"But that's perfect!"

"How?"

"They sound ghastly. And ghastly people are certain to need help. Or money. Or both. I'll just have to find a way to make Mr. Trimble feel obligated to supply them."

My spirits began to rise. "You are the most intrepid soul I have ever met. Do you think you can do it?"

"I can try. Now then, do you know anything at all about who his family is or where they come from?"

I thought for a moment. "Well . . . he received a letter from a place called Eastleigh."

Miss Templeton's field club met the next week for an excursion, and I let myself be persuaded to join her. Mostly because Mr. Trimble didn't want me to. My head didn't pound like a drum anymore, and I really was anxious to be out, doing something.

The Admiral took us to church in his carriage and afterward delivered me to the train station. I met the group there, umbrella and vasculum in hand. Miss Templeton and I were soon joined by Mr. Stansbury and the rector. Upon arrival in a neighboring town, the field club gathered together on the platform to make a plan for our ramble. There was some discussion between the female members as to where would be the best place to come by mistletoe and among the male members about the possibilities of spotting one of the small linnet finches in the vicinity.

I found it quite distressing that no one had thought to organize the outing in advance. "We might find one or the other, or one on the way to the other, but it's unlikely they'd be found together." I muttered the words to Miss Templeton, since doing anything with any sort of vigor made my head begin to pound.

"Maybe Miss Withersby can lead the way to the mistletoe." Miss Templeton spoke quite loudly as she jabbed at me with her elbow. "She's a genius with botany."

The president blinked, like an indignant owl. "But I was hoping for some thistle seed or dock seed."

My head was throbbing again. "If you want those, then it would be much better to head toward the nearest mere, wouldn't it? To a place where they are known to grow?"

The mere was finally settled upon as our goal. But when we got to it, we found it overrun with members of the Irondale Foundry Field Club from the county of Shropshire, who had snuck into our county from their own. They looked very much like foundry workers in their smocks and caps.

Our president halted in outrage. "Good heavens! It looks as if they've already stripped all the seedpods!"

Which was why amateurs should not be allowed to partake in scientific pursuits, in my opinion.

He addressed himself to the president of their field club. "Perhaps you hadn't realized, but this is a Cheshire mere."

The other president came at ours, chin raised. "You don't own it."

"We plan on it being available, as it's in our jurisdiction."

"Nature knows no jurisdiction." The man was sneering now.

Our president took a step backward. "Why don't we be reasonable about this?"

The men from the visiting field club slipped the vascula from their shoulders and let them clatter to the ground.

Our president retreated further. "Look here. We'd made the plan to visit last June."

The rival club's president took a step forward for every step that ours took backward. "Maybe we made our plans last April."

"Then I suppose you'll welcome us next month to a field in Shropshire?"

He snorted. "Not likely!"

The longer I'd stood there looking at the picked-over field, the more reasons I'd found for dismay. I stepped between the two men and addressed myself to the visiting president. "Look at what you've done: you've stripped the place bare! You ought to be ashamed of yourselves!"

The visiting club's president halted in his approach. "It isn't your field."

I stabbed at him with my umbrella. "And it isn't yours either and now, thanks to you, it will never be anyone's. None of these will come back in the spring. Did you not think to leave even one?"

"We didn't—"

I appealed to the field club members who had come to stand behind him. "And how many of you actually know how to preserve your specimens? Or label them properly?"

He glanced over his shoulder at his club's members. "We weren't—"

"What are you going to do with all your seedpods and catkins? Take them home and . . . and stick them between the leaves of . . . of some big book and let them rot? Or put them in a vase and let them gather dust?"

"We hadn't—"

"You're not worthy even of being called amateurs of botany

and if you had any decency at all, you'd return those vascula to the vendor from which you got them."

"We won't—"

"I think the best thing would be for all of you to *leave*. Immediately."

"Now, wait just a minute!" The cry came from someone among the group from the neighboring county. "Why should we listen to some girl? We've as much right to all of this as they do."

Mr. Stansbury stepped up beside me. Given the chill of the day, I was surprised to see that he'd discarded his coat and rolled up his shirt sleeves. "The lady is right."

"Lady!" The man was jeering. "That's no lady!"

I couldn't say for certain who threw the first punch, but soon, all of our men were involved in a melee of grand proportions. Miss Templeton and I stood clutching each other as the brawl swirled around us.

Eventually the rival club was beaten back, and we found ourselves in possession of the field. A dubious prize considering how trampled the remaining plants now were.

One of the men sent up a cheer. "I say we need a new president!"

There was a murmur of general agreement among the club membership.

Miss Templeton fluttered her handkerchief. "All in favor of Miss Withersby, say 'Aye.'"

"But I don't want to—" My words were drowned out by an overwhelming chorus of shouts in the affirmative.

Miss Templeton was plucking at my sleeve. "I think your first order of business ought to be to suggest that we repair to one of those pubs down by the train station."

"But we haven't even picked anything yet!"

"And we won't at this late hour. Besides, no one wants to anymore."

"Then what is the purpose of a field club?"

"Just say it! Trust me."

The cheers had died off, and now everyone was looking at me. Miss Templeton jabbed her elbow into my side, and I found myself speaking. "I was thinking, perhaps, in light of all that has happened, maybe we should repair to one of those pubs down by the train station in order to plan the next outing."

Cheers went up again, and then someone broke out into song as we all marched toward the station. Though my head had begun to protest my movements quite painfully, I contemplated the possibilities for a true field excursion, perhaps to Tiverton or even out to Bidston.

Miss Templeton took up my arm as we walked along. "Mr. Stansbury and I were talking, and I think it would be quite agreeable if he were to lead a tour for the field club through his glasshouse, with a small reception to follow."

"That wouldn't really be a field outing though."

"But it would be so convivial! And it's turned too cold to spend time out of doors."

"It's just the time to find all sorts of berries in the wood."

"I really think the tour would be better. Just imagine: walking through the glasshouse to the accompaniment of music and the promise of tea and warm chocolate. Doesn't that sound divine?"

It sounded nothing like any field trip I had ever undertaken.

At the pub, Mr. Stansbury secured a table. Miss Templeton and I joined him, along with the rector. During the course of the conversation, Miss Templeton transformed the outing to

Mr. Stansbury's glasshouse into a town-wide field club sponsored charity event for the refurbishment of the church's chancel. There was to be a raffle for a prize, which remained to be determined. A subscription to *Curtis's Botanical Magazine*, perhaps. Or one of Mr. Stansbury's prized orchids.

The rector's eyes kept growing wider with each new detail. "That's extraordinarily generous of you, Miss Templeton."

"Don't thank me. It was Miss Withersby who first noticed the deplorable condition of the chancel."

I did? "It was?"

She smiled at me. "You must remember how you said the church could use some attention?"

I had?

"As the new president of the field club, she'll have to consult with both of you on the details." She looked at Mr. Stansbury and the rector in turn.

"I will?"

She nodded vigorously. "To ensure that the event is properly planned and that the money gets transferred to the rector once the tour is over. I'm sure it will occupy you for days."

I felt my spirits sink.

As we left the pub for the train, Miss Templeton leaned close to whisper in my ear. "You'll have to have tête-à-têtes with both of them! How the town will start to talk. You can thank me later."

I told Father and Mr. Trimble all about the outing that evening over dinner. "Someone even bloodied the rector's nose."

They were looking at me with horror. "This was . . . Did you say it was on a field outing?" Father's voice registered surprise.

"It was."

Mr. Trimble shook his head. "And I thought I had it tough in New Zealand."

"The other club really had no right to poach our field like that."

Mr. Trimble was regarding me with grave reprobation. "I hadn't thought you a ruffian, Miss Withersby. And you say you brought Mr. Stansbury and the rector into your scuffle?"

"It wasn't my scuffle."

"You really are a bad influence."

"What would you have had me do? Just let them pick all the plants they wanted and leave the field barren?"

"Of course I would not have wanted that."

Somewhat mollified, I continued to eat. At least my appetite was well recovered. "Oh, and they elected me president of the club."

A corner of Mr. Trimble's mouth curled up. "So now you've gone and staged a coup."

"And Miss Templeton got Mr. Stansbury to agree to host a benefit for the repair of the chancel . . . centered on a tour of Overwich Hall's glasshouse." I was still rather unclear as to how she had worked that all out. "And I'm to help him plan it. So we'll be having quite a few"—what was it she'd called them?— "tête-à-têtes. Which is saying quite a bit about my prospects, I should think."

Mr. Trimble's brow had a skeptical tilt to it. "Perhaps. But is it what you wish to say?"

My father had been listening with what appeared to be great interest. "We'd all hoped you'd find a husband, Charlotte. It looks as if your efforts are working."

Mr. Trimble had continued speaking. "Of course you must help. If that's what you want to do. But . . . is it, I wonder?"

"Is *it* what? Is what it?" I was thoroughly confused.

"Is becoming more involved with that man what you wish to do? It would encourage him in his hopes. You do understand that, don't you?"

"Of course I understand it. I'm not simple, Mr. Trimble."

"I never thought you were."

My father's brows were folded and he was worrying his mustache. "Then we're backing the industrialist? Is that what we're saying?"

"I suppose it is." Mr. Trimble didn't appear happy to be saying it, which had the effect of making me extremely happy. Now was the time to underscore the consequences of their putting me out into society to marry. "I suppose if I married him I would have to go and live at Overwich Hall."

Father was nodding. "That's generally what happens. The bride goes to live with the groom."

"And I wouldn't be able to be here."

"No. Not any longer. But you'd have that nice glasshouse of his. And that project he's always talking about. With the trees? It was trees, wasn't it?"

"His stumpery." Bless me, I'd forgotten all about it.

Father smiled and reached over to pat my hand. "Have no worries about me, Charlotte. Mr. Trimble has me all put together and organized. In any case, I should think you'd be quite happy with the man."

But the point wasn't whether I'd be happy or not. The point was for him to understand just how miserable *he* would be if I were to marry. But this, too, Mr. Trimble had ruined. Now Father didn't have to worry about letters or bills or articles. He might not have a partner in research so much as he had a secretary, but he seemed to miss me not at all.

Mr. Trimble had been watching me all the while. "Are you then?"

"Am I what?"

"Happy with the industrialist?"

"Why wouldn't I be?"

"So this is what you want?"

"I suppose that's what I'm saying, isn't it?" I speared a morsel of roast to emphasize my conviction. And then I chewed it quite forcibly so he wouldn't be tempted to ask me anything else.

24

The field club excursion had tired me more than I wished to admit, and I was hoping for a sleep-in the next morning, but I wasn't to be allowed a moment's peace. Planning for the benefit started that very day. The Admiral came in his carriage, and whisked me away to Overwich Hall, his only advice being to avoid too much fuss.

Though I considered myself quite immune to it under normal circumstances, Miss Templeton seemed to create fuss wherever she went, so I was not overly optimistic. It had been her idea, after all.

Mr. Stansbury welcomed me, once more, to his glasshouse. "I have to think this is becoming a habit, Miss Withersby."

"It seems to be."

"And more than that, I like to think that we work well together. We ought to keep it up."

"We do. We should." His glasshouse was always quite pleasant.

His cheeks grew even more ruddy than normal, and he crooked his arm for mine. A secretary dogged our steps as we walked, scribbling down everything we said.

"So you do think placing the band right here would be good?" He indicated a gap in his shelves, between the orchids and the smaller potted palms.

"I think that would be fine."

We walked several steps before he paused. "And then serving the refreshments from here? I could clear this shelf beneath the *Dieffenbachia*."

"They drip poison from their leaves, you know."

"I didn't. Perhaps we should move them then."

"Or maybe you could place the food over there." I gestured toward the other side of the aisle.

"By the fountain? Would we not risk the food being ruined by the mist?"

"I suppose we would." I sighed. "I'm not very good at this sort of thing."

"I think you're doing splendidly."

"And I think you're being too kind. It's your suggestions you seem to be following. Not mine."

"How ungallant of me."

"I think it's entirely practical of you. Now, if we were speaking of hosting plants, it would be another thing entirely. I could tell you just how to arrange them and feed them and make them happy."

He glanced about as if surprised. "They could be happier than they are now?"

"Oh, much! Your palms haven't enough light and your orchids have too much shade."

"If it were up to Miss Templeton, she would have all my plants moved toward the waterfall so they could be aesthetically arranged in a semicircle around it."

"She means well."

A small smile softened his mouth. "She's rather extraordinary, isn't she?"

I quite agreed. And on the whole it seemed we spent a good deal more time discussing Miss Templeton than we did the reception.

Eventually, he nodded toward the windows that looked out onto a garden that sloped toward the river. "There goes the Admiral again." My uncle was pacing back and forth outside, hands clasped behind his back, pausing now and then to survey the river that glistened in the distance.

It struck me as a lonely stance. And rather forlorn. "He always seems to be gazing off at the horizon."

"I suppose it comes from a life spent at sea. I've half a mind to offer him a spyglass."

"Do you have one?"

"I have two. One carved from ivory and its match, from ebony."

"You ought to show them to him."

"I'll have the butler bring them out." He spoke to his secretary, who hurried off toward the house.

We went back to speaking of food and music and other things of which I had no firm opinion, and I soon saw the butler present Mr. Stansbury's spyglasses to the Admiral. He spent no little time fiddling with them and trying them out.

"Then it's all decided?"

"What's that?" I'd been feeling a bit sorry for my uncle. It seemed as if he was somehow shipwrecked here on the plains of Cheshire. It didn't seem he was truly unhappy, but I couldn't resolutely vouch for his happiness either.

After we were done with our discussion, I excused myself from Mr. Stansbury, gathered my mantle about me, and went outside to join my uncle.

"Is it difficult, not to be at sea?"

"Hmph?"

"Do you wish you were sailing?"

"Hmph."

"You can't even see the ocean from here."

"No. Probably best. Then I'd just want to be out in it. You forget the terrible parts. The fighting. The stench. Death. But there's something about standing on the deck of a ship and seeing nothing but the sea . . . Of course I miss it. But there comes a time when even the thing you love betrays you." He cast me a glance. "Some botanical society refuses a perfectly well-written article. A queen commands you to fight for the enslavement of an entire people." He shrugged. "You have to know when it's time to give it up, I suppose. Doesn't mean you love it any less, of course. Just means it's time to move on. When you can't agree with the decisions that bind you, then you have to take your talents elsewhere."

"What happened, exactly? In the war?"

He took so long in answering that I had quite decided he wasn't going to.

"It's complicated, my dear, in the way wars always are. I was ordered to fight for the opening of China's ports. What happened, as a result, was the debasement of her people. It's difficult to be proud of something like that. The Opium War was the best thing and the worst thing that ever happened to me."

He put a glass to his eye and stared through it for a moment, then he collapsed it with a tap from his palm and put it back down on the tray a servant was holding for him.

"In any case, I don't want you to have to go through what I did, never quite feeling a part of the family, but then never quite wanting to leave it either. I just want to see you settled. Accepted." He threw me a glance. "Loved."

"I never knew you—"

"My sister, your mother, had the mind for botany, you know. She was brilliant. And you're just like her."

"For all the good it does me. I can't get anything published."

"Your mother worked it out . . . all those books she wrote for children. Charming."

I didn't want to be *charming*. I wanted to be incisive and provocative. I wanted to be admired. I wanted my work to count for something other than lining the bookshelves of a child's nursery.

"The pursuit of science isn't an easy way to make a living. So I brought her a surgeon. I brought her a lieutenant. Even brought her a captain or two. But she wouldn't have any of them. She could have lived in luxury . . . or at least in less dire straits, but she chose your father instead."

He made it sound as if she had made a poor choice.

"I know how it is not to fit in, my dear. What it's like to have people going on about their hunting dogs when all you want to do is go sailing. But when you're pushed out, what else can you do but go? And when you do, you've got to look out for yourself. I'm in a position to help you now, so let me. Why not use my resources while you can?"

Mr. Stansbury joined us then, but only to excuse himself to meet with the mayor, and we left soon after.

Miss Templeton had insisted the rector would have much to say about raising funds for his chancel, and so she had told us to meet that afternoon as well. The Admiral took one look at the children, who were having a good romp outside the rectory, and escorted me into the house with great alacrity.

We spoke of the tour and the raffle for quite a while, until the rector finally looked me in the eye. "I wonder . . . is the chancel really so bad? Because if money is going to be raised for something, I was thinking that it ought to go to Widow Greenley, who needs a new roof, or even to old Mr. Gadstow, who could really do with a new chimney. Not, of course, that I'm dismissive of your attention to the chancel, but if the fading paint could be tolerated for another year, then perhaps we might do some real good and put the money in the benevolence fund."

"I think that's a splendid idea." I knew from experience how very necessary it was to have a sound roof over one's head.

"You do? You don't think Miss Templeton will be much aggrieved?"

"Why would she mind if our efforts are diverted toward those who are truly in need?"

"I'm so glad you agree. These things can get so contentious when the clergy feel one way about something and the parishioners another."

"You're the rector. I should think you have the right to say what ought to be done with the money."

"One would think so, wouldn't one?"

From the armchair near the fire rose a snore.

We turned to see the Admiral dozing.

The rector and I smiled at each other, and he inclined his head toward the coal hod. "About my collections . . ."

I discovered then that the spirit of generosity that had lately expanded within my breast in regard to him did not extend to his specimens.

"I was thinking about my speedwell and wondered if there might be any significance in the fact that, upon reflection, I remember I found some in a meadow as well as by a marsh."

"There might be, depending upon the variety. I have always been much more interested in the *why* of things than the *what*, and it's quite curious that it should have grown in two places so wholly unlike each other. It's too bad you don't have comparison specimens of each. Then I might have been able to learn something from them."

"I've always simply thought that God puts plants where He wants them."

"I shouldn't say He doesn't, but is it any sin to wonder why? And how?"

"*How?* Some would say that borders on blasphemy, Miss Withersby. Or at the very least on cheekiness." His eyes were twinkling.

"So I've been told. But I can't see why. There must be reason in nature, must there not? Some purpose for a flower being where it is? The question doesn't seem so contradictory to faith if your only argument is believing that God placed it where you found it. Why should the *how* of it matter?"

He looked at me as he seemed to ponder that thought. "Are you wondering perhaps how God could use circumstance to His benefit?"

"Perhaps I am."

"An interesting question. Quite interesting. And worth some further thought. Do you mind if I write it—"

"Not at all. Please write it down." If I couldn't be a regular contributor to a journal, at least I was a regular contributor to the rector's sermons.

"I find . . . I hope you don't think me too forward, Miss Withersby, but I find such pleasure in conversing with a like-minded soul."

He seemed to expect some sort of answer. "As do I."

His face flushed. "That's very . . . heartening. Thank you."

The following Saturday, the day of the benefit for the parish's benevolent fund, arrived, and I found myself wondering if perhaps I had been too hasty in pronouncing myself recovered from my injury. The stuffiness of the glasshouse and the unrelenting noise of music and conversation soon conspired to make my head ache with nearly constant pain. I spent most of my time hiding behind a cluster of ferns. They were arranged in a pyramid in an especially dark corner, well clear of the curiosity of a fishtail palm about which everyone seemed to have to exclaim.

Mr. Stansbury waved at me from afar, and then he must have asked one of his staff to keep me supplied with refreshments, for a steady stream of tea and biscuits was sent my way.

The Admiral paced, as before, just outside the windows, a wintery breeze ruffling the hem of his cloak.

Father and Mr. Trimble stood beside an orange tree, lost in conversation. Every so often, Mr. Trimble's gaze wandered my way, and I would redouble my efforts to look blissfully unaware of them and perfectly healthy. I could only imagine what they were discussing. Most probably something much more important than the fern about which Miss Templeton was exclaiming.

I was much surprised when she congratulated me on the event. "Well done, Miss Withersby."

"I have to say that, in spite of my involvement, the whole thing did go off rather admirably."

"I will admit that I had a few doubts, but I resisted the urge to guide you, since I decided you must learn from doing. In order to marry either man, you must put it around that you could be an effective hostess. Now everyone recognizes that fact. I daresay you may start to attract the attention of even more men."

"You mean this is what I would do, should I marry?"

She nodded.

"For a living? As a matter of course?" Horror swirled in my stomach.

"What else did you think you'd be doing?"

"Thank heaven I'm not in this for a marriage. I can't marry. I can never marry. I won't. It's much too exhausting!"

"Come now, don't tell me you've become fainthearted."

"I would never get any work done if I had to read up on

giving balls and creating guest lists and come up with ideas for benefits and raffles."

"And you won't have to. Surely after this, your father will understand what peril awaits if he insists upon pushing you to matrimony. You hosted the extravaganza of the season."

"Come now, Miss Templeton, it was in fact you who came up with the plans and you who told me what to do."

"But he doesn't know that. Perhaps I can persuade the newspaper to write it up on the front page. Your father *does* read it, doesn't he?"

"I don't think that he—"

"Seeing it in print ought to make quite plain to him the danger with which he's flirting."

"It ought to . . ." It had to.

"It's just a matter of time. You might even wish to pack Mr. Trimble's bags for him when you get home! The man will soon be but a fond memory."

"Fond?"

"I do so like the cut of his hair and shape of his chin. If only he came from a better family. If only he was a gentleman."

"I think you miss the point!"

"I understand your point entirely. It's just that I have my own. If his family weren't so dreadful, he might do quite well in society."

That was the problem. If they weren't so dreadful, then he could go back to them. "Have you achieved any success in pushing him back to his family?"

"I'm awaiting a reply from an acquaintance in Essex. But one way or another, I assure you, your problems will soon be behind you."

As I gained my strength, though I could not seem to interest myself in a true ramble, my walks took me increasingly far from home, and I often happened upon the rector as he made calls on his parishioners. As long as we did not speak of plants or of his collections, I found him pleasant company, and though he could not converse with any knowledge on botany, he did have a bent toward philosophic discussion that I enjoyed. We discussed birds and stars and the failings of the local paper as well as parliament and Lady Harriwick's inexplicable fondness for obscure hymns.

"And what are your thoughts on children?" he asked one day at the beginning of December as we walked along.

My nose had gone cold, so I had tucked it into the folds of my muffler. I pushed the folds down with a gloved hand as I replied. "Children? I don't. Think of them, that is."

"You are your parents' only child?"

"I am."

"But you do *like* children?"

"I don't *dis*like them."

His smile hesitated for a moment, and then it came on full-fledged. "You're very different."

I laughed and birthed a cloud of condensation. "A species of my own. That's what Mr. Trimble says."

"I'm sure he means it in a kind way."

"I'm not."

"But truly, I find children quite add to life, don't you?"

I wondered why he was so set on speaking of children. We hadn't ever discussed the topic seriously before. Upon reflection I supposed, as a father of eight, they must never be far from his mind. "I would have to agree. If it weren't for children, we would all go extinct."

He blinked. "I suppose that's true . . . but I was speaking of children in particular, not as a . . . not as a group."

"In particular?"

"My children, for example. I find them very . . . very dear."

I found them rather loud, although I was quite sure it would be rude to say so.

When I said nothing, he continued, "Some people might find their number daunting, but they're not so difficult as you might think."

"With adequate water and enough sunlight, I suppose almost anything will grow."

"That's a very . . . philosophical way of looking at things. But . . . what I'd really like to say, however, is that I think we work well together, Miss Withersby."

We did. Although following along behind him and fixing the mess he'd made of his collection and labeling required far more work than I was used to doing.

"I was hoping you would do me the honor of helping me for many more years to come."

Years! I hoped not. My fingers would be worked to the nibs. But a gracious invitation required some sort of polite response. At least that's what Miss Templeton's etiquette book had said. And he was looking at me as if everything depended upon my words. Gracious. I hadn't noticed before what nice eyes he had.

"I'd be pleased, Mr. Hopkins-Whyte. Truly I would." I wouldn't. Not really, but he was a nice man. "Perhaps I could even come help you with your collections tomorrow." I gave up my hold on the muffler, and my nose settled once more into its folds.

He grasped his Bible more tightly. "Splendid! Just . . . just *splendid*, Miss Withersby."

After the rector left me, I stopped in at Overwich Hall on my way home. I was interested in a new orchid Mr. Stansbury had acquired. I knew I should have gone with someone—the Admiral or Miss Templeton—but as it was on my way home, and since I really did wish to see the orchid, I didn't think my lack of chaperone too grievous a sin.

Mr. Stansbury was not long in appearing and he seemed quite happy to see me. We spoke for a while about his growing number of specimens, and he showed me his new acquisition. He had taken my advice and written to one of my father's correspondents for assistance, and I was quite happy to verify he had in fact received exactly what he had paid for.

As I took my leave, he stopped me. "I'd just like to say, Miss Withersby, that I have quite enjoyed our time together. I hope you have done the same."

"I have, Mr. Stansbury." Especially when I did not have to look at his stumpery.

"You have done a great deal of good here."

I had not been able to persuade him from his stumps, but aside from that, I *had* gotten quite far in putting his glasshouse to rights. "I hope so, Mr. Stansbury."

"I consider what we have started here to be a long-term project, and it is my greatest wish that you would do me the honor of continuing with me what we have begun."

"I would be delighted to." Then maybe I could turn his stumpery into one of those grottoes of which Miss Templeton was always speaking. Or a garden. Surely he could be reasoned with.

"Before you agree with such alacrity, I must tell you, Miss Withersby, that as a result of an unfortunate illness in my youth, I am . . ." His ears had gone red at their tips. "Rather, that is, my doctor has told me quite plainly that I will never be able to . . ." He paused to clear his throat. "That is, fatherhood will never be a part of my life."

I wasn't quite sure what his particular situation had to do

with his interest in botany, but it clearly disturbed him. I put a hand to his arm. "If that is the case, then just think, Mr. Stansbury, your stumpery will never be endangered by the whims of your heirs."

"*Our* stumpery, Miss Withersby." He patted my hand. "I must say, you are a marvelously understanding sort of woman."

25

After leaving Overwich Hall, I stopped in at Dodsley Manor, but Miss Templeton wasn't in so I decided to walk home by way of a field. It had been too long since I had given myself the pleasure of such a long walk, and I was both exhilarated by my time out of doors and dismayed that there was so little by way of plants left to behold.

All told, I was rather pleased with myself. I'd done quite well both at helping the rector understand what he had collected and planning the next stages of Mr. Stansbury's acquisitions for his glasshouse. Soon I forgot the state of my head altogether and found myself climbing over rocks and scampering down a clough in order to see what might be found.

Had I remembered to remove my gloves, it might have been all right, but thinking of the Christmas season later in the month, I found some ivy to pick and holly as well. Soon my gloves were stained beyond redemption and my boots were thick with mud. But what did it matter? Who did I have to impress?

My foot slid across a stone and I fell onto my knees.

What a perfectly useless botanist I'd become in the past few months! Really, there was no point to me now. Having received no intimations of proposals, I was a failure at society just the same as I was a failure at botany. I might be dressed in the latest modes, but for what purpose?

I spent several hours wandering about before I turned my steps toward home. And when I did so, it was with the intention of calling a halt to the search for a husband.

Upon my return, Father called out from his study for me, and I went in to see him.

"I must say, Charlotte, you've done exceedingly well for yourself."

"I rather thought so. The rector's collection is just about sorted out and Mr. Stansbury's plants are coming along rather nicely. He just got a new orchid." I took off my gloves, swept a sheaf of papers from a chair, and sat.

My father was chewing on the tip of his mustache. "Only . . . I cannot quite work out what you would have me say . . ."

"About what?" I wrenched my boots off and set them down beside the chair.

"About the proposals."

"What proposals?"

"For marriage."

"Whose?"

"Yours."

"Mine!" *Mine?* "I'm quite astonished. Who has asked to marry me?"

"Why, the rector and Mr. Stansbury."

"Then you'll have to refuse them both."

"But you already accepted."

"I did?" *I had?* "Whose?"

"Both of them."

"*Both* of them? Why would I accept two of them when I'm not even interested in one of them? In any case, I find it quite hard to believe I agreed to marriage, considering I just saw both men today and neither mentioned anything of the sort."

Mr. Trimble had been working at his desk in the parlor, but now he left his work and came in to stand beside my father. "So you did speak with them . . . ?"

"Of course I did. I spoke with both of them, just the way you taught me to."

"Of what did you speak?"

"Mr. Stansbury talked of plants and his ridiculous stumpery and he said how he thought I had done a great deal of good and wasn't I happy there and what an honor it would be to continue what we had started."

"That would do it."

"Do what?"

"You must learn to hear what people aren't saying, Miss Withersby!"

"And how am I to do that if they don't say it? Really, Mr. Trimble, how could it be *my* fault that I fail to realize what people can't bother to put into words?"

"And of what did you and Mr. Hopkins-Whyte speak?"

My father held up a finger. "I just . . . can't quite . . . How did you find a proposal in all of that, young man?"

"He quite clearly made it in that bit about Miss Withersby being happy there and what an honor it would be to continue what they had started." He turned to me. "He did ask for some reply didn't he?"

Had he?

"*Did* you reply?"

"I did, but—"

"In the affirmative?"

"I said I would be delighted to continue—"

"And when she agreed, she accepted his proposal."

"But I agreed to nothing of the sort! How could I when I understood him to be speaking only of what he was speaking about?"

Mr. Trimble sighed a drawn-out, long-suffering sort of sigh, of the kind I wished very much to make myself. "And what did you say to the rector?"

"It's not what *I* said, because I'm quite clear about that. Apparently, it's what *he* said."

"Then what did he say?" He asked the question with an infinite reserve of patience, as if he were speaking to one of the rector's children.

"I . . . well . . . I've been working on the rector's collection, helping him to understand where the gaps are."

"Yes, but what did he say?"

What *had* he said? "Well, he . . . he spent some time talking about children and then asked whether I liked them very much and what I thought of his in particular, and then he said that we worked well together and that . . ." How had he phrased it? "That he hoped we could work together for many more years."

"And you said . . . ?"

"I said exactly what I didn't mean, which was that I'd be truly pleased."

"Then you accepted."

"Accepted *what*? He didn't even ask a question. He made a statement. He expressed a *hope*, not a proposal."

"Yes! He expressed a hope of union."

"Union? It was a hope of my fixing his mess and filling in his collections."

"He asked you to marry him, and you accepted."

"Well, then I *must* protest. How am I to be responsible for a reply when he didn't even ask a question?"

"You must always be careful what you say in unguarded moments, Miss Withersby. I know, from unfortunate experience, how even the simplest phrase can be misconstrued."

"I hardly know how anyone ever dares to speak at all if you cannot say what you think and are not allowed to mean what you say. Polite society is rather rude!"

"What are *you* upset about? All you women have to do is say yes. It's the man who has to summon the courage, and think of what must be said, and fix a time at which to do so. It's no wonder those men had a difficult time coming around to the point of it all."

"The point of it all? The point of it all is, if a man can't bring himself to ask me to marry him in no uncertain terms, then why should he consider himself worthy of my hand? Is there nothing worth speaking plainly?"

He was ignoring me. In fact, he'd already turned to my father, who was mumbling to himself and blinking quite rapidly. "And what did *you* say, Mr. Withersby?"

My father started and looked up at him. "Say? About what?"

"What did you say about the proposals?"

"Oh! Well . . . I . . . congratulated him. Them. What else was I to have done? Charlotte kept going on about finding a husband, and I just . . . "

I kept going on about finding a husband? "You're the one who forced me out into society to find a husband. The only reason I kept on with it was because I was sure you would soon change your mind once you realized all the work I had been doing. Only he"—I pointed a trembling finger at Mr. Trimble—"came in and *stole* my position. And then he did it all so much better than I did, and I just . . . I've tried so hard to be what you needed, and now I've come to understand that I'll never be the kind of daughter you want."

"You've always been the kind of daughter I want. It's just that I was made to realize you should have so much more than this."

"But this is what I want."

"It can't be."

"And why can't it? It's all I've ever had. All I've ever known. It's the only thing I'm good at."

"It shouldn't be."

"But it is. And I am. In spite of what BAAS thinks, in spite of what all the others insist, I am good at botany."

He was staring at me quite miserably. "How was it that we came to all of this?"

I knew how. "It's the Admiral's fault. All of it. So let him figure it out."

"Then . . . what shall I tell your husbands-to-be?"

"Tell them anything you want."

"But which one did you want to marry?"

"It doesn't matter. I don't care. The point was to find a husband and I did. Have I not fulfilled my Christian duty? What does it matter who he is?"

Father was looking at me now with pity. "But of course it matters. You'll have to live with him for the rest of your life."

I felt a sort of wild panic rise in my throat. I looked toward Mr. Trimble. "I suppose changing one's mind about a proposal isn't done."

He shook his head quite gravely.

"Then let's hope I'll be short-lived." I never once thought I'd be envious of Miss Templeton for that particular reason.

Father was frowning. "I'm not quite certain . . . Which proposal are you saying I should accept?"

Mr. Trimble sent me a long glance. "Have you no preference, Miss Withersby?"

"None." I faced either trying to come to terms with one man's stumpery or trying to put in order the collections of a haphazard clergyman while I cared for his motherless children. At least I had some experience at being motherless. "The rector."

Mr. Trimble's brow arched. "The rector? But Mr. Stansbury sits atop a veritable fortune. He might not be a gentleman, but he is not unworthy of consideration."

"Which underscores how very little you know me." The image of a bluebell danced in my head, but I refused to be taken in by the wild imaginings of a sheep farmer from New Zealand. Picking my boots up, I rose and stalked upstairs.

I had almost succeeded in forgetting that I was twice betrothed as I drew, from memory, Mr. Stansbury's new orchid. And then someone knocked on my door.

"Enter."

My father stepped into my room and looked around as if he had never seen it before.

I followed his gaze as he took in all the new gowns that hung like pressed flowers from their pegs and the stack of hatboxes by my washstand. His eyes finally settled on my illustration. He took hold of it and turned it round. "I don't think . . . I mean . . . there's something different about your drawing, Charlotte."

No thanks to Mr. Trimble. "I've been experimenting with a lighter grip on my pen and a more relaxed interpretation, but I've decided I like things better the way they were."

"No. You must continue in this style. It's magnificent work. Now . . . that fine young fellow downstairs persuaded me that since I must refuse one of your suitors, I should try to determine, as best as you can help me, which man you in fact truly wish to marry. He is not convinced you meant what you said in choosing the rector."

"In truth, I wish to marry neither of them. But if it's impossible to refuse them both, then I prefer you do the choosing."

"You must have some opinion of the matter."

"I have none."

"But there's a great contrast in the life you could expect to live with both of these men."

"I know that."

"And yet you've no preference?"

"With neither man would I be able to do my own work. I might be labeling specimens or ordering exotics from the colonies. I could be raising orchids or raising children, but I wouldn't be doing any illustrating and I wouldn't be writing any papers."

"Neither would you have to write books on how to make wax flowers."

"I didn't mind those so much. Not really. At least I could say that they were mine. I've written seven books on topics like that, you know."

"I do know. And I'm quite proud of your work . . . but we were speaking of your suitors. Perhaps if you told them of your work they would be amenable to your continuation of it."

"When? In between dinner parties or parish functions? It doesn't matter to me which man you choose, because in the end, the result is the same."

"And what result is that?"

"Don't you see? I will step into someone else's life as I give mine up in forfeit. Have you never considered that the Admiral was the normal one and that we were the eccentrics? Did you never think that perhaps we were the ones in the wrong, insisting that he give up what he loved in order to accommodate our ideas?"

"Charlotte, I wish I could—"

"All I wanted was to do my work in peace."

"You have. You can."

"Then why have you taken it all away from me?"

Not an hour later, Miss Hansford was sent upstairs to fetch me. "The Admiral's here, miss."

Maybe he would take care of the mess he'd created.

I walked into the parlor head held high to find the men gathered around a microscope consulting about something or other. I stamped my foot.

They started, turning about to face me.

"After allowing myself to be talked into this by you . . ." I glared at my father. "After allowing myself to be squired about by you . . ." I turned to the Admiral. "And you!" I stalked over toward Mr. Trimble. "I hope someone has devised a way to extricate me from this impossible situation."

Mr. Trimble held up a hand as I advanced toward him. "I had nothing, whatsoever, to do with this."

"You had everything to do with this. You are the one who taught me—*everything*! If I hadn't been so intent upon being polite and trying not to say what it was that I thought and denying everything I felt, then I wouldn't be in the situation of having to refuse two proposals."

"One proposal."

"What?"

"One proposal. What you ought to have said is that you were in the situation of having to refuse one proposal since you can accept the other one."

My father began to splutter. "I don't quite understand . . . is it two refusals we have to come up with or just the one?"

"One." Mr. Trimble looked at me as if daring me to object.

I decided to ignore him. "Two. I have decided to accept neither."

"Neither?" My father looked to the Admiral and then to Mr. Trimble. "But hadn't we decided to back the industrialist fellow?" My father was scratching at his ear.

The Admiral was shaking his head. "I thought we'd decided upon the rector. Least, that's what I decided after I've heard him preach these past months."

"It doesn't matter which of you decided what. *I* have decided that I'm not going to marry either man. So how shall we go about rejecting them? That's what I'd like to know."

For men who were so eager to push me into marriage, not one of them offered any advice.

"Father, since you accepted the proposals, I think you should reject them."

"Oh . . ." He sighed. "I don't know as how I ought to do that. I didn't really know you'd accepted two proposals, you see, and they might not understand either, seeing as how I don't really know how to explain it. It's probably best if you do it yourself."

I looked at the Admiral and Mr. Trimble in turn, but they both glanced away from me.

"Fine." I strode to the desk that had once been my own, took up a piece of paper, addressed it to Mr. Stansbury, and spoke aloud as I wrote. "Dear Mr. Stansbury, I won't be able to marry you after all. Please accept my regrets. Sincerely, Miss Charlotte Withersby." After blotting the ink, I folded up the letter, shoved it into an envelope, sealed it, and waved it about. "Mr. Trimble, will you please do me the favor of posting this?"

"I don't think that's such a good idea. Your letter provides no explanation."

"And what would you suggest that I say?"

The Admiral and my father were looking at him as if they too were much interested in his reply.

"I don't know. I simply think the honor of a proposal should be responded to in kind."

"You mean with a mumble-jumble that doesn't quite make plain what it is that I mean but leaves it to him to decipher?"

"Well . . . no. I think it best if . . . that is, you might consider telling him the truth."

"The truth? The truth is that I never had any intention of marrying anyone at all. The truth is that all I really want to do is finish my illustrations for father's volumes and get my paper published even though no one seems to want it. The truth is that I have been entirely miserable gadding about in slippers and fancy gowns while I waited for father to come to his senses and re-call me to work. The truth is that the only one I have been waiting for is you, Mr. Trimble."

"*Me?*"

"Yes! I have been waiting for you to leave so that I can return. The truth is that I have tried my best to fit in with science, for which my sex has apparently made me ill-suited, and I have done my best to fit in with society, for which my passion for botany has made me equally ill-suited. The truth is that I seem to fit neither here nor there, and I deem it best, at this moment, to take myself upstairs. If you will excuse me."

The men parted to let me through, and I made my way up the stairs. I got to the top before my tears started, and then I saw little use in trying to stop them.

26

The next morning, I put on my boots and walked across the fields to Dodsley Manor. I needed to speak to Miss Templeton.

It only took fifteen minutes for her to appear. She fairly burst into the sitting room. "What is it! It's only half past nine, and *you* know that I usually sleep until ten, so *I* know you wouldn't call unless it were really, truly urgent."

"I need your help. I've been offered two proposals, and I don't know how—"

"*Two* proposals? But I thought you hadn't meant to receive any."

"I hadn't. But I did. In the same day. Within an hour of each other."

"Then you'll simply have to refuse them."

"Apparently I have already accepted them."

"*Both* of them?"

I nodded.

Her hands flew to her mouth.

"So what am I to say?"

"Well . . . you can't refuse them now that you've accepted them.'"

"I'm going to have to refuse at least one of them!"

"But how did this happen? This is all the fault of Mr. Trimble, isn't it? If he would have done you the favor of leaving, then none of this would have happened. And I've just been told where he . . . Oh! I've half a mind to—"

"It father's fault. He never asked me to stay."

"I wouldn't let Mr. Trimble go as easy as that! Not after what I have to tell you about . . . " She stamped her foot. "Oh! I still haven't forgiven him for being so handsome. And neither should you!"

"I'm not going to. But all and still, I wouldn't have gotten nearly as far as I did if he hadn't taught me about conversing and dancing and . . ." And everything else. Perhaps he *was* the one to blame. I wouldn't have been nearly as attractive a candidate for marriage if he hadn't taken it upon himself to tutor me.

Miss Templeton was looking at me as if waiting for something.

"I don't know what to do."

"It's just not done, refusing a proposal you've already accepted. I mean, I suppose it has been done, although it was probably due to dire circumstances. I suppose Mr. Stansbury's fortune is in no danger of a collapse . . . ?"

"Probably not."

"And the rector isn't already married . . . ?"

"No."

She sighed. "I just don't know, then."

"I am a menace to polite society."

"I wouldn't say you're a menace exactly. I'd just say that you're always saying the most unexpected things."

"I suppose the best thing to do would be to . . . ?" I looked to her hoping for guidance.

She simply looked back at me.

"What would *you* do?"

"I wouldn't have accepted the proposals in the first place."

"That isn't very helpful to me in my current situation."

"No." She sighed again. "I suppose you have no other choice. You'll just have to tell them both the truth."

"That's what Mr. Trimble said."

Her eyes narrowed. "I hate him even more now."

I turned to leave.

"But Miss Withersby, I have to tell you what I learned about—"

I walked out the door without another word. Whatever it was would have to wait until I became unbetrothed.

Tell the truth.

It was so much easier said than done, because the truth was not very flattering. In spite of what I had shouted at my father and the Admiral and Mr. Trimble, the truth was that I had toyed with Mr. Stansbury and the rector, employing their affections for my own gain. And that's exactly what I told Mr. Stansbury as I spoke to him later that afternoon.

"For my own gain. Do you see?"

"Yes. And I see something more as well. I see that I have done the same to you, trying to woo you with orchids and stumperies so that you might make my solitary life a little less lonely. We could say I was using you in the same way that you were using me."

"I didn't realize we were both so mercenary. Did you?"

He laughed.

"Are you very disappointed?"

He looked at me for a long moment. "I am. But not, perhaps, in the way a jilted bridegroom should be."

I didn't know whether to be offended or very grateful.

"I don't know how I'm going to do without you now." He gazed around his glasshouse with a sigh.

"Just because I won't marry you doesn't mean I can't help you, does it?"

His face brightened. "I suppose it doesn't."

"Although . . . I probably shouldn't do it right this minute, because I still have to refuse Mr. Hopkins-Whyte's proposal."

"Two proposals to refuse? In the same day? That might just be a county record."

"I know." The words came out quite as miserably as I felt about the whole thing.

Mr. Stansbury's brow arched as a smile tilted his lips. "Then I'll have to compliment myself on courting the belle of the season."

I walked from Overwich Hall down the road toward the rector's, pausing frequently to admire a variety of seed stems on the way, and eventually I found myself on the rectory's doorstep. I knocked and received a muffled response to enter. Opening the door, I gasped when I saw the rector. He was sitting on the floor, specimens strewn about him.

"Miss Withersby! I hadn't expected you until later in the afternoon."

He started to rise, but I joined him instead, kneeling on the floor. "I know. I'm sorry, I—"

"Which is not to say that I'm not delighted to see you. There's no way that you can fail to see that I need you."

"I do realize that, and I certainly don't mind trying to help you . . . but I wonder if you really, truly need a wife."

"I assure you that I do. With eight children and—"

"Your children may need a mother, and you may need some help with your botanical collections, but forgive me for asking when I wonder if you really need *me*."

"But I am so happy and . . . and honored that you consented to—"

"And there's that as well. I didn't really understand that I was consenting, yesterday, to anything at all. At least nothing of a matrimonial nature."

He blinked his surprise, eyes widening. "But I assure you that I—"

"You asked me to help you with your collections. What I agreed to was that."

"But I meant—"

"I wonder, Mr. Hopkins-Whyte, if you actually meant anything else at all."

"What is it that you're saying, Miss Withersby?"

"I just think it quite clear that your needs include a botanical assistant and a mother to your children, but they don't really include an actual botanist. And that is what I am . . . and what I will probably always be, no matter how contrary to the designs of God and nature."

"When you say . . . What *are* you saying?"

"I'm saying that I think it best if we don't marry. I think you should, when you find the right woman, but that woman is not me."

He took a handkerchief from his pocket and swabbed his forehead. "I must say, I am quite relieved."

"Relieved?" That wasn't quite the sentiment I had expected.

"Oh! I didn't mean to offend. Not relieved that you're not going to marry me, but I am relieved that I won't have to keep up with this collection."

"Keep up with . . . ?"

"Not that I wouldn't, you understand. Of course I would keep up with my rambles, but I might not . . . I mean, since you wouldn't expect it of me . . ."

"You mean to say that you would have married me in order to feign an interest in something in which you really have no interest at all?"

"I wouldn't say I have *no* interest. I am a rector, you understand. And I should be delighting in God's creation as a part of the job, you might say."

"But must we all be spoken to through flowers? Why could not some of us, like you, find inspiration in actual words? What needs illustration to the rest of us, is revealed quite plainly to you. I should think you ought to take some pride in that."

Appreciation shone from his eyes.

"Is it any shame to your Creator if you do what you do best? Would it not be an affront if you did not?"

"Are you saying I do this poorly?" He was looking around at the specimens that overflowed his parlor.

"Quite frankly? Yes."

He smiled.

I smiled.

And then we both began to laugh.

Sometime later, as we both wiped tears from our eyes, he offered me a hand and helped me to standing. "A rector who isn't enamored of botany? Do you really think that proper?"

"If he's a rector who preaches wonderfully stimulating sermons and has eight children, he has plenty enough to do of a day. Those who would criticize you for not seeing to your collections would be churlish."

He glanced round at the papers and specimens that littered the floor. "What a mess I've made of everything. I suppose there's nothing worth saving . . . ?"

"I don't believe so. No." At long last I was free to express my true opinion.

"Then if I can stuff it all back into these drawers, I will burn it for kindling. I daresay it should last me until spring."

"I don't mind saying that I think it for the best."

He gazed into my eyes for a long moment. "Thank you, Miss Withersby. I cannot tell you how grateful I am for your honest words. I might have just kept on doing what I thought I ought to. How liberating it is to realize that I don't have to anymore."

When I returned to the house, it was with a clear conscience. But though I went to sleep in peace that night, I woke at five the next morning and couldn't return to my slumber. I tossed about for a while before I gave up. What I needed was a good ramble. At that early hour in the morning, I navigated by old habit. It wasn't until I'd left the house and was on my way down the lane, trying to button up my shooting jacket that I noticed it was my new one.

"Miss Withersby!" Mr. Trimble hailed me from the grasses beside the road.

"Mr. Trimble, I had not known you to rise so early."

"After working these weeks with your father, it's become a bad habit."

We walked along in silence for a while, and then I noticed him glancing at me. And quite frequently. But then why should he not stare? I knew enough about fashion now to know that I was quite singularly dressed. "This new shooting jacket is abominable. I had no idea it would turn out the way it did." It was cut entirely too close to the body for my comfort. I suppose that's what one got when one went to a dressmaker for a jacket.

"It's quite . . . it's truly . . . It's very fetching."

"It is?" I glanced down at it. "I wish it had deeper pockets. What I really need is a coat that will carry a flask and a pocket glass." I held them up for his view.

"Would you like me to carry them for you?"

I was about to demur and then decided to let him. He owed me that at least. And then I decided he owed me a little more, so I asked, "How is it that you know so much about so many things? The command of servants, the rules of conversation, and the vagaries of fashion?"

"I grew up among people for whom those mattered very much. It's the reason I left them. One of the things I like most about New Zealand is that a man is measured by his own character rather than that of his family."

"Perhaps I shall go there someday. It sounds like a place I would enjoy."

He sent me a sidelong glance. "I believe you would, Miss Withersby. You would like it very much."

After breakfast, I was wondering what I ought to do with myself. My quest for my old position had failed and I had no books to write or correspondence to undertake. As I was considering my relative position in the household, my father called Mr. Trimble and me into his study.

"I have to say, Charlotte, that I have heartily missed being able to speak to you of our work. I feel I might be closer to finishing my volumes if I had thought you wanted to speak of classification and orchids."

"But I did. I would have."

"Perhaps we can pick up where we left off, then."

I glanced at Mr. Trimble. If we picked up where we left off, did that mean he was leaving? Apparently I was to be given what I most wanted. But if that was the case, why didn't I feel happier? "I would be happy to do so, but . . . in all truth, didn't Mr. Trimble do a much better job of things than I did?"

"I suppose it depends upon the things to which you refer."

"If I may?" Apparently Mr. Trimble was not yet done with his explanations.

Father nodded.

"Perhaps I found a way to better organize your father's papers and manage his correspondence, but I haven't nearly the grasp of botany that you do. You are much more philosophic than I could ever hope to be."

Father was nodding. "It's true. I had high hopes for you, young fellow, but . . ."

"But a few short months of immersion in a topic cannot make up for a lifetime of familiarity."

I was confused. "So you're saying . . . ? What *are* you saying, Father?"

Mr. Trimble did not hesitate in answering. "I think he's saying that we all ought to do what we're best at. You can't tell me that management of the butcher's bills and your father's correspondence are things you truly missed?"

"No, but—"

"Or that you were wishing you had been the one to release Mrs. Harvey from employment. Or complete the manuscript for that book on wax flowers."

"No, but—"

"Then why can't I do those things, which I am in fact quite good at, while you do those things that you do best?"

"But I—"

"My being capable at those things should not give you offense. We can't all be brilliant botanists, can we?"

"No, we . . . I mean . . ." What did I mean? And what did I want?

He took up several papers from Father's desk and moved toward the door. I followed him. "Does that mean you're going to stay?"

"For now."

It was that *now* that I wasn't quite clear on. "But what about your family? Don't you have some sort of obligation to them?"

"To my family? Strictly speaking, no."

"Then what about your sheep?"

"It's what I have a farm manager for. I am entirely at your disposal. Now, then. If you will excuse me, I need to see to some bills." He pulled the door shut behind him.

I turned back toward my father. "Is he really going to stay?"

"I should think so. He said he was going to, didn't he?"

A decision which would have caused me no little consternation a short month ago was filling my breast with . . . What was it, that welling up of . . . was it . . . It couldn't be elation, could it? If it was, surely it was because I had been given back my position. And more than that, I had been freed to do it.

27

I spent the day with my father, going over his notes. We enjoyed a lively debate over lunch with Mr. Trimble regarding the classification of the bloodwood: to wit, was it or was it not a *Eucalyptus*. Mr. Trimble had the temerity to suggest that it was not.

As we repaired upstairs for the night, we made plans to meet for a ramble in the morning. When we woke, however, a storm was blowing in from the west, and Mr. Trimble convinced us that it was wiser to stay inside. And so I worked on an illustration at the table in the parlor while Mr. Trimble worked at his desk with a microscope, and it was midmorning before I even realized I had let my tea go cold.

Someone pulled the bell around noon, and I heard Miss Hansford's steps in the hall. Several minutes later she hurried toward me and whispered, "There's a Countess of Cardington, here to see a Mr. Edward Trimneltonbury. I told her there is no such person here, but she insisted that there was. There isn't . . . is there?"

"Not that I've ever seen. Perhaps she's confused our Mr.

Trimble with this Bury man. Are you quite sure she's sound of mind?"

She leaned close. "Not only that, but she's quite certain about him being here too."

"Can't you tell her he's not here?"

"She says he is."

Mr. Trimble was examining a slide and did not give any appearance of hearing our discussion. I considered the woman apparently standing at our door, determined to enter. There was nothing so irritating as a person insisting upon the veracity of the completely impossible. "In such cases, Miss Hansford, it is best to be polite but firm."

I picked up my brush, trying to remember where it was that I had stopped.

She sighed and lifted her chin as if in preparation for battle. "I'll do my best, Miss Withersby." Squaring her shoulders in a way that would have made the Admiral quite proud, she went out toward the front hall.

Not long after, a great squawking arose.

"What's this fuss about?" Mr. Trimble asked from his desk. "Has Miss Templeton come by again?"

"For a man who insists upon kindness as the mark of a gentleman, you evidence a remarkable lack of that particular virtue."

"You confuse kindness with forbearance, Miss Withersby. The former may be exercised upon any occasion, while the latter may, by overuse, eventually find itself exhausted, with no virtue attributed to its former possessor."

A din of rising voices issued from the hall.

His eyes narrowed. "That's not Miss Templeton."

"It's some woman—the Countess of Cardington, Miss Hansford called her—inquiring after a Mr. Somebody-bury and insisting that we are harboring the man. I assured her we . . . Are you quite well, Mr. Trimble? You're looking rather peaked."

"The Countess of Cardington?"

"Do you know her, then? Perhaps you can persuade her to be reasonable about the matter."

Before he could rise from his chair, a clatter of footsteps approached and a woman wearing a fur-trimmed mantle and muff burst into the room.

"Edward! My dearest!" If Mr. Trimneltonbury could not be found, Mr. Trimble seemed a worthy substitute, for she sailed up to his desk and then turned her cheek to him for a kiss.

What's more, he did it. He rose and kissed her!

Then he turned to me. "Mother, may I introduce you to Miss Withersby? Miss Withersby, Lady Cardington."

Mother . . . ? That woman was his mother? If she were Lady Cardington and a countess, then would that not make him a . . . sir? At the very least? The question wasn't so much where was Mr. Trimneltonbury, but rather who was Mr. Trimble? "Mr. Trimble, I must confess that I don't quite—"

A commotion arose again from the hall, punctuated by an exclamation from Miss Hansford. Then a younger woman appeared and joined the countess. She was one of those prim, elegant varieties of the female species whom I had become accustomed to seeing among Lord Harriwick's hunting parties.

I turned to Mr. Trimble. "This must be . . . Is she a sister?"

"No." When the younger woman offered up her hand, he took it and kissed it. Then he turned to me, a look of resignation and unhappiness at work upon his face. "This is my fiancée, the Lady Caroline Dunsmere. Lady Caroline, may I introduce to you, Miss Withersby."

Fiancée? "But . . ."

There was a great cry and a show of tears from the younger

woman. Mr. Trimble made many convincing sounds and shows of encouragement as he patted her on the arm and concurrently nodded in response to everything his mother said. And then . . . they were gone. All of them. Mr. Trimble, his mother, and his fiancée.

When my father came out of his study a short while later, I was sitting in my chair, clutching my paintbrush, trying to figure out what had just happened.

"I discovered the most delightful article about orchids in southern Africa." He glanced about. "Where is Mr. Trimble?"

I looked up at him. "He's gone. And I'm afraid . . . at least, that is . . . I expect that he's not coming back."

Miss Templeton showed up later that afternoon, clutching a letter. "I received the most disturbing news about Mr. Trimble, and you didn't give me the chance to tell you the other day, but here!" She thrust it at me.

I turned and walked toward the fire. It was distressing how drafty the room was this winter. I fastened another button on the Admiral's shooting jacket. With the new one fitting so tightly, I hadn't been willing to give the old one up. "I suppose you're going to tell me that he's Lord Such-and-So or Sir Somebody?"

Her mouth dropped open. "But I've only just heard. How did you know?"

"They came to get him. His family did. And now they're gone."

"Gone? Gone where?"

"Home. Back to wherever it was that he came from."

"Eastleigh."

"It's to the east, then, I presume?"

327

She nodded. "In Essex." She sat in a chair as she chewed on her lip. "He didn't tell you anything about his family?"

"Nothing."

"He didn't even hint at who they were?"

"No."

"And here we were thinking he came from some disreputable sort of people! I always hated him, of course, but after I met him, I was almost inclined to feel sorry for him. I actually thought he was someone honorable, trying his best to live down his family's name. And then I read this!" She brandished the letter. "He's probably sitting at the queen's own table right now, laughing at all of us."

"Laughing?" Was he really?

"You ought to have been meaner to him, Miss Withersby. We ought to have been crueler. I just knew there was something about him!"

"So did I."

"You did? I always thought . . ." Her words trailed off as she peered at me. And then she got up and came close to hand me a handkerchief.

I waved it off. Little good it would do me now. I swiped at the tears dripping down my cheeks.

"I really truly did always hate him," she insisted.

"He was going to stay. He told us that himself, just yesterday. He was going to do all the bills and all the correspondence and help me color my illustrations, and I was going to be able to help father with his research. He was quite wonderful, really, with papers and people—"

"People?"

"—and roofs and—"

"Roofs?"

"—and servants and—"

"What did he do with the servants?"

"He did everything—everything I'd never done. And then he just . . . Now he's gone."

She gathered me into her arms and let me weep.

I'd had one perfect day in which I'd believed there might yet be hope. I had been led to dream there might be more for me. But now it was gone. I was relegated to the bills, relegated to correspondence, and to wax flowers. The rector's words echoed in my thoughts. *"I might have just kept on doing what I thought I ought to. How liberating it is to realize that I don't have to anymore."*

What if I didn't have to keep on doing those things either? What if I could choose? Why should I have to figure out how to make wax flowers? Or knit them? Or twist blossoms from crepe paper?

Because those kinds of books paid—that's why. And if we wanted to keep ourselves in food, then we needed the money.

Mr. Trimble was gone, and I had my work back, but now I was ruined for it. I wanted more. Or *less*, to be accurate about it. I wanted less of what wasn't botany and more that was science. I wanted to be recognized for my work. I wanted to be published.

In short, I'd accomplished what I'd set out to do. My wish had been granted, I'd gotten rid of Mr. Trimble. But I no longer wanted what I'd had. What was wrong with me?

Whatever it was couldn't be cured by tinctures or tea. Nor could it be cured by study. I found that I fairly despised the very plants that had once given me so much pleasure. I marched past stubbled fields and open meadows without suffering the temptation to pick even one plant.

I took a hard look at the notes and specimens and illustrations that had once more grown into piles on the desk around me. What good had any of my work done me? What good had it done anyone? Was there nothing of any lasting meaning or value? Had I made the world a better place through my efforts or given anyone a better, truer glimpse of God?

My father walked by the desk one day as I was gazing at a specimen. "There you are. I was wondering, could you help me with something?"

Is that all I was good for? Helping someone *else* do something? "Yes, of course." Is this all that I could expect from life? Even the two men who had proposed to me had couched that honor in terms of my assisting them. Did no one want me for who I was instead of for what I could do?

And why was it that I was expected to help everyone else and no one was expected to help me? That didn't seem quite fair. Christian duty, of course, required sacrifice on the part of everyone, but if that was the case, then everyone ought to be sacrificing something and everyone's needs would in turn be taken care of. But it felt as if I were the only one doing the difficult bits while everyone else reaped the benefits of my labor.

All in all, I had been in much better spirits when I hadn't been aware just how much I was being taken advantage of! My attempt at pretending an interest in marriage had ruined me for reality.

Father received a letter from Mr. Trimneltonbury a week after his abrupt departure. He handed it to me after he was done with it, but I simply dropped it into the dustbin.

"Rather extraordinary, really. Imagine, we had the son of an earl here under our roof the whole time."

Yes. Rather extraordinary that he idled away his hours writing letters and firing cooks and fixing roofs. And quite extraordinary that I should have believed him to be who he said he was. A sheep farmer. A colonial. An honorable man.

"I must say he was a fine young fellow, though." He glanced over at me. "He did some good work here."

I said nothing.

"I rather miss him. Don't you?"

I closed my book, stood, and shook out my skirts. "I think I'll go for a ramble."

A letter arrived for me the following day. I was occupied by finishing Mr. Trimble's drawing of that spider orchid. I couldn't seem to get it quite right. Miss Hansford had given the mail to my father, and he passed a letter to me. "From Edward. I rather miss him."

"What . . . what did you say?"

"Edward. It's from Edward, and I said I missed him."

It was the first time my father had bothered to remember one of his fine young fellows' names. A tremor shook my hand, and my paintbrush spread a swath of red across the paper before I could stop it. I would have to start all over. Unfastening the paper from the easel, I tore it in two and then crumpled the halves and threw them into the fire.

"Aren't you going to read it?"

If I had been alone, I'm not certain what I would have done with it, but for my father's sake I slit the seal and began to read.

Dear Miss Withersby,

I hardly know what to say or where to begin. I realize I have behaved terribly, and yet, in my defense, I presented myself as I truly am: a sheep farmer from New Zealand with a passion for botany.

331

Everything I told you about myself was true. My family is profligate. Our fortunes have diminished to a regrettable level. My brother's gambling led to the unfortunate circumstance of his proposing a duel to protect his honor. To my family's eternal shame, I tried to stop him—for which efforts I was exiled to a family holding in New Zealand. It was in boarding the ship for the colony that I met your father.

I did try to tell him I was a Trimneltonbury, but even during that brief, first meeting he was already calling me Trimble. I don't care to be known as my father's son, and so Trimble seemed as good a name as any other.

You know everything about my time in New Zealand. You know I discovered a penchant for sheep and how I further developed my interest in botany. Though you may try to convince yourself otherwise, please know that I also developed a penchant for you.

While I told you no lies, I did not tell you all my truths, and I must own my faults. My duty and affections are engaged to Lady Caroline and were before I left. I would ask you to forgive me, but I have not acted honorably and do not expect that you would grant such a favor. To do so would be a forbearance so great that I would have no other option but to call it a kindness. And that I do not deserve. My only regret from my time in Overwich is the way in which it ended.

Please do not forever hold my sins against me, and I shall strive to make myself worthy of your kind regards.

I remain ever, as always, sincerely yours,

Edward Trimneltonbury

"What does he say?"

"Nothing." I bent toward the fire and fed it to the flames, as I should have done from the first.

I was rummaging through my dresser later that day when I put a hand to that sketch he had once done of me as a bluebell. I traced his bold, graceful strokes with a finger and then pressed the paper to my bosom as tears leaked from my eyes.

A bluebell.

I considered the drawing for a moment and then propped it up against the wall. Such talent shouldn't be put to waste.

28

On New Year's Day, I roused myself from bed to accompany Father on the first ramble of the new year. It had been my mother's favorite day. Though there was hardly anything to be seen and nothing worth collecting, she had always spoken with delight about what was to come. Of the flowers that would bloom in the spring. Of species just waiting to be discovered.

She had energized our family with her enthusiasms and her vigor. But as if she were a specimen poorly pressed, I was at pains to come up with any adequate description of her essence. She had lived among us, she had enlivened us once. Now she was gone. It was difficult to find much to anticipate in the year that lay ahead; it seemed to promise nothing more than the years that lay behind us.

It was one of those days that dawns heavy, morning mists rising from the fields as clouds descended at the same time. Caught up in trying to find a Lenten rose, I came to gradually realize I had left my father behind.

I hurried back to him and held some tree branches out of the way. "I'm sorry. I wasn't thinking. Forgive me."

"There's nothing to forgive."

We did, eventually, find a field of Lenten roses. I bent to take up some samples while my father rested as he leaned against a fence.

"I think, my dear Charlotte, that perhaps I was wrong in pressing you to marry. That said, I am quite capable of managing my work. I wasn't at first . . . after your mother died. If it had not been for you, I don't know what might have happened to us . . . what would have happened to me. But you've been carrying the burden of our work—" he paused to clear his throat— "the burden of *my* work, for far too long. Though I can't deny that I enjoy your company and appreciate your contributions, when it comes to it, I'm a man grown, who ought to be able to look after himself."

"I didn't mind doing it."

"I know you didn't."

"I wanted to do it."

"I know you did. Your mother would have been so very proud of you. But the point is, you should not have had to do it all. Not by yourself. For that I am very sorry."

Slipping my arm through his, we proceeded on together.

The Admiral paid us his weekly visit that Friday.

He greeted my father with a glance, but it was me upon whom his gaze settled. "I've come to offer my congratulations."

Congratulations? "To me?" Had I accepted *another* proposal?

"To you." He was very nearly smiling as he placed a copy of the *Proceedings of the Botanical Society of London* before me and opened it to the Letters to the Editor section.

"What is it?" My father came over to join us.

"It's a letter to the editor by Charlotte. The first of the bunch!"

By me? "I never . . . I never submitted one." But in spite of all knowledge to the contrary, there it was. The letter I had thought Mr. Trimble was writing on behalf of himself had my name beneath it, not his. Miss Charlotte Withersby. "I've been published?"

The Admiral clapped me on the back. "You've been published."

Father took the journal from him and read it, nodding all the way. Several *Yes, yes, I see*s marking his progress. "Very fine work! If I weren't so involved with my volumes, you might have convinced me to join you in the investigation of distribution." He took the proceedings with him over to the sofa and began to page through it.

I'd been published. My own words, in my own name. True, Mr. Trimble had cut their number by half, but the result was more than I might have hoped for. I wished he were here to thank.

"In any case, it seems I've been prevailed upon to hold a dinner party."

He had? "By whom?"

"Your Miss Templeton. She said it would be just the thing to help you get over Mr. Trimble's departure."

"I don't need to be helped to get over anything, as I haven't gotten under anything to begin with."

He raised a brow, as if he could not agree with me.

"It is, however, quite kind of her to think of me."

He rocked back on his heels as he gazed about the room. "And what are you working on now?"

"Something I had noticed this summer past. But with all of the parties and balls I've been attending . . . and Mr. Trimble's presence . . . I hadn't had the chance to write it up for Father."

"Why don't you write it up for yourself?"

"I should think the idea is more important than the person

who writes it. With Father's name on it, the society ought to publish it immediately."

"Contrary to family opinion, I never despised botany, my dear. It's simply that I liked sailing better. I'm a fellow of the Royal Society, and—"

"You are?"

"I am. Don't be so astonished. I always welcomed botanists to my staff when I served in Her Majesty's Navy. And I've continued to follow the development of our science."

"You did? You have?"

He continued to speak. "In my opinion, there is nothing so vexing as an important opinion muddled by an obscure presentation. Perhaps *I* could help your father with his writing. If I can help lend a certain—frankly, needed—clarity to his words, then I would consider that I have done my duty by science."

"His works lack in clarity?"

"There appears to be an unconscious kind of obfuscation at work when a writer sits too close to his subject."

"But . . . the author of most of those articles was me."

There was no little kindness in his gaze as he looked upon me. "Yes. I know."

"Are you saying I'm not a good writer? That I've been doing my father a disservice?" There was a quaver to my voice that I couldn't control.

"No, dear child. I'm saying that sometimes the danger is to gaze unseeing at the solution that's right in front of you." He coughed.

"I was only trying to help you, in bringing you out into society, but I can see I have done you wrong. In spite of society's dictates, in spite of convention, this is your calling, just as the sea was mine. And it has done neither of us any good to pretend otherwise, has it. That doesn't mean I can't take pleasure in a bit of botany now and then or that you might not be able to find some happiness in the companionship of a good man—just so long as I can keep my sloop and just so long as you can keep on with your work. On our own terms. Not on anyone else's."

I rose on my toes and kissed him on the cheek. "You are a good man."

He harrumphed, though the tops of his cheeks had gone pink and he fumbled about his pockets for his pipe. "Good man in need of a good smoke, I should say, so I'll take myself away."

"Not too far, please."

Miss Templeton came the next day, a Saturday, to plan the Admiral's dinner party. She tried to cheer me with her commentary on the town's doings, and I tried to cheer her with evidence of my command of etiquette.

We stood together at the back of the Admiral's parlor a week later, during the evening of his party. "You would have made quite a fine Mrs. Stansbury or Mrs. Rector, Miss Withersby. I have to say that you are much improved from the first night we met."

I linked my arm through hers. "And I must say that I wish you didn't have to be a Mrs. Anybody."

She sighed as she laid her head on my shoulder. "I know. I share your sentiment, but one must do what one must do."

"Have you decided, then, on a husband?"

"I am left with the son of Father's friend, so I shall have to make him fall in love with me."

"That should not be difficult."

She patted my arm. "You are too kind, Miss Withersby. I've always said so." A certain vigor and enthusiasm seemed absent from her words, and her gaze was fixed on the far corner, where her father was speaking to Mr. Stansbury.

After all of the dinners and concerts and other events that I had attended, the image that remained pressed into my memory was that of Miss Templeton and Mr. Stansbury together. His head bent toward her. She with her chin tipped toward him, laughing. And that gave me an idea. She had tried, in every way possible, to help me with my plan. Why, then, should I not do the same for her?

I asked the Admiral to take me to Overwich Hall on Monday. As he excused himself to walk down by the river, I asked for Mr. Stansbury and was escorted out to the glasshouse. When my presence was announced, Mr. Stansbury looked up from a notebook in which he was writing. A smile lit his eyes.

"I hope I'm not intruding."

"Not at all. What might I do for you?"

Though I had rehearsed what I wanted to say, I found I could not quite remember how I ought to start. So I dithered. "The orchids are doing well?"

He turned from me to look out at them. "They are. You were right. Given the proper setting, they've begun to thrive. I have much to thank you for."

I did not feel the need to hear of his gratitude, and remembering the topic of our last conversation, I did not wish to linger on those things he owed me, so I resorted to the Admiral's favorite trick. "There is no way in which to be delicate about this matter, so I shall simply say it."

"By all means. I would hope that after all of this time we are friends enough for that."

"I was so hoping you would say that. Or something similar."

One of his brows peaked.

"You had once mentioned to me your . . . unfortunate . . . your . . ." How did one speak of such things?

Comprehension bloomed on his face. "Ah. You speak of my condition."

"Yes. Your condition. What I've come to find out is how certain you are of that diagnosis. What I need to know is . . . well . . . sometimes, you see, you can think a plant quite sterile, and all of a sudden, one spring, for reasons unknown, the snow disappears to reveal acres of them. Do you see what I mean?"

"Yes. But no. Such is not the case with me. I will never be able to reproduce."

"But how do you know it?"

"I have several doctors' opinions on the matter, and they were all quite certain."

"My father is a scientist, Mr. Stansbury, and I hope you won't think me impertinent, but on occasion, even he has been mistaken about matters in which he has no little expertise."

"I appreciate your concern. Beyond the doctors' diagnoses, you might say I put their theory to the test."

"So . . . you mean to say you've proved it?"

"In a manner of speaking." He paused as he cleared his throat. "You are a most uncommon woman, Miss Withersby. You do understand that this doesn't fall within the definition of polite conversation."

"I do know that, Mr. Stansbury. And I do apologize, and I hope you won't feel the need to protect my finer sensibilities, for I've discovered these past months that I truly don't have any."

He laughed. "How I would have enjoyed being married to you. We might have caused quite a scandal saying all the things we're not meant to say."

"It *is* rather a shame. I always found you quite congenial."

"Thank you. That's one of the kindest things anyone has ever said about me. Please believe that if I was not certain of my condition, then I would not have felt compelled to tell you."

"I am so very glad. I cannot tell you how relieved I am."

"Relieved that I can never—?"

"Yes. I'm . . . I'm absolutely delighted!"

"I wish I could say the same."

I could not wait to tell Miss Templeton what I had discovered, and so I went in haste to Dodsley Manor and asked if she might see me. Once shown to her room, I could not bear to keep the news to myself. "I've found the perfect suitor for you."

"You've found the perfect suitor? *You've* found the perfect suitor for *me*? Where?"

"Here."

"Here? Here in Cheshire?"

"Right here in Overwich."

"Is there someone new come to town?"

"No."

"Then do I know him?"

"Quite intimately."

"I must protest. I know no man in that manner!"

"It's someone quite perfect for—"

"But I've already told you, I shall only marry someone who adores me—someone who shall be enraptured with me for the rest of my abbreviated life."

"What if I told you that you might marry and live as long as God allows, without fear that you will ever die in childbirth?"

"Don't tease, Miss Withersby. It isn't kind."

"I'm not teasing."

"You do understand that I'm not interested in marrying Mr. Carew."

"Mr. Carew?" He was ninety years old, if he was a day.

"And I'm not interested in marrying Mr. Robinson, because I've become quite convinced he has consumption, even if he won't admit it. I wouldn't want it said that I married only because I was anticipating my husband's certain death. That would be too much like cheating, don't you think?"

"That thought had never occurred to me."

"I won't have less just because I might not live long enough to enjoy it. I have made that clear, haven't I? I will marry my handsome prince."

"On that point you've been quite clear."

"Then I confess that I have no idea who you've found for me."

"Mr. Stansbury."

"Mr. . . . *Stansbury?*" She blinked. "But he's not . . . he's . . . He proposed to you. He doesn't want me. And my one condition is that—"

"Yes, I know. Your one condition is that your groom be absolutely, madly, in love with you."

"Exactly. I know you're very clever, quite a bit more clever than I am, so I hope you won't take offense when I say I don't see how Mr. Stansbury meets that condition."

"He doesn't love me. He loves you."

"And still, he made his proposal of marriage to *you.*"

"Only because he can't have children, and he thought, my being rather older than the normal debutante, that I wouldn't mind."

"He can't . . . ? What do you mean he *can't* have children?"

"I mean to say he's incapable of it."

"Incapable . . . ?" Her brow furrowed, and then she gasped as her features rearranged themselves. "Oh. Oh! He's *incapable.* Is that what you're trying to say?"

"Yes."

"Oh. I see. And he thought it wouldn't bother you, being so old, but . . . where do I come in again?"

"You come in because he would never have considered that you would want him, if you knew about his condition."

"That's ridiculous! Of course when he first came here, I thought him uncouth, just like everyone said, but now I've come to know him."

"And his condition makes him perfect for you. That's what I've been trying to say."

"There's only one problem."

"But there can't be. It's too perfect."

"I think, in fact, there is."

"What is it?"

"I think, perhaps . . . I've become besotted by *him*! Oh, dear. What shall I do? It's all well and good to be adored, but to love someone in return? I don't . . . I haven't . . . That requires no little work!" Her chin began to tremble.

"Are you going to . . . Don't cry." I didn't have a handkerchief to offer her. "Please don't. I thought to make you happy, not to cause you sadness."

"But he would want to love me, wouldn't he? He's that kind of man. Oh! I can just see it now. The horror!"

Horror?

"What have you done?"

"I only wanted to help."

"Now I can't be brave and noble and be done with things before I've messed them up. Don't you understand? I'd have to . . . I'd have to *love him back*."

"But I truly think that he loves you."

"And I truly think that I love him! And it's all just too terrible for words."

"I don't quite understand—"

"You don't have to tell me I ought to be deliriously happy. I know I should be, but I just can't find it in my heart to be so just now. I hope you won't take offense if I ask you to leave."

"Of course not. You know I would never—"

"Then, please. Leave."

I walked back home in a sort of daze. I couldn't comprehend what had just happened. Hadn't Miss Templeton's fear been that she would die in childbirth? And hadn't I just given her a way in which to avoid it, and by marrying a man she claimed to love?

Why then wasn't she happy?

29

I puzzled over Miss Templeton that evening and through the next morning, but I came no nearer an answer. And then, that afternoon, she paid me a call. She was wearing what I had come to know was her favorite gown, of rosy orange silk with a lace-lined bodice and sleeves. She wanted to know would I come with her to Overwich Hall.

"I sent a note to ask Mr. Stansbury if we might come see his newest acquisitions and he's invited us to tea."

"But . . . but . . . I didn't think you'd ever want to see me again after what you said yesterday."

"Don't be foolish. Of course I'd want to see you again. I apologize for my hysterics. I was just frightened. You see, all my life I'd planned on dying, not on living. So to imagine that possibility presenting itself so suddenly and with a man I've come to . . ." A blush swept her cheeks. "In any case, you can see how it would be quite disconcerting. And how many things would have to be rethought. I'll have to convince my father and . . ."

"I hadn't really considered—"

She patted my hand. "Of course you hadn't. Because you are my dearest friend. You've offered me a gift I could never have imagined, and I didn't even have the courtesy to thank you for it. So thank you. And don't worry about Papa. I can talk him into anything." She leaned over to kiss me on the cheek. "Now then. Shall we go? Have you your gloves?"

We were in the carriage and very nearly to Overwich Hall when I realized that, though I had told Miss Templeton everything about Mr. Stansbury, I had never said anything about her to him. I gasped. "He doesn't know!"

"Who? Who doesn't know what?"

"Mr. Stansbury. He doesn't know about you. You know everything about . . . about *him* . . . and about how he's in love with you, but he doesn't . . . I didn't tell him about *you*. I'm so sorry. I've ruined everything."

"No. No, don't be sorry." She clasped my hand in hers. "You've done wonderfully. You've done perfectly. There would be no fun in it if you hadn't left something for me to do."

The carriage turned off the road and as it made its way up the drive, Miss Templeton drew a deep breath. "Is my hat straight? Are my cheeks too pale?"

"They're—"

"Oh, don't answer. But would you do me the favor of speaking to the butler? I don't know that I can do it just now. I've been dreading a betrothal for so long that I hardly know how to enjoy it. But I can. I must." She closed her eyes. "I *will*."

"You are."

She blinked as if in surprise, and then she broke out in a radiant smile. "I am, aren't I?"

The butler took us down the hall into the glasshouse and announced our presence. Mr. Stansbury appeared at the end of the building, from a grove of ferns. Miss Templeton nearly swooned beside me. As we stood watching him approach, she reached out and clutched at my arm. Then she whispered a word to me. "Adah."

"Adah?"

"That's it. That's my name."

"Your name is Adah?"

She nodded though she did not take her eyes off him. "I must claim it now, mustn't I, since I'll have to live with it." She lifted her chin, though it trembled.

"Adah is a lovely name, Miss Templeton."

"I never thought so before, but . . . do you think it will do?" She tore her eyes from him and looked at me beseechingly.

"I think it will do just fine."

As Mr. Stansbury reached us, she released her grip on my arm and extended her hand toward him.

He took it into his own, brought it to his lips, and kissed it. "Are you well, Miss Templeton?"

"Oh, yes. I'm quite the happiest I've ever been, Mr. Stansbury." Her smile was tremulous, but wonder lit her eyes. "Thank you *ever so much* for asking."

Neither of them moved, and still he kept hold of her hand. She glanced up at him. "And you?"

"Me?"

Her smile burst forth like the sun, and she threaded her arm through his. "Yes *you*, dear man."

I felt quite extraneous as they proceeded up the aisle leaving me to investigate his new palm quite on my own.

February plodded past with its long, dreary days. I was hoping to hear about a paper I had decided to submit to one of the journals. I told our publisher I would not be doing a book on wax flowers. They mailed back, asking if I would do one on knitted flowers instead. Seeing as how I did not knit and did not plan to learn, I declined that offer as well.

Mr. Trimble's spider orchid finally bloomed. As I knelt on the floor beside the Wardian case, I discovered that he had been right. It looked nothing like the illustration of its type. It was both more and less than I had anticipated. As he had predicted, the flower had bloomed below the leaves, and the petals did, in fact, droop. I spent a few moments admiring its form, and then I moved it into indirect sunlight, where it would be happiest, and went on about the day's work.

Though I continued to receive many invitations to dinner parties and dances, with Mr. Trimble's departure, work had quickly consumed me, and I found myself venturing forth less and less, which suited me just fine.

One morning in mid-March, while I was working on an illustration, the bell sounded at the door.

Miss Hansford was out doing the marketing, and I was not at all happy to have my work interrupted as I went to the door and pulled the latch. "Yes? What is it?" My annoyance died away when I saw it was not the morning post. It was Mr. Trimble.

He bowed. "Miss Withersby."

I nodded.

He looked more refined than when he had lived with us. He was wearing a grey top hat with an impeccably turned-out frock coat and a wide cravat tied up in a knot beneath his chin. "May I come in?"

I stepped aside, let him through the door, and gestured toward the parlor.

He took off his hat with a nod. Stepping into the room, he surveyed it as if he'd somehow missed its tight, drafty quarters.

Papers and journals were once again piled haphazardly about the room.

"You can see we're back to our old habits."

The corner of his mouth lifted in a smile.

I now realized that, as hostess, the burden of conversation fell upon me. "Are you well, Mr. Trimble?"

"I am, thank you."

Wasn't that just like him, to lecture me about speaking in questions and then not follow his own advice? "It's rather fine weather for this time of year, isn't it?"

"It is. Although I've been told rain is much more preferable to a botanist than fair weather."

"In the summer."

He blinked, as if startled. "Pardon me?"

"Rain in the summer is much more preferable. In the winter it's only depressing."

"Forgive me. I must have misremembered how you—"

"You must be anxious to speak to my father. I'll go get him for you." I turned in the direction of the study, but he grabbed hold of my elbow.

"*Please*, Miss Withersby. I would much rather speak honestly about—"

"It was you, if *I* remember correctly, Mr. Trimble, who taught me that people generally never say what it is that they're really feeling and that no one expects to be told the truth. I don't see why you should apologize for following that social convention."

"It was deplorable of me to leave you without saying one word on . . . Well, I could hardly say anything on my behalf, could I? But if I could have . . . I would have said something. I would have told you how very sorry I was to leave. How very sorry I was to leave *you*." He paused as he swallowed. "I was so sorry."

349

I glanced from his face down toward his hand, which had fixed itself to my sleeve.

He let go. "Will you say nothing?"

I looked him in the eyes, willing myself to remain immune to the pull of their deep blue depths. "Again, I must remind you of your own advice that conversations feed on questions prompted by those things the conversants wish to know. I can truthfully tell you there is nothing I wish to discover about you or anything you have said. I will say, however, that I never had the chance to congratulate you on your engagement, my lord."

He winced. "Please don't think you must do so now. I'm afraid I've gone and botched it."

"On the matter of botched engagements, I feel I might be able to offer you the benefit of my own unfortunate experience."

"I do not think you can help me, Miss Withersby. While I have made clear my intentions to return to the colony, Lady Caroline seems to feel that marriage to a sheep farmer from New Zealand is quite beneath her."

"I always said it was a preposterous line of work."

"Perhaps. But it generates a decent income. If my memory serves correctly, *you* once said those in polite society were rather rude, and I have to say I agree."

"That's an extraordinary thing to say, considering that you *are* one of them, Mr. Trimble."

"By birth, Miss Withersby, but not by inclination. Through my bloodline runs a tendency to spend rather more than our income allows. If you will not think me too free for saying so, the first Earl of Cardington left us with an enviable fortune that later generations quickly depleted. My elder brother, it appears, will be the last to be able to do so and even he will insist upon doing it in poor taste. He gambles and several years ago was rather slow in paying off his debts. When he was accused of being a cheat, he challenged the man to a duel. I could not see the situation ending well for either man, so I contrived to keep him from that meeting, believing the taking of some young man's life, or the end of his, would reflect poorly on the family's name."

"That may explain your deplorable family, but it has nothing to do with your engagement."

"*Former* engagement. Lady Caroline is a longtime family friend. Several years ago, while she was away on the Continent with her mother, her father died. I was the one dispatched to bring them back, and at that time I made the careless promise that she was not to worry, that I would personally see to it that she was always taken care of."

"And?"

"And what?"

"And what else did you say?"

"That's it. That's all I said."

"And from that she inferred that you were to be married?"

"She did."

"And you could not retract it? Say you did not mean it?"

"I did mean it. I did take care of her. I saw to it that her father's estate was honestly settled."

"That did not require you to marry her."

"It did not, but what is a gentleman to do? It did not matter to me at the time, since I assumed I would one day marry anyway. How was I to know that I would one day also fall in love?"

I could not stop a blush from suffusing my face.

"In any event, after thwarting my brother's attempt at a duel, I was shipped off to New Zealand and told to make something of myself."

"Which you seem to have done quite admirably."

Again his lips lifted in the promise of a smile. "I find the colony well suited to an honest life."

"But Lady Caroline did not share your opinion?"

"She did not. And to remedy the social humiliation of letting her not-inconsiderable fortune slip through my family's fingers, I have considered that I might have to get myself banished again."

Get himself banished? "How?"

He sighed as he turned his hat over in his hands. "I suppose the best thing, the quickest route, would be to take up with an unsuitable woman." His gaze darted toward mine.

"I have been told that people of your class do so all the time. And without any apparent shame."

He sent me a piercing glance. "Upon reflection, I would have to agree with you. But I was thinking . . . if I *married* the woman in question I might actually be ordered to go far away. Expected to even. I would have to consider it my duty as an honorable man."

He seemed to expect some sort of reply, but I had already conversed with him more than I had meant to.

Just as I decided to get my father, the echo of his words stopped me in my step. "Did you just ask me to marry you, Mr. Trimble?"

"I might have. Why? Would you accept such a ridiculous proposal from a preposterous sheep farmer?"

"I might. If I were given the courtesy of a proper proposal."

"Good heavens, Charlotte. I don't like games any more than you do. Marry me!"

"Though I have to say that I do not disapprove of your expression of ardor, that was an imperative statement, Edward, not a question. How can you do me the honor of asking for my hand when you do me a dishonor by assuming that—"

He took me by the shoulders, pulled me to himself, and kissed me. Rather thoroughly. Quite beyond what might be considered the bounds of appropriate displays of affection. Fortunately, there were none present to observe us. At length he released me. Or tried to, but I wound my arms about his neck when he would have let me go.

He put a hand to my cheek. "Will you?"

"Will I what?"

"Will you, for heaven's sake, marry me?"

"For heaven's sake? I hardly think so." Although I did rather wish to kiss him again.

"Confound it!" He grabbed my hands and sank to his knees. "You are the most maddening, most vexing, most exasperating woman I have ever met. Let me make this very plain for you, Miss Withersby. I love you. I need you. I wish to marry you."

"That's all very nice for you, Mr. Trimble, but do you not wish to solicit my opinion on the matter?"

He closed his eyes, took a deep breath in through his nostrils, and then opened his eyes and fixed that penetrating gaze on me. "Do you wish to marry me, Miss Withersby?"

"Yes."

"Yes? Is that all you're going to say?"

"Would you rather I said no?"

"No! It's just that I've declared to you my love and . . . and my devotion, and I just . . ."

"Like a flower in bloom, I've discovered that it's no good to try to adhere to some idealized type that has no basis in reality. I can only be what I am and offer up what petals I have, hoping that someone might look beyond what is supposed to be to what, in fact, actually is."

He stood, grinning. "That's altogether fanciful of you."

"It's meant to be poetical."

He took my hands in his and brought them up to his chest, where he bent his head to kiss my knuckles. "Yes?"

"Yes."

"You'll have to become a sheep farmer's wife."

"Or perhaps you'll have to become a botanist's husband."

He smiled as he bent to kiss me once more. "Perhaps I shall."

Epilogue

The Templeton-Stansbury marriage was the wedding of the century. At least, that's what was claimed in Cheshire. The nuptials were held that May at the church, presided over by the rector. A reception was given afterward in the stumpery, which was disguised, by the bride, with a breathtaking array of ferns and flowers for the occasion. The couple repaired to the Continent for a yearlong honeymoon, from which I was sent a constant stream of letters. Though Mr. Stansbury had intended to spend the year acquiring specimens for his collections, Adah prevailed upon him to take her to Paris, Berlin, and Vienna. It was my understanding that a cargo hold of trunks containing stylish gowns, Wardian cases of exotic plants, and crates of fashionable new furniture awaited them at Overwich Hall upon their return.

Mr. Hopkins-Whyte fed the remains of his unfortunate specimens to the fire during the months of February and March and then made a visit to his beloved Northumberland for a fortnight in April while the children's nurse and the cook put the rectory in order. To his great surprise, he got himself married to a third cousin while he was there. She has the makings of a very fine Mrs. Rector.

Out of respect for my father, Edward and I did not marry until he had settled himself in with the Admiral. And for the purposes of convention, we waited until Lady Caroline had found herself a suitable husband. With her family's connections, however, it did not take long. Before the end of June I was being called Mrs. Trimneltonbury. And I must say, I delighted in hearing it.

That summer, I undertook a journey I had never imagined. It took a full two months to reach New Zealand, and another month of provisioning in Christchurch, and only then, once we reached Edward's sheep farm in Canterbury, did I discover the parcel of letters awaiting me from home.

I confess that I will never fit with the Trimneltonbury family, but Edward and I have determined to cultivate our own species in a place that pleases us both, with a life we adore. I had not ever had the pleasure of acquainting myself with sheep, but I find they are not quite so dreadful as I had feared. And Edward himself is more wonderful than I had hoped. There is an abundance of flora just waiting to be discovered, and I conceive of at least several volumes that need to be written and illustrated in order to adequately represent them to the rest of the world. And on the whole, I find myself quite . . . happy.

Note from the Author

I have this great idea for a book about painting, and women, and botany!" I told my agent and my editor. It wasn't until I planned my research that I started having second thoughts. Because to understand science, you actually have to *read* about science. And I did. I read about botany, about the history of botany, and about the histories of the botanists who comprise the history of botany. I started my research back in the 1700s and read about what happened well into the 1900s. What a challenge I set for myself with this book: to have a main character who lived and breathed science, yet make botany interesting to people like me who have no particular interest in it.

This book is based on the stories of the multitude of women whose contributions to the field of botany have largely been ignored. Women, like Charlotte, who wrote books and created illustrations that were credited, upon publication, to men. My writing was fueled by outrage at the knowledge that in spite of all of their hard work, they were not given credit for it.

The mid-1800s was a turning point in the study of botany.

That area of science had chiefly been the purview of women and clergy who had an interest in the classification of plants. It was a safe pursuit whose study was meant to illuminate God and enrich faith. It was wrested from them, however, by professional academics more interested in the patterns of the distribution of plants.

The opening up of the study of botany to the "why" instead of simply the "what" struck fear in the hearts of many religious people of the era. They believed that investigating the distribution of plants somehow diminished the role of God in His creation. Although the distributionists came up with some dubious theories, they were matched in their doubtful rationale by responses from the religious adherents of the science. In some ways, religion's credibility was so damaged that it was effectively written out of the scientific debates of the period and, sadly, most of the scientific debates of today.

Botanists had a reputation during the era for being philosophic thinkers with hardy constitutions and a winsome sort of charm. In the wilds of the colonies, in search of rare specimens, they perpetuated a reputation much like that of Indiana Jones. Illustrating their discoveries was part of the job description, and many of them, like Edward Trimble, dashed off whimsical caricatures of flowers. From the world of botany sprang the genre of literary nonsense best exemplified by the works of artist/writers like Edward Lear and Charles Lutwidge Dodgson (Lewis Carroll), who socialized with the era's leading philosophers and amateur botanists such as John Ruskin (the famed patron of the pre-Raphaelite artistic movement).

Botany gave birth to a handful of dynastic families who often intermarried. The upbringing of members of those families was, much like Charlotte's, eccentric in the extreme. But if you grew up with botanists and socialized with botanists and married a botanist, how would you have known what was expected of you in society at large?

Victorians were known for their enthusiasms. They created stumperies and ferneries and all sorts of other overblown collections of objects both living and dead. And sometimes field clubs did come to blows over jurisdictions! It was not uncommon for a field club to sweep over a piece of property and leave nothing behind in its wake. Victorian collectors didn't look far enough ahead to think of preserving the very things they were trying to collect. Many species nearly went extinct before conservationism came into vogue in the later nineteenth and early twentieth centuries. But that, as they say, is a whole other story.

The Ranunculaceae family includes over a thousand species of plants, like ranunculus, clematis, larkspur, delphinium, and hellebore. The Orchidaceae family is the largest family of flora, numbering over 20,000 species. Some of them, like those Charlotte sought, grow as wild flowers in England and are treated as weeds. One gardener's nuisance can be a botanist's treasure.

Miss Templeton's extreme fear of childbirth may seem odd in our era of modern medicine, but in the nineteenth century the maternal mortality rate was 50 of 1000 births. If Victorians generally had five or six children, then the chance of dying during childbirth can be calculated at 20 to 25 percent. The monogram is often thought of as a symbol of status and wealth, but its origin is actually quite chilling. A woman would take care to place her monogram on items she brought to her marriage. After she died, were her husband to remarry, she could then be assured that her possessions would be passed on through the line of her own children instead of being given to her successor's.

The first Opium War took place from 1839 to 1842, as a reaction to an international trade imbalance. As the popularity of Chinese tea, silk, and porcelain grew in the eighteenth and nineteenth centuries, the Chinese found little of interest to import from Britain. That forced the British to pay for their imports with silver. By the early 1800s about 40 percent of the world's silver supply had been shipped to China.

By the 1830s, however, the British found something the Chinese were willing to pay for: opium. With the relatively cheap cost of opium and its highly addictive nature, the trade imbalance reversed to such an extent that Chinese silver was soon pouring into Britain. But the opium trade exacted heavy social losses, and it quickly grew too lucrative for the emperor to contain. From a single, approved port in Guangdong, the opium trade soon jumped official boundaries and was overtaken by corrupt officials, local merchants, and smugglers as it worked itself into the rhythms of daily life. Even missionaries came to rely upon opium smugglers for the delivery and posting of their letters and packages. The emperor was an opium addict, and so were nearly 30 percent of his officials.

Merchants and local officials supported legalization of opium and, therefore, taxation as a method of control. Opponents of the drug and those worried about the trade imbalance, however, argued for outright prohibition.

The emperor, deciding for prohibition, seized all opium in China and in international waters and burned it. British merchants, who were left with heavy losses, appealed to Parliament to reimburse them. When the conflict burst into war, although its basis was in the struggle to release trade from the emperor's authoritarian control, in effect British soldiers fought for the right to supply millions of Chinese opium addicts with the drug. As the Admiral himself stated, it was both the best thing and worst thing to happen to international trade.

At least a third of the world's population are introverts. While they can pretend to be extroverts for a while, frankly, the task is exhausting. I hope Charlotte accurately portrayed the complexities of this personality. Contrary to common belief, introverts are not necessarily shy. They are not misanthropists. Though they gain energy from solitude and quiet, they don't always like to be by themselves. They are, however, wonderful observers of the world around them, are quite self-aware, and prefer deep conversations to small talk. They are also inclined to think that there's something seriously wrong with them. Many times they desperately hope that if they just try hard enough, they'll be able to be like everyone else. I should know. I am one. Perhaps my novels always speak to questions of worth because so often I doubt my own.

As Mr. Trimble suggested to Charlotte, Eve's designation in the Bible as a *helper* should not consign women to a fate of eternal servitude. That word, *ezer*, is used only twenty-one times throughout the Bible. The first two are in reference to Eve. The other specific references are used when God refers to himself. Perhaps you are familiar with this one: "*I lift up my eyes to the hills. From where does my help [ezer] come? My help [ezer]comes from the Lord, who made heaven and earth*" (Psalm 121:1–2 ESV). It's a shame that the vitality and strength of that descriptor has been lost in translation. It lends a different slant to the idea of Woman to think that God gave that trait, that strength of His, specifically to the female of our species.

In the Victorian era, when you could be a man-scientist-professional *or* a woman-wife-mother, *or* was a safe though limiting word. It still is. *And* is much more dangerous because it requires more complexity.

Grace *and* mercy, faith *and* works, love *and* wrath.

Illustrator *and* female. Botanist *and* wife.

You *and* all the talents and abilities you were born with.

In the writing of this book, I've come to believe that God is much bigger than we often give Him credit for, just as people are so much more than their gender. In a world filled with questions, we shouldn't be afraid to articulate them. When we look for answers, I don't think it possible that we can find any less of God when there's so much more of Him to be discovered.

Acknowledgments

To my agent, Natasha Kern, for loving Charlotte just as much as I do and for understanding her even better than I did! To my editors, Dave Long and Karen Schurrer, for their wise advice and their generous encouragement. To Maureen Lang, who made me feel a lot less insecure about the grade I earned in high school biology when she said she loved this story.

To my street team members for their enthusiastic support of this book: Jamie Lapeyrolerie, Denise Harmer, Jaquelyn Scroggie, Kathleen E. Belongia, Amy Putney, Brenda Veinotte, Kelsey Shade, Debbie Wilder, Beth Bulow, Lindsey Zimpel, Melissa Tharp, Julianna Rowe, Lorraine Hauger, Martha Artyomenko, Nancy McLeroy, and Pattie Reitz read my sample chapters and provided feedback on the cover. Several of them even slogged through the manuscript. Thank you, ladies! It's been such a pleasure creating this book with you.

And to Tony. Thanks for seeing me. For looking beyond what's supposed to be to what, in fact, actually is. I love you.

Siri Mitchell is the author of over a dozen novels, three of which were named Christy Award finalists. A graduate of the University of Washington with a degree in business, she has worked in many different levels of government and lived on three continents. She and her family currently reside in the D.C. metro area. Visit her at www.sirimitchell.com.

More Fiction You May Enjoy

You May Also Like . . .

Shipwrecked and stranded, Emma Chambers is in need of a home. Could the widowed local lighthouse keeper and his young son be an answer to her prayer?

Love Unexpected by Jody Hedlund
BEACONS OF HOPE #1
jodyhedlund.com

To fulfill a soldier's dying wish, nurse Abigail Stuart marries him and promises to look after his sister. But when the *real* Jeremiah Calhoun appears alive, can she provide the healing his entire family needs?

A Most Inconvenient Marriage by Regina Jennings
reginajennings.com

A quiet Jewish scholar named Ezra is called upon to deliver his people from Babylon to Jerusalem, and to bring hope in a time when dreams of the future— of family and love—seem impossible.

Keepers of the Covenant by Lynn Austin
THE RESTORATION CHRONICLES #2
lynnaustin.org